SNATCHED

SNATCHED

MANDASUE HELLER

LARGE PRINT

Oxford

Copyright © Mandasue Heller, 2009

First published in Great Britain 2009
by
Hodder & Stoughton

Published in Large Print 2009 by ISIS Publishing Ltd.,
7 Centremead, Osney Mead, Oxford OX2 0ES
by arrangement with
Hodder & Stoughton
An Hachette Livre UK Company

British Library Cataloguing in Publication Data
Heller, Mandasue.
    Snatched
    1. Single mothers- -Fiction.
    2. Organized crime- - England- -Manchester- -
    Fiction.
    3. Suspense fiction.
    4. Large type books.
    I. Title
    823.9'2–dc22

ISBN 978–0–7531–8484–4 (hb)
ISBN 978–0–7531–8485–1 (pb)

Printed and bound in Great Britain by
T. J. International Ltd., Padstow, Cornwall

To dear friends,
Jaynie Maunsell and Ray Bello
— gone but never forgotten.
Also Conrad Morton.

Acknowledgements

As ever, love to my partner, Wingrove Ward; mum, Jean Heller; children, Michael, Andrew, & Azzura, and precious granddaughters, Marissa and Lariah; sister, Ava; Amber & Kyro, Martin, Jade, and Reece; Auntie Doreen, Pete, Lorna, Cliff, Chris & Glen; Natalie, Dan, & Toni. Our Heller family, USA; and the Wards: Joseph, Mavis, Valerie, Jascinth, Donna, & children. And love to the rest of my family — past and present.

A massive thank you to the Hodder team — Carolyn, Emma, Auriol, Lucy, to name but a few . . . You're all great.

My agents, Cat Ledger, and Guy Rose.

Nick Austin.

Hi to Betty & Ronnie Schwartz, Martina, Norman Fairweather, Wayne Brookes, Faye Webber.

And to the real Jackie Harris, who won the competition to have a character in this book named after her.

And lastly, a long over-due hello to the friends who shared the crazy ride through the Hulme of the 80's with me — good and bad, they were life-changing days indeed!

PROLOGUE

Squeezing through the gap in the railings, Nicky Day scrambled down the embankment and thrashed through the nettles standing guard below. Gritting her teeth when painful welts sprang up on her hands and legs, she stumbled over the tracks of the disused railway line and hauled herself up the facing bank, clambering over the chain-link fence into the field beyond.

The sky was already turning a deep stormy violet as the winter shadows closed in, making visibility poor as she picked her way through the overgrown bushes bordering the wasteland. Catching her foot in a tangle of roots, she went down heavily, gashing her cheek on a rock and catching her hair in the brambles. Sobbing, she tore herself free and hobbled on. There was no time to stop; Kelly Greene and her gang wouldn't be far behind when they realised that she'd come this way. And if they caught up with her now, she was dead.

Reaching the end of the bushes at last, she scanned the darkness ahead through her tears. There was an exposed area of some fifteen feet between here and the road, and she had to make sure that Kelly hadn't pre-empted her and gone that way to ambush her. No one seemed to be around, so she took a tentative step out into the open.

Squealing with fear when somebody grabbed her ponytail, snapping her head back on her neck, she flailed her arms to keep her balance. But the first savage punch knocked her clean off her feet — and the blows that followed made sure she stayed down.

CHAPTER
ONE

Pacing the living room floor, Sue Day glanced at her watch and cursed under her breath. It was almost 8.30 and the taxi was due any minute, but Nicky still wasn't home. And if she didn't get a move on Sue was buggered, because there was no way she could go out and leave Connor in the house by himself. She'd have to send the taxi away when it arrived — and there was no chance of getting another one at this time on a Friday night.

Going across to the window she yanked the curtain aside and peered out, only to find the road just as deserted as it had been every other time she'd looked out over the past hour. Snatching her cigarettes up from the window ledge, she lit one and exhaled loudly. Nicky was so selfish, sometimes, she really was. One night a week, that was all Sue needed. Was that really too much to ask?

Putting the finishing touches to her make-up at the mirror over the fire, Julie Ford glanced at her friend's rigid back and rolled her eyes.

"Oi, quit bloody stressing before you set me off," she scolded. "She'll not get here any faster with you glued to the window, so do something useful and spark me one of them before you drive me mental."

Sighing, Sue let the curtain drop and slid another cigarette out of the packet. Lighting it, she passed it over. Julie was right; she should stop worrying before she ruined the night. Nicky was a good kid, and if she'd promised to be home, she would be.

She'd *better* be.

Swiping a thick coat of gloss over her scarlet lipstick now, Julie turned to get Sue's appraisal.

"Well, what d'y think? Babe, or double babe?"

"Triple," Sue said, feeling a sudden twinge of envy.

Julie was a big girl, but she certainly knew how to make the most of her ample figure, and it was *her* that the men always made a beeline for at the club every weekend. Sue was much better-looking, and at least two stone lighter, but she rarely got much of a second glance — until closing time, when she invariably found herself lumped with the mate of whoever Julie had hooked for the night. Julie reckoned it was her own fault for giving off *I-belong-to-someone-else-so-back-off* vibes, and that considering it was almost a year since Terry had gone off with his teenage tart, it was high time she got back on the horse — and stopped complaining about the saddle. Which was all right for *her* to say, seeing as she got all the studs while Sue was left with the nags.

But tonight was as good a night as any to make a new start, because it was Julie's birthday, and she'd got them a double date with a couple of salesmen she'd met in town earlier that day. Sue wasn't holding out

6

much hope of hers being anything special, but she'd promised to make an effort and have a good time, and had even bought herself a new outfit to make a good impression. And she looked bloody good in it, even if she did say so herself.

Now all she needed was for Nicky to get home before she lost her nerve.

Curled up on the couch behind them just then, Connor's stomach rumbled loudly. Clapping a hand down on her enormous breasts, Julie said, "Christ, that was loud, mate. You got the hungry hippos in there, or what?"

Shaking his head, Connor cast a guilty glance at his mum. She'd shouted at him earlier for refusing to eat his dinner, but he didn't like tinned sausages and beans, and that was all she ever made these days. He was starving now, but he'd rather wait for Nicky to get home because she'd do him proper sausages, and mash with butter and milk, and everything. He just wished she'd hurry up.

"Don't tell me you haven't fed him yet?" Julie gave Sue a disapproving look as she flicked her ash in the general direction of the small wastepaper bin. "Leaving it a bit late, aren't you?"

"I offered him something when he got back from school," Sue told her defensively, watching as the ash missed its target and settled on one of her fluffy slippers. "He said he wasn't hungry."

"Well, he sounds like he is now," Julie said, holding the cigarette between her teeth as she turned back to the mirror to tease her hair. "Give him a biscuit. That always did it for mine when they wouldn't eat."

Yeah, and look how they *all turned out*, Sue thought meanly, remembering how disgusted she'd been the one time she'd met Julie's fat, unhealthy, hyperactive kids. Glancing at Connor now, she gave him a dark look, to let him know that if that had been his plan all along, to get a biscuit instead of proper food, it wasn't going to work.

A car horn hooted outside. Running to the window, Julie saw the cab and snatched up her jacket, saying, "Come on, girl, get a move on. They charge extra for waiting, you know."

"Er, aren't you forgetting something?" Sue jerked her head in Connor's direction. "I can't just leave him. We've got to wait for Nicky."

"Oh, yeah," Julie murmured. Then, clicking her fingers: "Try her mobile."

"I've already tried three times, but she's not answering," Sue reminded her irritably. This was the one thing that really annoyed her about Julie — that she couldn't remember even the simplest things from one minute to the next.

Sighing, Julie folded her arms. "Well, I hope she's not too long, 'cos you know what'll happen if we lose the cab. We'll have to get the bus instead, and they're not exactly reliable round here, are they?"

"Don't blame me," Sue muttered, snatching up her mobile and tapping yet *another* message into it telling Nicky to get her arse home right now.

8

"Great!" Julie complained. "First date I've had with a bloke who's got more money than sense in ages, and now I'm gonna be so late he'll have pissed off with some other bitch by the time I get there. And we won't get another chance, you know, 'cos they're only here for the weekend."

"Tell you what," Sue said tetchily, tossing her phone down onto the coffee table and reaching for another cigarette. "Why don't you just go by yourself, eh? I'll stop here and watch telly on my own for the rest of the night — like usual."

Sensing that her friend was on the verge of slipping into one of her moods, which would take days of coaxing to get her out of again, Julie danced up to her and gave her a cuddle.

"As if I'd leave you alone on a Friday night, mate. Anyhow, there's no way I'm going out with two blokes by myself. I'd get a right reputation."

"Like you haven't already," Sue snorted softly, only slightly mollified.

"Aw, shaddup!" Julie grunted, waddling back to the window to make sure that the taxi was still there. Turning back with a grin after a moment, she said, "Hey, I think we just got lucky, kiddo; it's Titty Man." Stubbing her cigarette out, she tugged on the elasticated neckline of her top, bringing it dangerously close to nipple territory. "Think I'll just nip out and keep him entertained while we're waiting. That should buy us a bit of time."

Calling after her not to go giving him a heart attack, Sue winced when the door slammed shut. Shaking her head, she said, "She'll have that door right off its hinges one of these days, you watch."

Thumb stuck firmly in his mouth, Connor gazed up at her. He was six, but he was so small and skinny that he only looked about four, and he seemed to have stopped growing altogether after his dad left. But he'd have to get used to Terry not being here one day. They all would.

"I thought you were going out, Mummy?" he said now, his words muted by the thumb.

"So did I," Sue murmured, sighing as she glanced down at her watch again. "But I've got to wait for your sister, haven't I?"

"She promised to play Superman with me," Connor said sleepily. "I hope she hasn't forgot."

"She won't have," Sue assured him, reaching down to stroke his mud-brown hair. It had been cut in the same close-cropped style as Terry's since the day he'd had enough hair *to* cut, and Sue had thought the "mini-me" thing was really sweet — *then*. Now she hated it, because it reminded her so much of his dad. But every time she left it to grow, Connor picked up nits from some kid at school and it all had to go again.

Gritting her teeth now to prevent the wave of misery that was washing in on her from taking hold, she said, "Anyway, don't you go dropping off, or you won't be playing anything when Nicky gets home."

"I'm not tired," Connor lied, his attention switching to the TV as the music for his favourite sitcom started up. "You can go now, if you want."

"Oh, can I now?" She snorted amusedly. "And who's going to look after you?"

"I'm a big boy now," he informed her earnestly. "Auntie Julie said."

"Auntie Julie said what?" Julie asked, coming back just then to let Sue know that they'd better get a move on because Titty Man had to leave in a minute for another booking.

"That he can look after himself until Nicky gets home," Sue told her. "Because, *apparently*, he's a big boy now."

"Well, he is." Julie tossed him a fond smile. Then, pursing her lips, she said, "Actually, that's not such a bad idea."

"What, leave him?" Sue frowned. "Don't be daft. He's six, not sixteen."

"Yeah, but he's smart," Julie countered, lowering her voice so that Connor wouldn't hear. "Come on, Sue, think about it. Have you ever met a more obedient child in your entire life? If you tell him not to move till your Nicky gets back, you know for a fact that he won't budge. And you said it yourself — she'll be back any minute."

"What if she's not?"

"You're kidding me, right?" Drawing her head back, Julie gave Sue an incredulous look. "This is your Nicky we're talking about. The girl who'd rather stop at home and play with her little brother than go out with her own mates."

"Only because she knows how much he's missing you-know-who," Sue whispered, not wanting to say

Terry's name out loud in case she upset Connor and really buggered up her chances of going out.

"Exactly," Julie said. "So, she'll be on her way home right now, won't she?"

"Probably," Sue conceded, shrugging lightly. "But it still doesn't feel right."

"Only 'cos you're an over-protective mum who thinks the roof's going to cave in if you take your eyes off him for two minutes," Julie said bluntly, reaching for Sue's jacket and shoving it into her hands. "I did it loads of times when mine were little, and none of them suffered for it, did they?"

Biting her lip, Sue gazed down at Connor thoughtfully. Julie was right about him being obedient, and if she said stay put, he would. So could it really do any harm to leave him on his own for a few minutes, knowing that Nicky would definitely be back soon?

"Well?" Julie was already edging towards the door. "Shall I tell Titty Man to wait, or let him go and take our chances with the bus when Nicky turns up as soon as he's gone?"

Hesitating for just a moment longer, Sue said, "Okay, I'll come. But I'm holding you responsible if anything happens."

"Which it won't," Julie said confidently. "Will it, Con-Con?" Dipping her head, she grinned at him. "'Cos you're gonna be as good as gold and watch telly till Nickers gets home, aren't you? And you can have a choccy biccy while you're waiting — can't he, Mum?" This she aimed at Sue, gesturing with a nod towards the kitchen.

"A Penguin?" Connor piped up hopefully.

Sighing, Sue flapped her hands and headed into the kitchen. Winking at Connor when she'd gone, Julie waggled her fingers and backed out of the door, whispering, "See you later, squirt. Be good."

Bringing two Penguin bars back, Sue handed them to her son and kissed the top of his head, telling him not to go out, and not to answer the door under any circumstance — unless it was Nicky and she'd lost her key. Then, slotting her cigarettes and lighter into her handbag alongside her purse and her make-up, she picked up her keys and headed out, calling back over her shoulder that she'd see him tomorrow.

"All set?" Julie asked when she jumped into the back of the cab moments later.

Nodding, Sue glanced nervously back at the house as they pulled away from the kerb.

"He'll be fine," Julie assured her. "So let's stop fretting and start practising our sexy smiles before we see those men of ours, eh?"

Grimacing when Julie gave her a cheesy grin, Sue said, "I wouldn't do that to yours if I was you — you'll scare the bloody life out of him."

"You don't really think he'll be paying any attention to my face when he cops an eyeful of these, do you?" Julie quipped, cupping her breasts and giving them a jiggle.

"Somebody's already copping an eyeful, by the looks of it," Sue said loudly, raising her eyebrows at the driver as he ogled her friend in the rear-view mirror.

"Concentrate on the road, you. I want to get there in one piece."

"Leave him alone," Julie chuckled. "He deserves a bit of fun after all the waiting he's had to do tonight. He even turned the meter off — didn't you, babe?" Leaning forward now, she pushed her breasts through the gap between the seats so that they were grazing his shoulder, and whispered huskily, "And who knows what you might get if you leave it off for the rest of the journey, eh?"

Shaking her head, Sue gazed out of the window — just in time to see a shadowy figure darting past. Pressing her nose against the glass as they reached the corner, she peered back. She was pretty sure it had been Nicky, but she decided to ring her again, anyway. To let her know that Connor hadn't had his tea yet, and to remind her that there was a fiver in the pot to top up the electric card before it ran out.

Frowning when she couldn't find her phone, she groaned when she remembered leaving it on the coffee table. But she couldn't go back for it now; Julie would go mad if she made them any later than they already were. Anyway, she didn't really need it. If there were any problems — which there wouldn't be, she was sure — Nicky was sensible enough to call her on Julie's phone.

Satisfied that everything was sorted, Sue shook off the last of her niggling doubts and settled back in her seat, all set for a good night out.

★ ★ ★

Craning her neck to watch as the taxi disappeared around the corner, Pauline Wilson tutted when a young girl from the other end of the road darted past her gate. Dropping the curtain back into place when the road was quiet again, she went back to her chair, muttering under her breath.

"What's that?" her husband murmured distractedly. He wasn't listening, it was just second nature to respond whenever she spoke, or she'd start accusing him of ignoring her. And if she got started with one of her rants, she wouldn't stop till the sun came up and chased her back into her coffin.

"Her next door," Pauline said disapprovingly. "Off out again with that fat lass. I don't know what they think they look like with everything hanging out like that, but it's not decent."

"Mmm," John said, his gaze fixed on the infinitely more interesting shots of a bloody American crime scene on the TV screen.

"I mean, I know she's had a bad time of it lately," Pauline went on. "But that's no reason to go putting yourself about like that, is it? Not when you've got children to consider. And that Maria from down the road's no better, the way she lets that lass of hers wander up and down the place. Black as coal it is out there tonight, and icy as all hell, but their Jodie's just gone running past in the thinnest jacket I've ever seen. It's a wonder she's not —"

"Isn't it time you got the kettle on?" John interrupted, sensing that she wasn't going to stop — with or without his interaction.

"Sorry . . .?" Drawing her head back, Pauline gave him an incredulous look. "Is it my turn again already? Only I could have *sworn* I'd made the last three."

"I'm watching my programme," he groaned, hoping that she'd take the hint and belt up.

"Aye, and I bet there's more of the same lined up for when it's finished," she said, wondering why she bothered trying to have a conversation with him at all, these days. Since they'd got that cable TV, it was nothing but wall-to-wall forensics in this house.

"That's right." Settling back in his chair, John raised the leg-rest an extra notch. "*CSI*'s Vegas and New York — and they're both follow-ups, so I'm going to need a bit of quiet in here, if you don't mind."

"Oh, well, don't let me disturb you," Pauline said sniffily. "I'll just go and do my duties while his lordship has a rest, shall I? Tea, is it?" She pushed herself out of her chair. "Or how about something a bit more exotic — like a nice mug of Ovaltine, or a little shot of arsenic?"

John ignored the sarcasm with practised ease.

"Tea's fine. But not too much milk, mind."

"You'll get what you're given," she muttered, adding, "And I'll take the bins out while I'm at it, will I? Even though you promised to do it hours ago."

"Aye, if you're up to it." Reaching for the remote, John pushed the volume up.

Shooting him a dirty look, Pauline went into the kitchen and slammed the door.

* * *

At the precise moment when Pauline switched on her kitchen light, the electric ran out next door, extinguishing the lights, the TV and the two-bar fire. Plunged into darkness, Connor shot up with a squeal of terror. He hated the dark, but he especially hated it when Nicky wasn't there to keep the monsters that lurked in the shadows at bay.

Heart beating painfully in his skinny chest, he eased himself down off the couch and stumbled across to the window. Standing on his tiptoes, he pulled the curtain aside and peered out at the road, but Nicky was nowhere to be seen, and the neighbours were all tucked away safely behind their own curtains, through which he could see the warm glow of lamps and flickering TVs.

Tears streaming down his cheeks, he rested his forehead against the icy pane.

Yanking her back door open, Pauline staggered up the path, cursing as the heavy bin-bag smacked against her shins with every step. Left to John, it would fester in the kitchen for the rest of the week and stink the house out. But did he care about that? Did he hell as like!

Heaving the bag up when she reached the gate, she shoved it into the wheelie bin and slammed the lid down on it. Wiping her hands on her skirt, she took a cigarette out of her cardigan pocket and lit up, feeling strangely cheated when the smoke was immediately stolen by the swirling winds. John had never smoked, so he didn't understand the pleasure she got from it — or the relief. And, *boy*, did she need all the relief she could get now he'd retired and was spending every waking moment under her feet.

Raising her hand to take another puff, she paused when the sound of muted crying floated to her. Sure that it was Connor, she peered round, only to see that next door was in darkness. Telling herself that she must have been mistaken, because Nicky always stopped in to look after Connor when Sue went out and would still be watching telly since it was only just gone nine, Pauline was about to turn to face the road again when a movement caught her eye. For a split second she was convinced that she'd seen the faint outline of a face at the window, but as soon as it was there it was gone again. And the crying had stopped, too.

Frowning now, she wondered if she ought to pop over to see if everything was all right. But she quickly dismissed the idea. It would be just her luck for Sue to come back and catch her. And she couldn't face that, not after the last time. All she'd done was ask if Connor was all right after one of his all-night crying sessions, but Sue had gone berserk, calling Pauline all the nosy bitches under the sun and screaming at her to stay the hell away from her family — and in front of all the neighbours, too.

No, she couldn't face that again. Any more than she could face the "*how many times have I told you to keep your nose out of other people's business*" lectures that she'd get from John for months to come.

Finishing her cigarette, Pauline flicked the butt out into the road and hurried back into the warmth of her house.

★ ★ ★

Huddled on the floor below the window, Connor held his breath until he'd heard Pauline's door closing. Sure that she'd spotted him just now, he'd ducked out of sight, terrified that she'd tell his mum he'd been peeping and get him into trouble. Or, worse, get Nicky into trouble for not being home yet.

Shivering as the chill of the winter night began to settle over the room, he got up. Making sure that the curtains were tightly drawn in case Pauline sneaked round for a nosy, he navigated his way past the couch and around the table into the kitchen. He was tired and hungry, and he wanted Nicky to come home and put the electric back on. But until she did, he'd just have to be a big boy and look after himself.

Licking at the bubble of snot that was dripping out of his nose, Connor rummaged blindly through the kitchen drawer for the candle his mum kept there. Finding it, he patted around on the side of the cooker for the matches. Feeling a surge of relief when the orange glow highlighted the familiar messy ledges and dish-filled sink, he lit the candle and secured it to a saucer with its own wax before carrying it carefully up the stairs.

Too scared to go into his or Nicky's bedrooms, because they were at the back of the house where there was no outside lighting to lift the terrifying darkness, he stood on the landing and gazed at his mum's door. He wasn't allowed in her bed since he'd pissed in it that time, but she always stayed over at Julie's on a Friday night and didn't come home till Saturday afternoon, by

19

which time Nicky would have got him up and changed the sheets, so she wouldn't even know he'd been there.

Pushing the door open, he ventured into the room and put the candle down on the bedside table before clambering fully clothed into the bed. Instantly soothed by the warmth of the quilt and the familiar scent of his mum's hair on the pillow, he closed his eyes and quickly fell asleep.

And if there was one thing Connor was good at, it was sleeping. Nothing could rouse him once he was gone.

Not the creeping heat that always spread out beneath him when he inevitably pissed the bed — sometimes two or three times a night.

Not Nicky picking him up and laying him on the floor while she changed his sheets.

And, tonight, not even the crackling sound of the candle flame licking at the torn fringe of his mum's bedside lamp.

CHAPTER
TWO

After putting the rubbish out and making John's tea, Pauline settled back into her chair. Bored by John's choice of TV viewing and the total lack of conversation, she drifted into a light doze, only to be jerked awake a short time later by the sound of shouting and running footsteps outside.

"What's going on?" she croaked, peering confusedly up at John as he made his way to the window.

"Sounds like someone's just smashed a window," he told her, pulling the curtain back and pressing his nose against the glass to see what was going on. "Looks like next door."

"Next door?" Pauline squawked, jumping to her feet. "Sue's or Irene's?"

"Looks like Sue's. A load of the neighbours are out there gawping."

Rushing to the front door, ignoring John when he called after her to stay out of it, she ran out to join the crowd that was already gathering on the pavement outside her gate. Gazing up to where all their eyes were trained, she gasped when she saw smoke pouring out through a hole in the centre of Sue's bedroom window, and bright flames licking at the bottom of the curtains.

Coming out of the house to the right of Pauline's just then, Irene Murgatroyd self-importantly informed everybody that they weren't to worry; that her Eddie had called the engines, and they should be here any minute. Exhaling loudly then, as if exhausted by her exertions, she waddled over to Pauline, muttering, "What a business, eh?"

"What's happened?" Pauline asked, holding her hair down as the wind whipped it this way and that.

"Not right sure," Irene said, pulling a little silver hip flask out of her dressing gown pocket and taking a sip from it. "But it looks like some sort of firebomb."

"You're joking!" Pauline gasped. "How do you know?"

"I heard the glass smashing when I was getting ready for bed," Irene told her. "And when I looked out, I saw someone running past, but I couldn't make out who it was. Then I heard Linda shouting fire, so I come out for a gander, and when I seen the smoke coming from Sue's window I got my Eddie to phone the brigade." Pausing for breath, she shook her head. "Good job no one's in, that's all I can say."

"Sue's not, 'cos I saw her going out earlier," Pauline murmured worriedly. "But I could have sworn I heard Connor crying after that. You don't think —"

"No, they're definitely all out," Irene said confidently, tightening the belt on her dressing gown. "Linda reckons it was dark in there when she come back from bingo at nine. And you know what that Nicky's like for watching telly when her mam's out, so there's no way she'd be sitting in the dark."

22

"I hope not," Pauline murmured, glancing past her when she saw two fire engines turning onto the road with their lights flashing. "But I really thought I heard him, and I could have sworn I saw someone at the window."

"Well, I hope you're wrong," Irene muttered, gazing up at the smoke that was still billowing out of the window. "'Cos my Eddie's already told them no one's in."

"Anyone seen the Jacksons?" another neighbour called out just then, diverting everybody's attention to the semi that was attached to Sue's.

"Oh, Christ," Irene said, giving Pauline a worried look. "They go to bed early, them two, so they probably don't know what's going on. And Lynne's room is right next to Sue's. She'll die in her sleep if that smoke gets through the wall — they both will."

Volunteering to go and knock on, Pauline hurried off down the pavement. But just as she reached Sue's gate, one of the burly firemen who were unravelling the hose ordered her to stay back.

"The woman on the other side hasn't come out yet, and she's got a disabled son," Pauline yelled up to him, hoping that he could hear her over the noise. "And I'm not sure," she went on, pointing at Sue's house now, "but I think someone might be in there."

"Any idea how many?"

"There's three of them live there, but it'll just be the two kids at home tonight, if they're in. I saw their mum going out earlier, and their dad doesn't live here no more."

Asking how old the kids were, the officer turned his back on her and relayed the news to his crew at a shout.

Offended by his rudeness after she'd gone to the trouble of alerting him about the kids, but pleased to see that her words seemed to have injected an edge of urgency into proceedings, Pauline went back to Irene, just as one of the crew kicked Sue's front door in, releasing thick clouds of black smoke into the air.

Clutching dramatically at her friend's arm, Irene said, "Oh, God, I hope Sue's not in there. That'd be all them kids need after losing their dad."

"She went out," Pauline reminded her. "And Terry's not dead, so don't talk like that."

"Might as well be for all them kids have seen of him since he took off," Irene retorted huffily. "And his new one not much older than his own daughter. Wants bloody shooting, he does."

"They're coming out!" someone on the other side of the road shouted, causing a mini-surge in the crowd around Pauline's gate as everyone strained to see what was happening.

Paramedics from one of the ambulances that were standing by rushed up to meet the fireman who emerged from the house. Seeing the small body in his arms, Pauline clapped a hand over her mouth.

"Oh, no, it's Connor! I *told* you they were in!"

Grabbing at one of the firemen who was rushing past just then, Irene said, "Oi, where's his sister? I hope someone's going back in there to look for her?"

Just as he was telling her that if anyone else was in there they'd find them, Sue's bedroom window shattered, sending shards of glass flying out in every direction.

Almost falling over when the fireman gave her a hefty shove back, Irene said, "Here, there's no need for that. I'll have you for assault."

"Do what you want," he retorted irritably. "But if you lot don't stop interfering and let us get this contained, the whole block's gonna catch."

"Is the boy all right?" Pauline called after him as he marched away. Getting no reply, she tutted and turned back to Irene. "Think they'd be a bit more civil, wouldn't you? I mean, it's not like we're not entitled to know what's going on. It's us who'll be picking up the pieces after they've gone."

"Makes you think," Irene murmured, not even pretending to listen to Pauline as she watched the flames leaping out from the hole where the window used to be. "All that money we spend doing our houses up, and, *poof*! It can be gone just like that."

John had just come out of the house. Wandering up to the gate in time to hear this, he said, "That's what happens when the council skimps on repairs, Reen. They're nowt but bloody cardboard, these houses."

"Oh, don't say that," Irene moaned, taking another slug from her hip flask before crossing herself superstitiously. "It's bad enough having to watch them fetch the boy out without a flicker of life in him, without thinking it'll be me next. I won't sleep a wink tonight, John, I really won't." Another sip.

"You will if you keep knocking that back," John said, pointedly eyeing the flask when he got a whiff of whisky. Resting his elbows on the gate then, he glanced contemptuously around at the faces in the crowd. "Incredible. You don't see half these buggers for weeks on end, but first sniff of excitement and they're out in their droves. Wonder they haven't fetched their chairs and knitting out."

"Do you have to?" Pauline hissed, digging him in the ribs with her elbow. "They're all worried sick about Nicky, and —"

"Eh up, cavalry's arrived," he said, cutting her off when he spotted a police car turning into the road. "Wonder what they called that lot in for?"

"'Cos it's arson, isn't it," Irene informed him. "Firebomb, like I told your Paul. But you'd never think anyone would do such a wicked thing when there's kids in the house, would you?"

"Don't you believe it," John replied darkly. "There's some proper evil buggers walking these streets, Irene. And you know what they say about crimes in the home, don't you? There's more chance of them being committed by them who live there than by a stranger, so think on."

It wasn't just John who turned to look now as, across the road, a pretty young woman with a sleek blonde bob and wearing a slate-grey suit stepped out of the passenger side of the squad car.

Oblivious to the interest she was attracting, Detective Constable Jay Osborne headed over to the chief of the fire crew to get an update.

"Six-year-old boy found at the bottom of the stairs," he told her. "Paramedics reckon he probably fell, judging by the bruise on his back. According to that lot," he went on, nodding towards the crowd outside Pauline's now, "the fifteen-year-old sister's supposed to be in there with him, but my guys haven't seen any sign of anyone else yet."

"Mum and dad?" Jay asked.

"Out, and non-resident," he said, adding darkly, "And the door was locked with a mortice, so if the girl's *not* in there someone needs to explain why a little lad like that was locked in on his own."

Telling him that she would put out an alert in case the girl had escaped before the crew arrived and was wandering around in a state of shock, Jay asked if they'd found any evidence that the fire had been started deliberately, as had been suggested.

"Neighbours reported hearing a smash and seeing someone running away," the crew chief said. "And the fire definitely started in that front upper room. But we haven't managed to get in there yet, because the stairs were well alight by the time we got here. Place is falling down around us; we'll be lucky to salvage anything. Only good thing is, there's no gas supply in the area or we really would have trouble."

Thanking him, Jay asked him to let her know as soon as he had any info about the cause of the fire and to give her a shout if he found the girl before she did. Heading over to the ambulance then, she had a quick word with the paramedics before going over to talk to the crowd.

Electing herself as spokesperson, because she was Sue's closest physical neighbour — apart from Lynne

Jackson and her son, who didn't count because they'd already been bundled to safety into one of the neighbours' houses across the road — Pauline told her about how she'd seen Sue going out earlier, and how she'd *known* that something was wrong and wished that she'd followed her instincts and checked.

Sure that it would probably turn out to be nothing specific, because it was amazing how many people experienced a "feeling" about something *after* the fact, Jay asked what had concerned her in particular.

"Connor crying," Pauline said, giving a little shrug as she added, "Not that *that*'s all that unusual, as such, because he cries quite a lot anyhow. But it was just a bit odd tonight."

"How so?" Jay asked.

"Well, I was sure I heard him, but soon as I looked over it stopped," Pauline said, feeling a bit like she was reciting from a book because she'd said these same words to so many of her neighbours already. "Then I saw there were no lights on, so I thought I'd imagined it," she went on, sighing heavily as she gazed back at the house. "But obviously I hadn't, eh?"

"So, it was dark in there. You didn't actually see anybody?"

"It was really dark," Linda Myers interjected before Pauline had a chance to reply. "I live directly opposite, and there were no lights on up nor down when I got home at nine."

"That's why I thought they were all out." Pauline jumped back in, glad that Linda had spoken out, because at least now she wouldn't be the only one in the firing line when Sue heard they had been discussing her with the police. "And that's too early for Nicky to have gone to bed, because she watches telly for hours when Sue's out — Irene will tell you that, won't you, Reen?"

Pushing herself forward, Irene said, "Oh, aye. Stops up for hours."

Jotting all this down in her notepad, Jay asked what time Pauline had seen the mother leaving the house, and if she had any idea where she might have been headed.

"Quart' to nine," Pauline said without hesitation. "But I don't know where she was going. Sorry."

"Probably the same place she goes every week," Irene commented scathingly. "Down town to pick up men."

Wanting to gauge if Sue Day had gone out socially tonight, in which case she could be gone for hours, or simply popped out on an errand, Jay asked if anyone had seen what she'd been wearing.

"I did," Pauline admitted reluctantly, aware that she probably sounded like a right nosy old so-and-so for knowing so many details. "She had a fairly short blue dress on, and black high heels, and a kind of glittery black jacket."

Writing this down, Jay's blue eyes were glinting like ice in the eerie glow of the emergency lights when she looked back up.

"And you say she regularly goes out and leaves the children alone?"

Shuffling her feet, unnerved by the intensity of the younger woman's gaze, Pauline said, "Well, no. I mean, yes, she does go out every week, but Nicky's always there to look after Connor, so she's not exactly leaving them on their own."

"Yes, she is," Irene contradicted her bluntly. "*She's* his mam, so she's the one who should be looking after him. Nicky's only fifteen; what's she supposed to do if something bad happens?" Turning to Jay now, determined to get her tuppence-worth in while she had the chance, she said, "And their dad's no better — taking off like that without so much as a by-your-leave. And, I mean, I'm no fan of Sue's, what with her buggering off out all the time and leaving the kids to fetch themselves up, but he's got to shoulder his share of the blame, 'cos neglect is neglect whoever's behind it. And if you want my opinion, you'd be as well to question that Leanne one if you're looking to find who broke the window."

"Sorry?" Jay's shapely eyebrows puckered with confusion.

"Terry's girlfriend," Irene said, as if Jay really should have known this already. "I wouldn't be surprised if she hadn't done this to get back at Sue for thumping her that time."

"Or one of her brothers," someone else chipped in.

"Mmm," Irene murmured, nodding her head and folding her arms. "Any one of that lot's capable. You mark my words, love, it'll be one of *her* lot behind it."

"I believe somebody reported seeing somebody running from the scene?" Jay said, looking around.

"Yeah, me," Irene told her. "I heard the smash, and looked out, and someone was legging it past my gate."

"Do you have a description?"

"Well, no, 'cos it was dark and I didn't have my glasses on," Irene admitted. "But I'd bet my life it was one of the Millers, 'cos they hate Sue. Anyone'll tell you that."

Flipping to a fresh page in her notepad, Jay asked for Irene's name and address.

"Irene Murgatroyd," Irene said, watching to make sure that she spelled it correctly. "Number seventeen, and I'm always in if you need to interview me properly."

Thanking her, Jay looked at Pauline.

"Er, no, I don't think so," John said before Pauline had a chance to open her mouth. "We don't speak to the Days or the Millers, so we can't help you." Gripping Pauline's arm now, he tried to pull her through the gate, intent on getting her inside before she got them mixed up in anything.

"I'll still need your names," Jay called after him. "It's just routine, sir. We'll be speaking to everybody in due course, not just yourselves."

Yanking her arm free, Pauline turned back and gave her name. Then, fearing that the policewoman might think that they all shared Irene's caustic opinion of the Days, she said, "I hope you don't think I'm accusing Terry and Sue of anything, 'cos I'm not. Sue would never hurt them kids, and Terry would never let anyone do anything to them, either."

"As I told your husband," Jay replied. "It's just routine to make a list of everybody who knows the family in these situations."

Nodding sadly, Pauline said, "When there's a death, you mean?"

"Nobody knows if there *is* a death yet," Jay told her quietly, sensing that she probably cared more about the neighbouring children than she felt free to express in front of her bossy husband and opinionated friend.

"So, he's alive, then," Irene declared — loudly, to make sure that everybody heard it from her first. "Well, thank the Lord for that. Now, let's just hope their Nicky's as lucky, 'cos she'll not stand much of a chance if that lot don't pull their fingers out and get back inside to look for her."

Assuring the crowd who were beginning to mutter their discontent that the fire crew would do everything in their power to rescue the girl if she was in there, Jay asked if anybody had the parents' phone numbers.

"If anyone's likely to have Sue's, it'll be Tina Murphy," Irene said, pointing out a younger woman who was standing in a garden further down the road. "She's about the only one who still talks to her round here." Folding her arms now, she nodded in the opposite direction. "You're best off asking Carole Miller for Terry's, though. She's in the dirty house down there; number thirty-two. She'll probably have his new address, an' all, 'cos him and the floozie are supposed to have gone and got themselves a fancy new flat, according to her. Not that they bothered inviting any of *us* lot round for the house-warming, mind."

"Yeah, 'cos they know what'll happen if they don't keep their heads down," someone else said nastily.

Thanking them for their help when she'd taken down all their names, Jay went to speak to Tina Murphy — who, it transpired, *did* have Sue Day's number. Ringing it, only to find that it was switched off, Jay left a message asking Sue to contact her urgently. Then she went back up the road to Carole Miller's house.

Frustrated to get no answer there after several minutes of knocking, despite being sure that she'd seen somebody moving behind the grimy nets covering the front-room window, she headed back to the station, hoping that she might find something there which would help her to trace the boy's parents.

CHAPTER
THREE

Terry was absolutely knackered when he finished his shift. It was gone eleven by the time he drove into the parking lot behind the flats and he just wanted to kick his boots off, eat his dinner, and go to bed. But one glance at the shadows dancing behind the curtains of his fifth-floor living room window as he traipsed wearily towards the main doors let him know that there would be no peace for him tonight.

Six weeks they'd lived here, which made six weekends of torture for Terry as Leanne filled the flat up with giggling girls, all trying to out-Mariah and out-Leona each other on the karaoke machine into the early hours. And he wouldn't have minded if any of them could actually sing, but they were all as bad as each other.

And the *mess* . . . he'd never seen anything like it in his life. Wine and beer spilled all over the new carpet, empty crisp packets and chocolate wrappers stuffed down the new couch cushions, ashtrays full to overflowing. It was like a kids' party, but way worse than it being your own kids, because at least you could tell them to shut up and clean up. But when it was your girlfriend, you had to respect her right to do whatever she wanted, whenever she wanted — or so Leanne kept telling him.

Letting himself into the flat now, Terry hung his jacket up in the hall and opened the living room door. Leanne and the girls were dancing around in the middle of the floor, while another was using the new coffee table as a stage, her words indecipherable as she belted out whatever song she was butchering through the echo-overloaded microphone.

Gazing around, Terry felt the irritation churn in his empty gut. Leanne had put them in a lot of debt furnishing this place, insisting that everything had to be brand new and top of the range. Washer/dryer, leather three-piece, flat-screen TV, king-size bed, designer sheets, copper-bottom pots and pans . . . The list had been endless, and Terry had no doubt that the paying back of the credit cards would be, too. And considering that *he* was the mug who was working every flaming hour under the sun to pay for it, he didn't appreciate her letting her mates trash it like this.

One of the girls suddenly noticed him standing there. Squealing, "Terry!" as if she knew him well enough to be so familiar, she rushed over to him and tried to hug him.

Snapping, "Leave it out, love. I'm not in the mood," Terry stomped into the kitchen, ignoring the calls of "Spoilsport!" from the girls. Kicking the door shut, he slammed his keys down on the ledge. It was bad enough trying to cope with Leanne when she'd had a drink, but the thought of being pawed by a whole gang of pissed-up teenage girls made his skin crawl.

Opening the oven door, he glanced inside, not in the least surprised to find it empty. His dinner had been waiting in there every other night this week, but he should have known better than to have expected Leanne to bother on a Friday night. It might be the end of his week, but it was just the beginning of hers, and she obviously had better things to do.

Wishing he'd thought to stop off at the chippy on the way home, he opened the cupboard and pulled out the bread.

Coming in just then, Leanne slinked towards him with a sexy smile on her face, purring, "Hey, gorgeous. Where's my kiss?"

Sidestepping her without a word, Terry opened the fridge and took out the margarine.

"Oi, grumpy!" she teased, coming up behind him and wrapping her arms around his waist. "What's up with you?"

"Don't," he muttered, prising her hands away and walking back to the counter.

Frowning, she pushed the door shut and folded her arms. "All right, what have I done?"

"Do you need to ask?" he said coolly, slapping two slices of bread onto a plate and looking for a knife.

"Well, *yeah*. Wouldn't bother if I already knew, would I?"

Turning, Terry peered at her. He could have reminded her that she'd promised not to have the girls round this weekend. And he could have pointed out that he was absolutely knackered after a week of twelve-hour shifts, which he'd only taken on to try and get them out of the debt *she*'d put them in. And he *could* have asked why she was so damn selfish that she couldn't even be bothered to make his dinner when she must have known he'd be starving. But he couldn't be arsed.

Tutting when he shook his head at her before turning back to his sandwich-making, Leanne said, "Oh, so it's like that, is it? You're not talking to me. Right, well, fine. If you want to be miserable, go for it. But don't think you're ruining my party."

"God forbid," Terry muttered under his breath.

Shooting him a dirty look, Leanne went back into the living room. Slamming the knife down on the ledge when he heard her turning the music up a couple of seconds later, Terry marched into the doorway and yelled at her to turn it down. Smiling defiantly, she reached down and turned it up some more, causing a barrage of protest from the next-door neighbour who immediately began to pound on the wall.

"Pack it in," Terry snapped, walking across the room to turn it down himself.

"Don't you dare," Leanne hissed, her chin lifted in challenge as she stood in front of the machine. "I mean it, Terry. It's mine, and I'll have it as loud as I want."

Aware that her friends were all watching, waiting to see how he would deal with this, Terry's voice was so low that he could barely hear himself when he said, "Stop being stubborn, Lee. Unless you *want* to get us evicted? 'Cos that's what'll happen if next door reports us to the council."

"He hasn't got the bottle," Leanne retorted unconcernedly. "Anyway, they can't just evict you like that these days. They have to have proof. And then you get warnings before anything happens, so stop being such a moany old man and chill out."

Knowing that there was no point trying to reason with her while she was being like this, Terry flapped his hands in a gesture of surrender and walked out of the room. Snatching his jacket off the peg, he was just pulling it on when Leanne followed him out.

"Where are you going?" she hissed, closing the door behind her so that the girls wouldn't hear — although she wouldn't put it past them to have their ears pressed up against the wood as she spoke.

"Out," he replied coldly. "And I expect that lot to be gone by the time I get back. And I *mean* it."

"Don't tell *me* what to do," she retorted childishly. "I'm not one of your stupid kids that you can order about. And don't ever talk to me like that in front of my mates again, either, because it's really embarrassing."

Growling, "Grow up," Terry yanked the door open and walked out.

Running to catch it before it slammed behind him, Leanne closed it quietly. She felt like going after him and telling him what a wanker he was being, but then the whole block would know that they were arguing again and she refused to give them the satisfaction. It was bad enough that her friends had seen him acting like that after she'd spent so long telling them how fantastic he was for an older man. But if he thought she was kicking them out just because he'd told her to, he had another think coming. So, plastering a fake smile on her face, she bounced back into the living room as if nothing was wrong.

"Terry all right?" her best friend, Goldie, asked, handing her a spliff.

"Fine," Leanne lied, taking a deep drag. "He's just a bit tired, that's all." Looking around then, she said, "What's everyone sitting down for? I thought we were supposed to be having a party."

"You're bad, you," Goldie said, chuckling softly as Leanne went to the karaoke machine to select a new song.

"Do I look like I care?" Leanne grinned, reaching for the microphone.

Outside, Terry had just realised that he'd left his car keys in the kitchen. Telling himself that it was just as well, because he'd probably end up killing someone if he got behind the wheel while he was so wound up, he tugged his collar up and headed out of the estate on foot.

It was impossible to walk in a straight line with the wind growing fiercer by the minute, but he put his head down and struggled on through Alexandra Park, keeping an eye out for gangs of lads on bikes. There had been a spate of muggings in the park recently, but Terry almost welcomed the thought of anyone trying to jump him. He'd probably get a good kicking, but at least he'd have had someone to vent his anger on before he went down.

And, *God*, was he angry right now.

Leanne was gorgeous and he loved her to bits, and when it was just the two of them, she was happy just to cuddle up on the couch and watch TV. But when she got around her friends she was like a spoilt kid: inconsiderate, loud, and more than capable of pressing all the right buttons to get him good and riled. Not that he'd ever dream of laying a finger on her, but he got enough aggravation off the guys at work without having to take even more off her when he got home.

Still, he only had himself to blame. If she'd been any other girl, the lads would have slapped him on the back and congratulated him for getting himself a fit young bird. But he'd had to go and get caught up with Dave Miller's daughter. And he really should have known better, because Dave was one of the biggest troublemakers in Manchester. Consequently, a year on, Terry was *still* getting shit from all sides. And, much as he loved Leanne, the way she acted around her mates, he couldn't help but wonder why he bothered.

Picking up four cans of beer and a pack of tobacco from the late shop on Great Western Street, Terry went back to the park and sat on a bench overlooking the dirty, rubbish-littered lake. Rolling himself a cigarette, he tore the tab off one of the cans and took a long drink. It was freezing out here, but he was determined not to go back until Leanne had had enough time to get rid of her mates. With any luck she might even be asleep and he'd escape the sulking. But it would be *way* too much to hope that she'd cleaned up. No doubt that would be left to him — as usual.

An hour, five smokes, and all four cans later, it started to rain. Drenched to the bone in minutes as the razor-sharp needles pelted down on him, he gave up and went home — only to be pissed off all over again when he came out of the lift and heard the music still pumping out from their flat.

Inside, Leanne had been making a good show of pretending that she was having fun, but she was still fuming about Terry walking out like that. And the longer he stayed out, the angrier she got. So when she heard the front door opening and closing now, followed by the sound of the floorboards creaking as he walked past the living room, she told her friends that she'd be back in a minute and went after him.

Terry had switched on the lamp and was getting undressed when she went into the bedroom. Scowling at him, she said, "Where the hell have you been? And don't say nowhere, because you've been ages. And you didn't take the car, so you must have been close by. So, where were you — and who were you with?"

"I was out," he replied flatly, stepping out of his jeans and peeling his T-shirt off over his head. "And now I'm going to sleep, so go back to your party."

Pursing her lips, Leanne cast a disapproving eye over the wet heap of clothes he'd dropped. "I hope you're not expecting *me* to pick them up and get myself covered in shit?" she said tartly.

Telling her that he'd do it in the morning, Terry pulled the quilt back and climbed into bed, reaching out to switch off the lamp before lying down.

Immediately flipping the overhead light on, Leanne folded her arms. "You still haven't told me where you've been."

Sighing heavily, Terry reached for the remote and turned the portable TV on. He felt like telling her that he'd been shagging another bird, because that's what she obviously *thought* he'd been doing. But he didn't have the energy to deal with the tantrum which would inevitably follow if he did.

Leanne's chest heaved with irritation as she watched him. Lying there, sulking like a baby just because he hadn't got his own way. It was pathetic!

"Why are you being like this?" she demanded. "You made a right show of me back there. Don't you care that they're all laughing at me behind my back?"

"So stop bringing them round when you've promised not to and it won't get to that," Terry replied reasonably, his eyes fixed on the TV, even though he wasn't really watching it.

Stepping in front of the screen to block his view, Leanne said, "That's not fair. You know I only get to chill with them at the weekend."

"You've got all day every day to *chill* with them," Terry reminded her, emphasising the word to let her know how stupid it sounded. "But the weekend's supposed to be *our* time, seeing as I'm working all the rest of the week and hardly get to spend any time alone with you."

"No one told you to go and change your stupid shifts," she countered moodily. "And I don't see why you bothered if you hate doing lates so much."

"You know exactly why."

"Oh, what, 'cos me dad threatened you?" Leanne said sarcastically. "Big deal! And I wouldn't mind, but he doesn't even work there, so you didn't have to change your hours at all. You were just being extra."

Giving her an incredulous look, Terry said, "No, 'cos he hasn't got all the lads at work having a go at me on his behalf, or anything, has he?"

"It's not my fault if they like him better than they like you," Leanne snapped. "So stop having a go at me all the time and deal with it."

"Like it's that easy," Terry snapped back, irritated that she was trivialising it when she wasn't the one who'd had to take all the flak that had been aimed at him for the last year. "Anyway, it's just as well I *did* go for lates," he added pointedly. "Seeing as the money's better, and we need every penny we can get while I'm the only one making any effort to clear the debts."

Narrowing her eyes, Leanne said, "Oh, so now I'm a gold-digger, am I? Well, thanks for that, Tez. At least I know what you *really* think of me."

Instantly regretting the words, Terry flopped his head back against the pillow and ran a hand over his eyes, murmuring, "I didn't mean that. And you know I don't mind the shifts, but would it kill you to show a bit of gratitude?"

"*Gratitude*?" she repeated scathingly. "What, like I'm supposed to thank you for keeping me, or something? Like a fucking dog."

"All right, consideration, then," he corrected himself. "I'm wiped, Lee, and all I want is a bit of peace and quiet when we get the chance of a night in together, instead of you fetching these idiots round all the time."

"They're not idiots. They're my friends."

"They're kids."

"They're exactly the same age as me, *actually*," Leanne said sharply. "Or is that your *real* point?"

Glancing up at her, Terry let his raised eyebrow answer the question.

"Christ, anyone would think *you* were my dad," she snarled. "It's your problem if you've forgotten how to have fun, but I'm *not* letting you turn me into a boring old woman!"

"As if," Terry muttered, closing his eyes. His head was starting to pound, and the beers were beginning to churn in his stomach. "All right, can we just drop this now?" he said wearily. "I'm too tired for —"

Before he could finish, one of the girls knocked on the door and called through that Leanne's mobile was ringing.

Telling her to switch it off, Leanne waited until she'd heard her go back into the living room, then said, "I don't know what's wrong with you lately, Terry, but you're turning into a right miserable git, and it's getting right on my nerves."

"And you're a selfish bitch."

"Bollocks! You're not the only one who's had to make sacrifices, you know. I lost all my mates, too."

"Oh, so the girls aren't really here, then?" Terry said sarcastically. "Well, shit, Lee, I wish you'd told me earlier, 'cos I wouldn't have had to go out in the fucking rain to get away from them, would I?"

"If you think you're going to bully me into making them feel unwelcome, you can piss off," she hissed. "I've already lost me dad over you. I'm not losing them as well."

Terry had had enough. Looking up at her coldly, he said, "Get out, Leanne."

"You what?" she squawked, glaring back at him. "Who the fuck do you think you're talking to?"

"I'm talking to you," he snarled. "So, go on, piss off back to your mates before we both say something we regret."

"The only thing I regret is getting myself hooked up with a tosser like you," she spat, marching to the door. "And don't think you're touching me again till you stop acting like a dick, 'cos you're not!"

"Thought I was acting like your dad," he reminded her, but she'd already flounced out of the room.

Groaning when he heard the karaoke starting up again a few seconds later, Terry glanced at his watch. It was one in the morning, but to hell with the neighbours. If he had to suffer, so could they.

He turned the TV up and had just rolled a cigarette and was reaching for his lighter when he noticed that his mobile was lit up on the bedside table. He hadn't heard it ringing because of the noise — and when he saw Leanne's mum's name on the screen, he wished he hadn't seen it, either.

He felt like switching it off, like Leanne had done hers. But, knowing that Carole would come round to see what was going on if she couldn't get hold of at least one of them, and she was the *last* person he wanted to see right now, he reluctantly picked it up.

"About time!" Carole gasped. "I've been trying to get hold of our Leanne but her phone went dead, and yours was just ringing and ringing."

"Yeah, well, I'm here now, so what do you want?" Terry said — as patiently as he could manage, given that the mere sound of her voice wound him up. They were almost the same age, so it was hard for him to treat her with the respect she seemed to think that she was due as his girlfriend's mother. But it was her nasty habit of forgetting all about Leanne and flirting with him whenever she got the chance that really turned his stomach.

But there was to be no flirting tonight as, sounding remarkably sober for once, Carole grimly informed him about the fire and Connor being taken to hospital.

"You what?" All trace of tiredness gone in a flash, Terry sat up and swung his legs out of the bed. "Where is he? What's happened?"

"He's all right," Carole assured him. Then, less confidently, "Least, I *think* he is, or the copper would have said, wouldn't she?"

"Copper?" Terry repeated confusedly, already pulling his damp jeans back on. "I thought you said it was a fire? What the hell have the police got to do with it?"

"*I* don't know, so there's no point having a go at me," Carole retorted huffily. "I just got back from our Lisa's and found a note through the door telling me to ring this copper. Our Lenny and Fred were both here when she called round earlier, but the ignorant little bastards didn't answer the door, so I don't —"

"Just tell me what she said!" Terry interrupted, dragging his T-shirt on and shoving his feet into his boots.

Tutting, Carole said, "Just that there was a fire and your lad's at the hospital, and she wants to see you. So, like I said, there's no point —"

"What about Nicky?" Terry cut in again, heading for the door. "Is she all right?"

There were several seconds of silence before Carole guiltily admitted that she didn't know; that she hadn't thought to ask.

Demanding to know when all this had happened, Terry burst through the living room door and pushed his way through the girls. Flapping his hand at Leanne to shut up when she started complaining, he muttered, "For fuck's *sake*!" when Carole told him that she thought it had been a few hours ago. "Why the hell didn't Sue let me know?"

"*She*'s not there," Carole replied caustically. "She's out with that mate of hers again, picking up diseases. Anyway, the copper will tell you more about it when she sees you, 'cos I had to give her your address. Hope you don't mind, only she said you haven't told your works where you'd moved to, so I had to."

Gritting his teeth, Terry asked which hospital Connor had been taken to. Hanging up without thanking her when she'd told him, he snatched his keys off the ledge and headed for the front door.

Following him out onto the communal landing, Leanne demanded to know where he was going. And who he'd been talking to just now. And, more importantly, why had he been talking about that bitch? Was there something she should know? And he needn't bother lying, because she'd find out.

"There's been a fire," Terry told her, marching to the lift and jabbing at the button. Slamming his fist into the door when he found that it had somehow broken down in the fifteen minutes or so since he'd used it, he turned on his heel and made for the stairs instead.

"A fire?" Rushing to the handrail, Leanne peered after him. "Where?"

"My house," he called back. "Your mum's just told me our Connor's in hospital."

Furious with him for referring to his ex's house as *his*, Leanne yelled that she was coming with him. Running back into the flat, she grabbed her jacket and told the girls to let themselves out when they'd finished, then legged it down the stairs after Terry.

If he thought she was letting him go to the hospital without her, he had another think coming. Sue would be there by now, and there was no way Leanne was leaving the bitch room to get her claws into Terry again. Everyone knew she was still after him, and this was the perfect excuse for her to throw herself at him in the guise of needing comfort now that something had happened to their brat of a son.

Terry was in the car with the engine running and his mobile phone to his ear when Leanne hurtled out of the main doors. Jumping into the passenger seat beside him, she scowled at him as she dragged her seat belt on, demanding to know who he was calling now.

Ignoring her, Terry rapped his fingernails on the steering wheel. Tossing the phone into the gap beneath the radio when it went straight to voicemail, he threw the car into reverse.

Instincts bristling, Leanne snatched the phone up and pressed redial. "I *knew* it!" she squawked, her head bouncing off the back of the seat as Terry backed out of the parking space with a squeal of rubber. "How come you've still got her number, you lying bastard? You *swore* you'd deleted it."

Keeping his stare fixed on the road, Terry drove on in silence. She was right; he *had* said that he'd deleted Sue's number, but only to get Leanne off his back. Everything was so cut and dried with her. He could either have *her*, or he could have Sue and his kids — no in-betweens, no ifs or buts. But she was too young to understand that he'd *had* to keep the number in case an emergency like this cropped up. And he was too old to waste his breath explaining.

Forcing herself to hold her tongue as they drove on through the backstreets of Rusholme at breakneck speed, Leanne dug her nails into the sides of her seat and held on for dear life. It sickened her to have caught him out in a lie about his ex, and he would pay for that before the night was out. But she wouldn't press him for answers right now — not when he was already driving like a maniac.

And definitely not when they were just minutes away from coming face to face with Sue. There was no way she was giving *her* the satisfaction of seeing them having an argument. No, she would walk into that hospital with her head held high and her hand in Terry's. And if Sue didn't like it — *tough*!

Sue wouldn't have liked it. But, fortunately for Leanne, she wasn't there to see it. She was still in town, and Terry — for once — was the furthest thing from her mind. Although, normally by now, when the club was closing and they were getting set to head back to Julie's place with whichever men they'd picked up, he'd be the *only* thing on her mind.

By now, she'd usually either be stone sober and wracked with guilt for even *thinking* about doing the dirty with another man; or pissed out of her head and sobbing that she couldn't live without Terry. Either way, she'd managed to ruin every date she'd had in the last year. But, so far, tonight's date was proving to be a whole lot better than she'd expected. Although she wasn't sure why, because her man, Chris, was nowhere near as handsome as Terry; and there was *no* excuse for the slacks and slip-on shoes that he was wearing. But he was so laid-back and easy to talk to that she'd felt herself warming to him as the night wore on. And unlike the losers she *usually* got lumbered with, who spent the night sighing and looking at their watches, and generally making it obvious that they were only tolerating her for the sake of their mate who'd copped off with Julie, at least he was making an effort to get to know her.

And it was working, because by the time the lights came up and the music stopped, she found that she was actually looking forward to continuing their chat back at Julie's. It remained to be seen whether anything *else* would happen when they got there, but it was a promising start.

At least, *Sue* thought it was, but Julie obviously didn't agree.

"I am so sorry," she apologised when they headed into the toilets to re-do their make-up before the doormen kicked everyone out.

"What for?" Sue asked, elbowing a group of younger girls out of the way so they could get to the mirror.

"For landing you with such a *gimp*," Julie replied guiltily. "I promised you a good one this time, and I *swear* he was better-looking this morning. But I think he must have had a fight with the ugly monster on the way over."

"Don't be tight," Sue scolded, taking her lipstick out of her bag and slicking a fresh coat on. "He's not that bad."

Snorting softly, Julie said, "Hey, I know I told you to behave 'cos it's my birthday, but you don't have to lie to me, mate. I bet you're dying to tell him to sling it. But I reckon you'll have a fight on your hands getting rid of this one, 'cos he's well into you."

"You reckon?"

"God, yeah. Haven't you seen the way he's been drooling over you all night?"

"Can't say I noticed," Sue lied, smiling slyly as she smacked her lips together.

"Yeah, well, he has," Julie said. "And if it wasn't for mine being so loaded, I'd be helping you to do a runner. But there's a nice pair of Pradas down the road with my name on them, and I reckon I'll be able to wangle them out of him if I play him right."

"You'll be lucky to get Shoes-R-Us, never mind Prada," Sue chuckled. "You know what they say about men with money — the more they've got, the tighter they hang on to it. Anyway, you don't even know if he *has* got money."

"Course he has," Julie said confidently. "And he'll cough some of it up if he wants a bit of what I've got to offer, don't you worry about that. Only thing is," she said now, giving Sue a sheepish grin, "he won't come back to mine."

Raising an eyebrow, surprised to hear that Julie's legendary pulling powers had failed her for once, Sue said, "So why the hell are we wasting time doing up our faces when we could be out there nabbing a cab?"

"I'm not saying he doesn't *want* to," Julie told her quickly. "But he's expecting some really important business call, or something, and he's got to be at the hotel when it comes through. So he wants us to go there instead."

Frowning at her in the mirror, Sue said, "I don't think so."

"Sorry, mate. I've already kind of said yes."

"Aw, *what?*" Sue groaned, giving Julie an exasperated look. "What did you do that for?"

52

"'Cos it's the *Lowry*," Julie said, as if that made all the difference. "And they've not just got a room, they've got a *suite*."

"Yeah, and you've got a whole flat."

"But I *want* to go. *Please*, Sue . . . you know I've been dying to see what it's like in there. And it *is* my birthday, so you've got to. Just this once, and I swear I'll never ask again."

Sensing that Julie wasn't going to quit until she got what she wanted. Sue flapped her hands. "All right, fine."

"Eh?" Narrowing her eyes, Julie drew her head back. "That was a bit easy, wasn't it? I thought it was going to take all night to persuade you."

Pointing out that the night was almost over already anyway, Sue said, "And I wouldn't start trying to put me off now I've agreed to it or I might just change my mind. Oh, and you can stop being mean about Chris while you're at it, 'cos he's not that bad."

"You what?" Julie squawked, her face a mask of disbelief and disgust. "I've hooked you up with loads of decent-looking blokes in the past few months, and you haven't had a good word to say about any of them. Now you get landed with Sir Dwayne of Dweebdom, and you reckon he's not that bad?" Shaking her head, she threw her hands up in surrender and headed into a toilet cubicle, muttering, "You must be more pissed than you look, mate!"

"Not yet," Sue called after her. "But I'm sure I will be once we've raided their minibar. It's all free at them hotels, isn't it?"

"Oh, aye? Planning on making a night of it, are we?"

"Well, you've been nagging me to make more of an effort for long enough, so you can't say I'm not trying. And, who knows . . . if he's good, I might just stretch it to *two*."

"Hey, hang on a minute!" Julie laughed, coming out of the toilet with her skirt hoisted around her waist while she tugged her knickers up. "I know I said I wanted a good crack at my fella, but don't you go committing me to a whole bleedin' weekend of him. A shag's one thing, but I'm not being bored to death having to look at the fat bastard in daylight, an' all."

"Not even for a pair of Pradas?"

"*No* man's worth that much sacrifice."

Laughing, Sue said, "You wouldn't say that if you'd met my Terry." Pulling herself up short, she cursed under her breath, wondering why the hell *he*'d come into her mind.

Wondering pretty much the same thing, Julie said, "What you thinking about *him* for, you silly bitch?"

"I wasn't," Sue lied. "It just slipped out."

"Yeah, well, slip it right back in," Julie told her bluntly. "He's getting on with his own thing, and you're supposed to be getting on with yours."

Muttering that that was exactly what she'd been trying to do, Sue turned back to the mirror and fiddled with her hair, to hide the fact that thinking about Terry doing his own thing had just made her feel sick.

He was probably having it off with the little slag right this very minute; kissing her, and touching her, and . . .

"Oi!" Julie prodded her sharply in the ribs. "If you ruin my birthday getting all miserable over that ex of yours, I swear to God I'll swing for you!"

Mumbling, "I'm not getting miserable," Sue took a deep breath. Then, turning round, she held out her hand, saying, "Right, give us your phone."

"Why? Who you gonna call?"

"Well, not *him*, if that's what you're thinking. But I can't just stay out all weekend without telling Nicky where I am, can I?"

"By God, I think she means it," Julie snorted, reaching into her bag and handing the phone over. "But won't she be in bed by now?"

"Which is exactly why they invented that little thing called *texting*," Sue told her sarcastically.

"Yeah, well, hurry up," Julie said, glancing around and seeing that they were the only people left in the toilets. "If I get out there and he's legged it before I get to see the inside of his suite, you're dead."

Sticking two fingers up at her, Sue dialled Nicky's number and left her message. Then, handing the phone back, she grinned.

"Right, then. Let's go and get this birthday party *really* started."

CHAPTER
FOUR

Jay Osborne was deep in thought when she reached the hospital. For a supposedly tight-knit community like that of the Fitton estate, where everybody dipped in and out of each others' business like biscuits in tea, it amazed her that no one had been able to tell her where to find Sue or Terry Day. But they'd had plenty enough to say *about* them.

Sue, despite the odd murmurings of sympathy, seemed to be looked upon as a "bit of a slag" by most of her neighbours — and a terrible mother by them all. While Terry was classed as scum for abandoning his family the way he had — and a pervert, apparently, for taking up with a girl less than half his age. And the kids hadn't escaped the venom, either, with Connor — now that the neighbours knew he wasn't actually dead — being labelled mardy; while Nicky, despite them all saying how good she was to her brother, was seen as a weirdo for spending all her time indoors instead of running wild with her mates. And, yet if she *had* been that kind of girl, Jay had no doubt that they'd be calling *her* as much of a slag as they called her mother.

Under the impression that she must be dealing with the family from hell, Jay had been surprised when she'd checked them out back at the station to find that they didn't have any major convictions between them. Sue had been cautioned for assaulting Leanne Miller some months earlier, but it had never gone to court, due to a lack of cooperation on both sides. And, apart from a couple of old convictions for fighting, the only recent notes on Terry related to allegations of domestic violence, and trespassing on his estranged wife's property without her consent — none of which had progressed to formal charges, because Sue had apparently refused to take it any further when push came to shove.

All of which seemed like the usual tit-for-tat games of an estranged couple, in Jay's opinion, which made her curious to know why everyone seemed to have turned against them so vehemently.

Traditionally, communities like that tended to be pretty evenly divided when there was a marriage breakdown; some siding with the victim, the rest with the villain. But, in this case, it seemed that neither of the Days had much support. And Terry's troubles seemed to have extended to work as well as home, according to his foreman, who had told her, when she'd contacted him to try and get Terry's address, that Terry had been forced to change shifts a few weeks back after suffering months of harassment from the workmates on his regular shift.

So, were they just horrible people who deserved everything they got? she wondered. Or were the neighbours and workmates just a particularly vindictive bunch? Either way, the Days certainly seemed to have a lot of enemies — any one of whom could have been the shadowy figure seen running from the scene after the window had been smashed tonight.

When Carole Miller had finally returned her call and given her Terry's address, she'd gone straight over there, only to find that Carole had beaten her to it and he'd already left — leaving several scantily dressed drunken teenage girls having a party there in his absence.

Wondering if maybe there was some truth to the pervert rumours after all, Jay had reminded herself as she headed over to the hospital that whatever Terry Day had or hadn't been getting up to with the Lolitas, at least he'd had the grace to tear himself away and go to his son in his hour of need. And one parent was better than none, given that the boy's mother still hadn't turned up.

Jay had left three messages on Sue Day's phone now, trying to convey the urgency of the situation without shocking her with actual details. Although she'd been sorely tempted to spell it out, if only to give Sue a kick up the backside for switching her phone off. Surely the whole point of having a mobile was to make sure that you could be reached in an emergency, so God only knew what her poor kids had been going through if *they*'d been trying to get hold of her tonight — which was very likely, Jay thought, since it had now been ascertained that the electric had run out at some point before the fire had started. But maybe that was the exact reason why she *had* turned her phone off: so that her kids couldn't interrupt whatever fun she was having with a trivial thing like needing money for the meter.

There was still no sign of Nicky, and the fire crew were convinced that if she *had* been there she'd left before they arrived. And, if that were true, then Jay could think of several possible reasons why.

She could have nipped out to get money off her mother for the electric, for example, unaware that someone had smashed the window and started a fire in her absence. Or maybe she'd panicked when the house was attacked and had run out to escape the fire, forgetting that Connor was still inside. Or she could have been injured, and was now wandering the streets in a state of shock. She might even have started the fire herself and run away. Or maybe she just wasn't as conscientious as everyone seemed to believe, and had simply sneaked out as soon as her mum's back was turned, leaving her little brother alone for the night.

Any of those scenarios was feasible, but Jay would still have expected Nicky to have come home by now, or at the very least been seen. But the fact that she hadn't been seen or heard from was worrying, because it wasn't safe for a fifteen-year-old girl to be wandering the streets at this time of night.

Hoping that Nicky's father might be able to throw some light on her whereabouts, Jay took the lift up to the intensive-care unit now. Directed to a side room at the far end of the ward, she tiptoed towards it, conscious of the patients whose lives were hanging in the balance all around her.

Terry Day was standing in the corridor just around the corner, his shoulders slumped, his head hung low as he gazed through the window at his son on the bed inside. Looking him over as she approached, Jay was struck by how handsome he was. He had thick, closely cropped brown hair, a strong nose, and just enough stubble to make him look manly rather than scuzzy. And he looked quite muscular, she thought, which indicated that he obviously took care of himself. Although, sadly, the same couldn't be said of his clothes, which were absolutely filthy, and — even from that distance — stank of stale sweat.

Sensing Jay's presence just then, Terry turned and peered at her with pain-clouded eyes. Knowing immediately that she was plain-clothes, a wave of dread washed over him.

"You've found her, haven't you?" he asked, his voice flat and low.

Guessing that he was expecting to hear that Nicky was dead, Jay shook her head. "No, sir, we haven't. But the fire crew are still at the house, and they'll find her if she's there." Gesturing towards a row of chairs against the wall behind them now, she said, "Do you think we could sit down for a minute? There are a few questions I need to ask you."

"*Questions?*" Terry repeated, confusion flashing through his eyes. "What can I tell you? I wasn't even there. If you want to question anyone, it's their *mam*." He spat the word out, leaving Jay in no doubt how he felt about his ex-wife.

Telling him that she hadn't managed to reach Sue yet, Jay walked over to the chairs. Following, Terry flopped down on one and sat forward, his elbows resting on his knees.

"Could I ask where you were tonight between the hours of nine and ten o'clock?" Jay asked.

"Work," Terry replied without hesitation. "Why?"

Assuring him that they were just routine questions, Jay said, "I've already spoken to your supervisor, and he's told me that your shift ended at ten. Is that right?"

"Officially, yeah," Terry said, his frown deepening. "But I didn't actually get away till half past, 'cos I had some stuff to clear up in the basement."

"Do you have any witnesses to that?" Jay asked.

"Didn't think I'd need any," Terry retorted indignantly.

"Did you leave the factory premises at any time before your shift officially ended?" Jay went on.

"Only for a smoke," Terry said. Then, "Jeezus, you think I've got something to do with the fire, don't you? I'm going out of my mind here with worry about my kids, and you really think I'd do something to hurt them?"

"I'm not accusing you of anything," Jay told him evenly.

"Doesn't sound like it," Terry muttered, running his hands through his hair. Then, "Right, I started work at two this afternoon, and stayed till half past ten. Got home about eleven, had a row with my girlfriend and went to bed. Then her mam rang and told me about the fire, so I got dressed and came straight here. So now you know everything, maybe you can go back to the house and find my daughter, instead of wasting time giving me the third degree!"

Sensing from the anger that was sparking in his eyes that he was telling the truth, Jay chose her next words with care, because she didn't want to raise his hopes only to have to dash them if she subsequently got word that a body *had* been discovered at the house.

"We're not absolutely sure about this," she said. "But we think there's a possibility that your daughter might not have been at home tonight."

"Course she was," Terry replied adamantly. "She's *always* there when her mam goes out. Sue thinks I don't know what goes on, but she forgets that Leanne's mam lives across the road. And *she* makes sure I hear all about everything." Pausing, he fisted one large hand and cupped the other one around it as if to control his anger before continuing. "It's all wrong, you know: making Nicky look after Connor when they could both come to me. But she reckons I've got no rights because I did the dirty on her. And she's already had me nicked for going round there when I thought she was out, so what am I supposed to do? *Demand* to see them, and have the lying bitch tell *you* lot that I've battered her again? I don't think so."

Jay could feel his frustration when he stared at her, challenging her to deny that he'd been given a rough ride. He had previous for violence, and there was no denying that there was something decidedly unsavoury about a man of his age surrounding himself with the type of young girls she'd glimpsed through the door of his flat tonight. But he obviously cared about his children, and that was no bad thing in a world where so many fathers walked away without a backward glance.

Slumping back in his seat after a moment, Terry stared up at the ceiling and blinked rapidly to keep the tears that were stinging at the backs of his eyes from bursting through. He'd been on a knife's edge since arriving at the hospital to hear that Nicky hadn't been brought in along with Connor, terrified that she was injured or dead. But, much as that thought grieved him, he equally couldn't bear the thought of Connor being alone in the house.

Waking up in the middle of an inferno with no one to comfort and protect him. Calling for his daddy and getting no reply . . .

Assuring him that the fire crew would do a much more intensive search of the house as soon as the site had been cleared for safety, Jay said, "In the meantime, can you think of anywhere else where Nicky might have gone tonight? Any relatives she might have decided to visit, or school friends? Or maybe she could have met up with her mother?"

"No way," Terry spat, his cheek muscles jumping as he clenched his teeth. "Sue might have got her own way with making me back off, but she wouldn't *dare* drag my kids into any of her shit."

Coming along the corridor just then carrying two steaming Styrofoam cups of coffee, Leanne narrowed her eyes when she saw the blonde talking to Terry. Quickening her pace, she marched up to them and demanded to know what was going on.

"She's from the police," Terry told her quickly, knowing from her expression that she was on the verge of kicking off. "They're trying to find Nicky, and they want to know if I've got any idea where she is."

"How are *you* supposed to know?" Leanne said sharply. Then, to Jay: "How's *he* supposed to know when he wasn't even there when it happened? He came straight home to me after work — and you can ask my friends if you don't believe me, 'cos they were all there."

Shaking his head surreptitiously to shut her up, because she was being too defensive and that was bound to make the policewoman suspicious, Terry said, "I'll tell you everything in a bit, but I need to get my head round it first. And I've got to try and think where Nicky might be." Looking at Jay now, he said, "No point talking to mine or Sue's families, by the way. They fell out with us before Nicky was born, so she doesn't even know where any of them live."

"Okay, well, we'll start with her friends," Jay said. "But don't worry if you can't think of any — I can always contact the school."

"I'll try," Terry said, pushing himself to his feet. "But I'm going to have a bit of a walk, 'cos I can't think straight while I'm so close to . . ." Trailing off, he gestured with a nod towards Connor's room.

Telling him to take his time, Jay tore a couple of sheets out of her notepad and handed them to him, asking him to write down any names he remembered.

Snatching at Terry's lapels as he made to walk away, Leanne planted a possessive kiss on his lips. Then, whispering a warning not to go chatting anyone up, she let him go, watching like a hawk until he'd passed the nurses' station. Going to his vacated chair then, she sat down and sipped at her coffee, peering at Jay over the rim of the cup.

Aware that she was being checked out as a potential threat although she couldn't understand why the girl was so insecure when she was so pretty, Jay said, "You must be Leanne?"

"Yeah. And?" Leanne held her gaze defiantly.

"Could you tell me where you were between nine and ten tonight?" Jay asked.

"At home," Leanne declared, a glint of victory in her eyes as she added, "And you can ask the miserable old git from next door if you don't believe me, 'cos I went round there at about half-nine to warn him to stop banging on the wall."

Nodding, Jay said, "Thank you."

"Where do you think Nicky is, then?" Leanne asked now, sipping at her coffee. "You don't reckon she's dead, do you?"

"We really don't know anything at the moment," Jay told her coolly, picking up on the complete lack of concern behind the words.

"Have you tried asking her *mam*?" Like Terry before her, Leanne spat the word out as if it stuck in her throat to say it. "We thought she'd have been here by now, but she obviously can't be bothered," she went on, her eyes flashing with spiteful hope as she added, "Unless this had something to do with her and you've already arrested her?"

"We haven't managed to contact Mrs Day yet," Jay informed her.

Sniffing contemptuously, Leanne said, "Too busy with her latest man, no doubt. Still, it's probably just as well she's not here because she's pushed Terry too far this time. You watch if he doesn't get them taken off her and put into care after this."

Raising an eyebrow, Jay wondered how Terry Day would feel if he knew what his girlfriend had in mind for his children. She'd barely known him for two minutes herself, but she sincerely doubted that he'd let them go without a fight if the social services *did* decide to remove them from their mother's care.

Coming back just then, Terry gave a sheepish shrug and said, "Sorry for getting shirty with you back there. I know you're only doing your job, but it just felt like you were accusing me, or something. Anyhow, here you go." He handed his list to Jay. "Sorry it's not much, but these are the only girls I remember our Nicky mentioning. And I've got no idea where any of them live, apart from Sophie Gordon. She was Nicky's best friend when I was still there."

Taking it, Jay stood up, saying, "Right, well, I'd best get on. I'll call round to see you as soon as I have any news about Nicky."

"Thanks," Terry murmured. "But you'd best ring first, 'cos I'll be stopping here till Connor comes round."

"Oh, *Terry*," Leanne complained. "That could be ages."

A flicker of irritation in his eyes now, Terry said, "Don't worry, I'm not asking *you* to stay."

Folding her arms, her lips pouting childishly as she cast a hooded side-glance at Jay, Leanne said, "I didn't mean it like that, and you know it."

Saying goodbye, Jay left them to it.

"Any joy?" PC Ann Hayes asked, starting the engine when Jay climbed back into the car a few minutes later.

"Same as the neighbours," Jay told her, pulling on her seat belt as Ann reversed out of the parking space. "Convinced Nicky would have been at home." Reaching up, she switched on the interior light. "He's given me a few names and an address. The handwriting's quite bad, but I think it says Derby Road."

Glancing at it, Ann said, "Yeah, it does. And that's just round the corner from the Days, so it's probably right."

Pulling up outside Sophie Gordon's house ten minutes later, Jay and Ann got out of the car and hurried up the path as the wind-driven rain pelted down on them. They rang the bell and were both shivering when the hall light came on a minute later and footsteps padded quickly down the stairs.

Opening the door an inch, Trevor Gordon peered out through sleep-crusted eyes. "Yes?"

Introducing herself through chattering teeth, Jay said, "Sorry for disturbing you, sir, but we need to speak to Sophie."

"You've got to be joking," he spluttered. "Do you know what time it is?"

"We realise it's late," she said apologetically. "But this really is urgent."

"What the hell's so urgent that you'd drag a fifteen-year-old girl out of her bed in the middle of the bloody night?" he demanded.

Jay started to explain about the fire, but he cut her off mid-sentence, saying, "Yes, I've already heard about that, thank you. And I can assure you it's got nothing to do with Sophie, because she's been here with me and my wife all night."

"We're not suggesting that your daughter was involved in the fire," Jay said evenly. "But Nicky Day is missing, so it's vital that we speak to as many of her friends as possible in order to find her." Taking the list of names Terry Day had given her out of her pocket now, she showed it to him, saying, "I believe these are some of your daughter's school friends."

Glancing at it, Trevor shrugged. "I don't recognise any of them."

"But your daughter might," Ann snapped, irritated by his seeming determination to obstruct them. "So, if you could just bring her down, please, sir?"

Sighing, Trevor shrugged in a gesture of defeat, and said, "Fine. As long as you don't have her up all night."

Assuring him that they would keep it as brief as possible, they followed him into the living room. Flicking the overhead light on, Trevor told them to take a seat, then headed back up the stairs, coming back a few minutes later with his daughter and his wife.

Sophie's eyes were dark with fear as her father herded her around to the front of the couch. She didn't think she'd done anything wrong, but her dad was already pretty mad at her for having the police round at this time of night.

"There's nothing to worry about," Jay told Sophie as she perched nervously in the centre of the couch between her parents. "We just need to ask you some questions about Nicky Day, if that's all right?"

Nodding, Sophie clutched her hands together nervously in her lap.

"I believe you've already heard about the fire?" Jay said when they were all settled.

"I've already told you that it's got nothing to do with her," Trevor chipped in before Sophie could answer.

"And we've already told you why we need to speak to your *daughter* about this, sir," Ann said coolly, holding his gaze until he looked away.

"Did you also know that Nicky went missing tonight?" Jay went on.

"No!" Sophie gasped, the shock in her voice telling Jay that the girl had genuinely had no idea. "God, I hope she's all right."

Reassuring Sophie that she was sure that Nicky would be fine, Jay held out the list of names and asked if she knew where any of the girls on it lived.

Nodding, Sophie said, "Kira and Cheryl live on Barton Road, and Michaela lives on Yates Close."

"That it?" Trevor said when Jay had written the addresses down. "Only I've got to get up for work in three hours."

Making no move to follow as he got up and walked towards the door, Jay said, "We have a missing child to find, sir. And I'm sure you'd appreciate as much help as possible if it were *your* daughter we were looking for."

"That would never happen," he replied sharply. "My daughter's not the kind of girl to go wandering off like that."

"And Nicky Day *is*?" Jay gave him a questioning look. "Only, that's not the impression we got from her neighbours or her father."

Sensing that they were going to get nowhere if her husband carried on like this, Marie Gordon said, "Why don't you go back to bed, love? I'll stop down here with our Sophie."

Gritting his teeth, Trevor shook his head and came grumpily back to his seat. He'd never get to sleep knowing that they were down here saying God only knew *what* to the police.

Keeping her focus on the girl while the father glowered at her from the sidelines, Jay said, "Nicky's dad tells me you're her best friend, so I'm guessing she'd have told you things that she wouldn't have told anybody else. Like, if there was anything troubling her at home. Anything which might have made her want to run away."

Bolstered by her mother's comforting hand on hers, Sophie said, "We don't really see all that much of each other nowadays, to be honest, but I know her and her mum get on okay."

"How about her dad?"

"Not sure. She hasn't really mentioned him since he left."

"I take it she wasn't very happy about it?"

"Not really. And her mum was a mess, so she had to kind of look after her as well as Connor."

"I've been told she's very good with Connor."

"Yeah, she's great. She does most stuff for him. Makes his dinner, and plays with him, and that."

Nodding, because this corresponded with what they had already been told about the Day children, Jay said, "She sounds like a nice girl."

"She is." Sophie smiled sadly. "I wish we still hung out together like we used to, but she's got too much on at home now, so I only ever see her at school. But we *are* still mates."

"Is there *anyone* you can think of who Nicky might have gone to see tonight?" Jay persisted. "A boyfriend, maybe?"

"Definitely not," Sophie said, blushing at the mere mention of what was a complete no-no subject in her own home. "And I can't see her going round to anyone's house, 'cos she hardly ever used to come *here*, even when we were best mates. I don't think her mum likes it, 'cos she thinks people are quizzing her about her dad, and that."

Guessing that Nicky had probably stayed away from *this* house more to avoid Sophie's less-than-friendly father than her own mother's displeasure, Jay turned to the subject of school.

"Your year have got exams coming up soon, haven't you? But if Nicky's been doing so much at home, I can't imagine she'd have had much free time for revision. Do you think she might have been worrying about that?"

Shaking her head, Sophie said, "No, she's always been cool with school work. It was more the stuff that happened with her dad that was bothering her. She went kind of funny after that. Sort of like a loner."

"Did that affect her relationships with the other pupils?"

"Not with *me*," Sophie said loyally. "But some of the others were a bit off with her because of her dad and Leanne."

"Because of the age difference?" Jay asked perceptively, guessing that the kids in the area probably mirrored the attitudes of the adults, in which case Nicky might have felt as if she was being picked on from all sides.

"I think it's more because some of Leanne's mates still go to our school, and they turned against Nicky after her mum went for Leanne." Hesitating, Sophie bit her lip before adding, "It's mainly Kelly Greene who's got a problem with her now, though. Most of the others have stopped going on about it, but Kelly won't let it drop. Nicky's never actually said anything, but I've heard Kelly having a go at her a few times. And yesterday . . ." Pausing, she cast a nervous side-glance at her father.

"Yesterday?" Jay prompted.

"Well, I heard that Kelly was supposed to be after her," Sophie said, her eyes beginning to glisten with tears. "I don't know what happened, though, 'cos Nicky ran out straight after the bell, and I didn't see her when I was walking home."

"When you say Kelly was after her, do you mean that she wanted to fight with her?"

Biting her lip even harder now, Sophie nodded. "They were all talking about it at school, how Kelly was going to jump her when she came out of the gates at home time, and that."

"I'd better not find out you were involved," Trevor said sharply.

"Course not," Sophie protested. "Nicky's my friend. I'd never do something like that to her."

"So, why didn't you tell someone if you knew what they were planning?"

"I *did*," Sophie sobbed. "I told Miss Newton, and she said she'd look into it." Swinging her gaze back to Jay now, she said, "Please don't tell Kelly I told you. She'll kill me if she finds out it was me who grassed her up."

Reassuring her that anything that was said in this room would stay here, Jay asked if Kelly had caught up with Nicky.

Dabbing at the tears with the tissue that her mother had just handed to her, Sophie guiltily admitted that she didn't know.

"I saw them all at the front gates when I was telling Miss Newton, but they were legging it onto the back field by the time I came out, so I think they must have sussed that she'd gone that way instead. And I know I should have gone round to see if she was all right, but I was scared they might be watching her house, 'cos that's what Kelly's like. If she wants you, she won't leave it alone."

"She'd better not touch you," Trevor said angrily. "Or she'll have me to answer to."

"I'm sure it won't come to that," Jay said quickly. "And if it does, I'd appreciate it if you gave us a call rather than try to deal with it yourself."

"Fine," Trevor said brusquely. "You keep my daughter out of it, and *I*'ll keep out of it. And you can look at me like that all you like," he went on. "But you obviously don't live round here, so you don't know what a battle it is trying to protect your kids from the gangs. They're like animals, smashing the place up and fronting up to anyone who dares pull them up about it. And God forbid we should lay a hand on one of the little bastards, 'cos you lot come down on us like a ton of flaming bricks."

"He's not blaming you," Marie said, jumping in apologetically. "We know your hands are tied, but it is really rough round here. And we'd love to be able to move the kids to somewhere nicer, but it's a vicious circle if you can't afford to buy. You ask the council for a transfer, and they just offer you something even worse, so what can you do?"

"It must be hard," Jay said sympathetically, fully understanding Marie's despair — and feeling a grudging respect for her husband, who was obviously only trying to protect his family. A little over-zealously, maybe, but Jay wished there were more parents like him in the area. It would certainly make her job a lot easier if there were.

Saying, "I think we're just about done," she stood up. "Thanks for your help, Sophie. And sorry again for disturbing you, Mr and Mrs Gordon."

Climbing back into the car a couple of seconds later, she said, "Sophie certainly seemed scared of this Kelly Greene girl."

"Probably got good reason," Ann grunted. "I take it you haven't had the pleasure yet, so be warned, she's a cocky little bitch. But if her mum's in, you'll soon see where she gets it from."

Back at the hospital, Terry was still out in the corridor. He'd been told that he had to stay out until the doctor had been and okayed it for him to go in. But every time he asked how much longer the doctor was going to be, he was told that he'd have to be patient; that the doctor was with a more urgent case right now and would be with them as soon as he could.

Pacing a tight circle in the corridor now, he was chewing his dirty nails to the quick. He desperately needed a smoke, but he didn't want to risk going down to the ground floor in case Connor woke up while he was gone. And he could have done with another brew, but there was no way he was asking Leanne to go and get it for him while she was being such a bitch.

Watching him with growing irritation, Leanne tutted loudly and said, "For God's sake, will you keep still? You're making my eyes hurt."

Snapping that keeping on the move was the only thing that was keeping him sane right now, Terry said, "Anyway, I thought you were going home?"

Lips tightening, Leanne folded her arms and jiggled her foot a little faster, muttering, "Yeah, I bet you'd like that, so you can chat up the nurses behind my back."

"Don't be so stupid," he hissed, casting a quick glance back along the corridor to make sure that nobody had heard her. "I just don't see the point of you being here when you obviously don't want to be."

"I'm not going till you do," she shot back stubbornly. "And don't talk to me like that or I'm going to get really mad, 'cos I still haven't forgiven you for making a fool of me in front of that snotty copper."

"Me make a fool of *you*?" Terry snorted. "That's a joke!"

"Hear me laughing?" Leanne snarled, her eyes flashing furiously. "No, 'cos I don't find it funny. You're lucky I didn't kick off, the way you were eyeing her up."

"You're off your fucking head," Terry retorted angrily. "Eyeing her up. As if!"

"You were. I was watching you."

"You always are, and you're always wrong. Just like you are now — *dead* wrong. 'Cos I've got better things to do than eye flaming women up."

"Like what?" Leanne demanded. "March round like a stupid caveman, making out like you're *oh so* upset. Like, boo hoo, look at me crying 'cos my kid's inhaled a bit of fucking smoke!" Sucking her teeth now, she gave him a dirty look.

Stopping in his tracks, Terry's face was paler than she'd ever seen it as he stared down at her, his eyes flashing a clear warning that she was going too far.

Unable to hold his gaze, she looked away. But there was no apology.

"You'd better go," he said thickly. "I mean it, Lee. Just go."

Folding her arms even tighter, Leanne shook her head.

"I need to be alone," Terry said, struggling to control the rage that was stirring in his gut.

Leanne's eyes were glistening with tears now and her voice was both accusing and hurt as she said, "You *won't* be alone, though, will you? You'll be with *them*." She gestured with a nod towards the duty nurses at the far end of the ward. "And they'll be flirting with you as soon as my back's turned."

"Will you get it into your thick head that I'm not fucking interested," Terry spat. "Not in them, not in that flaming copper, and not even in *you* at the moment."

Jumping to her feet, her cheeks flushed with indignation, Leanne said, "If that's supposed to be some kind of threat, you can fuck off, 'cos if anyone's going to finish with anyone round here, it'll be *me* finishing with *you!*"

Feeling the heat of embarrassment crawl up his neck, Terry grabbed her arm and told her to quieten down.

Yelling, "Get off me!" Leanne jerked away from him, her voice seeming to bounce back at him from every wall as she said, "You're always putting those stupid brats before me, but I've had enough! I've done everything for you, but if you don't appreciate me, I —"

Seizing her by the wrist, Terry hauled her down the ward and out into the corridor. Pushing her into a corner, he brought his face close to hers and said, "My son's in there on his deathbed, and my daughter's God only *knows* where, and all you want to do is talk *shit*! But it stops now, Leanne — do you hear me? I can't turn my back on them, and if you don't understand that, *tough*."

Unable to get free as Terry held her in his powerful grip, Leanne pursed her lips and glared up at the ceiling, refusing to look at him.

Exhaling wearily after a while, Terry let go of her and, shoving the stairwell door open, headed down to the ground floor. Going out into the cold night air, he sat down on a partially sheltered bench and rolled a cigarette. He hadn't wanted to leave the ward, but there was no way he could go back in there just yet. He was too ashamed.

Catching up with him a few seconds later, Leanne struck an aggressive hands-on-hips stance and glared down at him.

"Not gone yet?" Terry said coolly, knowing from experience that she was probably expecting him to apologise for shouting at her.

"Is that what you want?" she demanded, her breath pluming out around her head. Scowl deepening when he gave an unconcerned shrug, she said, "Right, you've had your chance, but you obviously care more about *him* than you do about me, so I'm off. And I'm not coming back."

Turning on her heel, Leanne stomped down the path towards the pavement. Pausing there, she looked each way along the road in search of a cab. Hissing, "*Shit!*" when she saw that the road was deserted, she closed her eyes. Then, taking a deep breath, she turned and marched back to Terry with her nose in the air and her hand outstretched.

"Keys."

Lighting his cigarette, Terry took a slow drag on it. "Sorry, I didn't quite catch that?"

"I said I want the keys," she repeated through clenched teeth. "You want me to go, so give me the keys. Unless you'd rather I *walked* home and got myself raped?"

"Yeah, right," Terry snorted. "Who's going to try it on with you when you've got a face like that on you?"

"Just give me the keys."

"Can't." He shrugged. "The car's not running right."

"Funny how it was fine when you needed it," Leanne sniped. Rolling her eyes when he still didn't move, she gritted her teeth and said, "All right, *please.*"

Taking the keys out of his pocket, Terry held them out, saying, "See, you *can* act like a grown up when you want to."

Snatching them from him, Leanne told him to go and fuck himself and walked abruptly away. Hearing his boots scraping against the concrete behind her and thinking that he was coming after her, she started running and didn't stop until she reached the car. Jumping in, she slammed the locks down and tore out of the parking lot.

Speeding all the way home, she'd just reached the perimeter of the Fitton estate when she spotted a police car ahead. Slamming her foot on the brake, knowing that she could get arrested and the car seized if they pulled her up and found that she didn't have a licence, she passed it at a more sedate speed, her stare glued to the rear-view mirror in case they decided to follow.

"Typical," Ann snorted, watching the retreating tail lights of the other car in her own rear-view as she pulled up to the kerb outside Kelly Greene's house. "You can hear them tearing about from miles off, but soon as they spot us they're down to little-old-granny speed in no time."

Smiling her agreement, Jay gazed up at the house they were about to visit. Catching the blue glow of a TV when the curtains at the front bedroom window twitched, she said, "Looks like someone's up."

"Damn," Ann muttered, grinning as she unbuckled her seat belt. "And I was *so* looking forward to disturbing them."

Maggie Greene was downstairs and at the front door before they made it up the path. Nipples jutting out from her saggy breasts like downturned coat pegs as the wind invaded the short silky dressing gown she was just about wearing, she folded her arms and demanded to know what they wanted.

"Your lass," Ann told her firmly, letting her know from the off that she needn't bother pulling any of her usual stunts. "She in, is she?"

"Why, what's she done now?" Maggie asked, sounding bored.

"We believe she was involved in a confrontation with another girl at school yesterday," Jay told her. "And we need to speak to her about it."

"A *confrontation*," Maggie repeated, a mocking edge to her voice as she jerked her head at Ann. "Christ, where'd you find this one? Down the encyclopaedia shop, or what?" Grinning nastily now, she took a cigarette out of her pocket and lit it, exhaling the smoke into Jay's face.

"Going to go and get her?" Ann said bluntly. "Or do I have to do it myself?"

"Got a warrant?" Maggie retorted coolly.

"Got any witnesses to say you didn't invite me in?" Ann shot back.

Taking another lazy pull on her smoke, Maggie lifted her foot and kicked back at the door, yelling, "*KELLY!* Get your arse down here!"

"I'm in *bed!*" Kelly yelled back.

"So was I, but I had to get up," Maggie snapped. "And it's not even *for* me, it's for you, so shift it."

"What's for me?" Kelly demanded grumpily, the sound of her bedroom door being yanked open and slammed back against the wall drifting down to them, followed by angry footsteps on the stairs.

"These *ladies* would like a word," Maggie said, her voice thick with sarcasm as she stepped back into the hall.

Narrowing her eyes when she saw them, Kelly said, "What d'y' want?"

"Do this inside, shall we?" Ann said, forcing Kelly to take several steps back as she walked in uninvited.

Jutting her jaw out in irritation as Jay immediately followed suit, Kelly slammed the door and marched past them into the living room.

"Go on, then," she snapped, flopping down onto one of the fur-cushioned armchairs and folding her arms. "Tell me what I'm supposed to have done."

"We'd like to ask you about an incident at school yesterday afternoon," Jay told her, sitting on the facing chair. "An alleged fight between yourself and Nicky Day."

"What fight?" Kelly said, the blasé look on her face matching the tone of her voice. "I didn't have no fight."

"But you were *intending* to," Jay said, fully understanding why a nice, sheltered girl like Sophie Gordon would be so afraid of this girl.

"Not me," Kelly lied. "You've got the wrong person."

"We know you were intending to have a fight with Nicky, and that there are witnesses who could verify that," Jay told her coolly. "And I'm sure the school's CCTV system will show you and your friends gathering at the school gates at home time. So, how about we stop playing games and talk about it sensibly?"

Shrugging, Kelly said, "Don't bother me. Anyway, even if I *was* going to have a fight, it's no one else's business so long as it's not on school property."

"So, you're saying the fight was outside school?"

"No, I'm just saying it'd be no one's business."

"But you did see Nicky yesterday?"

"*Duh!*" Kelly pulled a face. "Course I *saw* her. We go to the same school."

"But you're denying that you had a fight with her?"

"Yeah, I am," Kelly replied defiantly. "Not that I wasn't *going* to," she added, grinning slyly now. "But she shit herself and did one before I got the chance."

"Language," Ann chided, shooting the girl a warning look.

Jumping to her daughter's defence, Maggie said, "Don't you be coming round here telling my kids how to talk in their own house. You might think you're something out there, but you're nowt in here." Turning on Jay now, she added, "And you can pack in talking to her like that, an' all. We've got rights, you know."

Ignoring her, Jay kept her focus firmly on Kelly, who had a gloating grin on her face now, obviously loving the fact that her mother was defending her.

"When you didn't catch Nicky at the front gates, you went out the back way to catch her — isn't that right?"

Narrowing her eyes, wondering who had been blabbing details, Kelly said, "So what? It's not illegal."

"Did you catch up with her?" Jay persisted, sure now that this girl *had* been bullying Nicky, and wondering if that was why Nicky had run away — if she'd ever arrived home in the first place. And given that Kelly obviously relished causing trouble, it was entirely possible that she could have physically attacked Nicky, leaving her hurt and unable to get home.

"This is serious," she snapped when Kelly just shrugged. "Nicky is missing, and if that's got anything to do with what happened at school, you need to tell me."

"Don't be blaming me for that," Kelly snapped right back. "Last I heard the stupid bitch had burned to death in a fire with that mongy brother of hers."

"Oh, so, you've heard about the fire, but I don't suppose you'd know anything about how it started, would you?" Jay said accusingly. Then, "Where were you between nine and ten o'clock last night?"

"Oi, you'd best not be accusing her of having anything to do with that fire," Maggie said protectively. "She was here with me and her brothers all night. And I'll fetch them down so they can tell you themselves, if you want?"

Narrowing her eyes, Jay continued to peer at Kelly's face. This was the first time she'd met her, but there was something really familiar about her . . .

"So, you've been at home all night, have you?" she asked in a deceptively soft voice when it suddenly came to her.

"Yeah, that's right," Kelly replied truculently. "So?"

"So, perhaps you could tell me *how*, when I saw you at Terry Day and Leanne Miller's flat when I called round there earlier?" Jay said.

"You'd better bleedin' *not* have been!" Maggie barked, switching the glare onto her daughter now.

"I wasn't!" Kelly protested, throwing her arm up to protect her face when her mother raised her hand. "Honest, Mam! I was in me room."

"No, you weren't," Jay said firmly. "I saw you."

"You bloody little liar!" Maggie yelled, landing a thudding blow on the side of Kelly's head. "I've told you a thousand times to stay away from that pervert. And I don't want you hanging about with that slag, neither. Didn't I have enough bother with her when she was after copping off with your dad?"

"It was me Uncle Aidan she was after, not me dad," Kelly protested. "Ask our Rob if you don't believe me."

Jumping up when Maggie went to lamp Kelly again, Jay stepped nimbly between them and reached for Kelly's raised hand. Taking it firmly by the wrist, she peered at the knuckles.

"How did you get these scrapes?"

Tugging her hand free, Kelly stuck it under her arm, muttering, "None of your business."

"Have you been fighting with Nicky Day?" Jay demanded. "You can either tell me here, or I'll arrest you and take you down to the station for formal questioning."

"All right, I'll tell you," Kelly said, casting a resentful glance at Jay and a nervous one at her mother. "If you must know, I did it on my brother."

"You what?" Maggie barked. "What have I told you about hitting our Ben, you nasty little cow? He's only eight!"

"He winds me up," Kelly retorted, wincing when her mother raised her hand again. "He's a cheeky git, 'cos he knows you'll jump in and protect him no matter what he does. You let him get away with murder."

"I'll bloody murder *you* if you lay one more finger on him," her mother warned her.

Feeling a sudden urge to laugh out loud that this girl was actually indignant about another child getting away with murder when *she* quite obviously lived her own life by those same rules, Jay said, "You still haven't answered my question, Kelly . . . Where were you between nine and ten tonight?"

"Here!" Kelly and her mother shouted in unison. Then Maggie said, "And she was definitely in then, 'cos she come down to watch that film with me . . . that what's-it-called about the thick fella."

"*Rain Man*," Kelly said.

"Yeah, that's the one," Maggie said. "*Rain Man*! And it was on ITV if you want to check out what time it started and finished, but she was definitely here then." Giving Kelly another fierce glare now, she said, "If she snuck out after that, she's gonna bleedin' know about it. But that's our business, not yours, so you can both piss off now, can't you."

Standing up, Jay said, "We'll be back, Kelly, because I'm still not satisfied that you're telling the entire truth about what happened with Nicky at school."

"Yeah, well, make sure you've got a warrant next time," Maggie told her frostily.

"If need be," Jay said tartly, already heading out of the door.

Jumping back into the squad car, she bit her lip and glanced at her watch, saying, "Don't know about you, but I think we should leave the other girls for now and see about organising a search of the land behind the school. It's just a field back there, isn't there?"

"Old railway line and park," Ann corrected her. "Might as well be a field, though, because no one ever uses it except to dump their old rubbish. It's way too overgrown for the kids to play on."

"Kind of place where an injured girl could lie undiscovered for some time?" Jay said quietly.

"I suppose so," Ann agreed. Then she added grimly, "But I hate to think what state she'll be in if the rats have been at her. There's *thousands* of the buggers in there at night, and they're huge."

Shuddering at the image, Jay said, "Let's go back to the station and see what we can set up."

CHAPTER
FIVE

Standing at the window beside the drinks machine in the small waiting room, Terry sipped at his coffee and gazed out at the traffic below, mesmerised by the glimmer of headlights dancing across the puddles dotting the road.

It had stopped raining a couple of hours back, and a faint sliver of sunlight was beginning to appear on the horizon. People would be coming in before too long and filling up the chairs behind him. But right now he felt totally alone. Although there might as well have been ten people inside his head, the amount of thoughts that were flying around in there. Mainly concern about Connor, who still hadn't shown any signs of coming round. And dread about Nicky, who still hadn't been found. And, in between all that, worry about Leanne, and what he was going to do about this latest mess of theirs.

The nurses had been kind when he'd gone back to the ward after she'd left last night, telling him that he shouldn't feel bad about the scene she'd made, because relatives often reacted like that in the pressurised atmosphere of the ICU, where concern about loved ones sent emotions soaring. But, while he was grateful for their understanding, it didn't make him feel any better, because he knew that Leanne couldn't use that as an excuse for *her* behaviour. She didn't even like Connor, never mind love him. And she couldn't stand Nicky, either. But then, Sue hadn't exactly made it easy for her and the kids to get to know each other, so it wasn't entirely her fault.

"Mr Day?"

Jumping at the sound of the voice, Terry turned and looked at the young nurse.

"Sorry," she apologised, smiling up at him. "Didn't mean to shock you. I just wanted to make sure you were okay?"

"I'm fine," he lied. "But how's Connor? He's not had a turn or anything, has he?"

"No change," the nurse assured him. "But that's a good sign, so don't worry. The first twenty-four hours are the worst, but if there's no deterioration in that time there's usually a very good chance of a full recovery." Giving Terry a concerned look now, she said, "You must be exhausted. Why don't you nip home and have a bit of sleep? I've got your mobile number if we need to reach you before you get back."

Terry didn't want to go, but she was right about him being knackered. And he could really do with a shower, because the stench of sweat was knocking *him* sick, so God only knew what it was doing to her.

Nodding, he said, "Yeah, all right. Just — you know — call me if there's any change."

"Of course."

Dipping his gaze when she smiled at him again, Terry sidestepped her and rushed out.

Walking back to the flat, because he figured it would be quicker than waiting for a bus, he was half expecting to find Leanne's mates still there when he let himself in. But it was not only empty, it was also spotlessly clean — which made him feel like a complete bastard for all the nagging he'd done earlier.

Going quietly into the bedroom, Terry gazed down at Leanne as she lay sleeping. She was so beautiful, and he felt guilty about all the shit he'd been putting her through lately. *He* was the one who'd cheated on his wife, and it had been *his* decision to do it in his marital bed. And the fact that it had been a drunken mistake that he probably would have regretted as soon as he was sober made no odds. Sue had caught them, and he'd had to take the consequences when it had all kicked off.

And Leanne had stood by him when everyone else turned against him, despite her dad falling out with her over it — which had really hurt her, Terry knew, because she'd always been a daddy's girl. But instead of thanking her for her loyalty, Terry had spent the last few months making her life a misery; resenting her for getting on with her life and having fun, because he still felt too guilty to dredge up a smile.

He knew exactly what everyone thought of him for getting caught in bed with a sixteen-year-old, and he didn't blame them, because he'd have thought the same if he'd been looking at someone else in that position. And the fact that Leanne was almost eighteen now and that he'd grown to love her was beside the point, because the face he saw in the mirror every morning was still that of a dirty old man.

But that was his problem, not Leanne's, and if he didn't get a grip and stop punishing her for it, he would lose her as well as everything else.

Tiptoeing out of the room now, Terry cleaned himself up and got changed. Then he wrote a quick note for Leanne, telling her that he loved her, and was sorry about their row and wanted her to come to the hospital when she woke up. Leaving it and a ten-pound note for a taxi on the pillow, he crept out again, picking up the car keys on the way.

Stretching lazily when she woke up several hours later, Leanne rolled over to give Terry a kiss. Frowning when she found that his side of the bed was empty, it took her a moment to remember what had happened the night before.

Snatching the note up when she saw it, she read it with a sneer, then screwed it up and threw it across the room. If he thought she was letting him off the hook that easily, he had another think coming! He'd been completely out of order shouting at her like that, and he'd have to do a damn sight better than say sorry in a poxy letter before she would even *think* about forgiving him. And if he seriously thought she was going to waste that tenner on a taxi to the hospital so she could sit and watch him moping over his brat of a son all day, then he was more stupid than he looked.

Shoving the quilt aside, Leanne got up and padded through to the living room to find her phone. Switching it back on, she rang Goldie to ask if she was still having the party she'd mentioned last night.

"Don't tell me you're actually going to come?" Goldie teased. "Wow, I'm honoured. You haven't set foot in my place all year."

"Not that easy when you're dragging a fucking great ball and chain around," Leanne said flippantly. "Anyway, never mind all that, who else is going?"

"Everyone," Goldie told her. Then, lowering her voice as if afraid that Terry might be listening, she said, "You're not planning on bringing Terry, though, are you? Only I don't think that'd be such a good idea."

"He's not coming," Leanne assured her, sliding a cigarette out of her packet and lighting it. "He's still at the hospital."

"Oh, right." Goldie sounded relieved. "Everything okay?"

"Fine," Leanne said offhandedly. "Anyway, what you wearing?"

Hanging up when she'd found out what she wanted to know, Leanne switched the phone off again to prevent Terry from getting hold of her and putting the mockers on her plans. Finishing her cigarette, she went back into the bedroom to root through her clothes.

Settling on a pair of skin-tight black satin pants that she hadn't worn in ages because Terry reckoned they were indecent, and a red halter-neck top that he hated her going out in because it made her boobs look amazing and he couldn't bear the thought of all the

92

lads getting a free eyeful, she laid them out on the bed and ran herself a bath.

Sod Terry. If he wanted to move into the hospital for the duration, that was his business. But Leanne had a life to be getting on with, and she was going to start enjoying it for a change.

Back at the hospital, Terry sat beside Connor's bed for the rest of the day, listening to the bleeping machinery and trying to block out the cries of the other patients and relatives who were suffering their own nightmares in the adjoining rooms.

Focusing all his attention on Connor, he willed him to come round, and prayed like he'd never prayed before. And not just the usual "Do this for me, God, and I swear I'll never smoke or drink again" kind of praying; but a deep, heartfelt plea for his son's recovery — and for Nicky's safe return.

And it seemed to be working — in Connor's case, at least — because the doctor had been really pleased with his progress when he'd checked on him that evening, calling it a miracle that Connor had escaped without more serious injury. And when Terry had asked why he still hadn't come round if he was doing so well, he'd said that it was quite normal; that patients — particularly children — tended to stay under for quite a while when they had experienced the kind of shock that Connor had suffered.

"Sleep is the body's way of repairing itself," he'd said. "Without the added stress of the conscious mind reminding it of the trauma that it's suffered."

That seemed plausible enough to Terry, but he still couldn't relax. Not until he was sure that Connor wasn't suffering any of the other things that the doctor had mentioned they were looking out for. Like *pneumonia*.

Just the word alone scared the hell out of Terry, who had always associated it with certain death. And the doctor's assurance that they very rarely lost patients to it these days did little to ease his fears. He wished Leanne would come and take his mind off it all, but she still hadn't turned up, and every time he'd tried to call her, her phone had been switched off. And Carole wasn't answering hers, so he couldn't even get her to go round to the flat and check if everything was all right.

Worn out with worrying about Connor, and with frustration about not being able to contact Leanne, Terry didn't even realise he'd fallen asleep until he was woken by a faint whimpering sound some time later. Confused by the darkness, unaware that a nurse had been in and switched the light off and drawn the blinds, he peered at the strange silhouettes in the room, trying to figure out where he was.

Hearing the noise again, he realised it was Connor and jumped to his feet, saying, "That you, son? You awake?"

Forcing his gluey eyes open at the sound of his father's voice, Connor peered blurrily up at him.

Resisting the urge to hug him, because he was terrified of dislodging any of the tubes or wires, Terry turned to the door and yelled for help.

Bustling in seconds later, the nurse flicked the overhead light on. Smiling when Connor winced in the sudden brightness, she said, "Well, hello there, little man. Had a good sleep, did we?"

Opening his mouth to answer, Connor immediately started to gag.

"What's happening?" Terry yelped, afraid that his son was choking. "Do something!"

Placing a gentle hand on Connor's shoulder, telling him to try and lie still until the doctor came to take a look at him, the nurse reached over and pressed a button on the wall behind his bed.

Trusting the caring tone of her voice, even though he felt like he had something really big and horrible stuck in his throat, Connor gazed up at her fearfully, trying his best not to struggle.

"What's wrong with him?" Terry asked again, wringing his hands together behind her.

"Nothing," the nurse assured him quietly. "This is the usual response when patients wake up with the tube." Smiling at Connor again now, she said, "But you're being a whole lot braver than some of the bigger boys we have in here, I can tell you. You wouldn't believe the fuss some of *them* kick up. But you're being really good, and I bet your daddy is really proud of you."

"I am," Terry mumbled, swiping at a tear that was trickling down his cheek.

Coming in a few seconds later, the doctor took a quick look at Connor then turned and headed for the door, jerking his head at Terry to follow.

"Everything looks fine," he said quietly. "But I'm going to remove the tube and take a look down his throat with a camera to make sure there's nothing nasty lurking down there. Now, you're quite welcome to stay, but I warn you it isn't the most pleasant of sights, so I'd advise you to go and get yourself a drink if you don't think you're up to it."

Reluctant to leave Connor who looked every bit as scared as he himself was, but unable to bear the thought of watching the procedure they were about to perform, Terry opted for the drink. Backing guiltily out of the room, he called out to Connor that he'd be back soon.

Getting a coffee from the machine, he carried it down to the ground floor and out to the bench that was beginning to feel like part of his own furniture because he'd visited it so many times over the last few hours.

Jay and Ann had just come out of a burger shop on Oxford Street when they got the call telling them that Connor had regained consciousness. Jumping into the car, they headed straight to the hospital.

Telling Ann to park up and eat her burger before it got cold, Jay got out of the car and walked towards the main doors — too deep in thought to notice Terry staring at her from the bench a few feet away.

The search of the field had gone badly, and she'd been thoroughly humiliated when one of the PCs had pointed out — loudly, to make sure that everyone heard him putting Jay in her place — that the "signs of disturbance" she'd thought she'd found near the bushes edging the perimeter fence were most likely the result of all the feet that *she* had directed into that area in her first frantic push to locate the body she'd been so sure they would find there. And as for the blood she'd found on the rock, and the clump of hair tangled in the brambles, well, they could have come from anyone or any*thing*. And even if the material *had* belonged to her "invisible murder victim", it was already so contaminated by the bad weather and whichever animals had traipsed through the scene between it being deposited and subsequently discovered that it would be absolutely unusable as evidence.

That bruising to her ego had kept Jay awake long after she'd climbed into bed that morning. Not to mention the rollicking she'd had off DI Hilton for wasting manpower and hours on the basis of nothing more substantial than an instinct. So, after tossing and turning for several hours, she'd given up on trying to sleep and had headed out to do in her own time what she should have done during her shift the night before.

Calling on each of the girls in Kelly Greene's gang in turn, Jay hadn't been surprised that they had all been expecting her. Or that they all mirrored Kelly's version of events about the alleged fight at school. Yes, they *had* known that Kelly wanted to "get" Nicky, they'd admitted. And, yes, Jay probably *would* see them on the CCTV footage running across the field if she checked. But no, they hadn't caught up with her then, and nor had they gone round to her house later. And between nine and ten that night, they had all been watching *Rain Man* with their parents.

Whether or not they were telling the truth, Jay still thought that the fear of Kelly's threats might have been a factor in Nicky's disappearance. But without proof, Kelly was off the hook. And Jay had nobody but herself to blame, because she'd given Kelly ample opportunity to coach her friends while she'd been busy conducting her abortive search.

Annoyed with herself about that, she'd pushed the girls to the back of her mind and had turned her attention to finding out which cab firm Sue and her friend had used. Which turned out to be a simple matter of asking Pauline Wilson, who knew both the company name and number, having seen it on the top of the cars that regularly picked Sue up on Friday nights — as, Pauline said, she could have told Jay yesterday, had Jay thought to ask.

Speaking to the actual driver, Jay had been disappointed to hear that he didn't know which club Sue and her friend had gone to, because they'd got out at the bus station to buy a pack of cigarettes from the machine and he'd had to leave them to make the rest of the way on foot because he'd already been late for another pick-up. But he *had* been able to tell her the friend's name. And, even better, her address.

Julie Ford's flat was on the third floor of a crumbling block in Cheetham Hill — a fair few miles from the Fitton estate in Rusholme, which probably explained why none of Sue's neighbours had known her. Getting no answer when she knocked, Jay had tried the flat next door, hoping that the tenants might know where Julie was, or have a phone number where she could be reached.

The neighbour hadn't been able to help Jay with any of that, but she *had* told her that, every Friday without fail for the last seven or eight months, Julie and her friend had been in the habit of bringing men home at all hours of the morning — and making a hell of a lot of noise about it. But *last* night there had been none of the usual commotion, and the neighbour had managed to sleep through the night undisturbed — an unusual enough occurrence for her to think it worth mentioning.

Getting the same story from the neighbours on the other side, Jay began to suspect that something sinister might be going on. Because if Sue had done the same thing every Friday for months, then surely it couldn't be a coincidence that she should suddenly break that pattern on the exact night that her daughter disappeared.

But did that mean that Sue had done something to Nicky, Jay wondered, and gone out as usual that night knowing that the neighbours would see her, only to slip back in a short time later and start the fire to destroy the evidence — maybe even throwing the brick that had been found in the debris through her own window, in order to make it look as if someone with a grudge had done it?

But if that were the case, then Nicky's body would have been found at the scene. And even if Sue had changed her mind and dragged it out before the fire brigade got there, she'd have had a hell of a time getting rid of it without somebody seeing her — even with her friend's help. They could hardly have dragged it along the streets looking for a safe place to dump it. They would have needed a vehicle — which neither of them had.

But Terry Day did. And when the fire started, it would have been parked up behind the factory where he was working. No one around to see if an ex with a spare key came along and "borrowed" it for half an hour.

Reaching the doors now, Jay pressed the buzzer, just as Terry called out to her.

Still on the bench, his heart was pounding and he could feel the sweat literally pouring off him. She'd said that she would come to see him when she had news about Nicky, so did this mean that they had found her? And if so, was she alive or dead?

Peering at Terry, not immediately recognising him because he looked so much fresher than he had the night before, Jay frowned when she realised it was him. Considering his son had only just come round, she'd have thought that he'd have been more concerned about spending time with him than feeding his nicotine addiction.

Unless Connor had taken a turn for the worse in the few minutes it had taken her to get here?

"Is everything all right?" she asked, walking quickly over to him now. "Connor is awake, isn't he? The nurse just rang to say he was."

Relieved that she wasn't here to give him bad news, Terry nodded, and said, "They reckon he's okay, but they're just taking the tube out to have a proper look down his throat. That's why I'm out here," he added guiltily. "The doctor told me it'd be best not to watch."

Agreeing that it was probably for the best, Jay said, "I'd like to talk to him, if that's okay? See if he can tell us anything."

Saying, "Yeah, course, I'll take you," Terry waved her towards the doors.

The nurse was just coming out of Connor's room when they got there. Barely glancing at Jay, she gave Terry a warm smile.

"It's all done, and he's had a little drink, but his throat will be sore for a while, so Doctor's given him something for the pain. He'll probably start to get drowsy again fairly soon, but, all in all, everything's looking good, so you can relax."

"Do you think he's up to talking?" Jay asked.

"He should be okay," the nurse told her. "But you'll have to keep it to an absolute minimum. No more than five minutes."

Thanking her, amused that Terry hadn't seemed to notice the adoring way the nurse had been looking at him, Jay followed him into Connor's room.

Connor's huge dark eyes seemed to be engulfing his entire face as he gazed out from beneath the covers. Ruffling his hair and squeezing his shoulder — the best he could manage for a show of affection in front of a stranger — Terry said, "This lady's from the police, and she wants to have a quick word about the fire."

Hearing the word "police", Connor's eyes widened even more, and his skinny little chest began to heave.

Guessing wrongly that it was the mention of the fire which had freaked him out, Jay gave him a reassuring smile and walked around the bed to sit on the chair and get more on his level.

"Don't worry, I won't keep you too long," she said. "But I just want to ask a couple of questions about what happened last night, if that's okay?"

Connor didn't even try to open his mouth, and several long moments of silence passed before Terry decided to answer for him.

"Course it is," he said, giving Connor's shoulder another squeeze. "The nurse says he's been really brave already, so I'm sure he won't mind talking to a pretty lady like . . ." Trailing off, Terry blushed and dipped his gaze, sure that she'd think he was flirting with her — which he wasn't.

Ignoring the slip, Jay kept her focus on Connor, asking, "Do you remember what happened, Connor?"

Terrified that he was in trouble, that they had found out that it was him who'd started the fire and were going to send him to the home for naughty boys that his mum was always threatening to send him to if he was bad, Connor squeezed his eyes shut.

"You must have been scared when the electric went off," Jay persisted gently, working on the assumption that he'd still been awake at that point, given that the neighbour had recounted hearing him crying when the house was already in darkness. "I bet Nicky made you feel better, though, didn't she?"

Still getting no answer, Jay decided to take a more direct approach. She didn't like to put words into people's mouths, but this was serious enough to warrant it.

"Is that why she went out, Connor?" she asked gently. "To try and find your mum, to get some money for the electric? Or was she hurt by the brick that was thrown through the window?"

Tears were rolling down Connor's cheeks now. Nicky hadn't been there when the electric went off, but he couldn't tell the policewoman that, because then they'd be angry with Nicky and lock her up in the bad girls' home. But everything was fuzzy after that; all he could remember was waking up and coughing really bad because the room was full of smoke, and trying to get down the stairs. Then nothing till he woke up in here.

"He must be tired," Terry said apologetically. "Maybe you'd best leave it till he's properly awake."

Nodding, Jay stood up. Giving the little boy one last smile, she said, "I'll come back to see you when you're feeling a bit better. And don't worry, everything will be fine."

"Sorry about that," Terry said when they were back out in the corridor. "He's usually got more to say for himself. But I'll have a go when you've gone; see if he'll talk to me."

"Okay, well, that's my mobile number," Jay said, taking a card out of her pocket and handing it to him. "Call me if he tells you anything. And it doesn't matter how small or insignificant you might think it is. He's the last one who saw Nicky, so whatever he remembers it's got to help."

Nodding, Terry slipped the card into his back pocket. His voice low now, he said, "What you said in there just now — is that what you think might have happened? That Nicky went out to get money for the electric?"

"I don't know," Jay admitted. "We *do* know that the electric had run out before the fire started, so I'm hoping that might be why she wasn't there when the crew went in."

"And the brick. You don't think it hit her as well, do you?"

"It's a possibility, if she was in the bed with Connor at the time," Jay told him. "But I really don't think it's wise to jump to conclusions until we've heard what Connor's got to say."

Nodding, Terry said, "Yeah, I know." Then, folding his arms, he said, "I, er, meant to ask if you've found his mam yet? Only he's bound to start asking for her now he's awake, and I don't know what to say."

Telling him that Sue's phone was still switched off, and that nobody had seen or heard from her, Jay decided not to mention that she'd been to Julie's flat because then she'd have to explain that the women hadn't been seen there either. And if Terry put two and two together and came to the same conclusions that she herself had reached about Sue's possible involvement in the fire, God only knew what he'd do if he got to his wife before she did.

Going back into the room when she had gone, Terry sighed when he saw that Connor was fast asleep again. Checking his mobile only to find that he still had no messages or missed calls from Leanne, he sat down and gazed at his son, praying that he wouldn't be asleep for too long this time, because there were loads of questions he needed to ask him.

Goldie's party was in full swing when Leanne arrived. She'd been ready for hours before setting off, but she'd wanted to get there late in order to make as big an entrance as possible.

The small flat was overflowing with people and there were more out on the balcony, dancing to the heavy Niche music that was pumping out through the open door as the strong scent of weed drifted through the air. Surrounded as soon as she walked in, Leanne found herself being hugged and kissed by friends she hadn't seen since leaving school. Feeling as if she was right back where she belonged, she was soon boasting about her new flat, proudly describing all the new furniture, the flat-screen TV, and the amazing stereo.

When the lads from the Fitton Crew arrived half an hour later, she broke away from her girlfriends and rushed to greet them. Having been one of only three girls who'd ever been properly allowed into the gang when they were at school, she considered these lads amongst her oldest, dearest friends. With the exception of Zak Carlton, who'd been her actual boyfriend until he'd decided to cheat on her, but he didn't appear to be with them, so that was okay.

"Hey, babe," Lance Thompson drawled, a flash of gold glimmering out from his whiter than white teeth as he swept her up in an affectionate hug. "Didn't know you were coming."

"What, stay away and miss seeing you?" Leanne beamed. "Never!"

"So, where you been hiding?" Lance asked, putting her down at last and looking her over with approval.

"Oh, you know, here and there," she said evasively. "Anyhow, never mind me, what have *you* been up to?" Stepping back, she gave him the once-over he'd just given her. "You look fantastic. Have you been living at the gym, or what?"

"Nah, man," he grinned. "'S all natural."

"You were never this buff at school," she teased, reaching out to give his newly developed muscles a squeeze — noting, with a little hint of pride, that they weren't as solid as Terry's.

"And you were never this *hot*," Lance drawled, his eyes raking over her body. "Mmm *mmm!*"

"Don't you be getting fresh with me, Lance Thompson," Leanne scolded. "I'm not one of them pushover white gals you can sweet-talk out of her knickers, you know. Anyhow, shift and let me see the rest of them," she said then, pushing him out of the way to get to Jase Brittax.

Still cooler than cool, Jase slipped an arm around her waist and gave her a kiss, drawling, "Long time no see, babe. You're looking good."

"So are you," she said, feeling a little tearful now as she hugged him. "You all are. I can't believe how much you've changed."

"We're the same old guys from way back," Lance laughed, putting a hand on her back and guiding her towards the couch. Jerking his head at the people who

106

were already sitting there to move, he sat down and patted the cushion beside him, saying, "So, come on, tell us what's been happening in Lee Land?"

Loving being the centre of attention, Leanne was soon telling them all about her wonderful new life, unaware that Zak had just walked in.

Getting himself a bottle of beer from the kitchen, Zak leaned in the doorway and watched as Leanne laughed and joked with his boys. He hadn't seen her since he'd heard about her getting off with the old-man neighbour of hers, and that had vexed him, because he'd wanted to confront her and find out if she'd had the hots for the dude while she'd been seeing him. Goldie had told him that it hadn't gone down like that, but he hadn't known whether to believe her because girls would say anything to protect their friends. But now Leanne was here, looking better than ever and acting like she'd never been away, he didn't know how he felt. But there was definitely anger in there somewhere.

Oblivious to the chill air blowing from Zak's direction, Leanne was laughing at something Lance had just said when Kelly Greene suddenly appeared in front of her. Instantly irritated, because it seemed like she couldn't get rid of the girl since she'd made the mistake of agreeing to let Kelly's cousin Neela bring her to one of the karaoke parties, she peered coolly up at her and asked what she wanted.

"Where's that bitch Nicky?" Kelly demanded.

"What the fuck are you asking me for?" Leanne snapped. "And what's with the attitude?"

Blushing when the lads started sniggering, Kelly's lips tightened. If anyone else had spoken to her like that she'd have kicked their head in. But Leanne was older than her, and probably harder. And, anyway, Kelly really liked her.

Making an effort to temper her tone now, aware that she'd probably been a bit too pushy, Kelly said, "Sorry. It's just that I had the pigs round at mine last night, asking all sorts of questions."

"What's that got to do with me?" Leanne said, not even trying to pretend that she gave a toss.

"I thought you might know where she is, that's all," Kelly muttered, sticking her hands deep into her pockets.

"Yeah, well, I don't," Leanne informed her dismissively. "And if you don't mind, I'm *trying* to have a good time here, so piss off."

"I'm only saying," Kelly retorted sulkily. "Only they were making out like I've done something to her, and I haven't."

"Maybe you should have," Leanne flipped back disloyally. "I'd give her a slap myself if I could, but I'm not *allowed*."

"They know I was at yours," Kelly blurted out as Leanne turned her attention back to the boys. "The policewoman recognised me."

"*And*?" Leanne sounded positively bored now.

Shrugging, Kelly said, "I'm just saying."

"Right, well, thanks for letting me know. Bye."

Confused by Leanne's coldness, but unable to stand there any longer with all the lads laughing at her, Kelly slunk away. She hadn't meant to upset Leanne, but she'd obviously pissed her off by asking about Nicky when everyone knew how much she hated her. But if Leanne fell out with her over it and stopped her going round for the karaoke parties, Nicky was dead — however long it took the shit-arsed little bitch to show her face again.

"What was all that about?" one of the lads asked when Kelly had gone.

"Oh, nothing," Leanne tutted. "Just that fire last night. One of the brats has gone missing, and the pigs are trying to find her."

"Wasn't she supposed to have started it and done a runner?"

Jumping at the sound of Zak's voice, Leanne's stomach did an involuntary flip when she peered up at him. He was just as fit as she remembered — if not *more* so, since he'd had his hair cut short. And the flashy diamond stud in his ear looked really sexy. But those lovely blue eyes that had used to melt her heart held no affection as they gazed back at her now.

"Her, or her *dad*," he said pointedly.

"Don't talk shit," she muttered. "Terry was with me all night."

"Only saying what I heard," Zak said quietly, taking a slow drink from his bottle.

"Yeah, well, whoever you heard it from, you can tell them they're wrong," Leanne retorted, anger giving the strength back to her voice. "And don't be saying it to anyone else, or you'll start a war."

"Like I care," Zak said scornfully. "The cunt deserves everything he gets."

"Why's that?" Leanne demanded. "And don't bother coming out with any of that shit about him being a *whatever*, 'cos I'm nearly eighteen, in case you've forgotten."

"I think the word you're looking for is pervert," he replied coldly. "And, yeah, that is what I was about to say, 'cos you weren't that old when you started fucking him, were you?"

"Get lost!"

"Whoa, chill, guys," Lance interjected, grinning to ease the tension that was sparking between them. "This is supposed to be a party."

"Tell *her*, not me," Zak said.

"You're lucky Terry's not here listening to the shit you're saying about him," Leanne snarled, shooting daggers at him. "He'd kill you if he was."

"And I'm supposed to be scared by that, am I?" Zak sneered, flinging his arms out and looking around as if expecting Terry to walk in. "Well, where is he, then? I'm waiting."

Coming in just then lugging the crate of beer she'd just been out to buy, Goldie took in Zak's aggressive stance and the tears glistening in Leanne's eyes, and said, "I hope you're not being a knob, Zak, 'cos you can fuck off if you think you're ruining my party."

"It ain't me," he retorted. "It's your friend there, defendin' the child molester."

"Aw, not all that shit again," Goldie groaned, handing the crate to one of the lads to take into the

110

kitchen. "How many times have you got to be told? She wasn't with *you* when she got with *him*, so get over it."

Sucking his teeth to let her know exactly what he thought of that, Zak said, "You don't think I'm bothered about *that*, do you? She wasn't worth worryin' about then, and she sure as hell ain't worth it now."

Coming to Zak's defence when Goldie started threatening to kick him out, Lance said, "Yo, he's only saying what everyone else is already saying."

"What, so Terry falls in love with me, and that makes him a pervert?" Leanne gasped, giving him an incredulous look. "Well, thanks for that, Lance. I thought you were supposed to be my mate."

"Yeah, well, now you know better, don't you?" Zak informed her nastily. "You lie with dogs, you get fleas, an' then *no* one wants to know you."

"Shut up!" she snapped. "You don't know anything about me and Terry, so keep your fucking big nose out!"

"I don't know what you're defending him for," Zak retorted. "You can't think that much of him, flashing your tits at everyone like that."

"Like I'd flash anything at a dickhead like *you* when I've got a real man at home," Leanne spat.

"Coming here dressed like that?" Zak said, looking her up and down. "I've seen less flesh on show in a fucking lapdancing club!"

Feeling the heat rise to her cheeks as the music suddenly stopped and everybody turned to watch the argument, Leanne said, "Sounds about right for you, that. Always knew you'd turn out to be the kind of sad twat who'd have to *pay* for it!"

"As if!"

"Yeah, well, I'm dressed exactly the same as all the rest of the girls here. So what makes me so different?"

"Oh, I don't know," Zak drawled. "Maybe the fact that everyone in here with a dick has already had you."

"Oh, like you're such a virgin," she shot back. "You've probably shagged every bitch in here, *and* their mams."

"I haven't had her," Zak said coolly, gesturing at a girl who was standing behind her. "Or her . . . or her . . ."

Tears of humiliation pouring down her cheeks now as the onlookers began to snigger, Leanne snatched up her bag and her jacket and shoved her way out of the room.

"See what you've done now?" Goldie hissed, punching Zak on the arm before running out after Leanne.

"Leave me alone," Leanne sobbed, struggling to get free when Goldie caught up with her halfway down the road and grabbed her. "I'm going home."

"Not like this," Goldie said concernedly. "I know you're upset, but you shouldn't let him get to you. Anyway, it's not like you haven't heard it all before — about Terry, I mean. And all that other shit was just Zak mouthing off 'cos you hurt him. You know he doesn't mean it."

"Yes, he does," Leanne cried, swiping at the tears with the back of her hand. "It's been horrible for the past couple of days, and I just wanted to chill with my mates, but he's ruined everything."

"Come back in and stop being so soft," Goldie urged. "It'll have blown over by now, you watch. And Zak will be crawling up your arse trying to make it up to you."

Shaking her head, Leanne said, "No, I'm going home."

"Well, at least wait till I've got my coat so I can walk you," Goldie said. "Please, Lee, you're my mate and I don't want to leave you on your own like this. I know how hard it's been for you lately, and you know I haven't got a problem with Terry. Well, not till he starts moaning, anyhow. But I can see why you fancy him, 'cos I wouldn't say no. And neither would any of the other girls — which is probably what's got Zak's back up."

"Stupid bastard," Leanne muttered, sniffing softly. Then, half-smiling through the tears, she said, "And I'd best not catch you trying it on with Terry behind my back now I know you fancy him."

"As if," Goldie snorted. Then, more seriously, "You gonna come back in, or what?"

Shaking her head, Leanne said, "No, I need to be by myself for a bit; get all that shit Zak was saying out of my head." Gazing at Goldie sincerely now, she said, "I wasn't doing anything wrong, you know. I was just happy 'cos I haven't seen them for so long. It's their business if they thought I was flirting, but nothing was ever going to happen, 'cos I love Terry too much to cheat on him."

"I know," Goldie said softly. "But you know what blokes are like. They get the wrong end of the stick, then beat you round the head with it when you knock 'em back. Anyhow, here," she said now, sliding a tiny flick knife out of her back pocket. "Take this. But if you have to use it, make sure you wipe it, 'cos I don't want it coming back to me."

Laughing softly, Leanne said, "You're such a drama queen."

"Better safe than sorry," Goldie insisted, pushing the little switchblade firmly into her grasp.

Thanking her, Leanne slipped the knife into her pocket and set off for home, rerunning the argument she'd had with Zak in her head as she walked. She wished she'd whacked him one, because he deserved it for what he'd said about Terry — and even more so for what he'd said about her, making her out to be the local bike like that. But, pissed off as she was about that, it was something *she*'d said that was niggling at her just now. Something that was lodged at the back of her mind . . .

Terry! she realised with a start. She'd told Zak that Terry had been with her for the whole of Friday night, so couldn't have been involved in the fire. But he *hadn't* been there the whole time. He'd come home from work later than usual, for a start. And then he'd gone out for ages, and refused to tell her where he'd been when he got back. And that was *before* they'd heard about the fire, so could it be possible that —

"No way!" Leanne muttered, shaking her head to prevent the thought from taking hold. Terry would

114

never start a fire knowing that his kids were in the house.

Unless it had happened by accident?

He could have had an argument with Sue, and things could have got out of hand — which would explain why *she* still hadn't turned up, because he'd *killed* her and hidden her body somewhere; giving himself enough time to get home before anyone found out he'd even been there.

Yeah, right! And if it was anyone but Terry she was thinking about, she might have believed it. But she knew him inside out and upside down, and he just wasn't capable of doing something like that.

Just as he wasn't capable of beating a woman up, like Sue had accused him of doing to her last year. And Leanne ought to know, because they'd had some terrible rows and she'd said some horrible things, but he'd never so much as raised his hand to her.

But the police didn't know that. All they knew was that he'd been in prison for fighting in the past, and had more recently been accused of battering his wife. And if they decided to ask the wrong person the right question . . .

Like Kelly Greene, who was already upset with Leanne for dissing her in front of the crew back at Goldie's just now. What if she decided to get her revenge by grassing Terry up?

Thoughts racing now, Leanne headed into the subway, oblivious to how dark it had suddenly become. But when she heard footsteps behind her a few seconds later, her fingers instinctively closed around the knife.

115

Yanking it out of her pocket, she released the blade and spun around to face whoever it was.

"Whoa!" Zak said, catching the flash of metal and stopping in his tracks. "It's only me. I'm not going to do anything."

"What the *fuck* are you sneaking up on me like that for?" she gasped, shaking furiously.

"Goldie told me to come after you and make sure you got home all right. But I guess I should have known you'd have it covered, though, eh?" Grinning now, Zak pushed her hand aside so that the knife was no longer pointing at him. "Since when did you start carrying a blade?"

"Since I heard there were idiots like you running round," Leanne retorted angrily. "What do you want, Zak?"

"To walk you home," he told her again. "And to say I'm sorry for kicking off like that. Peace offering?" he said then, taking a spliff out of his pocket.

Shaking her head, Leanne set off walking again.

Easily catching up, Zak said, "So, you accepting my apology, or what?"

Folding her arms as he strolled along beside her, Leanne didn't answer. He was one of the best-looking lads she'd ever been out with, and under different circumstances she'd be flattered that she could still get him running round after her like this. Despite being one of the only white guys in the crew, Zak was just as cool as the rest of the lads and all the girls fancied him — which was saying something, because the black lads had cool down to a fine art. But she just didn't trust him. Not now he'd made it so clear that he was still thinking stupid things about her and Terry.

"I'm making an effort here," Zak went on. "And I don't have to, you know. Not after what you did to me back in the day."

"What *I* did to *you?*" Leanne snorted. "You're the one who couldn't keep your dick in your pants."

"All right, so I cheated," he conceded. "But at least the girls I slept with were the same age as me. And I reckon you're only touchy about what I said about *him* 'cos you know I'm right."

"No, you're *wrong*," Leanne insisted — genuinely meaning it, because tonight's run-in with Zak had reminded her that Terry was the only man she'd ever met who didn't make her feel threatened, stupid, or cheap. And that was because he *was* a man, whereas Zak and the crew were still just boys; children who thought that their new muscles and bad-ass attitudes earned them automatic respect.

Looking into Leanne's eyes, Zak detected a dullness that hadn't been there before. Saddened that she'd allowed herself to be dragged down like that, he said, "You've changed."

"Course I have," Leanne snapped. "That's what happens when you grow up. But you wouldn't know that, because you and the crew are still stuck in the old days."

"You're wrong," he said earnestly. "You might think you've passed us by, but we've all moved on, too. You just can't see it."

"Hey, I looked. But all I saw was the same old shit going on that used to happen way back."

"Yeah, and I've apologised for that. But I've still got a right to my opinion."

"Even if you're wrong?"

"In *your* opinion."

"There's no point having this conversation," Leanne said flatly. "Yeah, I've changed, but my life's better for it. I've got my own place, and a man who loves me, while you're all still living at home with your mummies and daddies."

"And you're not?" Zak gave her an incredulous look. "Come off it, Lee, the dude might as well be your dad."

"Oh, what, because he's older than me?"

"No, because *he*'s the one who's paid for all the shit you've been bragging about tonight."

"I do my share."

"Cleaning up now and then, and opening your legs," Zak said scathingly. "Who you trying to kid?"

"It's an equal relationship, actually," Leanne spat, resenting the way he was trying to cheapen what she had with Terry.

"If you say so," Zak replied without conviction. "But don't be knocking me and the crew, 'cos at least we've earned everything we've got."

"You call mugging people *earning*?" Leanne sniped. "Do me a favour."

Genuine anger flashing in his eyes now, Zak said, "We've never mugged anyone in our fucking lives, and you know it. I can't believe you even said that."

"Oh, really," Leanne snorted. "So, where did you get the money to pay for all the flash gear?"

"From working," Zak told her bluntly. "We've all been grafting our bollocks off since we left school, while you've been playing queen of the castle and taking handouts from your old man. So who's the grown-ups now? Us, or you?"

Leanne could feel the heat burning her cheeks, but there was no point trying to defend herself because Zak wouldn't understand what she had with Terry. It wasn't about who earned what, it was about just being together.

And she wished she was with him right now, because he was worth ten of Zak. But she couldn't go to him in this state. She'd have to go home and sleep off the booze and the weed before she could face him again.

Stopping when they reached the mouth of the subway, Zak watched as she carried on walking.

"This isn't over," he called after her. "We had something, and I'll be seeing you again. Believe."

Ignoring him, Leanne kept on going.

CHAPTER
SIX

Connor slept right through the night and late into the next morning. Waking up, he was thrilled to find his dad asleep in the chair beside the bed. But the thrill only lasted as long as it took for his dad to wake up and start throwing questions at him.

Did Nicky go out to get the money for the electric?

What time was that, and when did she get back?

How did the fire start?

Were you alone, or was Nicky back by then?

Did she start it?

Did she have someone else in the house and they started it?

Who threw the brick through the window?

On and on they came. And Connor couldn't answer a single one of them, because they all led to Nicky being to blame for the fire. So he just lay there, tears streaming down his cheeks, praying for the torture to end.

At his wits end when the doctor came by later that day, Terry said, "What's wrong with him? I've been talking to him for hours, but he hasn't said a single word. He just lies there staring at me, like he's terrified of me, or something."

Reiterating what he'd already told him several times over, that it was just the shock and that Connor would speak when he was good and ready, the doctor said, "But, in the meantime, I'd strongly advise you not to push him too hard. Not only because it's probably quite painful for him, right now, but also because it might cause irreparable damage to his vocal cords."

Which left Terry feeling like an absolute shit for how hard he'd *already* pushed him.

Still, at least if Connor couldn't talk, he couldn't start asking for his sister, which was a relief.

Or for Sue.

And Terry was absolutely fuming with her. It was Sunday, and Connor had been here since Friday, but she still hadn't turned up. And what kind of a bitch was she, that she could waltz off and leave her kids alone in the house for a whole weekend? And she *must* have heard about the fire by now. It had made the front page of yesterday's *Evening News*, and Terry had even caught a glimpse of it on the local TV news last night, so surely Sue must know something.

Or maybe that was precisely why she hadn't come back yet, because she was scared of facing up to the consequences of neglecting the kids. Either way, she'd blown it this time. And she'd better hope that the police got to her before Terry did, because he was already struggling to keep the image of himself strangling the life out of her at bay.

As it happened, Sue hadn't seen or heard a thing. Having sneaked past the hotel's reception desk on

Friday night, she and Julie had been holed up in the men's suite for the entire weekend, too busy partying to bother with the TV or newspapers.

She had thought about the kids, of course; suffering little pangs of guilt every time she tucked into the fantastic food the men had ordered up from room service, or when she'd been watching cable films on the massive flat-screen TV that Connor would have *died* for. But Julie had quickly nipped that in the bud, reminding her that the kids had plenty of food in the freezer, and a fiver for the electric so Connor could watch TV all day and night if he wanted to. So, conceding that they must be okay or Nicky would have rung by now, Sue had put them out of her mind and got on with enjoying herself.

And she was surprised to say that she actually *had* enjoyed herself — for a change. Chris might not have been the best-looking of blokes, but he'd made up for it in sweetness; running around after her like she was a princess while she lazed about on the bed, refilling her glass every time she emptied it, and telling her not to worry about the cost of anything because they would claim it all back as company expenses.

All in all, a nice, generous, reasonable-in-bed-despite-his-looks kind of man — whom Sue had absolutely no intention of seeing again, despite having promised to meet up with him next time he came to Manchester.

Sweet as he was, she'd realised that she wasn't ready to get into anything serious. Not yet; maybe not ever. It wasn't fair to the kids. Not after Terry had already hurt them so badly.

Making her way home that evening, blissfully unaware of what was waiting for her, Sue was praying that Nicky would have already put Connor to bed so that she could slope off to her own without a fuss. She'd missed her kids but she was too tired to pay them the attention they deserved tonight, so she thought she'd pick them up after school tomorrow instead; treat them to a McDonald's with the money that Chris had slipped her before she left the hotel, and maybe throw in a trip to the bowling alley afterwards. Or the pictures. Or both.

Smiling at the thought of the delight on their faces when she sprang her surprise on them tomorrow, Sue gazed dreamily out of the window as the taxi cruised along the road, her gaze dancing over the familiar outlines of the houses they were passing. It was only seven o'clock but it was already pitch dark, and the condensation on the window was distorting the view. So when she saw the gap in the skyline where her roof was supposed to be, she had to look twice.

Already fumbling with the door handle when the driver slowed to a stop at the kerb, Sue almost fell out of the car.

"My house!" she gasped. "What's happened to my house?"

"What about my fare?" the cabbie called out as she staggered towards the gate. "Oi, lady! You owe me seven quid."

Sue gaped back at him in disbelief. Her house had been destroyed, and all he could think about was his *fare*. What a heartless, heartless bastard!

But when she opened her mouth to say that to him, the only sound that came out was a long, drawn-out, wounded-animal scream.

Cursing under his breath, the driver rammed his foot down on the accelerator and tore away from the kerb. Sod the fare. He wasn't hanging about for some nosy do-gooder to come out and accuse him of rape — which was exactly what had happened to one of the other drivers recently. And he was fucked if he'd be picking up any more lone female fares from now on. Not a chance!

Back on the pavement, Sue had no idea that the scream was coming from her mouth. She didn't even register the sharp sting of the first slap across her cheek. But the second slap was much harder, jarring her enough to make her inhale sharply.

"Are you all right?" Pauline asked, her hands shaking wildly as she held onto Sue's arms — as much to steady herself as to prevent Sue from lashing out in retaliation.

Gaping back at her, Sue opened and closed her mouth, but nothing came out.

By now, several of the neighbours had come out to see what was going on. Aware that one of them might say something stupid and tip Sue over the edge, Pauline jerked her head at John who was still hanging back by their own gate.

"Don't just stand there. Help me get her inside."

"Inside where?" he asked stupidly.

"Where do you bloody think?" she snapped, shaking her head in despair when he finally got moving.

Taking an arm each, they guided Sue up the path and into their house, closing the door firmly on the prying eyes. Ushering her into an armchair, Pauline hurried into the kitchen to make her a cup of sweet tea.

The heat of the living room enveloped Sue like an electric blanket, but did little to stop the shivering. Vaguely wondering why this house was so much warmer than her own, in which you had to have the fire on full blast and be sitting on top of it to get the benefit, she gazed numbly around. In all the time she'd lived next door to Pauline, she'd never actually been inside her house before, and yet it looked exactly as she'd imagined it would: a fussy old people's nest, crammed with grossly outdated furniture and bursting with old-fashioned ornaments. And they had radiators, she noticed, a flicker of confusion crossing her brow. How come they had radiators when no one else on the estate did?

"Here you go," Pauline said, bustling back in a couple of minutes later with a steaming cup in her hands. "You drink that. It'll make you feel better."

"The kids," Sue murmured, her hands shaking violently as she reached for the cup. "Where are my kids?"

"They're safe," Pauline lied, casting a surreptitious glance at John to warn him not to contradict her. "Connor breathed in a bit of smoke so they had to take him off to the hospital, but he's doing all right."

"And N-Nicky?"

Casting another quick glance at John, Pauline gave Sue a small, tight smile. "She's fine, pet, don't you worry about her. Now, drink up, there's a good girl."

Sipping at the hot liquid, Sue burst into tears as the relief of knowing that her kids were safe overwhelmed her — not to mention the guilt that she hadn't been here to prevent whatever had happened from happening in the first place.

Snatching the cup away from her before she spilled it all over herself and the carpet, Pauline placed it on the table and squatted down beside her — wincing as her knees and hips cracked simultaneously. She'd have a hell of a time getting up again, but sometimes you just had to forget about your own troubles and concentrate on helping someone else.

"There, there," she crooned, holding Sue's icy hands in hers. "You get it all out. It's been a big shock for you, I know. But everything's going to be all right, you'll see."

"What happened?" Sue sobbed. "I need to know what happened."

"There was a fire," Pauline explained. "But let's not talk about it now, eh? Let's just get you settled down."

"No . . ." Sue moaned, shaking her head from side to side as the tears streamed through her make-up. "No, no, *nooo* . . ."

Edging towards the fire, John stuck his hands deep into his pockets and watched in uncomfortable silence as his wife ministered to the neighbour. He didn't know what else to do. Hysterical women had never been his strong point.

Looking up as Sue continued to bawl, Pauline caught his eye and mouthed, "What should we do?"

Shrugging, in a *what-you-asking-me-for* gesture, he said, "Whatever you think best, love."

Tutting softly, Pauline bit her lip. Then, jabbing a finger towards the dresser against the far wall, she said, "Get that policewoman's card out of the tin."

Finding the card after rooting through the rest of the rubbish that Pauline kept in the old biscuit tin, John held it out to her. Rolling his eyes when she flapped her hand at him dismissively, he wandered off into the kitchen to make the call, muttering under his breath.

Jay was becomingly increasingly frustrated in her efforts to find Nicky Day. Everywhere she turned, she seemed to hit the same brick wall. She'd spoken to everybody on the Fitton estate several times over by now, and to the teachers at Nicky's school, and even to her doctor to see if he thought that she was depressed or suicidal. But everybody had said the same thing: that Nicky was a quiet girl who adored her brother, and that she definitely would have been at home with him if she was supposed to be. And yet she definitely *hadn't* been there by the time the fire crew arrived.

Desperate for some kind of breakthrough, Jay was spending every waking moment on this case, visiting police stations and hospitals across Manchester, looking at girls who fitted Nicky's description who'd been brought in.

On the way to see one such girl — who had been arrested for shoplifting over in Longsight — when John

Wilson's call came through, she told Ann to turn the car around and put her foot down.

Pauline was standing in the doorway, nervously wringing her hands, when Jay and Ann pulled up. Calling out in a loud whisper as they got out and hurried up the path, she said, "Thanks for coming so quickly. I didn't know what to do for the best."

"How is she?" Jay asked, wiping her feet on the mat as she followed her into the hall.

"Quietened down a bit now. But she was in such a state when she got here that I thought she must be in shock, so I didn't want to tell her too much. I thought I'd best ring you instead."

Assuring her that she'd done the right thing, Jay asked exactly what she *had* told Sue.

"Not a lot," Pauline admitted. "Just that the kids are both fine. And I know that was a lie, but I didn't want to set her off again by telling her about Nicky. I don't suppose you've had any news yet?"

Shaking her head, Jay gestured towards the closed inner door. "Through there, is she?"

Nodding, Pauline opened the door, releasing them from the confines of the tiny hallway into the equally claustrophobic living room.

Still huddled in the armchair, Sue had a blanket around her shoulders now. Clutching it to her throat when Jay and Ann walked in, her stare darted nervously from one to the other of them.

Introducing herself, Jay asked Sue if she was up to talking, or if she'd prefer to see a doctor first.

"I don't need a doctor," Sue murmured. "I just need to see my kids. Are you going to take me to them?"

"Soon," Jay said, perching on the edge of the chair facing hers. "I need to ask you a few questions first."

Fear skittered down Sue's spine like ice water. Oh, God! They were going to arrest her for leaving the kids on their own.

Looking guiltily down at the carpet when Jay asked where she'd been since Friday night, she said, "I, er . . . I've b-been with my friend. It was her birthday, and we . . . we were at her f-flat."

"Would that be flat six, Monsall House, Monsall Street, Cheetham Hill?" Jay asked, reciting the address from memory. "Only, I've been there several times over the last couple of days, and the neighbours are claiming that nobody has been there all weekend."

Aware that she'd been caught out, Sue blushed. "Oh, yeah, sorry. We *usually* go to hers, but we, er, we were with some other people, and we went back to theirs instead. Sorry, I can't seem to think straight right now."

Taking out her notepad, Jay asked for the names of the people she'd been with, and the address she'd been at.

"Why do you need to know that?" Sue spluttered. "They don't know anything about this. They don't even know my kids."

"We need to verify your whereabouts," Jay told her. "It's just routine; nothing to worry about."

Licking her lips, Sue flicked a hooded glance in Pauline's direction. Her voice little more than a whisper now, she said, "It was just a couple of blokes my friend met. They were staying at a hotel, and we . . . well, we kind of spent the weekend with them."

"Which hotel was that?"

"The Lowry," Sue muttered. "But no one saw us, 'cos we sneaked in." Half burying her face in the blanket now as the flush of shame spread down her neck Sue couldn't bring herself even to glance at Pauline, because she was bound to tell everyone, and they'd all think that Sue was even more of a slag than they already did.

"And the names of the men?" Jay asked impassively.

"Chris and Greg," Sue croaked. "But I don't know their surnames or where they live. They're from London, and they were only here for the weekend."

Writing this down, Jay said, "And your children knew where you were, and how long you'd be gone?"

It was asked innocently enough, but Sue felt the full weight of the disapproval and accusation behind the words. Blush deepening, she said, "Course they knew. And I haven't done anything wrong, because Nicky's old enough to look after Connor."

"And Nicky was at home when you left on Friday evening?" Jay looked directly at her now.

"Yeah," Sue lied, hunching deeper into the chair. "I wouldn't have gone out otherwise, would I?"

"I don't know," Jay said evenly. "Would you?"

Sue's mind was racing. The woman obviously knew what she'd done, but if she was trying to get her to admit it so that she could arrest her for neglect, she'd have a long wait. And if it came to her word against

Nicky's, Sue would front it out and convince Nicky that the shock of the fire had confused her.

Turning her guilt into a more productive indignation now, she said, "Why are you asking me all these questions? My kids are in hospital, and I need to see them. But if you won't take me, I'll get a taxi."

Watching as Sue made a show of flinging the blanket aside and looking for her shoes, Jay said, "Do you know where your daughter is, Mrs Day?"

"Yeah, at the hospital, like I just said," Sue muttered, slipping her jacket on and zipping it up. "And I bet you haven't been grilling their *dad* like this, have you?" she went on self-righteously. "It's all right making out like *I've* done something wrong just because I had a bit of a break, but what about *him*? He's not shown his face round here in months, but I bet you haven't accused him of neglecting the kids. And they're just as much his as mine, so what's the difference?"

"I'm not accusing you of anything," Jay pointed out calmly as Sue stomped to the door. "I'm just trying to find your daughter."

Hesitating, Sue turned back. "What's that supposed to mean? She's at the hospital. Pauline said she was — didn't you, Pauline?"

Dipping her gaze guiltily, Pauline reached into her pocket for her cigarettes. John wouldn't like it, but sod him. Hands shaking, she lit up, grateful when the policewoman started talking again, drawing Sue's attention back to her.

"Nicky wasn't in the house when your son was rescued. And she hasn't been seen since. So if you're claiming that she was there when you left —"

"She *was*," Sue gasped, convinced that it was true, because she'd *seen* Nicky from the taxi.

Hadn't she?

Head swimming as the seriousness of the situation really began to dawn on her, she staggered back to the chair and slumped down heavily. Nicky was hardly ever late home, and even when she was, she always *came* home, she never ever stayed out. She didn't have anywhere else *to* stay. But if she hadn't gone home *then*, and she still wasn't home *now*, where was she?

"Oh no," Sue muttered, sounding as sick as she felt when something else suddenly occurred to her. "You're not telling me *she* started the fire, are you? You don't think she did it and ran away? Please don't tell me that's what happened."

Telling her that they couldn't speculate about that until they had more information, Jay said, "But it would be helpful to know if Nicky was upset about anything the last time you saw her. Did she mention that she was worried about anything? Maybe something that had happened at school?"

Shaking her head as fresh tears welled up in her eyes, Sue said, "No, nothing."

"And did you speak to her at any point after you left the house that night?"

Sniffing loudly, Sue wiped her nose on the back of her hand and said that she'd called Nicky just before the club closed.

"That would have been at about two a.m.," Jay said. "But your phone was switched off every time I tried to reach you before and after that. And surely, if you switched it back on to make that call, you'd have seen my missed calls and messages?"

"It wasn't my phone," Sue told her, swiping at a tear as it trickled down her cheek. "I'd left mine at home, so I had to use Julie's."

"But Nicky didn't mention the fire when you spoke to her?"

"I didn't actually speak to her. I knew she'd be in bed by then, so I just left a message."

"So you don't know where she was at that point?"

"No."

Feeling sorry for Sue when she started to sob again, Pauline plucked a couple of tissues out of the box and carried them over to her.

Peering up at her gratefully, Sue dabbed at her eyes, saying, "My Nicky's a good girl, isn't she, Pauline? And you know she's always there when I go out. I never leave him on his own, do I?"

"Not that I know of," Pauline murmured supportively, rushing back to her seat.

"Did Nicky have your friend's number?" Jay asked now. "Only, I'm wondering if she might have tried calling you prior to your calling her — to let you know that the electric had gone, for instance?"

"She knows the number," Sue said, blowing her nose loudly. "But she wouldn't have called for something like that, because she knows I keep a fiver in the pot on top of the cupboard. She'd have just taken that and nipped out to the garage if it had gone."

Asking how far away the garage was, in order to gauge how long it would have taken Nicky to get there and back, Jay turned to Ann when she heard that it was just around the corner.

"Best call in there on the way to the hospital — see if we can take a look at the CCTV tapes."

"No point," Sue murmured. "They're dummy cameras."

Telling her that she'd still have to check, on the off chance that someone might remember seeing Nicky, in which case they might know if she'd been with anybody else at the time, and in which direction she'd headed off in when she left, Jay said, "In the meantime, can you think of anywhere where she might have been staying since Friday? Your husband gave me the names of some of her friends, but none of them have seen her since school finished that afternoon."

"I don't know," Sue moaned, shaking her head from side to side and rocking backwards and forwards in her seat. "I don't know, I don't know, I don't *know* . . ."

Sensing that they probably wouldn't get anything else out of her right now, Jay said, "All right, we'll take you to see your son. But I will need to talk to you again at some point."

Exhaling shakily, Sue nodded her agreement. She was really worried about Nicky, but at least the girl wouldn't go to prison for starting the fire. Not like Sue would if they knew she'd left Connor alone in the house.

Following them out into the hall as they prepared to set off, Pauline asked Jay where they'd be taking Sue after they'd been to the hospital.

"I mean, she obviously can't go back home, can she?" she whispered. "And I'd offer to let her stay, but it's a bit difficult with . . ." Trailing off, she jerked her head backwards, to indicate that she was referring to John.

Jay was just telling her not to worry, that they would sort something out through the homeless unit, when Sue blurted out that there was no way she was going into a hostel. Turning to Pauline then, she said, "Can you do me a favour and ring my friend? Let her know what's happening and see if it's all right for me to stay at hers for the night."

Saying, "Course I will, pet," Pauline rushed back into the living room to get a pen and paper.

Dave Miller was just driving past when the door opened and the women came out. Spotting Sue between the policewomen, he screeched to a halt and jumped out of the car. He had a kilo of fresh skunk and two ounces of coke in the boot, but he wasn't concerned. Even if the pigs could smell it, they'd need a warrant to search the car, and he'd have done one long before they got it.

"Everything all right, love?" he called out now as he approached Sue.

Shivering wildly again as the cold air bit into her, she glanced warily up at him and nodded.

"I'm really sorry about what's happened," he said, peering down at her with seemingly genuine concern.

"I've only just got back from London and heard about it or I'd have come to see you sooner. But if there's anything I can do, you know you've only got to say, don't you? *Anything*," he added meaningfully.

Murmuring, "Thanks," Sue eyed him with suspicion as she climbed into the back of the police car, wondering why he'd suddenly decided to talk to her after so long. And why he'd been so nice, considering that he'd been an absolute bastard to her the last time their paths had crossed. She'd just caught Terry in bed with Leanne at the time, but instead of supporting her as she'd expected, Dave had turned on her, accusing her of having known that Terry had been shagging his precious daughter when she was underage and letting him get away with it. It was an absolute lie, because Sue would have castrated Terry with her bare hands if she'd thought that he'd been messing about with anyone, never mind a child. But she'd been too stunned to defend herself at the time — which was probably just as well, because Dave had been so mad he'd probably have killed her.

Waving as the police car pulled away now, Pauline said, "It was nice of you to show your support, Dave. Pity you weren't so thoughtful when your Leanne nicked her husband off her, though, eh? You gave her a proper rough ride of it, if I remember right."

"Yeah, well, we're all guilty of pointing fingers in the wrong direction sometimes, aren't we?" Dave replied smoothly, reminding Pauline that it hadn't been all that long since she herself had been spreading rumours

136

about Sue. "Can't hold grudges for ever, though, can you? Not when you think about what's just happened."

"Suppose not," Pauline murmured sadly. "And she needs her friends more than ever right now, 'cos she's only just found out about it all, and she's still in a right state."

"What do you mean, she's only just found out? Where's she been?"

"Some hotel, apparently, celebrating her friend's birthday. Just got back tonight and found the house like this."

"Jeezus, that must have been a bit of a shocker," Dave said, gazing at the debris still littering the next-door garden. "So what are the police saying about it?"

"Nothing much," Pauline said, an edge of disapproval in her voice as she added, "They were too busy quizzing her. And it's wrong, that, isn't it, because you'd think they'd give her a bit of time to get her head around it all first. But no. They want to know where she's been, and who she's been with. And the questions they asked about *Nicky*. Going on and on about whether she was in the house when Sue went out. And all the time Sue's crying her heart out, desperate to get to Connor. I felt that sorry for her."

"Do they think Sue had something to do with the fire?" Dave asked, frowning down at Pauline. "Only I heard they were blaming Nicky. Wasn't she supposed to have started it and done a runner?"

"No one knows anything for sure yet," Pauline told him wearily. "But I don't think they're blaming Sue. I think they're more concerned about whether she'd left Connor in the house by himself, the way they kept asking her if she was sure that Nicky was there when she went out. But we all know she'd never do something like that, so Sue'll be all right."

"What a mess," Dave murmured, shaking his head. "And what about the other one? Haven't they questioned *him* yet?"

"Course they have, but he was at work when it happened, so they know it was nothing to do with him," Pauline said. "And he went straight home to your Leanne after that, didn't he?"

Shrugging, Dave said, "No idea, love. I couldn't tell you the last time I spoke to either of them. Suppose I should give her a call, though. See how she's coping."

Giving him a direct look now, Pauline said, "I would if I was you. I mean, I know you had your reasons for falling out with her, but she's still your flesh and blood at the end of the day. And if this has taught *me* anything, it's that we should treasure our nearest and dearest before it's too late."

"Even your John?" Dave gave her a wry smile.

"Aye, even him," Pauline murmured. Then, "Anyhow, best get myself inside and ring that friend of Sue's like I promised. Poor girl can't even do that for herself no more, 'cos she lost her phone in the fire."

Pursing his lips thoughtfully, Dave said, "Don't suppose you'd do me a favour and pass my number along to her, would you? Only I wouldn't mind keeping in touch — to make sure she's okay, and that."

"I'll certainly pass it on," Pauline said, taking the pen and paper she'd just written Julie's number down with out of her pocket. "But I wouldn't hold my breath if you're expecting her to ring you, 'cos she didn't look right impressed when she saw you just now. And you can hardly blame her after the last time, can you?"

Amused that she was being so protective of her one-time enemy, Dave said, "Me and Sue got along just fine before all that shit happened, so the least I can do is let her know it's all forgotten on my part. Just give her the number and tell her I want to apologise properly, yeah?"

Phoning ahead to make sure that Terry wasn't at the hospital — in order to avoid a nasty confrontation — Jay took Sue up to the ward where Connor had been moved to and left her there, telling her that she'd be waiting for her outside.

Getting herself a coffee from the machine, Jay carried it into the waiting room and, choosing a seat from where she could see all exits and entrances so that she could intercept Terry if he came back while Sue was still here, she sat down and mulled everything over, trying to figure out what it was about Sue's account of Friday night that didn't quite add up.

Sue obviously realised the need to prove that she had left Connor with a responsible person that night, but the way she'd gone on about it, it had seemed to Jay that she was more concerned about *that* than about Nicky having gone missing. Terry, on the other hand, had reacted exactly as Jay would have expected — with absolute horror at the thought of his child lying dead in the house, or wandering the streets injured. But those thoughts didn't seem to have crossed Sue's mind, and Jay couldn't help but wonder why.

But then, maybe she was being too hard on her: projecting her own frustrations about her lack of headway onto Sue and reading something suspicious into her reactions. The woman had just had the shock of arriving home to find her house burned to the ground, so how awful must it have been to then find herself facing a barrage of questions from the police about where she'd been and who she'd have been with? Of *course* she'd have been concerned about proving that she'd provided adequate childcare for her son. Just as she'd have been more concerned to get to him at that moment, knowing that he *had* been hurt, than to speculate about where the one who probably *hadn't* been injured had gone.

And if Connor loved his mother as much as she obviously loved him, then that might explain his continued silence. Because he'd been waiting for the one person in the world that he could truly trust; the one person who could reassure him that everything was going to be all right. And, now that she was here, he might just tell her what they all needed to know. Jay certainly hoped so.

Inside the ward, Sue was holding Connor's hand and talking to him in a whisper, her eyes flicking frequently towards the door in case someone came in and heard what she was saying.

"Please, son, just tell me what happened. I promise I won't be angry, but I really need to know. Did Nicky do something bad? Was she smoking? Is that what started it?"

Tears trickling slowly down his cheeks, Connor shook his head from side to side on the pillow. He'd been so happy to see her, but straight away she'd done what everyone else had done and blamed Nicky. But he couldn't tell her that it was his fault, because then she'd be mad at him for lighting the candle when he wasn't allowed to touch the matches. And mad at Nicky for forgetting to come home and look after him. And then his dad would get mad at his mum for going out when Nicky wasn't there. And his mum would be mad at him again for grassing her up. And everyone would just be going mad at everyone, and they'd take him away and lock him up, because it was all his fault. And that was why he couldn't speak. Not even to her. Because, if he didn't open his mouth in the first place, then he wouldn't be able to say anything stupid.

"You haven't told anyone about me leaving you on your own for a minute that night, have you?" Sue was asking now, peering solemnly into his eyes, terrified that his silence indicated that he felt guilty because he'd already said something which would incriminate her. "You know I'd never leave you alone on purpose, don't you? And, anyway, I saw Nicky running past when I was in the taxi, so that was all right, wasn't it? You weren't on your own for long — just like I promised."

A flicker of confusion flashed through Connor's eyes. If his mum had seen Nicky, then she must have been in the house all along. But why would she hide from him? And why hadn't she come out when the electric went, when she knew he was scared of the dark? *Unless she didn't love him any more.*

"Promise you haven't told anyone?" Sue said now, squeezing Connor's hand to bring his attention back to her. Exhaling shakily when he shook his head, she said, "God, I hope you're telling the truth, Con, because I'll get into a lot of trouble if they find out. So if they ask, you've got to say she was there. Do you understand, son?"

Nodding now, Connor raised a hand to swipe at the snot that was dribbling from his nose.

Jumping when the door opened behind her, Sue gave the young nurse who came in a guilty smile. "I was just talking to him."

"That's good," the nurse said approvingly, "'Cos he's been dying to see his mummy, haven't you, sweetie?" Wheeling a little trolley over to the bed now, she smiled at Sue. "Sorry, but I'll need to get in there to take a little look at his back."

"What's wrong with his back?" Sue asked, standing up to give her room.

"We think he might have been hit by the brick," the nurse whispered, turning Connor gently onto his side.

"Brick?" Sue repeated confusedly.

"The one that got thrown through your window," the nurse told her, frowning now. "Don't tell me you didn't know about that?"

"I was away for the weekend," Sue explained guiltily. "I've only just got back and found out."

142

"And no one thought to tell you about that?" the nurse asked. Tutting softly when Sue shook her head, she said, "Well, I can only imagine they were trying not to worry you, but I know *I'd* want to be told if it was one of mine who'd been hurt."

Gasping when the nurse raised Connor's pyjama top now, revealing a huge, angry purple bruise that ranged from just above his hip to just below his shoulder blade, Sue clapped her hands over her mouth. "Oh, my *God!*"

"Don't worry, it's not hurting him," the nurse assured her. "We've been giving him plenty of painkillers to make sure of that."

Gazing sadly down at her son's wounded body, Sue felt the tears welling in her eyes again. He looked so tiny and vulnerable, and she couldn't imagine how scared he must have been when that brick came through the window and hit him. But who would do such a terrible thing? Surely not Nicky.

"I'm going to give him his medicine now," the nurse said, jolting Sue out of her thoughts. "And he tends to get sleepy quite quickly afterwards, so you might want to say goodnight while you've got a chance." Smiling now, she added, "This boy of yours certainly likes his sleep."

Murmuring that he always had, Sue leaned down and kissed Connor, whispering, "Night-night, darling, I'll see you again tomorrow. And don't forget what I said — not a word. I might have lost Nicky, but I won't lose you as well." Kissing him again, she turned and walked quickly out of the room.

Leaving Connor staring after her from the bed, petrified that something awful had happened to Nicky, because why else would his mum say that she'd lost her?

Looking up when Sue came out of the ward, Jay said, "Did he say anything?"

Shaking her head, Sue slumped down onto a chair and buried her face in her hands as the sobs wracked her body.

Waiting until she'd calmed down enough to speak again, Jay said, "We will find Nicky, Mrs Day. But the important thing right now is that you and your husband are here for Connor."

"Terry's here?" Sue gasped, her voice thick with dread as she jerked her head up.

"Not at the moment," Jay assured her. "But he'll probably come back fairly soon, because he's only been nipping home for the odd hour since Connor was brought in."

"He's been here the whole time?"

"More or less," Jay said, wondering if the odd tone of Sue's voice was due to guilt that she hadn't been here while he had, or fear of his reaction when their paths eventually crossed.

Murmuring, "Oh, God," Sue started chewing on her thumb nail. "Has *she* been here, as well?"

"Only on the first night," Jay told her. "But I believe your husband's been coming alone since then."

"I don't want her anywhere near my son," Sue muttered, a glint of anger in her eyes now as she turned to look at Jay. "And that's my right as his mum, isn't it? To say who's allowed to see him?"

Telling her that it wasn't really a police matter, Jay suggested that she discuss it with Terry.

"I can't," Sue said edgily. "There's been too much trouble."

Sensing that Sue was genuinely scared of her ex, Jay sighed. She didn't really want to get involved in their marital disputes, but the situation was tense enough without them fighting in the hospital if they bumped into each other when no one was around to separate them.

"Okay, look, I can have a word with him — if you like?" she suggested. "Let him know that you'd rather he didn't bring his girlfriend in to see Connor, and see if he'll agree to setting up a schedule so that you can keep your visiting hours separate."

Thanking her, Sue exhaled shakily. Jay was right: she *was* scared of Terry. Although not because he was the unreasonable wife-beater she'd made him out to be, but because he was precisely the *opposite*: a reasonable man who loved his kids, and would do whatever it took to get them away from Sue now that he knew she'd left them alone for the weekend. And to make sure that didn't happen, she would have to carry on lying about him — even if by doing so she blew any hopes she still harboured of one day getting him back.

Glancing at her watch now, Jay said, "I really think we should get moving if you don't want to see your husband."

"I don't," Sue muttered, getting up and walking quickly to the lift. Stabbing at the button, she said, "What'll happen about my house? Do you think they'll give me another place?"

Telling her that she'd have to speak to the council about that, Jay waved her into the lift — wondering why, as the doors slid smoothly shut, she still hadn't said anything to indicate that she was concerned about her daughter.

Julie was waiting for them when they reached the flat a short time later. Yanking the door open before Jay had a chance to knock, she said, "Are you all right, babe? That woman who rang said there'd been a fire."

Bursting into tears at the sight of her friend, Sue fell into her arms and clung to her.

Pulling her inside, Julie jerked her head at Jay and Ann, saying, "Come in if you're coming."

Leading them through to the living room, she sat down on the couch with Sue and waited for somebody to tell her what was happening.

"Mrs Day's going to need a place to stay for the night," Jay said, perching on the edge of one of the armchairs as Ann stayed by the door. "Is it okay if she stays here, or would you like us to contact the council's homeless team?"

"God, no, course she can stay," Julie said immediately. "But what about the kids? Only, I've only got two bedrooms, and they're not exactly huge."

Guessing that Pauline Wilson had been sparing with the details, given that Julie didn't know about the

146

children, Jay gave her a brief rundown of the situation, sure that Sue would tell her the full story when they'd gone.

"Can you just confirm your name for me?" Jay said then, taking out her notebook. "And give me your account of what happened on Friday night?"

"Julie Ford," Julie told her, frowning. "But what do you mean, 'my account'? Account of what?"

"Just the sequence of events leading up to you and Mrs Day going out."

"Same as always," Julie said, shrugging. "I got there around eight, and did my make-up while Sue was getting dressed. Then we waited for Nicky . . ." Trailing off when she sensed Sue's body tensing, her frown deepened.

"So Nicky wasn't there at that time?" Jay pounced.

"Well, not when I got there, no," Julie blustered, trying to guess what her friend must have already told them. "But she was there before we went out, obviously, 'cos she was babysitting for Connor."

"So, if you got there at eight, and you both left when the taxi came at eight forty-five, what time did Nicky actually arrive?"

"*I* don't know," Julie said, as if it were a ridiculous question. "Sometime between eight and quarter to nine, obviously. But I wasn't clock-watching, so I can't give you the exact time." Looking at Sue now, she said, "What do you reckon? About quarter past?"

Nodding, Sue chewed on her thumbnail, too afraid to look at the policewomen because she was sure they knew that Julie was lying.

"And was it usual for her to come home so late?" Jay asked, directing the question at Sue now. "Only I was under the impression that she usually comes straight home from school."

"She does," Sue mumbled. "But she'd been hanging about with her mates, or something."

"Do you know the names of those friends?"

Shaking her head, Sue buried her face in Julie's chest as the sobs started up again.

"Is this really necessary?" Julie asked, giving Jay a disapproving look. "Only you can hardly expect her to know the names of everyone Nicky hangs about with, even if she was in any fit state to think about stuff like that right now — which she's obviously not."

"Okay, we'll leave it for now," Jay said, repocketing her notepad. "But you're definitely sure that Nicky was in the house when you and Mrs Day went out?"

"I've already said, haven't I?" Julie retorted irritably. "I got there at eight, she came in at quarter past, we went out at quarter to. End of. Now is there anything else you want to know, or can I get my mate settled down?"

Saying, "No, that's fine for now," Jay stood up. "Don't get up. We'll see ourselves out."

Waiting until she'd heard the front door closing behind the policewomen, Julie said, "Jeezus, whats the hell's going on?"

"They're lying," Ann said flatly, trotting down the stairs and shoving the heavy main door open.

"I know," Jay murmured, glancing thoughtfully back at the windows of the flats as she followed her out to the car. "But why? What have they got to hide?"

"No idea, but the mother gets edgy every time you mention the girl. And there's something not right about it, if you ask me."

"I agree," Jay said, shrugging as she added, "But I don't suppose we'll really know what's going on until Connor finds his voice again."

Back in the flat, Sue had just finished telling Julie everything that had happened.

Muttering, "Jeezus," Julie got up and went to get her cigarettes from the mantelpiece. "You could have bleedin' warned me," she said then, lighting up and sucking on the smoke agitatedly.

"What do you mean?" Sue asked, peering up at her in confusion.

"I mean, you could have worded me up before you let me go and lie to the coppers," Julie said snappily. "You've landed me right in it now."

"How could I have warned you?" Sue asked, wondering why Julie was being so unsympathetic. "I didn't exactly get any warning myself. I just got home and found . . ." Trailing off, she bit her lip as her chin began to quiver.

"Aw, don't start that again," Julie complained. "I've got a right headache without you bawling your eyes out every two minutes." Pacing up and down now as Sue sat in stunned silence, she said, "So what did you tell them?"

"Pauline told me the kids were fine," Sue murmured guiltily. "So when the police kept asking me if Nicky was home when we went out, I just panicked and told them that she was, 'cos I thought someone must have said something about us going out and leaving Connor on his own."

"And you didn't think that Nicky might have already told them that she'd got back late and you'd already gone?"

"Not straight away, no. But then I thought if she had, I'd just front it out and make out like she was confused. Christ, you don't think I wanted it to end up like this, do you?"

"Obviously not," Julie tutted. "But shoulda-woulda-coulda's not going to help me, is it? And, all right, so Nicky's not there to tell them what happened, but Connor is. And what's to say he hasn't already told them everything?"

"He's in shock," Sue told her quietly. "He's not spoken to anyone in days."

"Well, he won't be in shock for ever," Julie reminded her grimly. "They're gonna be asking him all sorts when he starts yakking again, and I can really do without getting dragged into it."

"You're already in it," Sue reminded her, hurt by her attitude because Julie was supposed to be her best friend.

"Yeah, well, thanks for that, *mate*."

"Why are you being like this?" Sue asked, peering at Julie as she stomped up and down. "I didn't even want

150

to go out that night. I wanted to wait for Nicky, but you made me."

"Don't even go there!" Julie gave her a fierce look. "You're not blaming me for this. No way!"

"It's true," Sue shot back self-righteously. "And you know it is, so don't try and deny it."

"Oh, right, 'cos I dragged you out of the fucking house by your hair, did I?"

"No, but you went on and on about losing the cab, and how you'd miss out on your stupid date if we didn't go right then. I said I didn't want to leave him, but you'd done it to your kids, so it was all right for me to do it to mine, wasn't it?"

Closing her eyes, Julie inhaled slowly. Then, holding up a hand, she said, "Right, stop. There's no point us blaming each other. It's happened, and we've got to work out what to do about it."

Nodding, Sue lit a cigarette and sucked deeply on it, waiting for Julie to tell her what to do next.

"First things first," Julie said after a moment. "We've got to find your Nicky."

"How?" Sue asked. "If the police can't find her, what chance have we got?"

"Well, I don't know, but she's got to be somewhere," Julie said impatiently. "You ought to know where she hangs out. You're her mam."

"Yeah, well, I don't," Sue muttered, the guilt settling over her again. "You know what she's like, she never goes anywhere. She's always at home watching telly or playing with Con."

"I bet she's done a runner," Julie declared. "She must have started the fire and legged it, scared you'd beat the crap out of her when you got home."

"That's what I thought," Sue said quietly. "But I just can't see her leaving Connor like that."

"Maybe it was too late to reach him by the time she realised. All the more reason to stay well out of the way now, if she thinks she's left him to burn to death."

Wincing at the image, Sue said, "Well, what about that brick getting thrown through the window. Or do you think she did that as well? 'Cos I don't."

"Who knows what's been going through her head lately?" Julie said coldly. "She's not exactly the life and soul, is she? She's probably got all sorts of weird shit stored up in that head of hers. You're lucky she didn't snap while you were there and stab you in your sleep, or something. And don't look at me like that, 'cos it happens."

Murmuring, "Not in my family," Sue bit her lip as another thought occurred to her. What if Nicky hadn't come home that night? What if something had happened to her on the way back from school? Like the policewoman had said, she *always* came straight home, so it was extremely unusual for her not to have been back by the time they'd left the house.

Shaking her head when Sue voiced these thoughts, Julie said, "No, you saw her running past the taxi, so you know she went home. She was just late, that's all."

"I *thought* I saw her," Sue countered worriedly. "But what if it wasn't her? I went out and left my baby on his own."

"He's not a baby," Julie reminded her. "He's six, and he's a smart lad."

"But he's not, though, is he?" Sue said, tears rolling down her cheeks again. "He's dead soft, and he can't do anything for himself. He could have been alone in the house all weekend and anything could have happened. And Nicky could be dead for all I know."

"Well, she's not, or the police would have found her body by now," Julie pointed out impatiently.

"She could be anywhere," Sue sobbed. "I've got to tell them the truth."

"What, and make us both out to be liars?" Julie said sharply. "No way. You're not doing that to me."

"This isn't about you," Sue cried, wiping her eyes on her sleeve.

"Yes, it *is*," Julie snapped, her cheeks flaming red with frustration. "You saw the way that copper was looking at me. If she finds out I was lying, she'll probably accuse *me* of starting the fucking fire."

"Don't be stupid."

"Don't call me stupid. You haven't got a fucking clue about these things."

"So you'd rather I carried on lying?" Sue peered at Julie accusingly. "And risk them not finding Nicky, just so they don't think you had anything to do with the fire?"

"It's not that simple," Julie said darkly. "And, believe me, you don't want them looking in my direction, or you'll probably end up losing Connor."

"What's that supposed to mean?"

153

Sighing, Julie said, "I didn't want to have to tell you this, because I'm not exactly proud of it. But haven't you ever wondered why my kids don't live with me?"

"Not really," Sue said, shrugging. "You said they wanted to live with their dads, so I presumed you were happy with that."

"I had no choice," Julie told her quietly. "It was either let them go to the bastards, or have them put in care." Swallowing loudly now, her cheek muscles jumped as she said, "I got accused of burning a mate's baby with a fag. And don't look at me like that, 'cos it wasn't fucking true. The bitch's boyfriend did it."

"So why didn't you report him?" Sue gasped, momentarily forgetting her own troubles.

"Because I didn't know at the time," Julie said defensively. "I reckon *she* did, though, 'cos the baby was already crying when she fetched him round and asked me to watch him. She said he was teething and told me to give him some Calpol. But he wouldn't settle, so I thought I'd give him a bath — like you do. Anyhow, it must have hurt like hell, 'cos he started screaming his head off. Then I saw the burn on his leg and called an ambulance, and they called the police. And would they *hell* believe I hadn't done it."

"And you lost your kids over it?"

"Not right away, 'cos they couldn't actually prove I'd done it. But then some of the neighbours decided to grass me up to social services for beating my lot, and I couldn't deny it, 'cos I did used to hit them. But no more than anyone else does, and only when they were being naughty. But, there you go . . ." Trailing off, Julie shrugged. "Mud sticks, doesn't it? So if you want to tell the police that we were lying now, you'd best be prepared to lose Connor, 'cos they'll probably think we were in it together."

Realisation landing on her head like a dark cloud, Sue gaped at her friend. "Christ, Julie. What am I supposed to do now?"

"Keep quiet," Julie replied simply. "Sorry, mate, but it's the only way. It'd be one thing if you'd told them from the off, but you can't go changing your story now or you'll do more harm than good."

Biting down on her knuckles, Sue shook her head. She couldn't believe this was happening, and there was nothing she could do about it but keep up the lie she'd started — because the fallout from telling the truth would be so much worse. And it was all Julie's fault for persuading her to go out that night. And hers for agreeing, she supposed. But if Julie had been honest about her past it would never have happened, because Sue would have avoided her like the plague. Not because she believed that Julie was guilty of hurting that baby, but because — as Julie herself had said — mud sticks. And all it would have taken was for one of *Sue's* neighbours to find out, and they'd have had the social services down on her in no time. Terry definitely would have.

"Anyway, Nicky's fine, or your instincts would have told you different," Julie said now, her breezy tone at complete odds with the despair that Sue was feeling. "So stop torturing yourself and go to bed while you've got a chance, 'cos things are probably going to be pretty hectic for the next few days." Picking up her cigarettes and lighter, she headed for the door. Pausing there, she said, "Oh, by the way, that woman who rang gave me some bloke's number to pass to you. It's on the pad on the table. His name's Dave, and she said he wants you to ring him."

"Dave?" Sue repeated numbly. "What does he want?"

"Dunno." Julie shrugged. "Something to do with an apology, or something. Wasn't really listening. Who is he, anyhow?"

"Leanne's dad," Sue told her.

"The one who had a go at you when Terry left?" Julie asked, a look of pure indignation on her face as she marched back across the room and snatched up the number. "Well, you won't be needing that, then, will you!" she declared, screwing it up and tossing it into the waste-paper bin. "And you can tell that cheeky bitch neighbour of yours not to try and trick me into doing her dirty work for her again, an' all!"

Staying where she was when Julie waddled off to her bed. Sue felt the silence descend on her like a two-ton weight. She didn't know what she'd expected when she'd come here tonight, but she certainly hadn't imagined that her so-called best friend would make everything so much worse than it already was. And what made it all the more horrible was that Julie hadn't shown the slightest shred of sympathy or understanding about the agony Sue was going through. She'd been irritated by Sue's tears, and she hadn't given a toss about Nicky, because she was too busy trying to protect herself. And with her past record, she'd as good as guaranteed that Sue would be tarred with the same brush if she decided to tell the truth, which meant risking having Connor taken off her. And the thought of losing him on top of everything else was unbearable.

More alone than she'd ever felt in her life before, Sue stared into space as the tears streamed down her cheeks, going over and over what had happened in her mind, trying to figure out how it had all gone so horribly wrong. She'd never left Connor on his own in the house before, and she couldn't forgive herself for letting Julie talk her into it. She should have waited for Nicky and let Julie go to the club alone. But, instead, she'd put her friend's desire for a night out before her children's safety, and now look . . . One had almost died, and the other might well be dead already, for all she knew. But Julie didn't even care enough to say she was sorry, which showed Sue just what kind of a friend she really was.

But, good or bad, Julie was her *only* friend right now, and it depressed Sue to think that she had nobody else in the world to turn to for the comfort and support that she so desperately needed. Her family had turned their backs on her for getting pregnant before she was married, and the neighbours were a bunch of nasty hypocrites, always gossiping about her and slagging her off behind her back. And Pauline might have been really good to her tonight, but that didn't mean that she could be trusted with a secret like this. Even Tina Murphy, who Sue *would* class as a friend, wouldn't do, because it wasn't the kind of close friendship that allowed this kind of personal confidence.

Jumping when a car backfired outside just then, Sue's gaze flitted towards the waste-paper basket. Biting her lip, she wondered if it might not be worth retrieving Dave's number and giving him a call. She and Terry had been good friends with him and Carole before it all fell apart, and Sue had always found him easy to talk to. *Too* easy, according to Terry, who had had the cheek to accuse her of flirting with Dave a couple of times — which hadn't been true — but Sue now believed that he'd only said it to cover up the fact that he'd already started screwing Leanne behind her back.

All that aside, she'd always got along fine with Dave, because they had grown up on the same streets and spoke the same language. He was the kind of man she understood: a real man's man, who protected his territory with violence, and treated his women like precious jewels. But only while he loved and respected them, and God help them when that died, because the fists were just as likely to fly in their direction as in that of any of his male enemies — as Sue had almost found out to her cost when he'd lashed out at her over Terry. But if he'd said that he wanted to apologise now, then he must mean it, because Dave Miller would keep a vendetta going for ever if he believed he was in the right. But he was also man enough to admit when he was in the wrong.

Reaching into the bin for the number now, Sue smoothed it out and stared at it for a while before getting up and reaching for Julie's phone. Tiptoeing into the kitchen, she closed the door quietly and tapped in the number, her heart already pounding as she heard the first ring, because she had no idea what she was going to say when he answered — if he wasn't already in bed.

"Hello, Dave?" she said quietly when he picked up on the third ring. "I'm not disturbing you, am I?"

"Course not," he said, sounding genuinely pleased to hear her voice. "And thanks for getting back to me, 'cos I wasn't sure you'd bother after all that shit last year."

"Pauline said you wanted to talk to me," Sue whispered. "So I thought I'd best ring in case you thought I was being rude."

"I wouldn't have thought that," Dave assured her, vaguely wondering why she was speaking so quietly. "I know you've got a lot on your plate, so I appreciate you taking the time out to talk to me. Truth is, I've been feeling guilty about being such a cunt to you, and I know I should have told you sooner, but you know what blokes are like — all talk, no bollocks. But, anyhow, I am sorry, and I hope you can forgive me?"

"Nothing to forgive," Sue murmured, feeling suddenly tearful again. "We all had a hard time dealing with it, but it's a long time ago now, so it's not worth talking about."

"Well, you're a bigger man than me for letting me off the hook that easy," Dave said, sounding relieved. "But, anyhow, never mind all that . . . how are you?"

"Not too good," Sue admitted. "Bit of a shock getting home to find the house burned down like that."

"I bet it was," Dave said sympathetically. "Take it you've seen the kids, though?"

"Well, Connor, yeah," Sue said, relieved that he hadn't asked where she'd been all weekend, and why she hadn't known what was going on back home. "But Nicky's . . ." Faltering as the tears suddenly started up again, she said, "Sorry, I just can't — can't talk about her without —"

"Hey, it's all right," Dave interrupted softly. "I'm a prat; I shouldn't have asked. Anyway, look, you're obviously in a state, so why don't I come round and see you? Give me the address; I'll be there in two minutes."

Struggling to pull herself together, Sue said, "You can't. Sorry. It's just that I'm at my friend's place, and we're having a bit of a weird time, so I don't think she'd like it."

"Tell me where you are and I'll pick you up instead, then," Dave suggested. "We'll go for a drive. Anywhere you want."

"Are you sure?" Sue asked, sniffing softly. "I don't want to put you out."

"Hey, that's what mates are for," he reminded her. "And if you can't put yourself out for one of your oldest mates, then you ain't no kind of mate at all, are you?"

Wishing that Julie had shown one ounce of the care that Dave had just demonstrated in that one short sentence, Sue said, "Okay, I'd like that. There's no way I can get to sleep, and I could really do with having someone to talk to."

Taking the name of the road, and arranging to meet her at the corner in fifteen minutes, Dave said, "See you in a bit, then."

Hanging up, Sue looked down at herself and frowned. She was still wearing the party clothes she'd gone out in on Friday night, and they were way too skimpy to protect her from the cold. But they were the only clothes she possessed since she'd lost everything else in the fire. Fortunately, she still had the money Chris had slipped her before she left the hotel, so at least she'd be able to buy herself a pair of jeans and a jumper tomorrow. But there wouldn't be much change, and there were all sorts of other things that she'd need apart from clothes. Like underwear, and toiletries, and a new phone. Not to mention clothes for Connor. And food, because she couldn't expect Julie to feed her when she only had her Jobseeker's allowance to see herself through the week. Subject of which, she didn't even know if she'd still be eligible for her benefits now that she didn't have a house to keep and children to feed.

Shivering as the enormity of her losses began to dawn on her, Sue slipped one of Julie's coats on and sneaked her keys out of her handbag, then crept out. Walking quickly down to the park at the end of the road, she hung back in the shadows, praying that Dave wouldn't be too long.

Pulling up alongside her a few minutes later, Dave pushed the passenger side door open for her. Grinning when she jumped in, he said, "Nice coat."

"Looks stupid, doesn't it?" Sue said, smiling, glad that there was going to be no awkwardness between them. "But it's better than freezing to death. And I could hardly stand around in what I'm wearing underneath, or I'd have probably got myself arrested."

"Take it you're still wearing the sexy skirt, then," Dave teased, turning the heating up. "Don't worry," he said. "You'll fit right in where I'm taking you."

"Oh?" Sue gave him a quizzical look.

"Little cafe I found that stays open all night," Dave explained. "They make the best bacon butties in Manchester. And they even serve prostitutes. Only joking," he added quickly as he set off. "You look great."

Blushing when her stomach suddenly growled, Sue folded her arms. She hadn't eaten since breakfast; hadn't even thought about food. But now that he'd mentioned it, she realised how hungry she was.

"Relax," Dave said, sensing her embarrassment. "We've known each other too long for airs and graces."

"I know," Sue agreed, settling back in her seat. "But it always happens when you don't want it to, doesn't it? At the doctor's, or the dentist's."

"Or in an old mate's car," Dave added. Reaching into his pocket now, he took something out and tossed it into her lap. "That might help."

Glancing down and seeing the small bag of weed, Sue shook her head. "Thanks, but I'd best not. I'm already struggling not to think horrible things, and that will send me right over the edge."

"What kind of things?" Dave asked, keeping his eyes on the road.

"Just stuff about Nicky," Sue told him sadly. "Wondering where she is, and if she's okay."

Reaching out, Dave squeezed her hand. "She'll be fine," he said reassuringly. "I know she will."

"I hope so," Sue said, gazing out of the window and blinking rapidly to try and stem the tears that were threatening to spill over again.

"Want to talk about it?" Dave asked perceptively. "You know I'm a good listener."

Biting her lip, Sue inhaled deeply. She wanted to talk, to tell him everything, because he would probably know exactly what to do. But she was too ashamed to admit what a terrible mother she was.

Glancing at her out of the corner of his eye, Dave sensed that Sue had a lot of shit going on inside that head of hers. But hc wouldn't push her, because she'd talk when she was ready. And when she did, he'd be there for her — all the way.

CHAPTER
SEVEN

Sue's mood went up and down like a yo-yo over the next few days. She was fine when she had someone or something to distract her, but as soon as she was alone, she'd find her mind straying into territories that no parent should ever have to visit; the shadow-land of her imagination, where terrible visions would play out in vivid detail across the widescreen of her mind's eye.

Nicky's mutilated body being dragged out of the canal in a bin bag — and Sue being made to identify her.

Somebody stumbling over Nicky's foot in the woods, unearthed by a foraging animal from the shallow grave she'd been flung into — and Sue having to identify her.

Nicky's skeleton hanging from a tree at the far, spooky side of the Red Rec where no one dared venture — apart from Sue, who had been drawn there by her instincts . . .

And the longer it went on with no word of Nicky, the more scared Sue was that one of the scenarios was going to come true, so she dreaded the policewomen calling round, because every time she heard the knock at the door she was convinced that this would be the day when they told her.

164

And yet, at the same time, she was equally convinced that Nicky wasn't in any danger, but had simply run away because she *had* started the fire. It was the only thing that made any logical sense.

The investigators had concluded that the fire had definitely started inside the house, and Sue knew that Connor couldn't have done it, because he would never dare disobey her and touch the matches. So that just left Nicky. And Sue suspected that Connor *knew* she'd done it, and that was why he still wasn't talking — because he couldn't bear to admit that his beloved sister had locked him in the house and left him to die a horrible death.

At least the police had stopped looking at Sue as a suspect since they'd seen her on the club's CCTV tapes and knew that she'd been there, both when the fire had started *and* when the brick had been thrown through the window. They still didn't know if the brick was linked, or if it was just a coincidence, but Sue would have thanked whoever had thrown it *whatever* their reason, because if it hadn't hit Connor and roused him he would certainly have died. Although, again, she suspected that Nicky might have been behind that; that, feeling guilty about what she'd done, she might have gone back to the house to get Connor out. But, finding it impossible to get in because the fire was already too advanced, she'd thrown the brick through the window — either to wake Connor up and give him a chance to escape, or simply to alert the neighbours to the fire, so that he would be rescued.

165

Sue hated to think that her own child could be capable of doing something so horrible, but at least Connor was alive, so she had to be thankful for that. Although she wasn't sure how she was going to manage now that the hospital had told her that they were ready to discharge him.

It wasn't her day to visit, according to the alternate-day schedule that the policewoman had arranged to keep her and Terry apart, but the nurse who'd rung had assured her that Terry had already been informed, so she wasn't worried about bumping into him. But she *was* worried about what life was going to be like after she brought Connor back to the flat.

As there was no physical reason for his continued silence, the doctors had decided that it was psychological, and had said that they intended to monitor his progress through a network of home-visiting health-care bodies. Which, to Sue, translated as having the social services set on her.

The thought of having her life invaded by these nosy do-gooders filled her with dread, because she was convinced that they would actually be monitoring *her*, not Connor. But she could hardly refuse their "help", because then they would probably say that she was being uncooperative or obstructive, and whisk Connor away to some foster home — for his own good.

But while she knew that she had no choice and would have to let them do whatever they wanted to do, she dreaded to think how Julie was going to react to the intrusion on *her* life. Things were already pretty tense between them, and Sue was actually starting to hate Julie for finding it so easy to act as if nothing had happened while Sue's life lay in tatters at her feet. She never asked how Connor was when Sue came back from the hospital, and she hadn't so much as mentioned Nicky since their row. But Sue couldn't come out and tell her how she felt about her, because Julie would kick her out, and she had nowhere else to go until the council pulled their fingers out and gave her the house they kept promising. So she'd gritted her teeth and pretended that everything was fine between them — thanking God when Julie dragged herself off to bed each night and she could sneak out and meet up with Dave.

He had been absolutely fantastic since they'd renewed their friendship, and she didn't know how she'd have got through the last few days without him. And he hadn't only helped in an emotional sense, he'd given her a fair bit of practical help, too; slipping her money to tide her over when — as she'd feared would happen — her benefits had been stopped, and buying her a new mobile phone to replace the one she'd lost in the fire. Not to mention dropping whatever he was doing to come and pick her up when she called — day or night.

That was what you called a *real* friend, and Sue blessed the day he'd asked Pauline to pass his number along.

But that was something else that was going to change now that Connor was coming home: no more sneaking out for those lovely long drives she'd been enjoying for the past five nights. There was no way she could risk leaving Connor sleeping in the spare room, because the chances were that he'd wake up as soon as she went out — and Julie would go absolutely ballistic if she had to look after him. And, yes, she could still call Dave on the phone and talk his ear off all night if she wanted to, but it just wouldn't be the same as being with him in person. And that saddened her, because things had been going so well between them up to now.

Not that anything had actually happened, because Dave had been the perfect gentleman, and hadn't so much as tried to *kiss* her, never mind anything else. But that just made him all the more attractive to Sue, and she couldn't help but wonder what life would be like if he was her man. And, despite the fact that he hadn't said or done anything, she knew that it wasn't just a foolish desire that had no chance of coming to fruition, because she could sense that he was beginning to feel something for her, too.

But that was as far as she had allowed herself to take the fantasy, because even if she'd been brave enough to raise the subject, she could already see a million reasons why it wouldn't be such a good idea for them to get together.

Dave's ex, Carole, would make their lives an absolute misery, for starters. And no doubt everyone on the estate would make a meal of it, presuming that Dave and Sue must have been at it behind Terry's back all along, and speculating about whether that was why Terry had gone off with Leanne in the first place. And, much as she liked Dave, and knew that he would never

168

hurt her now that they'd made their peace, she couldn't just ignore his bad reputation for fighting and drug dealing. The authorities certainly wouldn't. And if she got together with him, she could just imagine the social services slapping an "at risk" label on Connor's little head.

But that didn't mean she couldn't still talk to Dave, or ask for his help when she needed it.

Ringing him now, to ask if he'd mind giving her a lift to the hospital, Sue couldn't help but smile when he said, "Course I don't mind, darlin'. I'll meet you at the usual place in half an hour. But I won't just drop you off," he went on. "I'll fetch you both back, an' all — save you having to get the bus. And if you don't mind, I'll come in with you when you get him, 'cos it's been ages since I saw the little fella."

Touched that Dave seemed so eager to see her son when Julie didn't seem to give a toss if she ever saw him again, Sue told him that she didn't mind in the slightest.

The nurses had been busy clearing away the breakfast trays when Terry had arrived for his scheduled visit that morning, so nobody had noticed him going into Connor's room, or they might have been able to warn him that Sue would soon be on her way over. But even if they'd seen him, they would have presumed that he already knew and had decided to come anyway, given that they'd rung that morning and left the message with Leanne. Unfortunately, Leanne had taken the call while he'd been in the shower, and had promptly gone back to sleep and forgotten all about it.

Sitting with Connor now, Terry was telling him all about a new animated film he'd seen advertised that he thought Connor would like. It was hard holding a conversation when you were the only one talking, but at least Connor listened, so Terry didn't feel like he was wasting his time. And the occasional sparks of interest or excitement that flared in Connor's huge, desperately sad eyes made him all the more determined to carry on communicating — even if most of what he said was rubbish that he'd made up off the top of his head just for the sake of saying *something*.

But the film was real, and Terry had every intention of fulfilling the promise he'd just made to take Connor to see it when he was well enough to come out of hospital. And Connor obviously liked the idea, because he had one of those rare flashes of excitement in his eyes. But it soon disappeared when the door opened and Sue walked in.

Laughing at something that Dave had just said, she stopped in her tracks when she saw Terry, causing Dave to bump into her from behind. Blood draining from her face, she gaped at her ex-husband, wondering what the hell he was doing here when he knew that she'd be coming today. Or was that *why* he'd come — so that he could have a go at her while he had the chance?

Inhaling deeply as the heat of rage consumed him, Terry stared at the floor. This was the first time he'd seen Sue in months, but after her recent antics — not least getting the policewoman to mediate because she was supposedly terrified that he might "attack" her again — he hated her even more than he had before. He really felt like telling her to fuck off, that this was *his* day to visit and she had no right to intrude. And as for bringing Dave Miller with her, that was her lowest trick yet.

But if she'd hoped to goad him into kicking off so that she could let everyone see that she'd been telling the truth about him all along, she was sadly mistaken. Much as Terry wanted to jump up and kick seven shades of shit out of the man — and her — he wasn't stupid enough to do it. Not in front of Connor, who was already panting with terror in the bed beside him.

So, getting up from the chair, he calmly slipped his jacket on and gave Connor a kiss, then walked towards the door with as much dignity as he could muster.

Sneering victoriously, Dave said, "Give my love to Lee, won't you?"

Ignoring him, Terry kept on walking.

"Thanks," Sue murmured, peering up at Dave and exhaling shakily when Terry had gone. "I thought you were going to go for him."

"In front of your lad?" Dave replied, a look of innocence on his face. "Never. Anyhow, forget him," he went on, giving her a hug. "And don't look so worried. He won't give you any more hassle now he knows we're mates again. And if he does, he'll have me to answer to. Right?"

Nodding, Sue dipped her gaze guiltily. She'd forgotten that Dave had heard the lie she'd told about Terry beating her up, but it was too late to tell him any different now, so she'd have to let him go on thinking that Terry was that kind of man, even though he'd never so much as raised a hand to her in the whole time they'd been together, and she'd only said it in the first place to hurt him as much as he'd hurt her.

Remembering why she was here, Sue extracted herself from the hug and turned to Connor. Seeing the frightened look in his eyes, and thinking that he was probably nervous about Dave being here because he'd seen the argument they'd had that time, she forced herself to smile as she went over to him.

"Don't worry, sweetheart," she said, giving him a kiss. "Everything's all right. Me and Dave are friends again."

"Good friends," Dave added, winking at her as he approached the bed and ruffled Connor's hair. "And I hope you and me will be good friends too, because I'm planning on spending a lot of time with you and your mummy from now on."

Peering up at him, Connor felt the tears welling in his eyes. He didn't want to spend time with Mr Miller. He wanted to be with his dad.

Leanne was washing the dishes when Terry got home. Drying her hands on the tea towel when she heard him going into the living room, she smiled at him from the doorway as he slung his jacket over the back of the couch and sat down heavily.

"Everything all right, babe?"

"Don't ask."

172

"What's happened?" Leanne said, frowning now. "And why are you back so early? Has something happened to Connor?"

"I don't want to talk about it," Terry muttered, yanking his tobacco out of his pocket and rolling himself a smoke.

"Oi, don't take it out on me — whatever it is," Leanne snapped. "I haven't done anything to you."

Inhaling deeply, Terry mumbled, "Sorry. It's not you. It's Sue."

"What about her?" Leanne demanded, her nostrils already flaring at the mention of his hated ex.

"She turned up at the hospital," Terry told her, lighting his cigarette and sucking deeply on it.

"You what?" Leanne squawked. "But it's *your* day. I hope you told the cheeky bitch to do one."

"Don't think I didn't want to," Terry retorted angrily. "But I could hardly make a scene in front of Connor, could I?"

"Oh, right," Leanne barked. "So I suppose you just slunk out with your tail between your legs and let that bitch think she'd got one over on you. And you know she'll have done it on purpose, don't you? She knew damn well you'd be there on your own, so she probably did it to spite me. Wheedle her way back in with you while she had the chance. And you just keep your gob shut like a sap and let her think she's in with a chance."

Resenting the implication that he was stupid enough to let Sue manipulate her way back into his life, Terry narrowed his eyes as he peered back at her, saying coolly, "I doubt she'd have brought your *dad* with her if that was her intention."

"You what?" Leanne hissed. "My dad was with her? How come?"

"How am I supposed to know?" Terry snapped. "Unless you expected me to stop and ask."

"Don't be ridiculous," Leanne snapped back, chewing on her nails now as her mind began to race over the implications of her dad and Sue turning up at the hospital together. "How did they look?" she asked after a moment. "Were they, like, *together*?"

"No idea, 'cos I wasn't looking that hard," Terry retorted angrily. "But I wouldn't put it past her. *Or* him."

"No." Leanne shook her head. "He wouldn't do that to me. Not when he knows how much shit she's given me over you."

"He won't have been thinking about *you*," Terry pointed out bluntly. "This will be about rubbing it in *my* face."

"Oh, and why would he think that *that* would bother you?" Leanne pounced, her eyes flashing with suspicion now. "Unless someone's given him the impression that you've still got feelings for her. And the only one who could have told him something like that is *her*, and she could only have got it off *you*."

"Aw, quit with the Inspector Morse routine," Terry groaned. "You'll have yourself convinced it's true in a minute."

"Well, isn't it?"

"Course not! How the hell could I give her that impression when I haven't clapped eyes on her in months?"

"So *you* say," Leanne said suspiciously. "But I've only got your word on that, haven't I?"

Losing patience, Terry stubbed his cigarette out in the ashtray and stood up. "Believe what you want," he said, snatching up his jacket and heading for the door.

"Where you going now?" Leanne demanded.

"Out!" he replied curtly, slamming the door behind him.

Eyes narrowed with rage, Leanne snatched up her mobile phone.

"Hello, Mum. Guess what I just heard about my dad . . .?"

CHAPTER
EIGHT

Since taking Sue in when she'd arrived home last Sunday, Pauline had begun to feel personally involved in the whole thing — and more than a little guilty about the part she'd played in it.

Raking over the coals of her memories of the night of the fire, she'd managed to magnify the fleeting little cry she'd heard on the wind into a terrible howl of despair. And in her mind's eye, she could now quite clearly see that the face she'd glimpsed at the window had been Connor's.

Poor little Connor, with tears streaming down his cheeks, his eyes pleading with her to come and save him . . .

But she hadn't saved him. She'd allowed her fear of being accused of meddling influence her; turning her back on him in his greatest hour of need. And Pauline didn't know if she'd ever be able to forgive herself for that. Or for the way she'd treated his mum in the lead-up to it.

She and Sue had never been what you'd call friends, but she'd begun to feel very protective of the younger woman lately, and had to admit now that she'd probably played more than a small part in creating and stoking the animosity which had grown between them during the time they'd been neighbours. She hadn't exactly made Sue welcome when she'd first moved in, and had actually been behind some of the complaints that had been made to the council about her over the years. And while she'd felt quite justified at the time — because this had always been such a quiet road, mostly populated by middle-aged couples such as herself and John — in hindsight she knew that it had been more than a wee bit of sour grapes on her part. Yes, the Days had been young and noisy, but they'd been no worse than a lot of the other younger families who'd subsequently moved in around here. And whatever troubles she'd had personally with Sue, the girl was still a million times better than Carole Miller.

Truth was, Pauline had been an intolerant old bat at times, and she knew it. But if this terrible near-tragedy with the fire had taught her anything, it was that bridges had to be rebuilt and amends made before it was too late. Because the last thing she needed was to go to her grave with spite-fuelled, unapologised-for past actions on her conscience.

And that was why she had decided that it was her duty to help Sue to get back on her feet. If not her *mission*, because it couldn't be a coincidence that she'd recently been elected chair of the residents' association, just when she'd need to get the rest of the neighbours on board to do *their* bit. If *that* wasn't a sign that Pauline was being told to do something helpful, then she didn't know what was.

Not that she would tell any of the neighbours that, because they'd think she'd gone totally gaga. And she wouldn't start preaching to them about friends in need, either, because they'd all be quick to point out that Sue Day was no friend of any of theirs. No, she would have to do it craftily, make them think they had made the decision to help Sue all by themselves. And that wouldn't be easy when Pauline had had more than a small hand in turning them against her in the first place. But nothing that was worth doing was ever easy. Like marriage: a sacred vow which couldn't be broken under any circumstances — no matter how many times you imagined yourself choking the life out of your other half along the way.

Determined to get cracking, Pauline called a meeting at her house on the Monday morning, using the pretext of wanting to discuss ways of getting the council to do something about the unsafe state of their houses. Which was plausible enough, given that how the council spent so much on the surrounding estates while doggedly overlooking theirs was already such a contentious issue amongst the neighbours.

John had just come downstairs when the neighbourhood women trooped in that morning. Ignoring Pauline's hissed order to go and get dressed, he plonked himself down in his pyjamas and dressing gown and switched on the TV. He'd waited years for the luxury of indulging himself in daytime TV, and he was buggered if he was going to let the Fitton Witches disturb him with their gossip. And Pauline could call it a "meeting" if she liked, but he knew she'd only called them round to get them all gassing about Sue Day.

Making tea while the neighbours settled themselves on the semicircle of chairs that she'd arranged in front of the table in the living room, Pauline carried the cups through and handed them out, telling them to help themselves to biscuits — to get them good and relaxed.

Sitting at the table when everyone had been served, she kicked the meeting off by thanking them for coming at such short notice. Then, looking around with a suitably solemn expression, she said, "As you know, I called you round to discuss the quality of our houses, and —"

"*Quality?*" Irene sneered. "That'll be the day! It's been a year since they fixed my lavvy, and it's still not flushing right. And I have to have an umbrella to walk through my back room, the roof's leaking that bad."

Tartly reminding her not to interrupt the chair, Pauline said, "Anyway, because there's been so many complaints, I've decided to start a log, and I want you all to tell me what you've reported, and when, and what results you got. I know this has been a common subject at these meetings in the past," she went on, "and we've all suggested ways to get the council to pull their fingers out, but I say it's time to *make* them listen, because I for one am not willing to sit back and wait for something like what happened next door to happen to *me*."

As she'd fully expected, the mere mention of the fire got them all talking at once about how awful it had been to see the house go up in flames like that. Which inevitably led on to how horrified they'd all been when Connor had been brought out and they'd all thought he was dead. And then on to what everybody thought might have happened to Nicky, who still hadn't been found.

Sipping her tea, Pauline sat back, content to wait until they got around to the subject of Sue. Then she'd jump back in and tell them what she had in mind, while making out like she'd only just thought of it.

"If you ask me, it weren't no accident," Mary Holden from number nine was saying, echoing what most of them already thought. "I reckon Nicky started it."

"Oh, that's not true," Jackie Harris from number twenty-four countered softly. "She's not the kind of girl to do something like that. She's been great with Connor since her dad left, so there's no way she'd hurt him on purpose."

"Never can tell," Irene murmured, throwing the cat in amongst the pigeons for the sake of it. "They say it's the quiet ones you've got to watch. And she's quiet to the point of being downright bloody mute, that one."

"What, just because she doesn't spend all her time gassing like you lot?" Carole Miller scoffed. "Anyway, you're all way off the mark, if you ask me. If anyone started it, it was Sue. She's not been right in the head for months, her."

Jumping back in here before they took it in the wrong direction and started to blame Sue, Pauline said, "No, now you're wrong about that. Sue might be guilty of a lot of things, but you all know she'd never hurt her kids."

"Bloody hell, you've changed your tune," Irene snorted incredulously. "It was only the other day you were going on about what a bad mother she was for going out with that mate of hers of a weekend."

"Yes, well, I've been thinking about that, and maybe I was a bit harsh," Pauline admitted shamefacedly. "Maybe we *all* were," she added, gazing around at them. "I mean, we've not exactly been nice to her lately, have we?"

"We've not exactly had *reason* to," Irene pointed out bluntly. "Come on, Paul, don't try and make her out to be some kind of saint just because she's had a bit of bad luck."

"A bit of bad luck? She's lost her bloody house, Reen. How much worse *could* it be?"

"At least the kids are alive — *that* would have been worse."

"Yes, but one of them nearly wasn't. And no one even knows where the other one is, so anything could have happened to her by now."

"That Nicky's her mother's daughter, all right," Carole said darkly, reaching for the biscuit tin. "They probably thought it up between them, knowing them. How to get the social to give us more money — oh, I know . . . let's start a fire and lose everything, then they'll have to give us a big fat cheque."

"Don't be ridiculous," Pauline snapped. "Sue had no idea what was going on. She left Nicky babysitting while she went out for her friend's birthday, that's all. And Nicky's fifteen, don't forget, which is perfectly legal. But that's not the issue," she went on, prodding a finger down on the table to emphasise her point. "The issue is, Sue had no idea. And if anyone thinks different, they'd only have to have seen the state she was in when she got back and saw the place to know that it's true."

Snorting softly as she dunked her biscuit, Irene said, "Some of us *did* see her, but she didn't convince anyone, 'cos we can all make ourselves cry if it makes us look less guilty about something. My Eddie says —"

"Your Eddie says a lot of things, but it doesn't mean he knows what he's talking about," Carole muttered.

Flicking her a dirty look, Irene said, "He knows a damn sight more than *you* do. Anyway, what you doing here? You don't even live on this side. This has got nowt to do with you."

"It's still my road, so it's just as much my business as yours."

"Yes, but you're not on the residents' committee, are you, dear?"

"So?"

"So, you shouldn't *be* here."

Irritated with Irene for veering them off course, Pauline reminded her that the meetings were open to all the residents.

"Well, tell her to keep her opinions to herself, because none of us is interested in anything she's got to say," Irene replied snottily.

"I know more about this than any of you lot, so my opinion counts for more than yours any day," Carole informed her smugly. "And if anyone needs to keep their big gob shut, it's you."

182

"*I've* got a big gob? That's rich, coming from a mouthy git like *you*."

"Eh, I might be mouthy, but at least I can back myself up. Not like *you* — flapping your gums all over the shop, then hiding behind your husband when someone comes after you!"

"Least I've still *got* a husband. But then, yours never got so far as to put a ring on your finger before he took off, did he?"

"And you've only still got *yours* 'cos he's too fucking fat for anyone to want to pinch him off you."

"Didn't I hear a rumour that your Dave got very friendly with someone lately?" Irene sniped, a vindictive smile on her wrinkled face. "Can't quite remember who — oh, yes, that's right. It was Sue, wasn't it?"

"No, it fucking wasn't!" Carole growled, her eyes flashing a clear signal of warning. "And if you ever try and mug me off like that again, I'll —"

"STOP IT!" Lynne Jackson blurted out. Blushing when everyone turned to gawp at her, she flapped her hands nervously. "Sorry, but I really can't stand all this shouting."

Listening to all this with glee, although he was still pretending to be watching TV, John gave a little chuckle of amusement. Mousy Lynne Jackson standing up for herself — well, well, well.

Flicking him an irritated glare, Pauline said, "Lynne's right. We shouldn't be arguing, we should be making decisions."

"I propose a petition," Jackie said, thinking that they were finally getting back to their real reason for being here: the council. "If enough of us sign it, we should be able to get them to do something."

"Wouldn't hold my breath," Irene said, picking biscuit out of her teeth. "I've been here a lot longer than you, and I've still not got central heating or double glazing."

"I'm more concerned about all the old wood frames," Jackie said worriedly. "None of us is safe, and after what happened at Sue's I'm seriously thinking about moving into a private let as a protest."

"I wouldn't do anything hasty," Irene warned her. "If you let your place go, you'll never get back in with the council."

"We've got to do something," Lynne said quietly. "I can't wait till they tell me it's safe to go back to my house, but at the same time I'm terrified I won't be able to sleep once I get there. I'll probably just lie awake all night, every night, thinking about what could have happened to me and David if we hadn't got out when we did."

"Yes, but you *did* get out," Pauline reminded her gently. Then, "Anyhow, getting back to Sue . . . I've been thinking while you've all been talking, and I reckon the least we can do is get a collection going."

"You're joking," Irene snorted, looking at her as if she'd gone mad. "Who's going to put money into a pot for *her*?"

Wondering how she could be so cold, Pauline said, "She's lost everything. And she didn't know what was going on. She's in a right mess."

"She *would* have known, if she'd been at home like she was supposed to be," Irene pointed out self-righteously. "And Nicky might be fifteen, but she should *never* have been left to look after the boy for the whole weekend. And you know I'm right, Paul, so I don't see why you're sticking up for her."

"I'm not."

"Yeah, you are," Carole said — in rare agreement with Irene. "Sue's a lying bitch, and them kids nearly died because of her. And I should know, because my Leanne tells me everything. Sue was out with some bloke when it happened, and didn't give a toss that she'd left them with no food or electric, and no way of getting hold of her — *that*'s the truth of it."

"That's where you're wrong," Pauline argued. "And *I* should know, because I was here when the police talked to her. She'd left money for the electric, and the kids *did* know how to get hold of her."

"So *she* says."

"And why would she lie?"

"Oh, come on." Drawing her head back, Carole gave a cynical smirk. "She's not going to admit that she took off and left them to fend for themselves, is she? You want to talk to Terry if you want to know what she's *really* like. It's a wonder them kids haven't starved to death by now, 'cos she's never got any food in. All the money she gets off the dole goes on booze. And don't get me started on what she does with the maintenance money she gets off Terry, 'cos the kids sure as hell don't see a penny of it."

"I wasn't aware he was paying maintenance," Irene slipped in snidely. "As far as I know, he's not paid a penny since he took off with *your* lass."

"Bollocks!" Carole shot back aggressively. "He gets half of whatever he earns taken straight out of his bank and handed to that bitch before he brings a penny back to our Lee."

"That's not true," Tina Murphy interjected quietly. She'd kept out of the discussion so far because she didn't want to risk getting into an argument with Carole, who was one of the most unreasonable and volatile women she'd ever met. But, as one of the few neighbours who still considered Sue a friend, she just couldn't sit back and let them assassinate her like this.

"You calling me a liar?" Carole demanded, turning on her nastily.

"No," Tina replied calmly, determined to stand her ground. "I'm just saying that it's not true that Sue gets half of Terry's wages. He might get some taken off him, but it doesn't get handed to her. It doesn't work like that."

"Like you'd know."

"I *do*, actually," Tina said firmly. "And I know what a struggle it's been for her since Terry left." Looking earnestly around at the other women now, she said, "I know you've all fallen out with her lately, but she's not as bad as you all make out. She's probably not been as friendly as you think she should have been lately, but you can hardly blame her, can you? Think how *you'd* feel if your husbands left you and everyone started whispering behind your back like it was your fault?

She's in *bits* about Nicky. She's not slept in days, and she's lost so much weight it's awful. So, unless you've talked to her like I have, please don't tell me she doesn't care, because she really, really does."

A silence had fallen over the room by the time Tina had finished speaking, only broken by the sound of the TV that John was still staring at. After a moment, Jackie Harris stood up. Taking a ten-pound note out of her purse, she walked over to Pauline and put it down on the table.

"That's all I've got till I get paid, but she's welcome to it. And I'll have a sort-through of the kids' stuff when I get home from work — see if I can find any clothes or shoes to fit Connor."

Gazing at the other women when Jackie had gathered up her things and left, Pauline said, "Now *that's* what you call a good neighbour. And if we all thought like her, this estate would be all the better for it — don't you think?"

Even Irene couldn't disagree with that. But Carole could.

"She'll get nowt off me," she declared, munching on yet another biscuit. "And as for clothes for the kids, she'll get plenty of handouts off the state, don't you worry about that."

Shaking her head in disgust, Pauline got up and snatched the biscuit tin out of reach. Slamming the lid onto it, she reached into her bag and took out her purse.

"There," she said, resolutely slapping a twenty-pound note down on top of the tenner. "Not much, I know, but none of us is rich, and anything's better than nothing . . . No matter how small . . . I'm sure it will all be gratefully received . . . Won't it?"

Persisting until she'd shamed at least a fiver out of each of them — apart from Carole, who stubbornly refused to budge — Pauline gathered the money together and put it into a tin.

"That'll do for starters, but it's not nearly enough. So, as chair, I'd appreciate it if you could all start thinking up ways to make more."

"How about some kind of function?" Lynne suggested. "I've still got that man's number — the one from the paper, who organised that thing to send my David to swim with the dolphins the other year. He might be able to get hold of some local celebrities if we ask him."

"That's a belting idea," Pauline said approvingly. "Fetch his number round later and we'll give him a call."

"Ooh, see if he can get Take That," Irene leered. "I'd love to see *them* in the flesh."

"Think you've still got it in you, do you?" Carole muttered snidely.

"Hey, don't be fooled by appearances," Irene flipped back with a sly grin. "There might be snow on the roof, but the fire's still burning down below."

"Jesus!" Carole snorted. "I bet your Eddie's never heard you talking like that."

Raising a painted eyebrow, Irene said, "Why do you think he's stuck around so long, my dear?"

Amazed that Irene and Carole were being almost civil to each other after years of open feuding, Pauline thought that she'd better seize the precious moment before it passed — which it would.

"So, we're all agreed?" she said. "We're going to do a fundraiser, and we're going to lay off Sue and help her get her life back on track instead of all the bitching and gossiping?"

Grinning from ear to ear when they all said yes, Pauline gave herself a mental pat on the back. It looked like something good might come of this tragedy, after all. And that was fantastic, because if there was one thing this estate needed it was for everyone to start pulling together instead of always pulling each other to bits.

And it was all down to her.

For the next week, John got to watch whatever he liked on the box without interference as, bit wedged firmly between her NHS teeth, Pauline busied herself with her fundraiser. If he'd taken the slightest bit of notice of what she was doing, he might have been impressed as she managed to secure not only the use of the local community centre as a venue — free — but also the services of a local catering firm, who promised to supply a simple buffet — again free, providing their name was prominently displayed in any publicity.

Putting Irene in charge of setting up a refreshments tent, Pauline set some of the younger women the challenge of organising a jumble sale, and a bouncy castle, and various other activities for the daytime. Jackie Harris knew the wife of the man who'd been voted North-West's Best Bingo Caller 2004, and Pauline was thrilled when she got him to agree to come along and give them a couple of games. Bingo was big business round their way, and it was sure to be one of the highlights of the event. That, and the live band called Street-Wyze that Lynne Jackson's journalist friend had managed to line up for them. Pauline was a bit disappointed that it wasn't somebody she'd actually heard of, but the journalist assured her that they were very well known among the younger generation, so she agreed to let them come — on the understanding that they didn't start any of that head-banging nonsense, because she wouldn't be putting up with any of *that*.

To finish the night in style, Pauline persuaded a local hospital-radio DJ to do a set, and was ecstatic when he offered to run an *X-Factor*-type karaoke competition — bound to be a massive hit, given how many Mariah Carey wannabes lived on the estate.

With all that in the bag, Pauline got a local printer to make a batch of posters to stick up around the area, and secured several mentions on the radio in the week leading up to the event. But her greatest achievement by far was to get herself interviewed by the *Evening News*. That really iced her cake, and made her feel like something of a local celebrity as people on the street started to recognise her from her picture on the front page.

All in all, it looked like they were heading for an enjoyable and successful event, and Pauline couldn't have been more proud of herself — or her ladies — when the big Saturday finally came around.

CHAPTER
NINE

Feeling younger and more vital than she had in years as she leapt out of bed that morning, Pauline ignored John's groans of protest and drew the curtains back, smiling broadly when she saw that it was already fairly sunny outside — and dry, which was fantastic, because they'd been forecasting rain. She'd been dreading that, knowing that most of the people around here would rather sit at home and watch telly than risk getting wet. But there would be no excuse for absences today.

Peeling off the hairnet which had protected her newly styled hair throughout the night, Pauline was washed, dressed, and out of the house before John had a chance to rub the sleep from his eyes. Arriving at the community centre a short time later with her clipboard in hand and a bossy look on her face, she opened the doors with a flourish — all set to whip her volunteers into shape, and make this the biggest fun-day the community had seen in a long time.

Over on the neighbouring Grafton estate, Terry was still in bed. He'd been awake for ages, but he was struggling to summon up the energy and enthusiasm to get up. It was so hard to make yourself do even the simplest of things when every fibre of your being was resisting.

He really didn't want to go to this fundraiser of Pauline's, and if he could have got out it, he would have. But he figured that things had been bad enough in the last year without making himself look like an ungrateful bastard by snubbing Pauline when she was making an effort to do something positive — even if she was one of the people who had made his life hell lately. Maybe not as much as her friends had, but she'd had her moments, and he hadn't entirely forgotten — or forgiven — the things that had been said and done in the past.

Still, he'd agreed to go, so he would. But there was no way he was staying till the end. He'd show his face and thank those who deserved thanking, then slip quietly away before people started to get tanked up and loose-lipped.

And, despite Pauline's insistence that everyone was coming along to show their support and not to cause trouble, he wasn't stupid enough to believe that they had all miraculously dropped the grudges they'd been harbouring all year. Someone was bound to start mouthing off before the day was through, but he planned to be long gone by then.

He just hoped that Sue didn't turn up before he managed to escape, because she was one person he could definitely do without seeing again this side of the millennium.

It still infuriated him when he thought about her turning up at the hospital with Dave on his visiting day.

And it didn't help that he'd since found out that Leanne could have prevented it, if she'd only remembered to pass on that message. But, contrary to what Leanne had thought, he hadn't given a toss about Sue and Dave, and whether or not they had been *together* together; his anger had been aimed wholly at Sue, for waltzing off for an entire weekend without giving the kids a second thought.

As it happened, Carole had confronted Dave and he'd denied that there was anything going on with him and Sue. He'd merely bumped into her on the way to the hospital and given her a lift, he'd said. And Carole reckoned it was true, because, despite splitting up, Dave still visited her regularly for sex, and she *always* knew when he had another tart on the go.

Leanne had calmed down a bit after hearing that, happy to go back to her "my dad wouldn't betray me" fantasy. But Terry wasn't so happy, because Sue hadn't let him see Connor since. She had whisked him straight round to her mate's flat, knowing full well that Terry didn't know where it was. And just in case he somehow found out and decided to turn up, she'd made damn sure that he knew he wouldn't be welcome by sending that exact message through Tina — which had caused yet *another* argument with Leanne, who was furious that Sue had given his number out to anyone, never mind to another woman.

All in all, it had been one of the most stressful weeks of Terry's life. He felt like he had a noose wrapped around his throat and Leanne and Sue were pulling at it from opposite ends, choking the life out of him. And if it hadn't been for the kids, he'd have been tempted to turn his back on the pair of them. But there was no way he could take off while Nicky was still missing. However long it took, he had to be here for her when she came home. And he had to be here *now* for Connor.

And that was the real reason he'd agreed to go today — to see Connor, and make sure that he was all right; that he was eating and sleeping properly, and maybe even talking again, which would be great.

Looking forward to that — and only that — Terry got up at last. Creeping around the room, because he didn't want to disturb Leanne who was still curled up on the other side of the bed, he gathered his things together for a shower. She'd been fairly mellow for the last couple of days, and he was hoping that the good mood would still be with her when she woke up today, because it was going to be hard enough facing all his old enemies without her adding to the stress by starting the day off in a strop. And to give himself a running chance, he decided to let her sleep for a little while longer, then wake her with a cup of tea and a cigarette — giving her no excuse to moan about anything.

Unfortunately for him, Leanne was already awake, and she'd been lying there for ages doing exactly what he'd been doing: thinking about how much she didn't want to go to the fundraiser today. But where Terry had Connor to motivate him, Leanne's only reason for even considering it was to support him. And given that she was already highly suspicious about his motives for agreeing to go in the first place, when he started

195

creeping around the room now she immediately suspected that he was going to try and sneak out without her.

Jerking up in the bed when Terry tiptoed out into the hallway, closing the door quietly behind him, Leanne listened out for the sound of the front door opening. But all she heard was the sound of the radio going on in the living room, followed by him whistling his way into the bathroom. Unaware that he was forcing himself to whistle in an effort to cheer himself up so that Connor wouldn't see how upset and worried he was, she took it as a sign that he was happy about going out today — which just made her all the more suspicious.

Coming back ten minutes later, Terry's heart sank when he saw the look on Leanne's face. Sighing when she snatched the cigarette he'd lit for her out of his hand without thanking him, he put her tea down on the bedside table and walked back round to his side of the bed. Taking a set of fresh underwear out of his drawer, he pulled it on without speaking, because there was no way he was going to ask what was wrong and risk having her bite his head off.

Watching as he went across to the wardrobe and took out his suit, Leanne puffed agitatedly on the cigarette. After her run-in with Zak at Goldie's party, she'd been determined to show Terry how much she loved him. So she'd told her friends to stay away so that they could spend some quality time alone together, and had thrown herself into pampering him, cooking and cleaning, and making an effort to look really nice when he came home from work. And she'd even been

196

supportive when he'd talked about his kids, even though she couldn't stand them and wished they'd never been born. But, hard as she tried to pretend that she and Terry were the only two people who existed, something always seemed to get in the way.

Like Sue trying to trick her way back into Terry's life by turning up at the hospital on his visit, knowing full well that Leanne wouldn't be there.

And Connor needing constant attention because he still wasn't talking — and Leanne knew the little brat was putting *that* on.

And the cheeky bitch of a policewoman turning up any time she felt like it, asking for Terry, and refusing to discuss what she wanted with Leanne if he wasn't there.

Right down to Tina flaming Murphy ringing him on his mobile to pass along messages from Sue. And that had *really* pissed Leanne off, because no woman should have had that number except her.

So, despite her very best efforts, the last two weeks had been difficult. And today looked set to be even more so, as, seeming not to care about how she was feeling, Terry continued to get dressed.

Feeling a bubble of rage well up in her chest when he calmly zipped up his trousers and took *her* favourite lilac shirt out of the wardrobe, Leanne jumped out of bed and marched out of the room, slamming the door behind her.

Exhaling wearily, Terry buttoned his shirt and tucked it into his pants. Then, looping his tie around his neck, he picked up his jacket and followed her out. She was sitting on the couch, with a deep scowl on her face.

"Don't you think you should start getting ready?" he said.

"I'm not going," Leanne replied tartly, folding her arms.

"Oh, please, let's not do this today," Terry groaned. "You know how important it is."

"Not to me," she retorted, her mouth puckering into a tight knot. "Anyway, I never said I *would* go, I only said I'd think about it."

"Yeah, and you've had all week, so why start playing up about it now, when you can see I'm ready to go?"

"I'm not playing up," she spat, giving him a reproachful look. "*Kids* play up."

Fighting to keep the frustration out of his voice, Terry said, "You said you were coming yesterday, so what's changed?"

"My mind," Leanne told him bluntly. "I don't *want* to go, so I'm not going."

Peering down at her, Terry shook his head in despair, wishing she'd just make up her mind and stick to it, so at least he'd know what he was dealing with from day to day.

"I don't see why *you're* so keen to go, anyway," Leanne sniped. "I'd have thought you'd be happier huddled away in a corner somewhere *crying*, seeing as that's all you've been doing for the last two weeks."

Terry felt the heat of anger rise to his cheeks. Sulking was one thing, but that was just plain vicious. So what if he'd cried? Who wouldn't if one of their kids had almost died in a fire, while the other was still missing? Of course he was upset, and if she couldn't understand that, there was something seriously wrong with her.

"Hadn't you better run along?" she said now, pushing him even closer to the edge when she added, "*Wifey* will be waiting for you. And we don't want to upset *wifey*, do we?"

"Pack it in," Terry warned her, his voice dangerously low. "I've told you a thousand times, I am *not* interested in her."

"Like I'm supposed to believe that," Leanne spat. "If you didn't want anything to do with her, you wouldn't be going to this stupid thing when you know she's going to be there. If you ask me, that's *why* you're going — 'cos you're desperate to see her again."

"That's shit, and you know it," Terry growled. "I'm going for my kids — and that's the *only* reason. If I wanted to see her, I'd have gone looking for her."

"What's to say you haven't?" Leanne said, crossing her legs and jiggling her foot wildly. "Once a liar, always a liar."

Something snapped, and Terry felt a sudden calm descend on him. He'd been trying so hard to keep her happy, to do things her way and not give her cause to argue. But nothing ever worked, so what was the point?

"Have it your own way," he said, looking around for his shoes. "But I'd have a serious think if I was you, 'cos one of these days you're going to get what you're looking for."

"Which is what?" she demanded, giving him a challenging look. "You gonna *hit* me, or something?"

"What, so you can go running back to the estate and tell everyone what a big bad bastard I am?" Terry replied softly. "Sorry, sweetheart, it's not my style. If you want someone like that, you'd best go get with one of your little hoodie boys."

"You mean one of the lads I *used* to hang out with before I tied myself down with an old man like you?" Leanne spat back. "'Cos that's what really gets to you, isn't it, Terry — that they're all so much younger and fitter than you, and all I'd have to do is click my fingers and they'd all come running."

"Don't let me stop you."

"Yeah, 'cos you don't give a toss about me." Leanne's chin was wobbling now, her eyes full of tears.

Refusing to rise to the bait and tell her that of course he gave a toss about her, because that was what she was expecting, Terry slipped his feet into his shoes and sat down to tie the laces.

Watching him out of the corner of her eye, Leanne wanted to scream, but she knew it wouldn't do any good. She'd gone too far, and he was going to go without her. And the only way she could stop him would be to apologise. But he'd already gone cold on her so he'd probably just tell her to piss off, and her pride couldn't take that.

Sniffing loudly as the first tear trickled slowly down her cheek, Leanne brought her knees up to her chest and hugged them as a wave of self-pity washed over her. She couldn't bear the thought of Terry going anywhere without her, especially not like this — all dressed up in his suit and looking really gorgeous. He'd have all those bitches back on the estate falling all over themselves to get at him. And God only knew what stunts that whore of an ex of his would pull to get near him.

Standing up now, Terry decided to give Leanne one last chance to snap out of her mood and come with him. Saying, "Are you coming then, or what?" he sighed when she carried on staring resolutely the other way. Shrugging, he walked out, calling back over his shoulder, "You know where I am if you change your mind."

Leanne waited for a few moments, then got up and rushed to the window. Gazing down, she watched as he emerged from the main doors below and headed for the car. Just as he reached it, another car pulled in beside him, and two women who lived on the floor below got out. Her eyes narrowed jealously when they started talking to him and she opened the window to hear what they were saying. She couldn't hear anything, but she didn't need to. She could tell just by looking at them that they were flirting with him. And if that could happen here, right under her nose, what the hell would happen when she wasn't there to keep an eye on him? Oh, no . . . she wasn't having that.

Flinging the window even wider as the women walked away and Terry started to climb into the car, Leanne yelled at him to wait for her. Then, running into the bedroom, shedding her dressing gown on the way, she pulled on the dress she'd always intended to wear and slipped on her shoes, before snatching up her make-up bag and handbag and running down to join him.

Across town, Sue hadn't even started to get ready. Pacing Julie's living room floor in her nightclothes, she was chewing on her thumbnail, wondering how she could get out of going without offending Tina. Or Pauline, who had been really good to her since the fire — despite having been such a nosy old bitch before it.

According to Tina, Pauline had worked really hard to get this event up and running, and had bugged everyone to donate the clothes and toiletries that had been sent over the previous week for Sue and Connor. But, grateful as she was, Sue still didn't think she could face Pauline today. And she definitely didn't want to see any of her other old neighbours.

Especially not Carole, who was already on the warpath about Dave taking her to the hospital that day. Dave had told her that Carole had come at him like a wild dog, accusing him of all sorts, but he'd protected Sue by saying that they'd met up by chance and he'd just given her a lift. Not that Sue needed protecting in a physical sense, because she wasn't scared of Carole. But she was going through a tough enough time already without the added burden of having to listen to Carole mouthing off.

Carole didn't really have cause to say anything, as it happened, because still nothing had happened between Sue and Dave. Sue had thought that an affair with Dave was what she wanted, and yet when she'd seen Terry, she'd realised that she still had feelings for him, too. So the barriers had gone back up, preventing Dave from making the move that she'd sensed he was getting ready to make. And, ever the gentleman, he hadn't pushed it.

Not that he'd had too many opportunities since Connor had come home, because they'd only managed to meet up a couple of times over the last week, and both times had been during the day, with Connor present, which had made it awkward to really talk. But Sue was still glad to have Dave on her side, and she was looking forward to seeing him today — even if they *would* have to play it cool so that the gossipmongers couldn't get hold of the wrong end of the stick and turn their friendship into something dirty.

And Sue desperately didn't want that to happen, because Dave was the only thing that was keeping her sane as things went from bad to worse with Julie.

The Nicky issue aside, the cramped living conditions were really starting to take their toll, because the flat only had two tiny bedrooms, a minuscule bathroom, and a walk-in closet of a kitchen. Which was absolutely fine for Julie on her own, and just about bearable for the two of them when Sue had used to stay over after a night out. But it was a completely unsuitable place for two adults to actually live together on a day-to-day basis, and since Connor had joined them there, it had been absolute murder.

Julie was trying not to let it get to her, and Sue was genuinely grateful that she was still willing to make the effort. But it was obviously pissing Julie off, because she'd started to make narky little comments about the mess, and to moan about the amount of time Sue spent in the bathroom, and how much her electric bill had gone up recently. And she'd all but given up on trying to communicate with Connor — although Sue could hardly blame her for that, because she was finding it hard enough to cope with him herself, and she was his *mother*.

The silence was frustrating enough, but now he'd taken to making little grunting noises when he wanted something, and Sue found that both irritating and — ashamed as she was to admit it — repulsive. It was almost as if he'd gone into hospital a boy and come out an animal, and she was his keeper, having to coax him to eat, and clean up his shit — which, to her disgust, he'd gone back to doing in his pants.

The social workers reckoned it was quite normal under the circumstances, but Sue just couldn't deal with it. The pissy beds had been one thing, but at least that had only been at night — and Nicky had been there to change his sheets and make sure he had clean undies. Now it was a twenty-four-hour job, and as Julie obviously had no intention of getting involved it was left to Sue to deal with it all. And she really wasn't coping half as well as everyone seemed to think she should be.

Already depressed about losing everything she owned, and still alternating between worrying about Nicky and cursing her for her wickedness, there were times when she felt as if she was hanging off the edge of a cliff by her fingertips.

And today was one of those days.

"Bloody hell, Sue!"

Jumping when Julie's voice penetrated her thoughts, Sue snapped her head around and gaped at her guiltily.

"What have I done now?"

"Don't you think you'd better get that sorted before it gets infected?" Julie said, nodding towards Sue's thumb as she unravelled the woolly scarf she was wearing from around her neck.

Looking down at her hand, Sue frowned when she saw the blood. She'd chewed right into the flesh, but she hadn't felt a thing.

"I know it's hard," Julie went on, draping the scarf over the back of the couch and shrugging out of her jacket. "But you're not doing yourself any favours with all this moping about." Waddling past Sue now, she said, "Anyhow, I'm putting the kettle on. Tea or coffee?"

"Tea," Sue called after her, wiping the blood onto her dressing gown and wincing as the pain finally filtered through.

"Might as well get dressed while I'm making it," Julie called back. "And make sure you put something nice and warm on Connor, 'cos it might look sunny but it's bloody freezing out there. I only went out for milk, but my nipples are like bleedin' torpedoes. No wonder that Malik was staring at me the whole time I was in the shop."

Grimacing at the image, Sue rushed into the bathroom to put a plaster on her thumb and have a wash. Going back into the bedroom, she got dressed before reluctantly waking Connor up to get him ready.

205

She hadn't really wanted to take him with her, but Julie obviously wasn't volunteering to watch him so she had no choice. But, oh, well . . . at least he'd give her a good excuse to leave early.

There was already a fair-sized crowd milling about on the field when Terry and Leanne pulled into the car park. Leanne hadn't spoken during the drive because she'd been too busy concentrating on getting her hair and makeup done. But she'd given Terry plenty of accusing looks whenever they went over a bump in the road, as if she thought he was deliberately trying to sabotage her efforts to make herself look nice, when, in fact, he'd been doing his damnedest to *avoid* them, sure that the next one would be the one that killed the struggling car off once and for all.

Cheering up when she spotted Goldie and some of the other girls making their way through the gates, Leanne bit her lip and cast a furtive side glance at Terry. She hadn't spent much time with the girls lately, and she could really do with a good chill-out. But Terry would probably expect her to stay with him, and she knew she probably should, because she was all he had right now. But it would be so *boring*.

"Go ahead," Terry said, guessing what was going through her mind.

Trying not to grin too widely, Leanne said, "Are you sure? I'll stay with you if you want me to."

Assuring her that he'd be fine, Terry said, "No point both of us being miserable, so go on. Have a good time."

206

Saying, "Thanks, babe," Leanne kissed him and hopped out of the car.

Watching as she caught up with the girls and hugged them all before linking arms with Goldie and disappearing around the corner, Terry sighed. It was at times like this that he really noticed the age difference and felt guilty for tying her down when she should be out there having a laugh with her mates. But he doubted whether she'd leave him even if he opened the door and shoved her out with her suitcase. And he couldn't finish it, even though he sometimes felt like it would be the right thing to do for her sake, because despite all the petty squabbles and jealous rages she did love him. And he loved her. And, anyway, it would just prove all the doubters right if they split, and he didn't want to give them the satisfaction.

Rolling himself a cigarette now, Terry got out of the car and, slipping a hand into his pocket in an effort to look relaxed, even though he was really nervous about being among so many of his enemies in one place at one time, he strolled around to the field.

There were more people than he'd imagined there would be. A whole load of bric-a-brac stalls had been set up along one side like a mini car-boot sale, facing which was a large play area for the kids, complete with a giant bouncy castle and a colourful little carousel ride. And, in the centre of it all, a huge refreshments tent.

Amazed that Pauline had managed to pull all this off in one short week, Terry made his way towards the tent to get himself a drink. Further surprised when people started nodding at him and saying hello as he passed, he nodded back. But that was as far as he was willing to go, because these were the same people who'd been giving him dirty looks for the past few months and he didn't trust them.

And he especially didn't trust Irene Murgatroyd, who was serving behind the makeshift bar when he entered the tent. Jackie Harris was there, too, but while he knew that Jackie would be polite, Irene was a different kettle of fish. And if anyone was capable of upsetting the fragile balance of acceptance that Pauline seemed to have achieved amongst the locals, it would be her.

As it happened, Irene had no intention of rocking the little love-boat that Pauline had launched here today. In fact, as soon as she'd realised that Pauline had the backing of the other neighbours, Irene had jumped on board with relish, determined to snatch some of the credit for herself.

Pushing Jackie aside when she saw Terry now, she gave him a big smile as he approached the counter, saying, "Hello, my love. And what can I get you?"

Unnerved as much by her friendly tone as by her newly dyed blonde hair, bright red lipstick and heavy blue eyeshadow, which all looked so wrong on a woman of her age, Terry asked if she had any lager.

Telling him that it was soft drinks only until the official bar opened later on, Irene cocked her finger to bring him closer, and whispered, "But I've got some Scotch in my bag if you fancy a nip?"

Guessing by the smell of her breath that she'd already had more than a couple of nips herself, Terry said, "I'll just take a Coke, please."

Pulling a tin out from below the counter, Irene put her hand over his when he tried to pay, saying, "Don't be so silly, I'm not taking your money. What'd be the point of that when it's all going to you in the end, anyway? Well, to *Sue*," she corrected herself, giving him another smile. "But you know what I mean."

Murmuring, "Thanks," Terry tried to get his hand back, but she held on to it.

"Ooh, you're bloody freezing," Irene said, as if he didn't already know. "Should have put a proper coat on. Mind, I don't suppose you'd want to cover up a belting suit like that, would you?" Giving what Terry could only assume was meant to be an enticing smile now, she added, "You look proper handsome, I must say. Don't he look handsome, Jack?"

Giving him a sympathetic smile, Jackie looked the other way, aware that he was embarrassed enough about Irene fawning over him without her adding to his discomfort by joining in.

"I'm so sorry about your loss," Irene was telling him now — with too much sincerity in her voice for it to be genuine, he thought. "And if there's anything I can do, you only have to ask — you know that, don't you? I mean, I know we've had our differences in the past, but none of us would have wished something like this on you. And I can't think of anything worse than losing one of your children like that."

Terry felt like reminding her that Nicky wasn't dead, but he couldn't bring himself to say it — just in case it wasn't true. It was a full two weeks since Nicky had gone missing, and he was clinging to the hope that she would be found soon — even if everybody else seemed to have already decided that she was dead.

Thanking Irene again, he yanked his hand out of hers and snatched up the can of Coke. Nodding at Jackie, he made his escape.

Squinting in the bright, heatless sunshine, Terry skirted around the edge of the crowd. There was a fantastic turnout, and everyone seemed to be enjoying themselves. But he was under no illusions that the air of camaraderie would last beyond the day, because these weren't the sort of people to forgive and forget so easily. And when the bar opened and the beer started talking, the knives would come out with a vengeance.

Looking around for Leanne, to make sure she wasn't getting any hassle — or giving any — he smiled when he spotted her leaping around on the bouncy castle with her friends. She'd either forgotten, or just didn't care that most of these people had blamed her as much as they had him for breaking up his marriage. But, hey, if she could shrug it off and get on with her life as if nothing had ever happened, good on her.

Going inside the community centre now, in search of a quiet place to sit and gather his thoughts, Terry peeked through the inner door before going into the hall, to make sure that Sue wasn't already in there.

Pauline was refilling the tea urn at the bar on the far side of the hall. Spotting Terry when he came in, she abandoned what she was doing and bustled over to greet him.

"Well, hello," she said, beaming and giving him a warm kiss on the cheek. "I'm so glad you decided to come. How are you?"

"All right," he said, forcing himself to smile. "You?"

"Oh, I'm absolutely wonderful," Pauline told him gaily, linking her arm through his. "Beautiful day, isn't it? And I'm so glad about that, because we needed to get everybody here to get the fund up and running. Anyway, let's go and say hello to the girls, because they're all dying to see you."

Feeling uncomfortable as she dragged him across to the women who were busy putting the finishing touches to the decorations, Terry began to wish he hadn't come.

Whisking him away again when everyone had said hello and gone back to work, Pauline said, "We've got so much planned for tonight; you'll be amazed when you see it all. We've got a professional DJ, and an award-winning bingo caller. And we've managed to get a fantastic band called Street-Wyze. Have you heard of them? They're supposed to be very good."

Shaking his head, Terry felt the tell-tale throb of an impending migraine behind his eyes. And that wasn't good when he had a full day of "niceties" to get through, some — like Pauline's — probably genuine, the rest positively fake.

Noticing how pale he'd become, Pauline said, "Are you all right, pet? You're not looking so good. Why don't you go and sit down and I'll fetch you a cup of tea."

Thanking her, Terry unhooked his arm from hers and headed for a table set right back in the corner furthest away from the activities. Flopping down onto a chair, he exhaled tensely, wondering how much he would be able to take before he had to get the hell out of there.

Outside, Sue and Connor had just arrived. Clutching at Connor's hand when her old neighbours immediately started to cluster around them, she held him in front of her, using him as a shield in case any of them decided to ask awkward questions.

"Yes, we're fine . . ." she heard herself saying numerous times over the next few minutes. "No, we've not been given anywhere to live yet . . . Yes, Connor's getting better . . . No, he still hasn't spoken since it happened, but they reckon it's the shock . . . No, still no word on Nicky . . . Yes, it's terrible, and I haven't slept for days, but you have to keep going for the sake of the little one, don't you?"

Leanne and the girls had just got off the bouncy castle and were making their way over to see what was going on. Spotting Sue in the middle of the crowd, Goldie stopped walking and jerked her head at her friends, saying, "Let's go back this way."

But it was too late; Leanne had already seen Sue. Eyes flashing angrily, she said, "She's got a fucking nerve showing her face today!"

Looking their way just then, Sue felt a rush of nausea and rage rise up from her gut to her throat. She hadn't laid eyes on Leanne in months, yet she felt the same depth of hatred towards her now as she'd felt back then. And if there hadn't been so many people around, she'd have launched herself at the bitch and punched the brazen look right off her face. How *dare* she come here today. This was nothing to do with her, and she had no right to push herself into it like this.

But if she was here, then Terry must be, too.

Glancing around for him now, Sue didn't know if she was relieved or disappointed when she didn't see him. In a perverse way she *wanted* him to be here, but at the same time she was dreading it, because she didn't want to see that look of loathing that had been in his eyes at the hospital that day.

Pauline had just heard that Sue was here. Coming out of the hall to look for her, she saw her in the middle of the crowd and guessed from her expression that she was probably feeling a bit overwhelmed by all the attention. Pushing her way through to get to her, she said, "Sorry, folks, I just need to steal her away for a bit."

Murmuring, "Thanks," when Pauline had taken her off to the side, Sue exhaled tensely. "I think I need a cup of tea. Is there anywhere I can get one?"

"In the hall," Pauline told her. "But I'll have to warn you, Terry's already in there. Though I'm sure he won't mind if you don't. I mean, this is for you as a family, isn't it?"

"No, it's all right," Sue said quickly, sure that Terry very much *would* mind. "I don't want to see him just yet."

"In your own time," Pauline said understandingly. "Let's go and get you something cold instead for now, then, eh? And how about I take the little one inside for a bit?" she offered then, keeping her voice low so that Connor wouldn't hear as she added, "Let him see his daddy for a few minutes while you have a break. Irene will look after you till you're ready to start mingling."

"I'm not sure that's such a good idea," Sue murmured as Pauline led her towards the refreshment tent. "She hates me."

"No, she doesn't," Pauline said gently but firmly. "That's what this is all about today, pet — putting the past to rest. Irene knows she's been rough on you; we *all* do. But we're trying to put it right, if you'll let us."

Sue felt the tears welling up in her eyes. Chin wobbling, because she genuinely hadn't expected this level of kindness, she said, "Thanks, Pauline. I don't know how I'd have managed without you lately. You've been really great."

"Oh, I haven't done anything," Pauline said modestly, flapping her hand.

"Yeah, you have," Sue insisted. "I know this was all your idea, and I think you've done an amazing job."

"It *has* come out pretty good, hasn't it?" Pauline gazed around proudly. "And I've right enjoyed myself, so it didn't really feel like work. But we'll sit down later and have that cup of tea and a good old chat, eh?"

Nodding, Sue dabbed at her eyes with the back of her finger.

Pausing when they reached the tent, Pauline said, "Right, well, let's hand you over to Irene, 'cos I need to

214

get back inside. The girls are doing a grand job, but they don't half need watching, otherwise they start moving things out of place, and it drives me up the wall. Now you know where I am if you need me. And if anyone says anything out of line, you just come and get me and I'll sort them out. Okay?"

Sue hadn't forgotten all the ill feeling of the past, and she didn't know if she'd ever truly forgive, but it felt good to be back in the fold — for now. So, reaching out, she gave the older woman an impulsive hug.

Across the field, still watching her enemy intently, Leanne sneered when she saw her hugging Pauline before heading into the tent. So the bitch thought everything was hunkydory again, did she? Well, they'd soon see about that!

Turning to Kelly Greene, who had just come back from the off-licence with the litre bottle of cider that the girls had pooled together to buy, she snatched it out of her hand and unscrewed the cap.

"Go easy!" Goldie squawked when she took a long drink. "That's got to go round five of us, you know."

Coming up for air, Leanne shrugged. "So, I'll buy another one," she said, tipping the bottle up again.

"Pack it in!" Goldie scolded, trying to take the bottle off her now. "I mean it, Lee. I know what you're doing, and I'm not letting you. Not today."

"*Yes*, today," Leanne hissed, jerking the bottle out of Goldie's reach. "She's had it coming for long enough."

"Not *today*," Goldie repeated firmly. "Not with all these kids around."

215

"Leave her alone," Kelly butted in, her eyes flashing with excitement at the thought of a confrontation. "She can have a drink if she wants one."

"Was I talking to *you*?" Goldie snapped, glaring at the younger girl. "No! So keep your fucking nose out."

"Get lost," Kelly retorted cheekily, sure that Leanne and her cousin Neela would back her up if Goldie kicked off.

"You fucking what?" Goldie snarled.

"Just shut up, you two," Leanne said irritably. "I've had enough of everyone trying to tell me what to do. I'll do what I want — all right?"

"And what *do* you want?" Goldie demanded, turning back to her.

"A bit of fun," Leanne muttered, casting a malevolent glance in the direction of the refreshment tent. "Anyone want to join me?"

"Too right," Kelly said, immediately up for it.

Shaking her head, Goldie said, "You're out of order. And your Terry won't be too pleased to know what you're planning, seeing as it's his kid who'll be watching it."

Muttering, "Don't fucking remind me," Leanne took another swig of the cider.

"I thought you were growing up," Goldie said, the disappointment in her voice piercing Leanne's anger like a dart as she added, "But you're still just as much of a kid as *her*, aren't you?" She jerked her thumb in Kelly's direction.

"No, I'm not," Leanne protested quietly, unable to meet her friend's direct gaze. "Anyhow, I never said I was going to do anything. I was just going to go in and stare her out, or something. That's all."

"Yeah, well, do it without me, 'cos I'm here to have a good time, not get myself arrested for stupidity," Goldie said. Then, to the rest of the girls, "What about you lot? You here for a laugh, or are you after starting shit?"

Most of them murmured that they were here for a laugh. Apart from Kelly, who declared that she was with Leanne.

Aware that she'd upset Goldie, which she genuinely hadn't wanted to do, Leanne sighed. "All right, I'll leave her alone. But you can't blame me for being pissed off, 'cos she shouldn't be here."

"Yeah, and she's probably saying exactly the same thing about *you*, seeing as this is about her and her kids," Goldie pointed out. "So, just chill out and forget about her. At least you know you've pissed her off by being here, so she hasn't won anything, has she?"

"Suppose not," Leanne agreed, handing the cider bottle to her, with a sheepish smile. "So, what now?"

"Get stoned?" Goldie said, grinning as she pulled a pre-rolled five-skin spliff out of her pocket.

"Size of *that*!" Leanne gasped, drawing her head back and gazing at it. "But I'd like to know where you're planning on smoking it without every copper from here to bleedin' Levenshulme seeing us."

Nodding towards a thick bank of bushes at the far end of the field, Goldie set off towards it. Turning back after a few steps, she glared at Kelly who was tagging along behind.

"Where d'y' think you're going?" she demanded. "You're not invited, so why don't you fuck off and play with someone your own age?"

Looking to Leanne for support, only to see her smirking, Kelly felt her cheeks flaming with humiliation. She hadn't seen much of Leanne since Goldie's party, and she'd really hoped to get back on track with her today. But she was being a bitch again, and that wasn't fair, because Kelly knew she hadn't done anything to deserve it.

"What you waiting for?" Goldie snapped, still eyeballing her aggressively. "Fuck off before I kick your head in."

"Right, I'm going," Kelly spat, folding her arms defensively. "You lot piss me off, anyway!" Turning, she stomped back across the field with her nose in the air.

"Thanks for that," Neela tutted, giving Goldie an accusing look. "You've landed me right in it now. Her mam'll be straight on the phone to mine, and you watch if I don't get it in the neck when I get in."

"Sorry, mate, but don't you think it's about time you told your mam to back off and let you make your own mind up who you hang about with?" Goldie said, twisting the cap off the cider and taking a little swig before passing it to her.

"Easy for you to say when you've got your own place to escape to," Neela pointed out enviously, taking a sip and passing the drink on. "And I don't see what you've all got such a problem with her for, anyhow. She's not that bad when you give her a chance."

218

"Come off it," Goldie snorted. "She's a pain in the arse, always running round after us like a little dog. And I'm sure she's got the hots for Lee, the way she sucks up to her all the time."

"So, she likes her," Neela said defensively. "What's wrong with that? You like her, an' all, or you wouldn't call her your best mate." Turning to Leanne now, she added, "And she was only trying to back you up just now, so you didn't have to take the piss out of her like that."

Biting her lip, Leanne gazed thoughtfully after Kelly. She hadn't said anything about Terry to anyone yet, but who was to say that she wasn't pissed off enough to do it now?

"Back in a minute," she said, setting off after Kelly to make it up with her before she did something stupid.

Too busy looking for Kelly, who had got lost in the crowd, Leanne didn't notice her dad and three of his mates coming towards her, and she almost fell over when she walked straight into him.

"Whoa!" Dave drawled, reaching out to steady her. "What you rushing round like a blind blue-arsed fly for?"

"Just need a word with someone," Leanne said, almost tasting the leather of his jacket and his strong aftershave as he gave her a hug.

"They can wait," Dave said, Scotch fumes floating down into her face as he continued to hold onto her. "I haven't seen you for ages, so the least you can do is spend a bit of time with me now I'm here. You remember the lads, don't you?"

Glancing up at his mates, Leanne felt suddenly nervous. They were smiling, but they all had the same dark gleam in their eyes that told her they had been drinking. And drinking spelled trouble when this lot got together — and it didn't take a genius to guess who would be on the receiving end of it.

"Why are you here, Dad?" she asked, struggling out of his grip. "You're not planning anything stupid, are you? Not today. We're only here for the kids."

Giving her a look of wounded innocence, Dave said, "And I'm here to see you."

"Promise?" Leanne murmured, giving him the stern look she'd always used on him when she was a kid and wanted to get her own way. "'Cos if you do anything, I'll never forgive you, and I mean it."

"As if I'd do anything to upset my little darlin'," Dave chuckled, pulling her into another hug. "And you *are* still my darlin', aren't you?"

"Course," Leanne gasped, wishing he wouldn't get like this when he'd been drinking, because it made her feel uneasy. He always got way too affectionate, and then he'd kick off if you didn't respond how he thought you should.

Saying, "Good, 'cos we're both too stubborn for our own good, me and you, and we shouldn't be falling out over shit," Dave gave her a kiss.

"Aw, *Dad*!" Leanne complained when he went on to ruffle her hair with his hand. "It took me ages to get that right, and you've ruined it now."

"It's gorgeous," he said, laughing at her indignant expression. "And so are you, so quit plastering all that

220

shit on your face before you end up looking like your mam."

"Take it you've had another row, then?" Leanne said wearily, licking her hand to try and flatten her hair.

"When are we ever not rowing?" Dave retorted, lighting a cigarette and squinting as he gazed around. "Anyhow, never mind her . . . where's lover boy?"

"I don't know," Leanne told him truthfully. "I haven't seen him since we got here. But why do you want to know?"

Shrugging, Dave said, "Thought he might want to join his old mates for a drink, that's all."

"You're not his mates," Leanne said warily.

"Course we are," Dave scoffed. "Me and Tezza go back years. Don't you remember how he used to come back to ours for a few after we'd spent the night down the pub?" Pausing, he slapped a hand on his forehead. "Oh, no, you wouldn't, would you, 'cos you were only a baby."

"Don't start," Leanne snapped, folding her arms now. "I'm not a baby any more, and I love him."

"I know that," Dave said easily — as if he had no problem with it, which they both knew he did. "Anyhow," he said then, rubbing his hands together, "all this talking is making me thirsty, so we'll catch up later, yeah? And don't forget to pass my regards on, will you?" Winking at her now, he jerked his head at the lads and set off towards the refreshment tent.

Pauline was just coming out with Connor. Seeing Dave and his friends heading her way, while Leanne gazed after them with a worried expression on her face, she pursed her lips. She'd spent too long organising this event for Dave Miller to start any of his shenanigans and mess it up. And he might have put things right with Sue, but he obviously still had issues with Terry. And he'd come mob-handed, which could only mean one thing.

Stepping neatly in front of him now, Pauline gave Dave a pleasant smile as his mates fanned out to get around her.

"Hello, Dave, what you doing here? Wouldn't have thought this would be your cup of tea."

"It's not," Dave admitted, giving a little shrug. "But you've got to do your bit for the community, haven't you?" Grinning down at Connor now, who peered back at him with dark eyes, he said, "Hi, there, fella. How's it going?"

Covering Connor's ear with her hand, unaware that Dave had probably seen more of him since he'd come out of hospital than she had, Pauline whispered, "No point talking to him, 'cos he won't answer. Poor little thing's still suffering the shock. I'm just taking him inside to see . . ." Pulling herself up short before she mentioned Terry, she said, "To see if we can find him a little job while his mum has a rest."

"Sue's here, then, is she?" Dave said, as if he hadn't expected to hear that. "She all right?"

"She's fine," Pauline told him, giving him a pointed look as she added, "So don't you go upsetting her."

"Why am *I* going to upset her?" Dave asked, giving Pauline a hurt look. "Would I have bothered going to the trouble of apologising if I was just going to flip it back round and have another go at her?"

"I'm just warning you, that's all," Pauline said firmly. "We all know what you're like when you've had a drink."

"Yeah, well, I've not had that much," Dave said, getting a bit irritated now. "And I've already held my hands up to what happened before, so you don't have to keep going on about it every time I see you."

Holding his gaze for several moments, Pauline saw the look in his eyes and realised that he was being genuine. Nodding, she said, "Okay, I believe you."

"Well, thank fuck for that," Dave snorted, wiping imaginary sweat off his brow. "Thought I'd slipped back in time for a minute there, and I was back at home getting a good old roasting off me mam."

"Mmm, well you're never too old," Pauline said, giving him a mock-stern look. "Anyway, best crack on," she said then. "Will you be staying around? Only we've got loads lined up for later. There's a professional band, and a DJ, and bingo. Oh, and we've got someone from the police dropping in, which will be nice, because they've been ever so good to Sue while all this has been going on. They seem to be taking it really personally, for a change."

"That's nice of them," Dave drawled, exchanging an amused glance with his mates who were making wanker gestures behind Pauline's back. She'd obviously slipped that in to warn him not to cause trouble, but she needn't have bothered, because he'd only popped in to see Sue and have a couple of drinks before he and the lads headed into town to watch the footy on the big screen in Albert Square.

Satisfied that she'd got her message across, Pauline said, "Right, well, I'll see you later. Oh, and don't forget to buy your raffle tickets. They're a pound apiece, but it's all in a good cause."

Sticking two fingers up at her back as she walked away, Dave headed into the refreshments tent — leaving Leanne exhaling with relief on the grass behind him. So, the police were coming — great! Even *he* wasn't stupid enough to start anything with the law around. But she'd still best warn Terry that he was here, just in case. If she could find him, because he seemed to have disappeared off the face of the earth.

Forgetting all about Kelly and the conciliatory talk she'd meant to have with her, she set off to look for Terry instead.

Irene was making as big an effort to be friendly with Sue as she'd made with Terry. And she was enjoying herself almost as much as she'd previously enjoyed slagging her off, because it made her look good that she could be so magnanimous.

Rattling on now, oblivious to the look of incredulity on Sue's face, Irene told her how sorry she was about the fire, and how worried she was about Nicky, and how sad she was that Connor was still suffering the shock, and how awful she felt about the misunderstanding that had arisen between them after Terry had left, because she'd never meant to offend her in any way and hoped that Sue didn't think that she was one of the

224

ones who'd been talking about her behind her back, because she wasn't.

Sue could hardly believe what was coming out of the old witch's mouth, considering everyone knew that she'd been one of the main instigators of the gossip. But Irene's overt change of attitude seemed to be having a positive effect on the rest of the neighbours, so Sue wasn't about to risk getting their backs up again by telling her that she was talking shit. So she smiled, and thanked her, and drank her whisky — hoping that it might take some of the edge off her nerves.

But it didn't seem to be working. If anything, it was making her feel sick again. Or maybe that was just the fact that she hadn't eaten in the last two days?

Topping up their plastic cups under the counter now, Irene spotted Dave and his mates, and murmured, "Eh up, look what the cat's dragged in." Glancing at Sue, she said, "You and him all right, or do you want me to get rid?"

Shaking her head, Sue said, "No, we're fine. We had a little chat when he gave me a lift to the hospital the other week, and everything's sorted."

"If you're sure," Irene said protectively. "But if he starts any of his nonsense, you just give me the nod and I'll have him."

Turning now as the men reached the counter, she said, "Yes, boys, what can I get you?"

Giving her a cheeky grin, Dave said, "Some of that Scotch you've got stashed under there will do nicely, thanks."

Informing him that there was nothing under the counter but pop, Irene folded her arms. She'd known Dave Miller since he was a baby, and had never had a problem with him. But her loyalties lay with Sue — for today, at least.

"Come on, you auld cow, don't try and kid a kidder," Dave chuckled, his nostrils flaring as he inhaled exaggeratedly. "You know I can sniff it out at a thousand paces. And you've already been at it yourself, if I'm not very much mistaken."

"And so have you, by the looks of it," Irene retorted. Then, lowering her voice and glancing around to make sure that she wasn't being watched, she said, "All right, you can have one glass each. But you'll have to pay, and if anyone asks, it's ginger beer. Got that?"

Saluting her, Dave reached into his pocket for his wallet. Looking at Sue now, he said, "All right, darlin'? Nearly didn't see you hiding in the shadows back there. Everything okay?"

Flicking a nervous glance at Irene, sure that she would pick up on the slightest sign of over-familiarity, Sue said, "Fine, thanks. You?"

"Same old, same old." Dave gave a casual shrug. "Any word on your lass yet?"

"No, nothing," Sue said quietly, aware that he was only asking because it was the first thing everyone else had asked when they'd seen her today, so it would probably look strange if he didn't.

"Really sorry to hear that," Dave said, peering deep into her eyes. "But you know where I am, yeah?"

Bringing the plastic cups from under the counter just then, Irene said, "That's a tenner, if you please, chaps."

"You what?" Dave snorted. "There's only five of us, not bleedin' fifty."

"And you'd be paying twice as much as that in the pub," Irene told him firmly.

"You probably paid less than that for the whole bottle, you stingy boot."

"Hey, we haven't got a licence for liquor, you know. And if you think I'm getting myself locked up for you, you can think again. A tenner, or pop — you choose."

Shaking his head, Dave slapped a ten-pound note down on the counter. "There, and buy yourself some new lipstick with the change, 'cos the last lot's all over your teeth." Winking at Sue now, he said, "See you later, love," before heading back out into the daylight.

Slipping her teeth out when the men had gone, Irene gave them a wipe on her cardigan before slotting them back into her mouth. Sitting down next to Sue then, she said, "He's a rum bugger, that Dave, but I'd take *ten* of him over that Carole any day. Don't know what he ever saw in her, I really don't. And her still using his name, like he'd ever made an honest woman of her. And he didn't, you know. Not like my Eddie and your Terry did with us, eh?"

Smiling sadly, Sue gazed down at the faint pale line where her wedding ring had been. She'd carried on wearing it for months after Terry had gone, but had finally taken it off a few weeks back — under pressure from Julie, who claimed it was probably the reason why she was having so much trouble getting a new man. She still missed it, though, because it had made her feel worthwhile. Even if it hadn't meant anything to Terry.

"Should have heard her going on about you the other day," Irene was saying now, her conspiratorial tone bringing Sue out of her thoughts. "I could have slapped her, I really could; trying to make out like *you* were behind the fire. But I wasn't having that, I can tell you. Oh, no! I put a stop to that right then and there! I said . . ."

Standing off to the side, Jackie's eyebrows rose as she listened to Irene's revised version of the association meeting. The two-faced old mare was not only claiming to have put Carole Miller right about Sue, but she was now trying to claim that she'd come up with the idea for this event. And that wasn't fair, because it was Pauline who deserved all the credit.

Jackie needn't have worried, because Tina had already told Sue exactly what had happened at that meeting, and who had said what. Anyway, Sue wasn't listening; she was too busy trying not to throw up all over the old bag.

She didn't know if it was the whisky on her empty stomach, or the tension of having to talk to Dave as if they hadn't seen or spoken to each other recently that was getting to her, but she was starting to feel really hot and nauseous.

Seizing her opportunity when Irene paused for breath at last, she blurted out, "I think I'd better go and check on Connor."

228

Reluctant to lose her audience, Irene said, "Oh, he'll be fine with Paul and Tina. Here . . . have another drink."

Shaking her head, Sue put her cup down on the counter and stood up. "No, I really need to go. I get nervous if I can't see him after . . ." Trailing off, she shrugged. "Well, you know how it is."

Nodding sagely, Irene said, "Go on, then, love, you pop off and see him. But come back when you're finished, 'cos I've still got loads to tell you."

Promising that she would, Sue squeezed out from behind the counter and dashed outside.

Turning to Jackie when she'd gone, Irene said, "Did you hear all that rubbish she came out with when I asked her where she was when the fire started?"

Giving her an incredulous look, Jackie murmured, "I heard *some* rubbish, yeah."

Rushing through the crowd, Sue darted around the corner to the car park and slipped into a dark corner. Leaning back against the wall, she closed her eyes and exhaled wearily. This was turning out to be even worse than she'd thought it would be, and if she had to listen to any more of Irene's bullshit she would scream.

When a car turned in off the road and parked up just a few feet away from where she was standing, Sue held her breath and pushed herself further back against the wall, praying that the driver wouldn't walk this way, because they'd probably take one look at her hiding there and think she was cracking up. And then Pauline would be all over her like a rash, and she couldn't cope with any more fuss.

Relieved when the footsteps went in the opposite direction, she glanced at her watch, dismayed to see that she'd only been here for half an hour. It already felt like triple that, and it was going to drag on and on, because there was still all the night-time stuff to come yet. But she couldn't even grab Connor and sneak away, because he'd be with Terry by now.

But if she had to stay, there was no way she was listening to any more of Irene's relentless gossip. She'd stay back here for as long as she could and let them get on with it without her. Sue just hoped that Pauline had enough on her plate to keep her occupied, otherwise she'd probably send out a search party.

Pauline was just walking through the reception area when she spotted Jay knocking on the door. Rushing over, she unlocked it and brought her inside, saying, "How lovely to see you, Detective Constable Osborne. I didn't think you were going to make it." Resisting the impulse to hug or kiss her as she had everyone else who'd arrived so far — because it didn't seem proper, somehow, even if this girl with her lovely hair and her smart suits didn't look old or ugly enough to be in the police — she said, "Anyway, come in and let me get you something to drink. There's tea, coffee, or juice."

Saying that coffee would be great, Jay followed her into the main hall and gazed around, amazed by how much the old woman had achieved in such a short space of time. There were glittery strands of tinsel

230

draped all around the walls, and bunches of balloons pinned above the windows, and the tables and chairs which were usually stacked in the storeroom had been set out in neat rows. A bingo machine was in position to the right of the stage, and the DJ's decks had been set up to the left, fronted by a bank of lights which were spraying rainbow colours out across the ceiling as the engineer tested them. And on the stage a couple of roadies who looked like they could have jumped straight off the cover of a Hell's Angels magazine were busy setting up the band's equipment.

"Looks fantastic, doesn't it?" Pauline beamed, barely able to contain her excitement or mask her pride. "I can't *tell* you how hard everyone's worked today. And the little one's not been doing too badly, either," she added, nodding towards Connor, who was helping Tina with something on the other side of the room.

Glancing across at him, Jay noticed how frail he still looked. His cheeks were pale and drawn, and the bags under his eyes were as dark as charcoal smudges even from that distance. But at least he was getting a bit of fresh air, which was good, because he'd been in bed the last few times Jay had called round to the flat, and the stench of his soiled pyjamas had been thick in the air. And sorry as Jay felt for him and his mother, she couldn't help but pity Julie Ford as well, because the flat would be reeking of shit long after her guests had moved out.

"He's still not said a word," Pauline told her conspiratorially, sounding as concerned as if he were her own grandchild. "Poor thing must have really gone through the mill in that fire. I hate to think what must have been going through his little head, I really do."

"I'm sure he's probably forgotten most of it by now," Jay told her kindly, sensing the guilt behind the words. "Children are much stronger than we give them credit for."

"Oh, I know," Pauline murmured, flapping her hand. "Anyway, let me get you that coffee. Milk and sugar?"

Telling her one sugar and not too much milk, Jay asked if Sue had brought Connor along. Last time Jay had spoken to her, she hadn't decided if she was going to come, or if she would just send her son along with her friend.

"Irene's looking after her outside," Pauline said, leading her towards the long bar area at the back of the room where the tea and coffee urns had been placed. "She looked a bit frazzled, so I thought I'd bring Connor in here to give her a bit of a break." Lowering her voice now, she added, "I don't think she was ready to see Terry just yet."

"Oh, is he here as well?" Jay said, her eyebrows lifting in surprise. "I had the feeling one of them would stay away if they knew the other was coming."

"I think they're both wishing they had," Pauline murmured. "Sue didn't look too happy when she heard he was here; and he's been sat in here since he got here — probably to avoid her." Nodding towards a dark corner of the room, she said, "He's over there if you want to see him."

Glancing around when the door opened behind her just then, Pauline saw that the caterers had arrived.

Telling Jay that she'd best show them where to put things before they messed up her arrangements, she put her hand on Jay's back and gave her a gentle push in Terry's direction, saying, "Go on and see him, pet. I'll fetch your coffee over."

Walking towards Terry, Jay couldn't help but feel sorry for him when she noticed the sadness in his eyes as he gazed at his son. It was a painful situation for the whole family, but in some ways it must be worse for him. They were both suffering the loss of their daughter, but at least Sue still had Connor, whereas this was the first time Terry had seen him since he'd left the hospital.

Reaching the table now, she said, "Hello, Mr Day. Mind if I join you?"

Giving a little wave of his hand to indicate that it was fine by him, Terry gave her a tight smile, his gaze immediately drifting back to Connor. Pauline had brought him over earlier, so they'd had a bit of time together, but it hadn't left him feeling very positive because Connor seemed to be sinking more into himself than ever. Terry had asked if everything was all right, but Connor had just nodded. And with him still not talking, there was nothing that Terry could do to get to the root of what was troubling him. So he'd told him that he loved him and that he was always at the other end of the phone if he needed him. Then he'd let Pauline take him over to help Tina, figuring that it was better for Connor to be occupied than to be sitting in this dark corner like a stiff little soldier battling his unseen demons.

Feeling awkward as the silence pulsated between them, Jay cleared her throat, and said, "Have you been outside yet? There seems to be a very good turnout."

"I was out there for a bit," Terry murmured. "But everybody's being a bit *too* nice — if you know what I mean."

"Must be difficult — for you *and* them," Jay said. "When people don't know what to say, they either don't say anything or they say too much."

"Well, this lot are definitely saying too much. And I think I preferred it when they were giving me the cold shoulder, 'cos at least I knew where I stood."

Bustling over just then with two cups of coffee, Pauline handed one to Terry, saying, "I thought I'd best bring you one as well, pet. You've been nursing that empty can for long enough. Shall I pop it in the bin for you?"

Handing the can over, Terry forced himself to smile when she patted him on the shoulder before walking away.

"See what I mean?" he said to Jay. "You wouldn't believe the trouble we've had with her over the years, but anyone would think she was my mam, the way she's acting today."

"She's probably just trying to show that she cares," Jay said, tearing the top off the sachet of sugar that Pauline had placed on her saucer and tipping it into her cup. "I know she's been working really hard to get this event off the ground."

"Yeah, and I am grateful, but it still feels a bit weird," Terry said, pouring two sachets into his cup and picking up the spoon. "Seen Sue yet?" he asked now, giving the coffee a slow stir.

Intrigued to note that he hadn't spat his ex-wife's name out like he usually did, Jay said, "Not yet, but Mrs Wilson told me she's outside, so I'll probably go and say hello when I've finished this."

"I hope her and Leanne haven't spotted each other," Terry said, sitting heavily back in his seat as if he had the weight of the world on his shoulders. "That'll be all I need — them two scrapping like a pair of idiots."

"I'm sure Mrs Wilson will be on the lookout for any signs of trouble," Jay said quietly, her eyes flashing with a rare hint of amusement.

"Knowing her," Terry agreed, smiling wryly as he looked over at Pauline, who was bossing one of the caterers around on the other side of the room.

Jay's mobile began to ring. Excusing herself, she got up and moved a few feet away to answer it.

Glancing at her, Terry couldn't help but notice what a good figure she had. It wasn't the sexy kind of curviness of Leanne — and Sue in her heyday — but the toned slimness that he associated with the gym. And her hair was naturally blonde, like Leanne's, although a cooler shade than Lee's dark honey. But where Leanne's was long and wild and required hours of brushing and straightening and general fiddling with, Jay's was cut into a simple sleek bob, which suited the shape of her face. And it was a surprisingly pretty face for a copper; much softer than the female officers who usually strutted around the estate, trying to out-butch their male colleagues.

Blushing when Jay suddenly turned back to him, he dipped his gaze and took a long swallow of coffee, grimacing when the hot liquid burned his tongue.

"I've got to go," Jay told him, seeming not to have noticed that he'd been staring at her. "Could you tell Mrs Wilson I'll try and get back? But if I can't, I'll call in on her when I get a chance."

Nodding, still not looking at her, Terry said, "Yeah, no problem."

Thanking him, Jay walked quickly out of the hall — berating herself with every step for noticing how good-looking he was. And the more often she spoke to him, the more she realised what a nice man he was.

Shivering as the tiny bit of sunlight that had been reaching her dipped behind a cloud, Sue drew her knees up to her chest and hugged them tightly. Startled when someone suddenly walked around the corner, she blushed when she saw that it was Dave.

Peering down at her, he gave her a wry smile. "What the hell are you doing, you dozy cow? I thought you were a junkie having an OD, or something."

"I was hiding," she admitted, knowing that she must look absolutely ridiculous.

"From what?" Dave asked, squatting down beside her. Then, "Nah, let me guess . . . Irene?"

"She was doing my head in," Sue said. "Anyway, I thought you'd gone."

"Ah, were you missing me?" Dave teased, giving her an affectionate smile.

236

"Not really," Sue lied, glancing away quickly. She had actually been missing him for the past few days, but it was her own fault, because she'd asked him not to come around and beep the horn outside during the day in case one of the social workers or health visitors or child psychologists — or any of the other nosy sods — were around. And given that she could no longer see him at night, yes, she was missing him.

"Oh, well," Dave said, giving a mock-offended shrug. "If you don't care whether I'm here or not, I might as well go to town and catch the footy. Fancy a quick smoke before I go?"

"I'll have a straight," Sue said quickly, knowing exactly what kind of smoke he would be having.

Pushing himself to his feet, Dave said, "I left my gear in the car, so we'll sit in there — get you out of this cold. Oh, and I've got some voddy I won on the pub footy card last night, if you want some?"

"You hate vodka," she said, taking his hand to let him help her up.

Telling her that he'd intended to swap it with his mate for some home-grown skunk, Dave led her to his car. Ever the gentleman, he opened the passenger door for her before going around to the boot and taking out the bottle of vodka. Handing it to her when he climbed in behind the wheel, he said, "Your favourite, if my memory serves me right."

Smiling as she unscrewed the cap, Sue said, "Never heard of this one before, but it's got to be better than that crap whisky Irene's been dishing out. She might be acting like my new best friend, but I'm sure she put something in it to make me ill." Grimacing now when she took a sip and the strong alcohol seared her throat, she croaked, "Christ, that's strong."

"Came off the back of Deggsy's lorry, and it's supposed to be some mad percent — like, seventy, or something. Least it'll warm you up, though, eh?" Switching the engine on now, Dave pushed some buttons on the dash, turning on the CD that he'd been playing on the way over, and releasing a stream of hot air through the vents. "So how long you been out here, anyhow?"

"Ages," Sue admitted, taking another little sip from the bottle. "And I know everyone's probably wondering where I am, but I just can't face them."

"Sack 'em," Dave said flippantly. "They might say they're doing this for you, but we all know it's just an excuse to have a party."

Getting a waft of the familiar combination of Paco Rabanne aftershave and Scotch when Dave leaned across her to reach into the glove compartment, Sue's stomach did a little flip. Those scents stirred memories of Terry in better times. And she didn't want them stirred, because she'd genuinely thought that she was getting over him — especially since she'd found herself also having feelings for Dave.

Settling back in his seat, Dave glanced at her out of the corner of his eye as he started rolling his spliff. He hadn't seen much of her since Connor had come home, and she'd lost a fair bit of weight in the last few days. But it was her eyes that showed how unhappy she was.

238

They were duller and darker, and held none of the sparkle that he'd always associated with her.

"So, how's it *really* going?" he asked, his voice gentle. "And don't give me any of that guff about being fine, 'cos you're obviously not."

"It's just Nicky," Sue murmured, running her fingertip over the rim of the bottle. "I miss her. And Connor must be really fretting, 'cos he just keeps sitting at the window looking out, like he's expecting her to come walking up the street, or something."

"Can't be easy with him still not talking," Dave said, licking his Rizlas and sticking them together. "Do you reckon the doctors have missed something, or what? 'Cos I can't see him still being in shock after all this time."

"They just keep saying he'll talk when he's good and ready, and there's nothing anyone can do to speed it along." Shrugging helplessly, Sue took another drink.

"Well, you're doing better than I would if it was one of mine," Dave told her with a hint of admiration in his voice. "I know he can't help it, but it'd do my nut in if one of my kids didn't answer when I was talking to them. I'd be tempted to give them a right backhander."

"Drives me up the wall, to be honest," Sue admitted, feeling better for being able to say it out loud without fear of being judged.

"Don't they all," Dave chuckled. Then, "Subject of kids, have you seen our Leanne yet?"

Biting down on the instant anger that just hearing that name evoked in her, Sue said, "Yeah, but she was across the field, so don't worry, I didn't hit her."

"Hey, I wouldn't blame you if you did," Dave chuckled, taking a compacted clump of weed out of the small plastic bag. "She was out of order for fronting up to you that time, and she deserved everything she got." Laughing softly now, he said, "Carole saw it different, mind, but she's off her fucking head, so that's nowt new. That's kind of what put the nail in the coffin for me and her, though. She reckoned I should've supported our Lee, and I reckoned she'd got what was coming to her. So we agreed to disagree and went our separate ways."

"I never knew that," Sue said, glancing up at him, wondering why he'd never told her this before. She'd known that he and Carole had split up shortly after she'd had the fight with Leanne, but she hadn't known that it had had anything to do with her. Especially since by that time Dave had already had that go at her about Terry.

"Don't worry about it," Dave told her, shrugging it off. "I should have left years ago, but you know what a lazy bastard I am. So long as everything was getting done for me, I'd have stuck it out for ever if something better hadn't come along."

"Oh, I see," Sue said quietly, a tiny frown fluttering across her brow. "I didn't realise you'd met someone else. You never said."

"That's 'cos I haven't," Dave said, giving her a sly side-grin as he added, "Been a few auditions, but no starring ladies on my stage just yet. How about you?" he asked then. "How come you haven't got a new man yet?"

240

"Haven't been looking," Sue murmured, gazing down at her hands.

"Never mind *you* looking, they should be fighting to get at a gorgeous girl like you," Dave said, lighting up and filling the air with the strong sweet aroma of bush. His eyes serious as he looked at her now, he said, "He's a born fool, you know."

"Sorry?"

"Terry," Dave said, his lip giving the slightest twist of a sneer as he spoke the name. "He's an idiot for letting you go. And I know Leanne's my kid, but she's not right for him. She's only a girl, and men like us need a real woman — if you know what I mean."

Sue didn't answer. He was trying to compliment her, but his words had pierced her like darts, because she obviously wasn't woman enough for Terry if he'd found it so easy to dump her for someone whose own father thought wasn't right for him.

"You know I've always had a soft spot for you, don't you?" Dave was saying now, his eyes glowing darkly. "That's why the ex-bitch couldn't stand you."

"I didn't think she needed a reason," Sue muttered, taking another swig from the bottle. "I thought she just hated everyone. Except *Terry*," she added sarcastically. "Never could keep her eyes off him when we all used to go out. Or her hands."

"Yeah, well, she's always been a tart," Dave said dismissively, inhaling deeply on his smoke. "Talking of which, you seen him yet?"

"No, and I don't want to," Sue said, relaxing at last as the vodka began to soothe her frayed nerves. "It was bad enough having your Leanne giving me the evil eye, thanks."

"She's a right one, isn't she?" Dave laughed.

"She's a right *something*," Sue retorted, smiling herself now. "So, who d'y' reckon she takes after, then? You or Carole?"

Thinking it over for a moment, Dave said, "Looks-wise, me. Temper, definitely her mam."

"Trying to tell me you haven't got a bad temper?" Sue teased.

"Only when it's justified. But if folk treat me right, I treat them right. You know that."

"Oh, yeah, 'cos I've never been on the sharp end of your tongue, have I?"

"Not yet." Dave grinned. "But anytime you want to hop on, just say the word."

Slapping him playfully when he stuck his tongue out and waggled it suggestively, Sue gave him a mock-stern look.

"Aw, don't give me them eyes," Dave groaned. "Reminds me of being back at school with Mrs Dooley. I'll have a fucking hard-on all day now."

"*What?*" Drawing her head back, Sue peered at him incredulously. "You've got to be kidding. Dooley was a witch."

"Probably different for you girls," Dave said, grinning lewdly. "But me and the lads used to get into trouble on purpose just so she'd give us a bollocking. There's nothing like the sight of an angry woman with a cane in her hand when you're a horny little toe-rag."

Laughing, Sue shook her head, not sure if he was being serious or just teasing her now.

"Nice to see you happy again," Dave said softly, pleased that he'd been the one who'd achieved it. "Your eyes are gorgeous when you laugh."

Smiling shyly as her stomach did another little flip, Sue took a further sip from the bottle.

"Yep, that Terry's an idiot, all right," Dave went on. Then, chuckling softly, he said, "Hey, there's a thought . . . think what'd happen if me and you got married. It'd drive him fucking mental."

"Mmm," Sue murmured sadly, doubting that Terry would give the slightest toss.

"That would make you his step-mother-in-law, though, wouldn't it?" Dave went on. "And I'd be Leanne's . . ." Trailing off, he shook his head. "Nah. Can't figure that one out. Not while I'm this fucked."

Glancing at Sue now, his grin faded when he saw the tears in her eyes. Guessing — wrongly — that he'd upset her by coming on too strong too fast, he cursed himself. Damn! He'd really thought she was ready.

"Hey, what's up?" he said, squeezing her hand. "I was only joking."

"It's not you," Sue croaked, swiping at the tears as they began to spill over. "I don't know what's wrong with me today. Everything's getting to me."

Reaching for her, Dave pulled her to him and held her as she cried. Relaxing against him, soothed by the smell of him and the feel of his strong arms around her, Sue reached into her pocket and pulled out a tissue.

Dabbing at her nose, she said, "Sorry. You must think I'm a right idiot."

"Don't be daft," he murmured, stroking her hair. "You're having a bad day, that's all. But it'll get better. And you've always got me when you need to soak someone's shirt," he added, chuckling softly.

Apologising again, Sue sat up and pulled the sun-visor down to check her face in the small mirror. "God, I look a right mess."

"You look fine," Dave assured her, taking a last drag on his spliff and flicking the roach out of the window. "Suppose you'll want to get back in there, then?"

Kicking herself for getting emotional and ruining what might well have been the moment she'd been half-praying for, Sue nodded.

Scooping up his weed and his cigarettes, Dave slipped them into his pocket and got out of the car. Taking his hand when he came around to help her out, Sue snorted softly when he asked how it was going with misery guts back at the flat.

"Not great," she said. "And I know I shouldn't complain, 'cos she didn't have to take us both in. But I can't wait to get my own place again."

"It'll come," Dave said confidently. "But in the meantime, just keep your head down and your gob shut, and if she wants to argue, let her argue with herself."

Glancing past him as a car turned into the car park, Sue saw who was behind the wheel and muttered, "Oh, God, I forgot she was coming."

"Who is it?" Dave asked, turning to look at the man and woman who had just stepped out of the car. Then, "Isn't that one of the coppers you were with when I saw you at Pauline's that night?"

"Yeah, and she's bound to want to talk to me," Sue whispered, hiding behind him. "But I've had too much to drink and I've got a feeling I might start laughing in her face if she gives me that serious look of hers." Slipping her arm through his now, she tried to pull him in the opposite direction. "If we hurry up, she might not notice me."

"If you're looking for a way not to get noticed," Dave said, seizing the unexpected opportunity, "try this." Pushing her gently up against the car, he lowered his head and kissed her, his tongue brushing against her teeth as he forced her lips apart.

Gasping for breath when he finally released her, Sue blushed when she felt his hardness pressing against her thigh — and the tell-tale tingle between her own legs.

Grinning sheepishly as he gazed down at her, Dave said, "Sorry, but it worked. They didn't see you."

"Thanks," Sue murmured, dipping her gaze as another blush spread across her cheeks.

Encouraged by the fact that she hadn't tried to stop him, and still hadn't pushed him away, Dave peered into her eyes, saying, "In case you're wondering, I've been dying to do that for ages."

"Me, too," Sue admitted shyly. "But I was scared."

"I'm not like Terry," Dave told her softly, thinking that she meant scared about getting into a relationship after being hurt. "If you give me a chance, I'm not going to ruin it by taking off with the first bird who gives me the eye. But there's no pressure. If you want more, you can have more. If you want to just stay mates for now, we'll just stay mates. Your call."

Sue was about to say that she'd meant scared of the trouble it would cause, when Carole's voice suddenly blared out, "Get the fuck out of my way, you moron!" from the other side of the car park.

"Oh, great!" Sue groaned. "That's all I need."

Glancing around and seeing his ex arguing furiously with the driver of a car that was blocking her path in the gateway, Dave said, "Don't panic, she hasn't seen you."

And it was true, Carole hadn't seen Sue, because Dave was so broad that he was shielding her from view. But she'd spotted *him*.

"What's going on over there?" she yelled, her head bobbing up and down as she tried to see if he was with anyone or alone. "Don't ignore me, Dave, you know I can see you!"

"I've got to get out of here," Sue said, pushing Dave off her. "I can't handle her today."

Saying, "Leave her to me," Dave turned Sue around and gave her a gentle push in the opposite direction, calling after her in a loud whisper to meet him at The George at ten for a lift home.

Dave was alone by the time Carole reached him. Face white with rage she swung her hand out and smacked him across the face, screaming, "Who was the bitch, and where have you hidden her? Come on, you stupid bastard, don't deny it. I *saw* her!"

246

Grabbing the front of her baggy T-shirt, almost lifting her off her feet, Dave said, "Who the *fuck* do you think you're talking to like that?"

His face was so close that Carole could feel the warmth of his breath on her skin — *and* smell the scent of the other woman on his. Bringing her arm up, she lashed out at him again, yelling, "I'm talking to *you*, you two-timing piece of shit! And I'm gonna fucking *kill* her when I get my hands on her!"

"You're off your head," Dave sneered. "There was no one here. You're imagining things   *again*."

"Don't try and lie your way out of this one," Carole hissed, her breath ragged as she struggled to free herself from his grip. "I saw her running away. And it won't take a genius to pick her out once I get round there, knowing what you usually go for. Blonde, was she? Big tits, no brain?"

Laughing, because it was a fair description of Sue, apart from the no-brain bit, Dave let go of Carole and stepped back. Dusting himself off as if she'd tainted him, he said, "Never change, will you? Always got to go in with all guns blazing."

"Believe me, if I had a gun it'd be blazing in your fucking face right now," she snarled. "You treat me like shit and think I'm just gonna sit back and take it. But you're wrong, mate. Very, very wrong. And God help you if it was Sue," she went on furiously. "Because I'll kill you *and* her if I find out you've been seeing her all along and lying about it."

"Do yourself a favour and go home before you make a show of yourself," Dave snorted, unfazed by her anger. "I left you months ago, so even if it *was* Sue — which it wasn't — it's got nothing to do with you."

"You might have left me, but that don't stop you coming round whenever you fancy a shag, does it?" Carole reminded him tartly. "Last night not good enough for you? Thought you'd come and pick up a bit of rough to finish the job, did you?"

"Last night was shit," Dave said coolly. "But don't worry, I won't be making that mistake again any time soon."

"Oh, right, 'cos now you've picked yourself up a slapper you think you don't need me, is that it?"

Saying, "Since when did I ever need you?" Dave walked away, ignoring her when she screamed after him that she'd find out who he'd been with just now and make sure he never looked at the bitch again.

Leanne had looked everywhere for Terry, but he was nowhere to be found. She knew he couldn't be inside, because the doors were locked, but he wasn't out here either.

Standing outside the centre now, she was just scanning the faces in the crowd for the umpteenth time, cursing him under her breath and thinking that he'd better not have gone home without telling her, when her dad strolled around the corner, followed seconds later by her mum.

Glaring after Dave as he headed off across the field to find his mates, Carole spotted Leanne and made a beeline for her.

"You see anyone run out of the car park a minute ago?"

Shaking her head distractedly, Leanne said, "I wasn't looking that way. Why?"

"'Cos I just caught your dad in there with some slag," Carole spat. "And the bastard as good as laughed in my face when I pulled him about it. But you wait till I find out who it was. I'm gonna kick her fucking head in."

"Thought you'd split up," Leanne reminded her irritably. "So what you going on with yourself about it for?"

"Whose side are you on?" Carole demanded, scowling at her.

"Mine," Leanne snapped. "And I've got better things to do than stand here listening to you obsessing about someone you claim to hate most of the time."

Grabbing her arm when she started to walk away, Carole said, "You seen him with Sue while he's been here?"

"No, he's been with his mates."

"Which mates?"

"Fucking hell, Mam, *I* don't know," Leanne hissed, yanking her arm free. "Them guys from Terry's works he hangs about with. Noxy and Stu, and that. Anyhow, I've got to go."

"Got any money on you?" Carole called after her.

"Why?"

"'Cos I've only got enough for a couple of drinks, and your brothers will be here in a minute, so if you see them can you slip 'em a couple of quid to keep them off my back?"

"If I see them," Leanne said, having no intention of giving either of them a penny, because the thieving little bastards probably had more money than she did.

Terry was still sitting at the table in the corner when Jay and the man came into the hall. Glancing up as they walked towards him, he nodded at Jay.

"I'd like to introduce you to Detective Inspector Hilton," she said, her eyes sending out a clear message of apology. "He'd like to have a quick word, if that's all right?"

Looking at the tall, thin man now, Terry didn't speak. He didn't trust coppers, but he especially didn't trust ones like this man, who wore their suits like badges of superiority and looked down their noses at those they considered beneath them. And he might have a smile on his lips, but Terry could read the contempt in his eyes as clearly as if it had been written there in black marker pen.

Reaching across the table to shake his hand, Hilton pulled out a chair and sat down, saying, "Pleased to meet you at last, Mr Day, and I'm sorry I haven't got around to you sooner, but we've all been up to our eyes with this case of yours. Anyway," he said now, looping his hands together on the table top. "That's why I'm here now — to tell you about an idea we've had."

"Oh, yeah?" Terry murmured, sensing from the look on Jay's face as she hovered behind the man's chair that

250

he wasn't going to like whatever Hilton was about to say.

"In light of how long it's been since anybody saw or heard from your daughter," Hilton said. "I think it's time we considered a televised appeal."

"What, you mean like on the news?" Terry was already frowning.

"Exactly," Hilton confirmed, the smile still not reaching his eyes. "You see, we've always found media coverage to be an extremely effective tool for jogging memories that might not yet have been stirred. Maybe someone who hasn't really been paying attention to the newspapers will see you and your wife asking for help, and suddenly remember that they saw something suspicious that day."

"Nah, I don't think so," Terry said coolly, folding his arms. "For starters, she's not my wife, she's my ex. And we're not exactly on the best of terms, so I can't really see it helping if we went on TV together. People will be so busy watching us trying to avoid looking like we hate each other, they won't have a clue what we're talking about."

"Oh, come now," Hilton drawled, drawing his head back and giving Terry a disbelieving look. "You're an intelligent man, so I'm sure you're not going to allow a little tiff with your ex-wife to deter you from participating in something which might well make all the difference as to whether or not we find Nicky."

"With respect, sir," Jay cut in, catching the look of rage which had sparked in Terry's eyes at the DI's patronising tone, "I've been working very closely with

Mr and Mrs Day, and he's got a point. They're really not in a good place at the moment, and it would be wrong to try and persuade them to do something they're uncomfortable with."

"We're all grown-ups here," Hilton shot back flintily. "And I'm sure Mr Day doesn't need babying into putting his personal feelings aside and doing his part."

"Even if *I* was willing to do it," Terry interrupted, disliking the man even more than he already had for the way he was speaking to Jay, "Sue wouldn't. She hates me so much she won't even let me see my own son."

"I'm sure it's very difficult for you both," Hilton said breezily. "But sometimes all it takes is for somebody with a little sense to mediate."

Knowing full well that he was having a dig at her for failing to bring them together, Jay raised her chin proudly. Catching the movement, Terry's frown deepened.

"Do *you* think it's a good idea?" he asked, directing the question solely to her.

Inhaling slowly, Jay gave a small, apologetic shrug. "Honestly? I'd have to say that the public are generally more receptive to TV appeals than the less visual forms of media. And, if you could bring yourselves to do it, I think it would be helpful. Apart from which," she went on quietly, "you really need to consider Nicky's age."

"What's her age got to do with anything?" Terry asked, confused now.

"She'll be sixteen in three weeks' time," Hilton answered for her, taking the blunt approach to get the man to see sense. "And once she hits sixteen, she'll no longer be classed as an at-risk minor. As it's a pretty fair bet that she ran away voluntarily after starting the fire, the emphasis of the search will shift to that of a general missing person."

"Which means what, exactly?"

"Which means that there will be no urgency for us to find her," Hilton said flatly. "If she's spotted, she'll be picked up. But if she decides that she doesn't want to come home, that will be her choice and we'll have to respect it."

Glancing up at Jay, and seeing from the look in her eye that the DI was telling the truth, Terry exhaled tensely.

"So, basically, you're saying this might be our last chance to get her back home?" he murmured. "That if we don't do this telly thing and jog people's memories, you'll give up on her in three weeks — unless you happen to bump into her one day?"

"Regrettable, but correct," Hilton confirmed.

"You can't do that," Terry said quietly, disgusted by what he'd heard. "You can't just assume she's run away and give up on her. What if something's happened to her?"

"Chances are we'd have found her by now if it had," Hilton told him, sneaking a surreptitious glance at his watch. "But in all honesty, there's no evidence to suggest that she left the house under duress, otherwise the door probably wouldn't have been locked. And we'd have found her by now if she'd wandered out injured. And we already know she was deeply unhappy about the situation between yourself and her mother.

Add that to the bullying she'd been subjected to at school, it pretty much looks like a simple case of her having run away, from a police point of view."

Biting his lip, Terry stared down at the table and mulled everything over. He'd rather have stuck a red-hot poker up his own backside than share the same breathing space as Sue after everything that had happened recently. But this wasn't about her. Or him. It was about Nicky, and he owed it to her to do whatever he could to try and find her before the police brushed her under the carpet and forgot about her.

"All right," he said, looking up at last. "If Sue will do it, so will I. But can you make sure we don't have to sit together? Because I really can't bear to be that close to her."

Saying, "Good man!" Hilton was practically rubbing his hands together as he stood up. "Right, well, just leave it with me, and we'll have it up and running within the hour."

"That fast?" Terry gasped.

"Sooner the better," Hilton told him, reaching across the table to shake his hand again. "There's a team already lined up at Granada just waiting for the go-ahead." Turning to Jay now, he said, "Do I need to speak to Mrs Day, or do you think you can handle that?"

Knowing that he was asking if she was capable of getting Sue to agree, as he obviously considered that he had managed to do with Terry, Jay forced herself to smile. "I'll speak to her, sir."

Nodding, Hilton said, "Make sure you prep them about the kinds of things we want them to say. And talk to your woman over there." He waved his hand in Pauline's direction. "Get her to have a word with the locals, because I want them in the hall showing their support. But no drunks or troublemakers, because it'll be my reputation on the line if this doesn't go smoothly."

"You're coming back, then?" Jay asked, praying that Hilton would say no, that he had something more important to be getting on with — like playing golf with the Super, which was where he could usually be found while the rest of them struggled on with their heavy workloads.

"Of course I'm coming back," Hilton said, as if it were a thoroughly stupid question. "You don't think I'm leaving it to *you* to speak on our behalf, do you?"

Watching as Hilton strode away, the air of self-importance streaming off him almost visibly in his wake, Terry muttered, "Smarmy cunt." Then, remembering that he had company, he said, "Sorry. Didn't mean to say that out loud."

Taking a deep breath to stop herself from laughing, Jay said, "It's me who should be saying sorry — for landing this on you like that. But DI Hilton didn't warn me when he rang; he just told me to pick him up to take him somewhere. I hope you don't feel like you've been railroaded?"

Shrugging, Terry said, "Not exactly looking forward to it, but I've said I'll do it, so I will. I think you'll have a job getting Sue to agree, though. And she's not too good at hiding her feelings, so you'll be lucky if she doesn't tell me to piss off in front of the camera."

"I'll speak to her," Jay said quietly, knowing that he was right; that Sue would be the more difficult of the two to persuade — and the far more likely of the two to let her emotions get the better of her and disrupt the whole purpose of the appeal.

"Rather you than me," Terry said, scraping his chair back. "Not that I'm going to have it any easier, 'cos I've got to try and explain it to Leanne — and *that* won't be fun."

Feeling for him, because he was trying so hard to do the right thing despite the opposition he was facing from all sides, Jay gave him a sympathetic smile, saying, "At least it won't take too long once it gets going. Hope you don't mind the thought of wearing a bit of make-up, though, because they're likely to want to put something on you for the cameras."

"Aw, you're joking?" Terry groaned, looking thoroughly unimpressed by the idea as he stood up.

"You might get lucky; they might decide it's more authentic for the concerned parents to be pale."

"Yeah, well, I'd prefer that. Mind, I bet your DI will have some on, though, won't he?"

Probably already in make-up as we speak, Jay thought scathingly. Keeping it to herself, because it was unprofessional to slag off a colleague — however much you loathed them — she glanced at her watch, and said, "I'd best go and find Mrs Day. Shall we meet back here in, say, fifteen minutes?"

Nodding, Terry came out from behind the table and waved her to go ahead of him. Following her across the hall, he left her having a quick word with Pauline, and set off outside to look for Leanne.

Expression thoroughly attentive, and suitably solemn despite the excitement that was coursing through her at the thought of her event being televised, Pauline listened to what was being proposed.

"Never mind all that," she said when Jay warned her that the TV crew would undoubtedly make a mess of the hall. "You just do whatever you need to do and let me worry about putting things back to rights. And I'll personally vet everyone before they get so much as a foot through that door, so don't worry about anyone causing trouble."

After nearly being caught with Dave in the car park, Sue had gone back to the refreshment tent, figuring that it would be the first place Carole would head for. And if Carole saw her sitting behind the counter with Irene, she'd assume that she'd been there the whole time, which would throw her off the scent.

Just as she'd predicted, Carole walked in a few minutes later. Already scowling, her eyes flashed with hatred when she saw Sue sitting there.

"How long have you been here?" she demanded.

"Who you talking to like that?" Irene jumped in before Sue had a chance to open her mouth.

"I'm talking to her, not you," Carole spat. "And this has got nothing to do with you, so butt out."

"It's got everything to do with me, seeing as she's been sitting with me all day keeping me company," Irene informed her icily. "Not that it's any of *your* business. And I'd thank you to take your nastiness elsewhere if you can't control yourself, lady, because this day is all about her and her kiddies, not you and your big gob!"

Sucking her teeth, Carole cast one last eye-dagger at Sue. Much as she'd have loved for it to have been her she'd seen with Dave so she'd be justified in giving her a good kicking, it obviously hadn't been, or Irene would have taken a great deal of pleasure from telling her and rubbing it in deep.

Turning on her heel now, she marched back out, brushing roughly past Jay who was just coming in through the entrance flap.

Shaking her head, wondering why some people had to be so rude, Jay headed towards the counter.

Sue had just lit a cigarette. Smiling guiltily, she said, "You're not going to arrest me for smoking inside, are you?"

"Not today," Jay assured her, returning the smile. "I just wanted a quick word, if you've got a minute. *Outside*," she added pointedly, for the benefit of Irene who was all ears.

Giving Irene a little shrug as Jay turned and walked away, Sue followed her out into the daylight, wondering what she wanted to talk about.

Going to a bench that was set some distance away from the crowd, Jay sat Sue down and explained what was being proposed. Pre-empting the immediate protest that she knew she would get, she said, "Mr Day's already agreed to do it if you will. And, given the high feedback these things generally bring, I would ask you to seriously consider it before you make a definite decision."

Face pale, hands visibly shaking, Sue said, "I can't believe Terry would agree to do something like that. He hates me."

Telling her that Terry was willing to put his own personal feelings aside for Nicky's sake. Jay explained about what would happen when Nicky reached the age of sixteen.

Having thought that they would just carry on looking with the same intensity until they'd found her, Sue couldn't believe that the search would get scaled down so drastically.

"Okay, I'll do it," she said, her voice shaking as much as her hands now. "But can you make sure I don't have to sit too close to Terry, or he might lose his temper and go for me."

Assuring her that they would be seated at a reasonable distance — without adding that Terry had already requested the same thing — Jay said, "I'll have to talk you through everything before the TV crew arrives, so if we could just go inside, I've arranged to meet up with Terry so we can all sit down and discuss it."

"Me and him together, *now*?" Sue murmured nervously. Biting her lip when Jay nodded, she said, "What about Leanne? I don't want her there."

"However you feel most comfortable," Jay said. "It's your call."

Seeming mollified by this, Sue said, "You'll be there, though, won't you? You won't leave us on our own?"

Telling her that she would be with her every step of the way, Jay waited for her to finish her cigarette, then walked her into the community centre.

Terry had been through the crowd twice now, but he still hadn't seen Leanne. And more people were turning up by the minute, making it hard to keep looking. Assuming that she had decided to go off somewhere with her mates, he felt a bit relieved. At least if she wasn't here, she couldn't kick off and mess everything up. He'd just have the sulking to put up with when he got home and told her about it later.

Heading back towards the community centre now, his heart sank when Leanne suddenly came into view up ahead. But she wasn't with her mates, she was with her mum and dad, and Carole was obviously in a foul mood about something, because she was swinging her arms around as she walked, shouting something that Terry could hear in volume if not in actual words. Wanting to avoid getting dragged into whatever was going on, he was about to take a detour round the back when Pauline appeared in the doorway with a microphone in her hand, and the static of the centre's PA system crackled out.

"Can I have everyone's attention . . ." Pauline said, her words badly distorted by the feedback she was creating by almost eating the microphone. "As you

260

know, we're holding this fundraiser today for Sue and Terry Day and their children. And I've been asked to tell you that there'll be a television crew arriving shortly, to film an appeal to help find Nicky."

Pausing for several beats to let that sink in, she said, "Now the police have asked me to invite some of you into the hall while Sue and Terry are filming. But not yet!" she added quickly, holding up a hand to prevent them all from running at her. "I'll give you the word when we're ready."

"Now, if I decide you can come in," she went on self-importantly, "you'll be expected to behave yourselves. No talking, no fidgeting, and no nonsense. There won't be room for everyone, so if you want to be involved, queue up outside the refreshment tent and wait for me to come and take your names. Thank you."

A deathly hush had fallen over the crowd by the time Pauline had finished speaking and gone back inside. But they all started talking at once now, their excitement about the impending arrival of a TV crew ringing out across the field as they made a mad dash for the refreshment tent — hoping to be first in line so they could bag a seat at the front of the hall and get themselves on camera.

Terry could see at a glance how badly Leanne had taken the news. There was no excitement on *her* face, just blind rage that he had obviously agreed to do this alongside Sue. Knowing that she was looking for him when she marched away from her parents with murder in her eyes, he put his head down and ran down the side of the community centre. He could have wasted time explaining, but she'd never have understood, so he'd just have to go ahead — and deal with the fallout later.

Knocking on the fire-exit door, he rushed inside when Tina opened it. Sue, Jay and Pauline were sitting at the table straight ahead of him, having a cup of tea. Joining them, he sat down and folded his arms.

Relieved that she'd finally got them in the same room, even if they weren't speaking to or looking at each other, Jay gave them a brief rundown of what would happen once the TV crew arrived — apologising in advance should anything happen differently and throw them off balance.

"I haven't done too many of these things myself," she admitted. "But DI Hilton's an old hand, so I'm sure he'll help you if you get stuck. He'll make the initial statement, detailing what's happened and what we're asking of the public. Then you'll both be asked to speak." Turning to Sue now, she said, "They'll probably want mum first, so just look straight at the camera, as if you're talking to Nicky herself. Tell her how worried you are, and how much you're missing her — that kind of thing. Then you'll pick it up from there." Jay turned to Terry. "Tell her not to worry, she's not in any kind of trouble, you both just want her to come home."

"Home?" Terry repeated quietly. "I'm not being funny, but if she's somewhere where she's able to watch TV, surely she'll have already seen the papers and she'll know that there's no *home* to come back to."

"We've got to keep it simple," Jay told him, hoping he wouldn't be pedantic about it when they started filming or it would alienate people. "We're aiming this as much at the viewer as at Nicky, because we need them to feel emotionally involved, as if they're sharing this experience with you. If it feels personal, they're more likely to really think about what they were doing the day Nicky disappeared. And, with any luck, someone might remember something."

"Like what?" Sue asked, her voice cracking because she felt so nervous being so close to Terry.

"Like, if they saw a young girl matching Nicky's description doing anything out of the ordinary," Jay said. "Maybe running, or crying — anything they might have considered odd at the time, but then forgot. Or somebody might remember seeing her talking to somebody after she left the house or the garage, which could point us in a direction we hadn't thought of. Anything is better than nothing."

Blushing with the guilt of still not having told the truth about Nicky not being home when she went out, Sue dipped her head and stared at her cup. She'd wanted to confess loads of times, but couldn't bring herself to do it because she was terrified of the police delving into Julie's past and tarring her with the same brush. And she definitely couldn't let Terry find out, because he would go crazy if he thought she'd had a suspected child abuser around his kids. And it wouldn't make any difference that she hadn't even known about it herself.

Seeing the misery etched on Sue's face, Pauline reached out and gave her hand a squeeze. "I'm so sorry you're going through all this," she said, glancing at

Terry to include him. "And if there was anything I could have done to prevent it, you know I'd have done it. But at least you're both talking again, and that's got to be better for Connor, because this has hit him hard, and he needs to see you pulling together as a family again."

Terry sighed and his gaze drifted to Connor who was sitting across the room with Tina. He was holding an ice cream, but he didn't seem in any hurry to eat it. In a world of his own, his eyes were huge and vacant as he stared off into space. There had to be some dark thoughts swirling around in that little head of his, but until he decided to start talking again Terry didn't have a clue how to reach him.

And neither did Sue. Looking at her son now, she suddenly saw him as other people must. Not an infuriating little boy who grunted and soiled his pants to piss her off, but an innocent child who had almost died, and who couldn't understand why his sister still hadn't come to see him — and his daddy had abandoned him again.

Knowing that she was totally to blame for the latter, her voice was hoarse with guilt as she forced herself to speak to Terry for the first time in months.

"I know I shouldn't have stopped you seeing him, but it's been really hard knowing what to do for the best since he came home. He's been so upset about Nicky, and I just feel like I've got to protect him."

"From *me*?" Terry asked, his eyes betraying the hurt that her words had caused him.

"No," Sue murmured, forcing herself to look at him now. "From *us*. Every time we see each other it ends up in a fight, and the kids have suffered enough, so I don't want Connor seeing any more of it. It's not fair."

Terry felt like pointing out that he wasn't the one who always started the arguments, but he held his tongue, because he knew that none of this would ever have happened if he hadn't been caught in bed with Leanne in the first place. He and Sue would still have split up at some point, because things hadn't been good between them for a while before it had happened. But, much as he loved Leanne and had no regrets about being with her, he *did* regret the way it had happened, because he should have done the decent thing and left Sue before he got involved with anyone else. But you couldn't change the past; you could only alter the way you dealt with it in the present.

As if echoing his thoughts, Sue said, "I'm not blaming you for everything. We both did things we shouldn't have done, but we've got to let go of all that and concentrate on the kids."

"That's what I've been trying to do," Terry replied, making a real effort not to sound accusing.

"I know," Sue murmured, her chin wobbling as she struggled to contain the tears that were threatening to spill over. "And I know I haven't made it easy for you. But it's been really hard for me, because I've not just had you to deal with, I've had *her* up in my face as well. And I'm sorry, Terry, but I just don't like her. And neither do the kids."

Terry didn't answer, because there was nothing he could say. It was true. The kids didn't like Leanne, and she couldn't stand them. In hindsight, he should have kept the two relationships completely separate until everything had settled down. But it wasn't that easy when you were dealing with someone like Leanne. If you tried to exclude her, she thought something was going on and made your life hell until you stopped doing whatever it was. And that was exactly what he *had* done when things came to a head between her and Sue: stopped seeing the kids. Not because he'd wanted to, but because it had felt like the right thing to do at the time — for them. As Sue had just said, they'd already seen too much nastiness, and he'd thought it fairer just to back off and let them get settled again.

"I'm sorry," Sue said now, her voice so quiet that they all almost missed it.

But Terry heard it, and his eyes were dark with his own guilt as he asked, "What are you sorry for? You didn't do anything wrong."

"I must have," Sue sniffed, reaching into her pocket for the already soggy tissue she'd been carrying around all day. "No, I *know* I did," she corrected herself, dabbing at an escaping tear. "I let myself go, and you found someone better. But, hey . . ." Shrugging, she dredged up a sad smile. "You're still with her, so it must have been the right decision."

It was the first time she'd smiled at him in months, and Terry saw a flash of the girl he'd once loved behind it. It didn't make him suddenly want to get back with her, but he was grateful that she was big enough to forgive him and wish him well like that. And if she could move on for the sake of the kids, then he would bend over backwards to do his part — whatever shit Leanne threw at him.

"Anyone for another cuppa?" Pauline asked, pushing her chair back and standing up. "I'm parched, and I doubt we'll get another chance once the film crew turns up."

Bustling away when they all nodded, Pauline bypassed the tea urn and rushed out to the toilets, perilously close to bursting into tears with the emotion of it all. She'd been happy enough just playing a part in bringing everybody together today, but she was so proud of herself for having had a hand in getting Sue and Terry talking again. And who knew . . . if they carried on communicating like they were right now, there might be a happy ending for that little family.

It was just a shame that they'd have to start again from scratch — next door to somebody who might not yet have reached Pauline's level of understanding, and who could make them feel as unwelcome as she once had. But if they made it that far, she was pretty sure they'd be strong enough to cope with whatever else came their way.

Fully aware by now that Terry was in there with *her*, Leanne was desperately trying to get inside. But the doors were locked, and Pauline's women were refusing to open up, telling her that there was official police business taking place. Infuriated, she started kicking the door — only for her dad to grab her and march her around to the car park.

"When are you going to grow up and stop being so flaming childish?" he barked, opening the passenger door of his car and shoving her in. "You know the filth are in there, so are you trying to get yourself arrested, or what?"

"I'm *trying* to get to my boyfriend," Leanne growled, folding her arms sulkily. "Not that it's any of your business."

Reminding her gruffly that she *was* his business, whether she liked it or not, Dave tossed a spliff to her, saying, "Get that smoked and chill the fuck out before you do something stupid."

Snatching the lighter out of his hand, Leanne lit up, even though she knew it would mellow her out — which she didn't want, because she desperately wanted to let Terry see how mad she was.

"I hate that bitch so much!" she snarled. "She's been trying to get her claws into Terry for months, and now the pair of them are locked away in there together. But she's not having him back. I'll *kill* her first."

"Don't talk shit," Dave said calmly. "No one's going to kill anyone."

"Wanna bet?" Leanne muttered, her dark tone letting him know that nothing he or anyone else said was going to deter her.

"Behave," Dave snapped, peering at her sternly. "I thought you'd have learned your lesson thinking you can take Sue on from the last time."

Furious with him for reminding her about the pasting Sue had given her, Leanne said, "She got lucky and caught me off guard. But it won't happen again. And there's no way she can take me *and* me mam on, so let's see how she copes with that."

"Leave your mam out of this," Dave warned her sharply. "I mean it, Lee. No more. Just let Sue be and get on with your own life. You've already got her man, so drop it."

Taking another hard pull on the smoke, Leanne glared at him with narrowed eyes. "How come you're always sticking up for her over me?"

Shaking his head, Dave stroked a finger down her cheek, saying, "What did I tell you earlier? Didn't I say you're my little darlin' and you always will be? Yeah, so quit talking shit about me taking sides, 'cos my loyalty's with you."

"No, it's not," Leanne retorted sulkily, jerking her head away from his touch. "Even me mam says you were out of order over that fight. That's why she kicked you out."

"She didn't kick me out, I left, and Sue had nothing to do with it," Dave told her coolly. "Anyhow, I'm not interested in what your mam thinks. I'm trying to get *you* to wise up, 'cos the more you kick off, the more you're letting Sue know you're scared of her."

"I'm not fucking scared of *her*!"

"Threatened, then," Dave corrected himself. "If you react like this every time Terry goes near her, she's bound to wonder what you're so worried about. And if she thinks that *you* think she's still in with a chance, she might just think it's worth holding out for him. So if I was you, I'd make out like you wouldn't care if she was standing in front of him bare-arsed naked, 'cos he's yours. *That* will let her know where she stands."

Chewing this over, Leanne realised that he was right. But it was hard to pretend you felt secure when you didn't. And what if she was wrong and Terry *did* still have feelings for Sue? If she backed off, wouldn't it make it easy for them to get back together?

"It's all in the way you play the game," Dave told her, smiling slyly. "You watch; it'll all come right in the end — for everyone."

Giving him a quizzical look, Leanne said, "Watch it, Dad. You almost sound like you don't mind about me and Terry any more."

Shrugging, Dave said, "Life's too short for me and you to be falling out. So if you want to be with him, I'll just have to swallow it, won't I? Like you said earlier, you're not a baby any more."

Unaware of his real reason for this sudden change of heart, Leanne felt a rush of love towards him. He talked shite a lot of the time, but when it really counted he always had her best interests at heart. And if he was finally getting used to the idea of her and Terry being together, then that couldn't be a bad thing, because there was nothing she'd like more than for her family to get back together. She'd always loved her dad, so it would be great if she could invite him round to the flat at last. Maybe tomorrow. She could cook a proper Sunday dinner, and it would be just like the old days —

her dad and Terry having a drink and a laugh, while Leanne and her mum . . .

No, sack that last bit. She didn't want her mum coming round any more often than she already did. But it *would* be good to see more of her dad. And if she could get him and Terry back to being mates, Terry might chill out — which would be fantastic.

"Eh up," Dave murmured, gesturing with a nod towards a large white truck that was turning into the car park. "Looks like Pauline was right about the TV thing."

Seeing the Granada logo on the side of the truck, Leanne felt a thrill of excitement course through her. It was *major*, getting yourself on telly. She'd been stopped once on Market Street and asked what she thought of some shit to do with the government, and loads of people had recognised her for ages afterwards. And she'd only been on screen for a few seconds that time, so how much better would it be to actually be involved in whatever they were reporting. And she *was* involved — whether Sue liked it or not. She was the missing girl's stepmother.

Grimacing as the word entered her head, Leanne pursed her lips thoughtfully. She might hate Nicky, but she didn't have to tell the TV people that. As far as they need be concerned, she was just as worried and upset as Terry. And Terry wouldn't contradict her, because he'd just be glad that she'd stopped having a go at him. *And*, it would get right up Sue's nose if she was there, supporting him, and showing the world how much in love they were. A total win-win situation, with the added bonus of getting her face on TV. But she'd have to be really careful not to cry, because that would ruin her make-up. And not too much worried frowning, or she'd end up looking as old and wrinkly as Sue. And no big smiles, either, because she was supposed to be concerned. Just a nice in-between level of caring, while still managing to look stunningly gorgeous.

Chuckling as he watched the thoughts flitting so openly across his daughter's pretty young face, Dave said, "If you're planning on getting yourself in on this, you'd best straighten up, 'cos your eyes are red enough to light a prozzie's doorway."

Grinning at his choice of words, Leanne handed the spliff to him and rolled the window down, breathing deeply to let the fresh air liven her up.

"Better?" Dave asked after a minute. "No more stupid ideas about Sue?"

"Nope." Leanne smiled contentedly back at him. "You're right. I've got to stop letting her think she's getting to me, then she might just get the message and piss off out of our lives for good."

Winking, Dave said, "That's the way. And, you watch: soon as she realises she's got no chance, she'll get herself a new man and you won't see her for dust."

"So long as it's not you, like me mam seems to think," Leanne said mock-sternly. "'Cos I'd have to *kill* myself if that happened."

"As if," Dave drawled, grinning secretively. No point telling her anything just yet. Anyway, there wasn't much *to* tell. But there *would* be — he was determined about that. However long it took.

272

"You coming in?" Leanne asked now, pushing the door open.

"Nah." Shaking his head, Dave glanced at his watch. "I was supposed to be in town before your stupid mam sidetracked me. But we're all right now, aren't we? No more falling out?"

Saying, "No chance!" Leanne threw her arms around his neck and hugged him.

CHAPTER
TEN

Terry felt sick. Up on the stage at the table the TV people had set up for them, he was sitting on one side of Sue, while DI Hilton was sat on the other. They weren't actually touching, but he was close enough that he could feel the fear pouring off her, and he could clearly see how badly she was trembling. But he didn't dare look at her or offer her any kind of reassurance, because Leanne was staring up at him from the front row.

She was smiling, but they hadn't had a chance to talk before she came into the hall with the rest of the audience, so he had no clue what could possibly be going through her mind. She was probably seething, though, and he had no doubt that he'd get it from both barrels as soon as she got a chance. But she was behaving herself for now — thank God.

"So, if anybody remembers seeing Nicky Day on or after Friday, the sixteenth of November, at any time from nine o'clock onwards," Hilton was saying, peering intently into the camera as he came to the end of his rambling speech, "please call one of the numbers displayed at the end of the programme." Then, pausing for several beats, he said, "Now Nicky's parents would like to make an appeal of their own."

Sue swallowed loudly when he turned and gave her the nod and her eyes danced with fear as she tried to locate the camera. Body and voice shaking with equal intensity, she said, "Nicky, if you're listening to this, I, um, just want you to know that we love you and want you to come home. We know you're probably scared because you think you've hurt Connor," she went on, a tear sliding down her cheek now, "but he's fine, sweetheart. He's just missing you so much. We all are. So please, *please* come home. Wherever you are, just come home."

On the back foot when she dissolved into sobs, and the camera panned towards him, Terry said, "Er, yeah . . . Nicky, if you're watching . . . like your mum said, we just want you to come home. I promise you're not in trouble, and nobody's been hurt, so there's nothing to worry about. We're just really worried about you, and we need to know where you are. And even if you don't want to speak to us, just call someone — anyone — and let them know you're okay. Whatever's wrong, we can fix it."

Standing off to the side of the stage, the newsreader looked suitably sombre as the camera panned to her now.

"That was an appeal for information about the whereabouts of fifteen year old, Nicky Day, who has been missing for two weeks, following a fire which destroyed the family home."

"As you've just heard, the family are deeply concerned for Nicky's safety, as are the police, who are working tirelessly to find her. There have been several reported sightings since her disappearance, but the police are asking the public to report anything they may have seen, or anything they've heard about Nicky, to them."

"Here on the Fitton Estate, members of the local residents' association have organised a fundraising event in Nicky's name, and I'm joined by the chairwoman, and Nicky Day's next-door neighbour, Pauline Wilson. Mrs Wilson, could you tell us how it's been going so far?"

"Oh, very good," Pauline said, casting nervous little glances at the camera. "Everybody's been very supportive."

"And you're expecting to raise quite a significant amount of money for the family, I believe?"

"Well, I don't know about significant," Pauline said cautiously. "I mean, none of us is exactly rich round here, so we wouldn't expect any massive donations, or anything. But we're all doing what we can, and that's what counts." Warming to her theme now, she said, "It's a bit like the old days, I suppose. If there was a crisis in the community, everyone got together to help their neighbours out. And that's what we're trying to do here — get things back to the way they used to be."

"Wonderful," the newsreader said, smiling as she turned back to the camera. "So, there we have it . . . a true display of community spirit. And if anybody would like to make a donation to the Nicky Day Fund, you should contact Pauline Wilson at the Fitton Community Centre here in Rusholme."

Holding the smile until she'd received the all-clear, the newsreader thanked Pauline and headed over to speak with her crew.

Going to Sue and Terry as they came down off the stage, Jay said, "That was really good. Well done."

"I thought I was going to faint," Sue said, dabbing at her nose with a tissue. Reaching for Connor's hand when Tina brought him over, she said, "Has he been okay?"

"Fine," Tina said. "And that was great — both of you."

Thanking her, Terry excused himself when he spotted Leanne heading their way. Intercepting her before she could get to Sue, he took her by the arm and walked her outside and around the corner. Just about to apologise for going ahead with the appeal without talking to her about it first, he was shocked when she threw herself into his arms.

"You were amazing," she gushed, kissing him proudly. "And you looked absolutely fantastic. Shame *she* looked such a mess," she added snidely. "But, oh, well . . . we can't all be gorgeous." Grinning excitedly now, she said, "Ooh, I can't wait to see it on the news. What time did they say it's going to be on?"

"Not sure," Terry murmured warily, wondering where this sudden change of attitude had come from.

"Well, see if you can find out," Leanne said. "'Cos I really don't want to miss it. Oh, and I'd best ring my dad to tell him to watch it."

"He wouldn't be interested," Terry said, taking his tobacco out of his pocket to roll himself a much-needed cigarette.

"He would," Leanne said, grinning at him now. "'Cos we've made friends again. And he's said he doesn't mind about you and me any more, so isn't that great?"

"Yeah, right," Terry muttered cynically.

"It's true," Leanne insisted. "Honest. I was sat in his car with him earlier, and he just came out with it. He said life's too short to be falling out, so if he's got to accept us to get things back on track with me, then he will."

"And you believed him?"

"Course — why wouldn't I?"

"Because he hates me," Terry reminded her bluntly. "And he's spent the last year trying to kill me, or get his mates to do it for him."

"Oh, that's all in the past," Leanne said breezily. "We're friends again, and I'm happy, so you should be too. Oh, and I want to invite him round for dinner next week, by the way."

"You've got to be joking!" Terry snorted, looking at her as if she'd gone mad.

"No, I'm serious," she said, a hint of a frown on her brow now. "And I hope you're not going to make things difficult for me after I just let you do that appeal with *her* without complaining?"

Sighing, Terry licked the Rizla paper to secure his cigarette. So *that* was why she'd been smiling up at him like that the whole time they'd been filming: because

278

she'd been planning to whack him with this and use her earlier cooperation as a tool to blackmail him into agreeing to it.

"Anyway, I'd have thought you'd be grateful that he's willing to forgive you," Leanne said now.

"*Grateful?*" Terry repeated incredulously. "Christ, you've got a short memory, haven't you? It's only a week since you were slagging him off for getting too friendly with Sue."

"Yeah, well, that was your fault for jumping to conclusions," Leanne reminded him. "Anyway, it wasn't true, so forget it."

Glancing around when someone came out of the community centre just then, Leanne folded her arms when she saw the newsreader heading onto the grass, followed by the cameraman carrying a hand-held rig. Biting her lip when they stopped to talk to some of the people who had come back outside, she wondered how to get herself into the frame without Terry accusing her of using Nicky's disappearance to get herself on TV. She was pretty sure they'd got a couple of good shots of her in the hall, but that wasn't enough. She wanted to be interviewed — to let them know who she was, and do the *I'm-so-concerned* routine she'd been practising in her head.

Interrupting her thoughts as he lit his smoke, Terry said, "Right, I'll have this, then I'll go and thank Pauline and we can get off."

"Aw, do we have to go now?" Leanne moaned. "Me and the girls were looking forward to seeing that band later. And I really, *really* want to do the karaoke, seeing as we can't do it at home any more."

She'd slipped that last bit in to make him feel guilty in case he had any objections, but she needn't have bothered, because Terry was actually relieved at the thought of having a few hours alone. It would give him a chance to think everything over — and there was a *lot* to think about. Not least, how he was going to pick Connor up for the day tomorrow without Leanne, as he'd arranged earlier with Sue.

And why the hell he'd asked Sue to keep the visit secret.

He'd only done it to avoid making Leanne feel excluded, but now if she found out she'd think that he and Sue were conspiring behind her back. And God only knew what *Sue* was thinking. But he couldn't undo it now, so he'd just have to pray that Sue didn't get spiteful and use it as a weapon to get between him and Leanne.

"*Terry?*" Leanne moaned, almost hopping with frustration now as she waited for an answer. "Can I stay, or what?"

"Yeah, sure," Terry said, forcing himself to smile. "I've got a bit of a headache, so I might go to bed early. You stay as long as you want and enjoy yourself."

Grinning, Leanne gave him a kiss. "Don't forget to tape the news for me."

Promising that he wouldn't, Terry watched as she tripped happily away and made her way through the crowd — trying to look like she wasn't even aware that she was getting closer to the newsreader and the cameraman with every step.

Rushing around the corner just then, Jay stopped in her tracks when she saw Terry. "Oh, you're still here?" she said, sounding surprised. "You disappeared so fast after filming, I thought you'd escaped."

"Will be doing in a minute," Terry said, smiling at her choice of words because he guessed that that was exactly what she was doing. "Just going to finish this, then I need to thank Pauline and make a getaway while I've got the chance."

Saying, "I don't blame you," Jay slipped her hands into her jacket pockets. "Everything okay?" she asked then.

Guessing that she meant with him and Leanne, Terry nodded. "Yeah, fine. Lee's staying on for a while. She wants to see the band and do the karaoke."

"Oh, well, at least she's enjoying herself," Jay said diplomatically. "And you must be relieved it's over?"

"You can say that again," Terry murmured. Then, looking at her, he said, "Thanks for your help, by the way. I thought it was going to be murder — with Sue, and that. But you made it a lot easier."

Telling him that it was her pleasure, Jay glanced at her watch. "I'd best go before DI Hilton changes his mind about going back with the TV crew and comes after me for a lift. I'll call round in a couple of days and let you know if we get any response from the appeal."

"Do you think it'll do any good?" Terry asked.

"I certainly hope so. At the very least I expect we'll have a lot of calls from people who remember seeing her that day. And that's good, because it'll give us more to work on." Looking into his eyes now, Jay said, "Don't worry, Mr Day, she will turn up eventually."

Holding her gaze for a moment, Terry said, "Thanks. But can you do me a favour and call me Terry? It sounds really weird to be called mister."

Smiling, Jay said, "I'll try to remember." Saying goodbye then, she left him there and headed into the car park.

Back inside the hall, Pauline was flitting around like a woman possessed, barking orders at her ladies as she tried to put the room back to rights before the evening activities got under way.

Sitting at the corner table where Terry had spent most of that morning, Sue gazed unseeingly out across the room, her mind too full of what had just happened to pay any attention to what was going on around her.

Things today had not turned out at all like she'd expected. She hadn't expected for everyone to be so nice to her, for a start. And then there'd been Dave kissing her like that — although she'd kind of expected that to happen at *some* point. But she'd never expected to suddenly find herself on TV. Or to be in the same room as Leanne without one of them trying to kill the other. But what had really knocked her back was the fact that she and Terry had managed to speak civilly to each other, with none of the accusations and dirty looks that usually accompanied their meetings.

Sue had never imagined that she would *ever* hear herself taking some of the blame for their split, because she'd only ever thought of herself as the victim until now. But now that she'd said it, she had to admit that she had played a part in the breakdown of their marriage. Terry had been the man of her dreams, yet she'd totally taken him for granted; leaving him to go out to work while she slopped about in her pyjamas crying post-natal depression. It was no wonder he'd stopped fancying her and gone after a girl who still took pride in her appearance. But it was too late for shoulda-woulda-couldas. She'd lost him, and she just had to accept it and get over it.

Still, she couldn't help but wonder why Terry had asked her not to tell anybody that he would be picking Connor up tomorrow. It could only be because he didn't want Leanne to find out. But if everything was so good between them, why would he hide something like that from her? Surely Leanne couldn't object to him seeing his own son. Or was it *Sue* she was objecting to him seeing? And if so, why? Unless she thought Sue was a threat.

But why would she think that, after everything that had happened? She'd won Terry's heart, stealing him away not just from Sue but from his kids as well. And he'd stayed with her, despite all the trouble that had arisen from it, so he must love her.

"Sue? . . . *Sue?*"

Glancing up when Pauline's voice filtered through, Sue said, "Sorry. I was miles away."

"Are you all right?" Pauline asked. "Can I get you anything? A cup of tea? Something to eat?"

"Tea would be nice, thanks."

"Right you are," Pauline said, giving her a motherly smile. "Oh, and in case you're wondering about Connor, he's had a sandwich, and I've just sent him outside for a bit before it gets too cold."

"Oh," Sue murmured, frowning now. "He's not on his own, is he?"

"I told Lynne to get Jackie and Irene to watch him, so he'll be safe," Pauline assured her. "And it'll do him good to play with some of the other kiddies, so stop fretting and relax. This is supposed to be a fun day."

Nodding, Sue smiled. "I know. And I am trying."

Saying, "Good girl," Pauline bustled away to get her a cup of tea.

Jackie and Irene were busy serving in the refreshment tent. Nodding at Lynne who was trying to tell her something, Irene said, "Of course, luvvie. Whatever you say."

"What was that about?" Jackie asked when Lynne had scuttled out again.

"God knows," Irene chuckled. "Talks like a mouse, so I couldn't hear a flaming word. Probably more orders from Queen Pauline, though, so I'm not really fussed."

Back outside the tent, Lynne leaned down and smiled at Connor. "Right, you go and have a play, and if you want anything, just ask Auntie Irene or Auntie Jackie because they're looking after you. Okay?"

Unnerved when Connor just peered blankly back at her, she gave him a tentative pat on the head and hurried away. She knew it wasn't his fault, but she'd been a bit scared of him since the fire. And every time she looked at him, she had an urge to cross herself, as if he were some kind of creepy little jinx.

Standing where Lynne had left him, Connor felt invisible as adults constantly barged past him on their way in or out of the refreshments tent. Almost knocked over by one man, he edged away from the entrance flap after a while, and sidled around to the back of the tent.

It was already shrouded in shadow round there, and most of the people who had been milling about had moved around to the brighter side. Glad of the solitude, Connor sat down and drew his knees up to his chest. Resting his head on them, he closed his eyes, wondering when this would be over so he could go home.

Not that Auntie Julie's flat *felt* like home. And she wasn't really like an auntie any more, either, because she never smiled at him, or called him by any of the pet names she used to have for him, or winked at him, or tickled him — or *anything* nice. She just walked around looking angry all the time. And then his mum would tell him off in that really quiet voice she used when *she* was angry, warning him to stop doing whatever he was doing to annoy Auntie Julie, or she would kick them out and it would be his fault.

Just like the fire.

She didn't actually say *that*, because she still thought that it was Nicky's fault. But Connor knew it was his fault, and not a day went by that he didn't wish he hadn't touched the stupid matches.

Just like he wished it could all go back to how it used to be; only not the how it was just before the fire, but the how it was before his mum sent his dad away. When Connor was still a good boy, and everyone still loved him.

"Give us it," a boy's voice hissed just then, jerking Connor out of the semi-doze he'd drifted into.

"Get to fuck!" another boy retorted. "I nicked it, so I'm having first dibs."

Holding his breath when he realised that it was Leanne's little brother Fred, and Kelly Greene's little brother Ben, Connor drew himself further back into the canvas, hoping that they wouldn't notice him if they came round this side. They both went to his school, and they were always picking on him. But that was the one good thing that had come out of the fire — that he hadn't had to go back to school yet.

"I'm not kidding," Ben was saying now, his voice getting closer. "Give us it, or I'll kick your fucking head in."

"Like to see you try," Fred snorted unconcernedly. "I'd batter the fuck out of you if we had a fight, and you know it."

"Wanna bet?"

"Do you?"

"Shut the fuck up and light the fucking thing!"

Laughing now, thrilled by the swearing they'd been indulging in, Fred and Ben came around the corner and squatted down to light their illicit cigarette at the other end of the tent.

286

Catching sight of Connor out of the corner of his eye, Fred jumped and hid the cigarette behind his back. Relaxing when he realised who it was, he said, "What you doing over there, dickhead? You'd best not be spying on us, or you're dead!"

"Oi, he's talking to you!" Ben joined in, following Fred who had got up and was swaggering over to Connor. Swinging his foot back, he kicked Connor in the thigh. "Did you hear me, dickhead?"

"Why you ignoring us, Dumbo?" Fred spat, kicking him in the other leg. "Still pretending you can't talk, are you?"

"Aw, look, the baby's crying," Ben jeered, hawking up in his throat and spitting on Connor's hair.

Grabbing one arm each when Connor raised them to protect his head, Ben and Fred wrenched them roughly down. Then, while Ben kept a lookout to make sure that no one was coming, Fred brought his face down close to Connor's and head-butted him.

"That's for your dirty pervert of a dad fucking my sister," he hissed, his eight-year-old face an ugly mask of vengeance. "And keep your slag of a mam away from *my* dad, or my mam's gonna rip her fucking head off."

"And stay out of his dad's car," Ben added, determined to get in on the action.

"Yeah, and stay away from him," Fred snarled. "'Cos he's my dad, not yours, and I'll *kill* you if you ever go near him or his car again!"

"And *I'll* kill you if you tell anyone what's just happened," Ben warned.

Hearing someone coming towards them just then, they kicked Connor one last time and ran away, their laughter ringing in his ears.

Bin bag in hand, Tina Murphy was picking up the litter that was strewn all around the tent. Eyes narrowing with suspicion when she saw the boys running away, she walked around to the back of the tent. She hadn't seen who the boys were, but it was obvious they'd been up to no good, and knowing the kids round here she wouldn't put it past them to have been setting fire to the tent.

Thinking that she'd caught one of them still at it when she saw the boy huddled in the corner, she was just about to grab him and give him a clip round the ear when she realised that it was Connor.

"You okay?" she asked, squatting down beside him. "Did those boys do something to you?"

Gulping back the sobs, Connor shook his head and buried his face in his knees.

"Come on, sweetheart, look at me," Tina persisted. "You can tell me what happened. Who was it?"

Shaking his head again, Connor refused to look at her. The head-butt hadn't been all that hard, because Fred hadn't mastered the art yet; but the kicks had been, and he could already feel the bruises flaring up beneath his trousers. But it was the bad thing Fred had said about his dad and Leanne that was really upsetting him. That, and what he'd said about his mum and Fred's dad, Dave. Fred had threatened to kill him if he ever went near him or his car again, but Connor couldn't help it if they bumped into him at the bottom of Julie's road and he gave them a lift to the café and bought them something to eat. That had happened twice since he'd come out of hospital, but now he'd be terrified of going for a walk with his mum in case it happened again.

"Let's go find your mum," Tina said, a frown of concern on her face as she reached for Connor's hand. "Or would you rather I go and fetch your dad?" she asked, wondering if he might just be upset because he hadn't seen much of Terry lately.

"No!" sprang to the tip of Connor's tongue, but he managed to keep it in his mouth. He didn't want her to fetch his dad, because he'd tell Leanne, and she'd tell Fred, and then Fred and Ben would come after him again because they'd think he'd grassed on them.

Shaking her head when Connor got up and lurched off in the direction of the community centre, Tina dropped the bin bag and followed him.

"What's wrong?" Sue asked when Connor came hurtling across the room and dived under the table.

Catching up a couple of seconds later, Tina said, "I don't know if anything happened, but I just saw two boys legging it away from the back of the tent, and when I got round there I found Connor in tears. He wouldn't tell me who it was or if they'd done anything, though."

"He can't talk, he's still in shock," Sue reminded her tersely, wondering what he'd been doing on his own behind the tent when Jackie and Irene were supposed to have been looking after him.

Saying, "Oh, sorry, I forgot," Tina gave her a guilty smile. Then, shrugging, she said, "Well, he's okay now, so I'd best get back to picking up rubbish before Pauline catches me."

Tutting when she'd gone, Sue leaned right down and looked under the table. Connor had forced himself to stop crying, knowing that she would start throwing questions at him if she saw that he was in a state. Peering back at her now, he nodded when she asked if he was all right.

"Are you sure?" she persisted. "Because Tina said she thought some boys might have been picking on you." Sighing when he shook his head, she flapped her hands in a gesture of defeat and sat up again.

Lying down, Connor closed his eyes and fell asleep — and stayed asleep for the rest of the evening.

Pauline was exhausted by the time the event came to an end. Exhausted, and exhilarated, although not everything had gone as well as she'd hoped. The bingo had been about as exciting as a wet weekend in Wigan, despite the caller being the so-called Best in the North-West. And the band had been horrendously loud, and really, really bad, so she'd been relieved when they'd been booed off mid-set. The DJ had been much better, though, and had rescued what could have been an awful night by getting everybody up and dancing to all the old Motown classics — a safe bet with any age group. And then he'd topped it off with the karaoke competition, which had been a resounding success.

Although Sue probably hadn't thought so, because Leanne had not only won, she'd then announced over the microphone that she couldn't wait to share her champagne prize with the love of her life when she got home. And there was no doubt that she had said this to get at Sue, because almost everybody else had gone home by that point.

As Pauline herself intended to do, as soon as the DJ had finished packing up his gear and she and her ladies had cleaned up.

Sue was still sitting at the table in the corner. Making her way over to her, Pauline hoped that she wasn't waiting for the money they'd collected, because she'd already given it to John to take home for safe keeping. She supposed that if Sue was desperate she'd have to take her back to the house and give it to her, but she really wanted to count it first — so that everyone would know what a good job she'd done. And how generous *they* had all been, of course.

Reaching Sue now, she smiled, and said, "You look shattered, pet."

"I am," Sue admitted, heaving Connor out from under the table. "Come on, son. Time to wake up."

"It's been a long day for him," Pauline said, seeing the dark sockets beneath Connor's sunken eyes. "But he's been good as gold, hasn't he?"

"Yeah, he has," Sue agreed, lifting him onto her lap and stroking his hair.

"And have you had a good time?"

"Yeah, it's been great." Standing up now, Sue smiled at the older woman. "Thanks so much for everything you've done, Pauline. And not just this today, but everything. I don't know how we'd have managed without you this last couple of weeks."

"Yes, well, like I said earlier, I haven't really done anything," Pauline told her modestly. "Anyway, you make sure you pop round tomorrow so I can give you what's been collected."

Embarrassed by the mention of money, because it made her feel like a charity case and that didn't sit easily with her, Sue thanked her and promised to go round in the morning. Then, saying goodbye, she made her escape — as quickly as she could manage with Connor weighing her down.

She would have left hours ago if she hadn't agreed to meet Dave at The George at ten. She'd actually tried to ring him several times to tell him that she would make her own way home, but he hadn't answered his phone, so she'd been forced to sit it out. Either that, or stand him up and risk having him fall out with her.

She just hoped that he hadn't forgotten. And there was always a chance that he would have, given that he'd spent the day drinking and watching football — two of the biggest causes of male amnesia. If he had, she was buggered, because it was almost ten o'clock so there was no chance of getting a bus back to Julie's. She couldn't afford a taxi, and there was absolutely no way she could carry Connor all the way back to Cheetham Hill — and even less chance of him walking.

Dave was parked up in the shadows at the side of the pub. Smiling when he saw Sue struggling down the road, he jumped out of the car and, holding his cigarette between his teeth, tried to take Connor from her arms.

Whimpering, Connor held on tight, almost strangling Sue.

"He's tired," she said, giving Dave an apologetic smile as she wrenched Connor's arms from her neck. "I'll just lie him down on the back seat."

Opening the door for her, Dave took his jacket off and laid it over Connor, saying, "There you go, son. You get your head down. Soon have you home and in bed."

Opening Sue's door for her now, he ushered her in, then went around to the driver's side. "So, how did it go?" he asked, climbing in behind the wheel.

"All right," she said, aware yet again of the comforting smell of aftershave and alcohol that always surrounded him. "Band was crap, and the bingo was awful, but the DJ wasn't too bad."

She didn't bother to mention the karaoke, or his daughter's spiteful victory speech. Not only because she didn't want to speak the bitch's name, but also because it had sickened her to hear what Leanne was planning to do with her prize.

But that was her and Terry's business, not Sue's.

"What about the TV thing?" Dave asked, easing the car out onto the road.

"It seemed to go well," Sue told him, embarrassed as she added, "I ended up crying, though, so I probably looked really stupid."

"Doubt it," Dave said reassuringly. "It'll just let people know how much you care."

"Hope Nicky does if she saw it. The police said to talk to the camera as if I was talking to her, but I felt really stupid. I just hope if she *was* watching, she'll realise I'm not mad at her and get in touch."

"Do they still think she started the fire?"

"Seems like it," Sue murmured. "That policewoman — the one we saw earlier when . . ." Catching herself before she mentioned the kiss, she flapped her hand. "Anyway, I was talking to her before they started filming, and she said the investigators think it might have been a candle. And if it was, there's no way it could have been Connor, because he knows he's not allowed to touch the matches."

"Not even if the electric's gone and he's alone?" Dave said softly.

"He wasn't alone, though, was he," Sue said tightly. "He was with Nicky. Anyway, can we talk about something else? This is starting to depress me."

"You choose the subject, then," Dave said. "But I'm warning you now, if you so much as mention footy, you'll be right out on your arse."

"Take it you lost, then?" She gave him a sly grin.

"Something like that," he muttered. Then, "Anyhow, how you feeling? About what happened earlier, I mean. Had any thoughts about it?"

Glancing shyly down at her hands, Sue said, "Well, yeah, I've thought about it."

"And?" Dave looked at her out of the corner of his eye.

"I don't know." She shrugged. "I just think it's a bit too soon."

"For who? You, or that lot back there?"

"Me. The kids. I don't know."

Driving on in silence, Dave narrowed his eyes thoughtfully. This wasn't the response he'd expected, and he wasn't sure what to make of it. She'd enjoyed that kiss, because he knew women well enough to recognise from the gleam in her eyes straight after it that she'd been turned on. So what was with the sudden cold feet?

"Did Carole say something to you?" he asked, wanting to get to the bottom of it. "Because you know she's full of shit, so if she said something to upset you, you shouldn't take any notice."

"She didn't say anything. She just wanted to know how long I'd been in the refreshment tent, but Irene jumped in and told her I'd been there all day, so that threw her off the track."

"Good old Irene. Sticking up for you today, back to tearing shreds off you tomorrow." Snorting softly, Dave shook his head. Then, "Leanne's not said anything, has she? Only I had a word with her earlier and told her to lay off you, so if she's been giving you any lip, I want to know."

"She hasn't said anything," Sue told him, wishing that he'd just drop it.

"Terry, then," Dave persisted, a dark edge to his voice now. "I take it you did this telly thing together?"

"Yeah," Sue said wearily. Dave had said he wouldn't pressurise her, but it was certainly starting to feel like it.

"So what happened? Because something obviously did. You're not acting the same as before."

Nervous now, because she could tell that he was getting angry, Sue said, "Nothing happened, Dave. I'm just tired, that's all."

"So you didn't speak to him?"

"Well, yeah . . . but only about Connor."

"What about him?" Dave asked. "I mean, it's not like he's got the right to start sticking his oar in after what he did, is it? He had his chance to be a dad, and he chose to walk out."

Frowning, Sue glanced over the back seat to see if Connor was hearing any of this. Seeing that he was fast asleep, she turned back to Dave.

"Terry didn't leave, I kicked him out," she reminded him, keeping her voice low. "And no matter what he's done, he's still Connor's dad, so it's only natural he'd want to know how he was getting on at a time like this."

Inhaling deeply, because this was going in the wrong direction, Dave said, "I'm sorry for getting wound up, but he pisses me off. He messes you about, then thinks he can just pick up where he left off."

"No one's picking up anything," Sue muttered, folding her arms.

"Yeah, well, I wouldn't put it past him," Dave sniped. "And you know how much I care about you and the kids, so I just want to protect you. And with everything that's happened lately, us getting as close as we have, it feels really personal. But if I've crossed the line, I'm sorry."

"You haven't," Sue assured him, sighing wearily. "I'm really grateful that you care so much, but we honestly don't need protecting."

"Yeah, you do," Dave said quietly. "You might not see it, but I was watching that lot back there today making out like they're all on your side. But they'll be back to bitching about you before you know it, and who's going to be there for you? Terry won't be, because he's too hooked up on our Leanne. And your mate Julie's a bitch. So that just leaves me."

Embarrassed to have it pointed out to her so bluntly that she didn't have any friends apart from him, Sue gazed out of the window and tried to blink back the tears that were stinging the backs of her eyes.

"I'm not trying to upset you," Dave said, his tone gentler as he glanced around at her. "I just want that lot to know that we're together, and that we don't give a toss what they say or think about it. And you feel the same — I know you do. You're just scared of getting hurt again."

Sue didn't say anything. She couldn't deny it, because it was true — part of her *did* want to throw caution to the wind and just go for it. But how could it possibly work when it was obvious that Dave still hated Terry? He'd got angry just now at the thought of her talking to him, so how would he react if she admitted that she had agreed to let Terry see Connor again. And she couldn't go back on it, because it would cause even more trouble, and that wasn't fair on Connor. But Dave would never accept her having any kind of relationship with Terry once she was *his* woman. And that was what she would be, because that was the kind of man he was: passionate, and territorial — and capable of beating any man who dared step out of line with her to a pulp.

Unbuckling her seat belt when Dave pulled up outside the flats a few minutes later, Sue turned to wake Connor.

Reaching for her hand before she had a chance to do it, Dave said, "Don't rush away. We need to sort this out before you go in." Switching off the engine now, he lit two cigarettes and passed one to her. "Right," he said, as if he'd been thinking really hard about what he was about to say. "I know I said I wouldn't push you for an answer, and I'm sorry if you think that's what I've been doing. But you've got to see this from my point of view. I've always liked you, but you were with Terry, so it never crossed my mind that I could have you. But now I know there's a chance, it's driving me crazy. I just want to be with you — to take care of you and your kids."

"I know," Sue said softly, aware that her hands were shaking and her heart was beating faster as she wondered if he was about to try and kiss her again.

Sighing now, as if he'd resolved something, Dave said, "Right, then. I've said my piece, so you know where I stand. The rest is up to you. Only try not to take too long, eh? Either way, I'd rather know soon as."

"I'll try," Sue promised, meaning it. Then, "Right, I'd best get him to bed before he wakes up, or I'll never get him off again."

"I'll carry him," Dave said, opening his door and jumping out. "And don't forget your voddy, by the way."

Biting her lip as she reached under the seat to retrieve the bottle she'd been drinking from earlier, Sue gazed up at Julie's living room window. The TV was on, which meant that Julie was still up — and alone, otherwise she'd be entertaining in the bedroom by now. She wouldn't like it if Dave came up, but Sue knew that she wouldn't manage Connor on her own, so she had no choice but to let him help her.

"Don't worry," Dave quipped, seeing the look on her face and guessing what was going through her mind. "I'm not expecting you to invite me in so Miserable can have a go at you. But if I was you, I'd get onto the council first thing Monday and start bugging the shit out of them, 'cos you don't have to live like this."

Nodding thoughtfully as she climbed out of the car, Sue said, "You're right. It's a joke."

Julie had her feet up on the couch, watching TV. Hearing the key in the lock, she popped one last chocolate into her mouth and shoved the box out of sight under a cushion. Narrowing her eyes when she heard hushed voices in the hall, she dropped her feet to the floor and waddled over to the door. If Sue thought she was bringing someone in without asking first, she had another think coming.

"I'm not stopping," Dave told her when she appeared in the living room doorway. "Just dropping them off."

Giving him a dirty look, Julie glared at Sue, then marched back inside, kicking the door shut behind her. Lighting a cigarette and puffing on it angrily, she stood by the fire.

Rolling her eyes at Dave as she took Connor from him. Sue said, "First thing Monday — without a doubt."

Winking, Dave said, "You do that. And who knows, I might even get a coffee next time I drop you off — at your own place," he added, loudly, sure that Julie was eavesdropping.

Shushing him, Sue pushed him further back onto the communal landing. Leaning forward, Dave stole a sneaky kiss. Then, winking at her, he trotted off down the stairs, calling back, "Want to meet up tomorrow?"

"No!" she called after him in a loud whisper. Then, thinking up a feasible lie to make sure that he didn't decide to drop by on the off chance, she said, "I've got the social workers coming round, and they stay all day and half the night. But how about Monday? You can give me a lift to you know where."

Saying, "My pleasure," Dave gave her the signal to phone him before letting himself out of the main door.

Smiling, glad that Connor was still asleep so he hadn't seen the kiss and couldn't tell Terry, Sue shut the door and carried him off to the spare bedroom. She knew full well that Julie was probably waiting in the living room to have a go at her, but sack her . . . Like Dave had said not so long ago, if she wanted to argue, let her argue with herself. And, with any luck, she could have her poxy flat back to herself before too long.

Laying Connor down on the bed now, she eased his pants down to put a clean nappy on him. Horrified when she saw the purpling bruises on his thighs, she shook him gently, saying, "Who did this to you, sweetheart? Was it those boys Tina saw running away from the tent tonight? Is this what they were doing?"

Eyes rolling sleepily, Connor shook his head.

"Please, Connor, just tell me," Sue implored. "If you don't tell me, I won't be able to do anything and they might do it again."

Sheer misery in his eyes now, Connor's chin began to wobble. Shushing him before he started crying, because that was the one noise that the shock definitely *hadn't* robbed him of, Sue said, "All right, son, go back to sleep."

Relieved when he quickly did, Sue gently traced the outline of the bruises with her fingertip. They looked like kick marks, she thought. Those nasty little bastards must have taken a good few swipes at him, and she wished she could get her hands on them and give them a taste of their own medicine. But if he wouldn't tell her who had done it, they had effectively got away with it. And what was to stop them doing it again? She couldn't keep him with her all the time. He'd have to go back to school at some point, and what if the boys went to the same school?

Dave's words about wanting to protect her and the kids sprang into her mind. She'd thought that she could cope with everything on her own, but this just proved how wrong she was. And how right *he* was that the people back on the estate would be back to normal before she knew it. The kids obviously hadn't dropped their malicious hatred of her family, and it wouldn't be long before some of the adults started to show their true colours again, she was sure.

Undressing now, she reached into her handbag for the sleeping tablets that the doctor had given her. She'd resisted taking any so far, fearing that she might get hooked and need more. But there were so many conflicting emotions coursing through her right now that she knew she'd never get to sleep unaided. And she really couldn't face yet another night of tossing and turning.

Popping one of the pills into her mouth, Sue washed it down with vodka. Then, switching the light off, she cuddled up to Connor and closed her eyes, waiting for the tablet to take effect. Praying that it would.

CHAPTER
ELEVEN

Terry was asleep on the couch when Leanne got home. The TV was still on, but the heating had gone off and there was a definite chill in the air. Kneeling down beside him, she kissed him softly on the lips, smiling when he immediately opened his eyes.

"Why didn't you go to bed? You must be freezing."

"I'm fine," Terry said, stretching and yawning at the same time. "And I thought I *had* gone to bed, but I must have been dreaming."

"Was I in it?" Leanne asked, trailing a fingertip over his lips.

"Course," he lied, reaching out to brush a lock of hair out of her eyes. Getting a strong waft of alcohol from her breath, he smiled. "I take it you had fun, then?"

"It was brilliant," Leanne said dreamily. "I won a tenner on the bingo, *and* I won the karaoke."

"Really?" Terry chuckled. "So who was your competition — Pauline and Irene?"

"Don't be cheeky," she scolded, giving him a playful slap and climbing up onto his knee. "It was just us girls from the estate. And my 'Rhianna' was the best, so I got the prize."

"Which was?"

"Da-da!" Reaching for the bottle she'd put down by the side of the couch, Leanne brought it up with a flourish.

"Champagne?" Terry raised an eyebrow. "Wow, you *must* have been good. Either that, or the others were really, really bad."

"Er, do you want some of this, or are you going to carry on being cheeky and make me not want to share it with you?" Leanne said, a mock-warning edge to her voice.

Grinning, Terry pulled her head down and kissed her. "Let's go to bed and get blasted."

"Why waste time going to bed when we can do it right here?" she whispered, pushing him back down. "It's our own place, don't forget. No more worrying about my mum or brothers walking in on us."

"What about the champagne?" Terry gasped when she started tugging at his fly.

"We'll have it when we've finished," Leanne said, pulling his jeans down and straddling him. "And then we can start all over again. In the bathroom, and the kitchen, and then in the bedroom. I just want you everywhere."

It was all over in minutes. Laughing when she collapsed onto him, Terry said, "Where the hell did *that* come from?"

"From me loving you," she murmured breathlessly. "I meant what I said earlier, I really, really love you, and I want to be with you for ever. And nobody's ever going to get between us again, because I won't let them."

Terry gazed into her eyes and said, "I've been trying to tell you that for ages."

"Yeah, well, I've got it now," Leanne said, rolling onto her side and pulling his head down onto her breast. "You're mine, and you always will be."

Listening as her heart gradually slowed to normal, Terry prayed that this was a turning point. He did love her, but if things carried on the way they had been going lately, he'd begun to fear that they wouldn't last another year.

Over on the Fitton estate just then, Carole was clumping heavily down the stairs. Yanking the bolts back, she opened the door just as Dave was about to knock again.

"What?" she snapped, folding her arms and glaring at him.

"What's with the bolts?" Dave asked, taking a last drag on his cigarette and flicking the butt into the overgrown garden.

"Oh, let me see," she retorted sarcastically. "Could I be trying to lock *you* out, d'y' think?"

Grinning, Dave stepped towards her. "And why would you want to do something stupid like that?" Nose to nose with her now, he carried on walking, forcing her to step back into the hall.

Tutting loudly, Carole walked around him and slammed the door shut. Then, turning to face him, she folded her arms again, saying, "I hope you don't think you're getting into my bed, 'cos you can piss right off after what you did today."

"Don't be like that," Dave crooned, making a sudden grab for her. Holding onto her as she struggled to get away, he said, "You know you want me."

"No, I don't," Carole hissed, putting her hands on his chest to hold him back when he tried to kiss her. "I hate you, and I wish I'd never met you."

"You know you don't mean it," Dave said softly, easily forcing her hands back against her own chest as he brought his face down to hers and ran his tongue between her lips.

"I do," she insisted, clenching her teeth together.

"You love me," he drawled, completely ignoring her protests and grabbing a handful of arse now. "Always have, always will."

"That's where you're wrong," she spat, her pride still smarting from the way he'd dismissed her at the fundraiser. "And you stink," she said now, trying to inject disgust into her voice even though she actually loved the smell of Scotch on his breath. "Anyway, what you doing here? The slag knock you back, did she?"

"Ssshhh." Touching a finger to her lips, Dave walked her backwards towards the stairs. "Don't wanna wake the lads up, do we?"

Resistance was futile, and Carole knew it. Sighing heavily, she flapped her hands, muttering, "You'll be the fucking death of me one of these days." Pushing him away then, she started to climb the stairs — squealing with delight when he came up behind her and slipped his hands up inside her nightdress.

It was gone twelve, and Zak Carlton had just left the snooker hall. Strolling down Wilbraham Road, he was about to cross over to take a short cut through the park when he saw a girl up ahead. The lighting was bad at this point of the road so he couldn't be sure, but he would have sworn it was Leanne. Quickening his pace, although he didn't have a clue what he was going to say to her given how they'd left it last time, he was just a few feet away when she heard him and spun around.

"Fucking hell, Zak!" Kelly squawked, her eyes wide with fear. "You scared the crap out of me."

Disappointed that it wasn't Leanne, Zak said, "Sorry, I thought you were someone else." Falling into step beside her now, he said, "What you doing out at this time of night? Shouldn't you be in bed by now?"

"I'm not a kid," she informed him indignantly. "I'm fifteen."

"Wow, that old," he teased, laughing softly.

Intrigued that he was still walking with her, Kelly glanced up at him from the corner of her eye. She'd always fancied him, but she'd never have admitted that to him in a million years, because he'd just go and tell his mates and they'd all take the piss even more than they already did. Anyway, he wouldn't look twice at her; not when he'd already had Leanne.

"Why you staring at me?" Zak asked suddenly, making her blush because she hadn't realised that he could see her.

"I'm not," she lied. "I was just thinking."

"About?"

"You and Leanne. You used to go out with her, didn't you?"

Shrugging, Zak said, "Yeah, so?"

"Bet you still fancy her," Kelly said, a hint of envy in her voice. "Most of the lads do, don't they?"

Peering round at her, Zak said, "Sounds to me like *you've* got a bit of a thing for her yourself."

"Piss off!" Kelly protested. "I've had loads of boyfriends."

"Yeah, right," Zak said disbelievingly. Reaching up to take a dimped spliff from behind his ear, he lit it and took a deep drag before offering it to her, saying, "So, what's with all the interest in me and Leanne?"

"Nothing," Kelly muttered, sucking on the smoke. "She's a mate, that's all."

"No way would she hang out with a schoolie," he scoffed.

"Honest," Kelly said earnestly. "You know Neela Jennings? Well, she's my cousin, and we go round to Leanne's every weekend. All the girls do. It's great."

"All the girls, eh?" Zak sneered, taking the spliff back. "Bet the old man gets off on that *big* time."

"What do you mean?" Kelly asked, frowning confusedly.

"Come off it," Zak snorted, looking her up and down. "Good-looking girl like you, and you can't figure out why he likes having you around?"

Thrilled that he'd said she was good-looking, but still confused as to what he'd meant about Terry, Kelly said, "I still don't get you."

"Do I have to spell it out?" Zak said patiently. "The dude likes them *young*."

Wrinkling her nose when it finally sank in, Kelly said, "Don't be disgusting. He's not like that."

"So, you're telling me he's never looked at you like that?"

"Never," Kelly said truthfully. "He's not even there most of the time. He's either at work, or he pisses off to bed."

"On his own?" Zak probed, handing the spliff back to her.

"God, yeah," Kelly said, already feeling the stone creeping up on her as she took another deep pull on it. "Leanne wouldn't do anything like that while we were there. Christ, she's bad enough about us hearing her arguing, never mind shagging."

"Oh, so they argue, do they?" Zak said, a hint of satisfaction in his voice.

"Never stop," Kelly told him, getting into her stride now. "If it's not him moaning about the noise, it's her accusing him of going with someone behind her back. She thinks we can't hear them because they go into the bedroom to argue, but the walls are dead thin." Giggling now, she handed the end of the spliff back to him, saying, "Should have heard her last time we went round, it was *well* funny. He went out for ages, and she went mad when he came back, demanding to know where he'd been, like he'd been shagging someone else, or something."

"And had he?"

"No way," Kelly said adamantly. "He'd never cheat on her. Anyway, that was the night of the fire round at his ex's house, and her mam rang to tell him about it, and they both went to the hospital, so they must have sorted it."

"What happened after that?" Zak asked, a thoughtful look on his face.

"Nothing." Kelly shrugged. "Leanne told us not to come round for a while, 'cos she wanted to spend more time alone with him. And we haven't been back since."

His mind really ticking over now, Zak said, "When you were at Goldie's party that night, you said something about the five-O questioning you."

"They thought I'd done something to that stupid bitch *Nicky*," Kelly said, spitting the name out. "And I wanted to know if Leanne had said anything, 'cos the copper remembered seeing me at hers that night."

Zak's eyes were narrowed to slits now as the thoughts began to slot into place. When he'd had that argument with Leanne at the party, she'd kicked off at him for accusing Terry of starting the fire; telling him that Terry couldn't have done it because he'd been with her all that night. But if Kelly was telling the truth, then he *hadn't* been there the whole time, which meant that Leanne was lying. But why? Unless she had something to hide.

Snapping out of his thoughts when he realised that Kelly had stopped walking, Zak turned back and looked at her.

"This is my house," Kelly said regretfully. This was the first time they'd actually spoken at length, but now he'd go on his way, and it would probably never happen again.

Pursing his lips, Zak said, "Got anything to drink in there?"

"What, you mean like alcohol?" Kelly asked, her heart pounding in her chest. Zak was gorgeous, and he could have his pick of any girl on the estate, so was he really asking to come in and have a drink with her?

Stepping closer to her now, close enough for her to smell the musky scent of his sweat working its way through the deodorant, Zak peered into her eyes, his voice low and husky as he said, "Anything wet will do. And you can tell me more about your girly nights round at Leanne's."

Too excited by the nearness of him and the prospect of what a drink might lead to to worry about his interest in Leanne, Kelly nodded and opened the gate.

Grinning slyly, Zak followed her up the path.

CHAPTER
TWELVE

Nicky's eyes felt as if they'd been glued together, but she forced them open when she heard the familiar sound of wood scraping on concrete coming from the pulsating darkness up ahead.

She wouldn't be able to see him, she knew that, but it made her feel better to have her eyes open when he came in, because at least she could see movement in the shadows and gauge where he was.

Holding her breath now as she heard locks being opened and the metallic rasp of bolts being drawn back, she gazed blindly in the direction of the door, from where, in a few seconds, the blinding light would appear, momentarily forcing her to close her eyes again.

It was the same every time: the scrape, the locks, the bolts, the light. Then, if he remembered, he'd toss whatever food and drink he'd brought for her onto the mattress.

And she'd ignore it, telling herself that she'd rather starve to death than take anything from him.

But it never worked. Hard as she tried, she always gave in to temptation in the end. Although she usually waited until he'd gone, if she could hold out that long, because it gave her pleasure to know that she'd deprived him of the satisfaction of seeing how hungry he'd made her. Which wasn't much of a victory, but it was the only thing that Nicky still had any control over.

Not that she cared all that much any more, because lately she'd found her thoughts straying more frequently towards death; it being the only way she could ever see herself getting out of this room that she'd begun to think of as her coffin. And she'd given up trying to count the days, because the continuous darkness made it impossible to distinguish day from night.

The light came now; a powerful torch beam aimed straight into Nicky's eyes. He came towards her, his movements disturbing the stale air and stirring up the stench of dampness and rot. They would settle back into the walls once he'd gone. But the other smells — the rancid scents of dead things — never went completely. They were on her. And sometimes she thought they were coming from within her.

The whooshing sound of her blood thundered through her ears now. When she was alone, she tried to pretend that she wasn't scared of him; that she would welcome it if he stopped playing whatever game he was playing and just got on with killing her. But the dread still came when he did, and her heart still felt as if it would explode with fear when she felt the movement of air on her skin as he got close.

He was just a few feet away now, and she could smell the alcohol on his breath; the leather of his jacket.

"How's it going?" he asked, sounding as if he were talking to an old friend. Waiting several seconds, as if expecting her to answer — which they both knew she wouldn't; he gave a soft chuckle. "Not in a talking mood, eh?"

Feeling the mattress depress beneath her feet as he sat down, Nicky swallowed loudly and eased herself further back against the wall.

"Thirsty?" he asked, still sounding like the genial host.

Nicky felt like screaming that, yes, she was thirsty . . . of course she was thirsty! What did he expect when he'd left her without a drink for God only knew how long? But she kept her mouth firmly shut.

Tossing a bottle of orange juice onto the mattress beside her now, he lit a cigarette. Watching the glow of the tip through half-lidded eyes, Nicky inhaled deeply. She'd always hated that smell when she'd been at home, but now she craved it because it reminded her of her mum. Later, she would cry as the memories swamped her. But, for now, she just wanted to savour it.

"You'll never guess what happened today," he said conversationally. "There was a big party round at your place, and everyone was there. Your mum, your dad, your brother."

"You're lying," Nicky croaked, her voice sounding alien to her ears because she hadn't spoken in so long. "She'd never let my dad in the house."

"No fooling a smart girl like you, eh?" he chuckled amusedly. "All right, you caught me out. It wasn't at

314

your house, it was at the community centre. And that is true."

Nicky's head was spinning. He sounded genuine, but how could it be true? How could her mum and dad go to a party while she was locked up in here? Didn't they care about her any more?

"Yep, it was a great party," he went on. "Everyone laughing and drinking. They even had a band, and a karaoke. Bet you would have liked that, wouldn't you? I know all the other girls did. Especially Leanne."

"I don't believe you," Nicky gasped, her breath ragged as her heart threatened to break.

"Tell you what, your brother's getting big," he went on as if she hadn't even spoken. "Dead spit of your dad, isn't he?"

Sobbing now as the tears she'd been trying so hard to hold inside came bursting through, Nicky cried, "Please let me go. I just want to see Connor."

"I know you do," he murmured, as if he actually cared. "And when I've done what I've got to do, you can. But till then, you'll just have to be a good girl and stay put, won't you?"

"I won't tell anyone," Nicky sobbed. "I swear I won't. Just let me go, and I'll do whatever you want me to do."

"You're already doing what I want you to do, darlin'," he told her softly.

"Well, let me go, then," Nicky begged. "Please, Mr Miller, I just want to go home."

"Not till Daddy's learned his lesson."

"*I want my mum,*" Nicky wailed, unable to stop the tears now. "*MUUUM . . .*"

"*Oh, now you're really pissing me off,*" Dave hissed, scrambling up the mattress and putting his hand over her mouth. "*What have I told you about that, eh? Do I have to get the gag out again? Is that what you want?*"

Shaking her head, Nicky's eyes bulged as the sobs caught in her throat. Taking his hand off her mouth when she started to choke, Dave gave her a couple of hard whacks on the back.

"*Do that again, and I will get the gag out,*" he warned her when her breathing had steadied. "*You promised not to make any noise, and I trusted you. But if you're going to prove yourself to be a liar like your dad, I'm going to have to hurt you. Got that?*"

Nodding, Nicky gulped loudly.

"*Yeah, well, make sure you have,*" Dave said, edging back to his seat at the foot of the mattress. "*'Cos it winds me up when you bitches say one thing then do another. And I wouldn't even mind if I'd done anything to you,*" he went on, lighting another cigarette and sucking on it agitatedly. "*But I haven't, have I? No! Because I'm not a fuckin' paedophile like your dad, that's why. But maybe I should try it, eh? Show the cunt what it feels like to have some bloke pawing his little girl.*"

Truly terrified now as he ranted on, Nicky tried not to make a sound, afraid that it might push him over the edge. He hadn't touched her yet, but if he decided to do it there would be nothing she could do to stop him.

316

Seeming to lose the rage as abruptly as it had come over him, Dave said, "Anyway, enough about me and my day. What have you been up to?" Sighing after a long, silent pause, he said, "And there was me thinking we were getting on okay. But, oh, well . . . there'll be plenty of time to get to know each other better when we're living together. Like the sound of that, do you? Me, you, your mum and Connor. Oh, and Leanne, of course — once we've got rid of your dad."

Sighing now, as if he could hardly wait, he stood up.

"Anyway, best let you get some sleep. See you soon. Oh, and, don't do anything I wouldn't do!"

Laughing, he walked towards the door, using the torch beam to guide him. Turning back when he reached it, he said, "Catch, by the way." Tossing a pre-wrapped sandwich onto the mattress, he let himself out.

Flopping down onto the rough pillows when he'd gone, Nicky squeezed her eyes shut as the burning tears slid freely down her cheeks.

"No . . ." she sobbed. "No, no, no . . . "

PART TWO

CHAPTER
THIRTEEN

Terry was feeling really positive about him and Leanne when he took a shower that morning. Which, in turn, made him feel twice as guilty about what he was about to do.

They'd had a brilliant night, and the sex had been amazing. He wasn't quite sure what had happened, but everything seemed to have really clicked into place between them. And after the stresses of the last few months that was fantastic, because he'd begun to seriously wonder if they had a future.

Now that everything was looking so good, he desperately didn't want to destroy it by deceiving Leanne. But how could he admit that he'd made arrangements with Sue behind her back without doing exactly that?

Still, it might all work itself out. Things were already looking up since Sue had called a truce and agreed to let him see Connor again. And, in time, she might even let him stay over at the flat with him. But Terry wasn't about to force it on her and risk having her change her mind. So he would play it her way for now — and hope that Leanne didn't find out before he was ready to tell her.

321

Which left him still needing a plausible excuse for getting out of the flat for a few hours without her today. And that wasn't going to be easy, given that he didn't work on Sundays and didn't have any mates to visit since they'd all turned against him in support of Dave. He couldn't even use his family as an excuse, because Leanne knew that he didn't have any contact with them. And there was no way he could say that he just wanted to be alone for a while, because Leanne would probably think that he was seeing someone else, and they'd be back to square one.

But he needn't have worried, because Leanne was about to make it really easy for him.

Still in bed, she was chewing her nails, wondering exactly the same thing as him: how she was going to get out of the flat without telling him where she was going, or who she was going to see.

Her mobile had rung a few minutes earlier and, thinking that it was probably her mum wanting to moan about her dad again, she'd glanced at the screen with every intention of ignoring it if she saw her mother's name. But when she'd seen a number she didn't recognise, she'd answered it, assuming that it was one of her friends letting her know that they'd changed their number again. Expecting it to be Goldie, or Janis, or Neela — or *any* of the girls — she'd been furious to hear Zak's voice.

Eyeing the door nervously in case Terry walked in and asked who she was talking to, she'd demanded to know how he had got her number. But Zak had told her that it didn't matter; that he wanted to see her.

322

"And don't even think about ignoring me," he'd warned, his tone letting her know that he wasn't messing around. "Because I know something about that fire that could get you and your man into serious trouble."

Telling her where to meet him then, he'd hung up, leaving Leanne in a quandary. Did she call his bluff and not go? Or lie to Terry and meet Zak to find out what he thought he knew?

She really didn't want to lie to Terry, not after last night. For months now she'd been terrified that they were drifting apart, but last night she'd felt closer to him than ever, and she didn't want to risk losing him over something stupid like Zak.

But if Zak *did* know something, and she pissed him off by ignoring him, then she might still lose Terry if Zak told the police and they arrested him.

The sensible thing to do, Leanne decided, was to meet up with Zak and let him say what he had to say. At least then she'd know what she was dealing with. And if it was just more speculative rubbish like the stuff he'd been coming out with at Goldie's party, she would tell him to get stuffed. But if it was something more dangerous, then she would just have to front it out and convince him that he was wrong. And smart as he thought he was, she had always found it easy to get round him when they'd been going out with each other. He was as much of a sucker for her wily ways as her dad was in that respect.

That's it! she thought, jerking upright in the bed. She'd tell Terry that she was meeting up with her dad.

He would believe her, because he knew that they had started talking again. And he definitely wouldn't ask to go with her, because it would take him a while to get used to the idea before he agreed to spend any time with her father.

Getting up now, pleased with herself for coming up with such a plausible excuse, Leanne slipped into a pair of jeans. Then, determined not to give Zak any reason to slag her off for flaunting herself, she pulled on one of Terry's jumpers.

Coming into the bedroom just then, Terry felt his heart sink when he saw that she was already dressed. Hoping that she wouldn't demand to come with him, he opened his mouth to tell her the lie he'd concocted about nipping into town to buy her a special present as a thank-you for all the support she'd given him this last couple of weeks.

But before he had a chance to speak, Leanne blurted out that her dad had just rung and asked her to meet up with him.

Looping her arms around his neck now, she said, "You don't mind, do you? Only I know you won't want to come, but if you'd rather I stayed here with you, I'll call him back and say I can't make it."

"*Go*," Terry insisted, hugging her tightly. "I know you've been missing him, so I'm not going to be selfish and say no, am I?"

Pressing her face against his chest as the guilt washed over her, Leanne murmured, "Thanks, babe. I'll try not to be too long."

"Be as long as you like," Terry said, holding her close so that she couldn't see the guilt that was written all over *his* face. "I was thinking of nipping into town, anyway."

"What for?" Leanne asked, pulling her head back and peering up at him, wondering if she should ask him to wait until she got home so she could go with him.

Smiling secretively, Terry said, "Never you mind. Just be ready to thank me when you see what I've got planned for tonight."

Pursing her lips, Leanne gazed coyly up at him through her lashes. "So, it's something for me, then? And is it nice?"

"Fantastic," Terry told her — cursing himself as soon as he said it, because now it would *have* to be special, which meant another battering for the credit card. But at least he'd have got to spend a bit of time with Connor, so it would be worth it.

Kissing him now, Leanne tripped happily out to the bathroom to get a wash — determined that whatever Zak had to say, she wouldn't let it spoil things between her and Terry.

Sue felt fresh and alert when she woke up, thanks to the sleeping pill, which had knocked her out so completely that she'd managed to sleep right through the night without being plagued by any of the usual nightmares.

Thinking more sharply than usual, she realised that she had a decision to make. Wait to see if there was still a chance with Terry — which might well mean being on her own for ever. Or accept that it was over, once and for all, and get on with her life.

She still loved Terry, and probably always would. But the thought of letting go of him didn't bring the heart-wrenching pain that it usually brought. Yes, there was a sense of sadness about it. But there was also a sense of hope, because letting go of the past meant that she was free to move on with the rest of her life. And, right now, the only person she could see herself spending it with was Dave.

There were still a million different reasons why it probably wouldn't work, not least the fact that Dave's daughter had stolen her husband, which would make family get-togethers an absolute no-no. And because everyone would immediately assume that they'd had something going on the whole time — and Carole would be the worst of the lot, Sue had no doubt about that. But like Dave had said last night, this was nobody's business but theirs, so it didn't matter what anyone else thought about it.

So, yes, she believed that she might just be ready to take the next step with Dave. But she would only make a definite decision after she'd seen Terry today and made sure that there really was nothing left between them. And she'd still want to wait a little while longer before she and Dave came out as a couple if she went for it. At least until she'd got somewhere of her own to live; and until she'd figured out a way to ease Dave into accepting that Terry was always going to be in Connor's life. And Nicky's when she came home.

If she came home.

Sadly, the new-found clarity of thought she'd woken up with today had all but stripped the rose-tinted faith away, leaving Sue to face up to the fact that she might never see her daughter again. But while she didn't want to believe that Nicky was dead, if she wasn't, and had just run away after starting the fire and nearly killing Connor, then she might as well be, because there would be no place for her in Sue's heart. And no excuse would ever be good enough for doing something so terrible. Not the bullying she'd supposedly been suffering at school; or the pain of losing her dad and having to help out at home while her mum recovered. Everyone had shit to deal with in life, but they didn't all take it out on their innocent baby brothers. And if that *was* what had happened, then Nicky could stay away for ever as far as Sue was concerned.

Getting up now, Sue pressed her ear against the door to listen for sounds of Julie being up and about. Hearing nothing, she crept out and took a quick shower. Then, dressing quickly, she woke Connor up and got him ready to go and meet his dad.

Sneaking out of the flat, she took him down to the café where she'd arranged to meet Terry, which was at the other end of the road from where she usually met Dave. Sitting Connor down at a table by the window, she ordered herself a cup of tea, and a small fried breakfast for him. She couldn't really afford it, and doubted he'd even eat it, but she couldn't let him go off with Terry with nothing in his stomach or Terry would think she was neglecting him.

Sipping at her tea while they waited for the food, Sue gazed out of the window, watching for Terry's car. The girl behind the counter was engrossed in a magazine and, with no prospect of getting any conversation out of Connor, Sue was glad of the tinny music coming from the radio, because it was the only thing that was stopping her from having to listen to her heart pounding in her chest.

Despite making her peace with Terry yesterday, she was nervous about seeing him again, because they both knew that she'd done some terrible things since the break-up. Knowing how much he loved the kids, she had used them as a weapon to punish him; telling him that if he wanted to see them it had to be on her terms — at *her* house, *alone*. She'd known that it would cause trouble between him and Leanne, but she hadn't cared because she'd wanted to split them up. But when that hadn't worked, she'd had him arrested for domestic violence — which had been an absolute lie, but it had seemed like the only way she could keep him away from the house. And although she'd stopped it from going to court, Terry must resent her for doing it in the first place. *She* certainly would, if the tables were reversed.

But now, much as she still hated Leanne and wished that she would do them all a favour and drop dead, she knew that the games had to stop — for her own sake as much as Connor's.

The food still wasn't ready when Terry arrived. Gripping her cup hard, because the sight of his handsome face never failed to give her butterflies, Sue watched as Connor jumped down off his chair and ran to him. Sweeping him up in his arms, Terry kissed him, oblivious to the look of envy that Sue was struggling to conceal.

Putting him down after a moment, he gave Sue a nervous smile, and asked if she was all right.

"Fine," she lied, forcing herself to return the smile. "You're early," she said then, trying not to make it sound like an accusation.

"Sorry," he murmured, wondering if it was.

"It's okay," she assured him. "It's just that I ordered breakfast for Connor and it's not ready yet." Squeezing her hands together nervously now, she said, "I was just going to get myself another cup of tea, though, if you want one. Or would you rather just take him?"

Terry wondered if staying for a cuppa was such a good idea, given that he already felt bad about being here behind Leanne's back. But it was unlikely that he'd see anyone he knew down this end. And anyway, it wouldn't be fair to drag Connor away without letting him eat first.

"Yeah, all right," he said. "I didn't think to get a brew before I came out, so I could really do with one."

"Not like you," Sue commented amusedly, pushing her own chair back. "You usually can't move without your morning cuppa." Blushing when she realised that she was talking in too familiar a way, she said, "I'll, er, just . . ." Trailing off, she scuttled over to the counter.

Sighing, Terry pulled out a chair and sat down. This was going to be a barrel of laughs if every time either of them spoke it was fraught with what was allowed to be mentioned and what wasn't.

Connor tugged on his sleeve. Looking down at him, Terry smiled. "What's up, little man?"

Connor pointed out of the window.

"What you showing me?" Terry asked, peering out. "The car?"

Keeping his mouth firmly shut, Connor shook his head and jabbed his finger more animatedly towards the glass.

Frowning, Terry shrugged. "I don't know what you want me to look at, son. Can't you just tell me?"

Giving up, Connor slumped down in his seat. Even if he'd wanted to talk, he knew it wouldn't happen now, because he'd tried before they came out, when his mum had sent him to the toilet to make sure his bladder was empty. Like he always did when he was in the bathroom alone, he'd peered into the mirror, pretending that the eyes looking back at him were Nicky's, because they were exactly the same. But then, when he'd opened his mouth to talk to her, the words had refused to come out, and all he'd heard was that stupid noise that his mum hated. So now he was terrified that he'd forgotten *how* to talk.

Coming back just then with two fresh cups of tea, Sue saw the sadness on Terry's face and asked what was wrong.

"He was pointing out of the window," Terry told her. "But I don't know what he was trying to tell me."

"He was probably just trying to show you where we've been staying," Sue said perceptively. "It's just up the road."

"Oh, right." Nodding, Terry picked up his tea and took a sip. Glancing at Sue and seeing the dark shadows under her eyes, he said, "It must be difficult trying to understand him. How do you manage it?"

"It's hard," she admitted, shrugging as she added, "But there's not a lot I can do about it, so I just have to get on with it."

"Haven't the doctors suggested anything?"

"Only what they said at the beginning: that he'll come out of it when he's ready."

"Isn't the counselling doing any good?"

"Is it hell," Sue said scathingly. "If we can't get him to talk, they sure as hell won't."

Sighing, Terry gazed at Connor. "Well, I wish you'd talk to *someone*, son, 'cos we're all really missing you."

Tears flooding his eyes, Connor stared down at his fingers. He missed his dad, and he missed Nicky. And he even missed his mum, even though he was still living with her, because she acted like he wasn't even there sometimes; as if she'd forgotten he existed just because she couldn't hear him. But when he made noises, she just got mad at him, so he tried not to do that now unless he really needed to get her attention.

"No point," Sue said resignedly. "And believe me, I've tried everything."

"Oh, well, I suppose we'll just have to wait till you're ready, eh, son?" Reaching out, Terry ruffled Connor's hair affectionately.

The girl came over just then, carrying Connor's breakfast. Putting it down on the table in front of him, she said, "There you go, gorgeous." Then, giving Terry a shy smile, she said, "He takes after you, doesn't he?"

"So they say," Terry replied proudly.

Patting Connor on the head now, telling him to enjoy his food, the girl went back to her station — where, Sue noted irritably, she had repositioned herself so that she was now sitting directly in Terry's eye-line.

Terry didn't notice. His attention firmly on Connor, he said, "That looks good, so eat up, and then we'll get going."

Eyebrows raised in surprise when Connor immediately began to tuck into the food, because she had a hard time getting him to eat anything these days, Sue asked where Terry was planning to take him.

"Thought we'd go into town for a bit," he said — without adding that this was a last-minute addition to his plan in order to pick up a present for Leanne. "Then I thought he might fancy a bit of bowling."

Smiling sadly when Connor's eyes lit up at the mention of bowling, Sue dipped her gaze as she felt the all too familiar sting of tears behind her eyes. That was exactly where *she* had been planning to take the kids when the taxi had pulled up outside her destroyed house that night.

"Are you all right?" Terry asked quietly.

"Yeah, I'm fine," she murmured, telling herself to snap out of it.

Connor made a sudden grunting noise. Looking at him and seeing him jiggling about in his seat, Sue said, "Do you need the toilet?" Pointing him in the right direction when he nodded, she was surprised when he jumped up and went on his own. Usually, he'd try and make her go with him, but he obviously felt braver in Terry's presence.

Seizing the sudden opportunity of being alone with Sue to broach the subject that had been playing on his mind all night, Terry said, "About yesterday . . . when I asked you not to tell anyone I was coming today. I hope you didn't think I was sneaking around behind Leanne's back?"

"I didn't think anything," Sue lied, sipping at her tea, determined not to react badly to the mention of his girlfriend.

"I hope not," Terry said quietly. "Because I'm just trying to do the right thing by everyone. I meant what I said yesterday; I am *really* sorry for what happened. But I still think it was the right thing to do. I just regret the way I went about it."

Inhaling deeply, Sue nodded. Well, there it was . . . straight from the horse's mouth. It was over.

Forcing herself to smile when Connor came back, Sue watched as he sat down and started to attack his food again.

"Wow, that's disappearing fast!" she said. "Isn't he a good boy, Dad?"

Happy that he'd had the chance to settle things, because now they all knew where they stood and everyone could move on, Terry said, "Very good. And if you carry on eating like that, you'll get nice and strong." Groaning then, he slapped a hand against his forehead, saying, "Oh, no! Now he'll be so strong he'll hammer me at bowling!"

Laughing, Sue said, "You'd have hammered him anyway, wouldn't you, Con?"

"Never!" Terry scoffed, reaching for the now-empty plate.

Taking out her purse, Sue said, "Leave that. I haven't paid for it yet."

Telling her not to worry about it, Terry took the plate to the counter and settled the bill. Then, coming back, he said, "Right, let's get moving."

Jumping off the chair, Connor pulled his coat on and rushed to the door. Calling him back, Terry said, "Say goodbye to your mam."

Running to her, Connor gave her a kiss, then ran straight back to the door. Telling Sue that he'd bring him back at half-four, Terry followed him out.

Staying where she was, Sue finished her cold tea and glanced at her watch. It was only ten o'clock, so that left her with six and a half hours to fill, but she didn't have a clue what she was going to do with herself. She didn't want to have to go back to the flat to look at Julie's miserable face, but she didn't have any money to entertain herself outside, and it was way too cold to just sit in the park or walk the streets. And she couldn't even go to Pauline's like she'd said she would, to pick up the money that had been collected, because Pauline would want to know where Connor was, and she'd promised Terry that she wouldn't tell anybody. And, anyway, she couldn't risk being seen on the estate, because someone might mention it to Dave, and then he'd wonder how come she'd left Connor alone with the social workers.

Resigned to having to go back to the flat, she got up and traipsed wearily back down the road. She'd just reached the block and was about to open the door when a car pulled up at the kerb behind her. Glancing back when the horn tooted, expecting it to be a taxi for one of the other tenants, she felt the blood drain from her face when she saw Dave grinning back at her through the open window of his car.

"All right, gorgeous," he called out to her. "What's a nice girl like you doing in a dump like this?"

"What are you doing here?" she asked, going over to him, trying to gauge from his eyes whether he'd seen her with Terry just now.

"Hey, don't look too pleased to see me," he quipped. "I might get the wrong idea and think you're happy, or something."

"Sorry," she murmured, slipping her hands into her pockets to hide the guilty shaking. "I just didn't expect you today. I thought we said Monday."

"Damn!" he said, frowning. "Don't tell me I've gone and got my days mixed up?" Laughing then, he said, "Stop panicking. I was only passing by on my way to my mate's. Then I saw this gorgeous bird, and thought, hey, why not stop and chat her up?"

"Oh, right," Sue said, forcing herself to smile now.

"So, where's my little mate?" Dave asked, looking around for Connor.

"Inside with Julie," Sue lied. "I, just, um, just nipped out to . . ." Stopping herself before she said that she'd been to the shop, because he'd want to know why she wasn't carrying anything, she said, "For a walk."

Nodding, Dave said, "Everything all right last night? Get any grief off moody hole?"

"Not yet," Sue said, sighing.

"Just tell her to piss off if she starts," Dave said, glancing at his watch. "Anyway, best get moving. My mate's just moved into a flat round the corner, and I said I'd help him do some painting. Unless . . ." He gazed at her thoughtfully. "You fancy letting me take you for a coffee? Only I'm not exactly looking forward to getting gloss all over my new trainers, and you don't look eager to go back in just yet."

"Won't your mate be expecting you?" Sue asked, thinking that she'd much rather go for a coffee with Dave than face Julie.

"Nah. He knows he'll see me when he sees me," Dave said flippantly. "Anyhow, he's lucky I said I'd do it in the first place, seeing as every other fucker he asked told him to do it himself. Come on . . . what d'y' say?"

Smiling, Sue nodded. "Okay, but only a quick one, because I shouldn't stay out too long. And, I, er, think we need to talk."

"Oh, yeah?" Dave gave her a questioning smile. "And am I going to like what I hear?"

"I think so," she said, smiling coyly as she climbed in beside him and pulled her seat belt on.

CHAPTER
FOURTEEN

Leanne was shivering as she stood in the bus shelter where Zak had told her to meet him. She'd been here for half an hour now, but he still hadn't turned up. She would give him ten more minutes, then she was off — and she didn't care *what* he might have to say about it.

Three minutes later, Zak sauntered up to her.

"About bloody time!" she snapped, standing up and facing him, her expression letting him know that she was mega pissed-off with him. "I've been waiting half a flaming hour."

"I know," Zak said coolly. "I've been watching you."

Screwing her face up in disbelief, Leanne said, "What? *Why?*"

"'Cos I wanted to see how long you'd wait," he said, the slightest of smiles on his handsome face. "And you waited *long*, man, so I reckon you must be well scared."

"Don't talk shit," she hissed, folding her arms defensively. "Why would I be scared of you?"

"Not of me, of what I know," Zak said, the smile sly now. "And you *know* I know, so you can drop the Little Miss Innocent act."

"And you can quit acting like Colombo, you stupid dickhead," Leanne spat. "You don't know anything. I don't even know why I bothered coming."

"Yeah, you do," Zak drawled, holding her gaze.

Rolling her eyes in irritation. Leanne said, "All right, then. Spit it out."

"The night of the fire," Zak said quietly, "your man wasn't with you all night like you said. He went out for a good couple of hours, and you don't know where he went."

"And who told you that?" Leanne said, fronting it out. "The same idiot who told you that he started the fire, I suppose?"

Narrowing his eyes, Zak peered intently back at her. "You're denying it, then? Only I reckon this *person* would be quite happy to back me up if I decided to tell the police. And I don't suppose you'd want that, would you?"

Gritting her teeth, Leanne glowered at him with hatred.

"Didn't think so," he said.

"All right, cut the crap and tell me what you want," Leanne said forcefully. "And don't bother asking for money, because I'm skint."

Laughing softly, Zak said, "Funny how things work out, isn't it? I mean, there's you making out like you're some kind of high-flyer just 'cos you bagged yourself an older man and got your flat all done out on credit. And there's me, who you look down your nose at, making a mint."

"Dealing drugs?" Leanne snorted. "Not the kind of money I'd want in *my* pocket."

"I don't deal," Zak told her truthfully. "I smoke, yeah, but I'm not gonna dirty my hands selling it. Nah, man. Everything I've got, I've earned — like I told you last time. But you've never had a job, have you, so you wouldn't know what it's like to pay your own way."

"Whoopi-doo for you," Leanne drawled, tiring of the conversation. "But if you don't want money, what *do* you want? And hurry up, 'cos I'm freezing."

"What I want," Zak said slowly, "is *you*."

"Don't talk crap," she retorted irritably. "You hate me, and I hate you, so just quit messing about and get this over with."

"I'm not messing," Zak told her, the look in his eyes letting her know that he meant what he was saying.

Frowning, she said, "I don't get you. We *hate* each other. We were nearly fighting back at Goldie's that night."

"Yeah, 'cos you've got a big mouth."

"So, why do you want me then?"

"Dunno." Zak shrugged. "I just do."

"For what?" Leanne demanded, staring at him. "'Cos if you think you're blackmailing me into having sex with you, you can forget it. I'd rather just go home and tell Terry what you're trying to do and let him deal with you."

Shrugging again, Zak said, "If that's how you want to play it, go for it. But you'd best hope you get to him before I get to the police. And don't test me on this, Lee, 'cos I mean it."

Leanne felt as if the sky was falling in on her head. She knew he meant it, she could see it in his eyes. But she couldn't agree to go along with him, because it would destroy her and Terry.

"Why are you doing this?" she asked, her eyes glistening with tears now. "What did I ever do to you?"

"You cheated on me," Zak said calmly. "And don't deny it, because we both know it's true. Maybe not physically, but you must have been checking him out while you were still my girl. You lived on the same road and knew him for years, so if you fancy him now you must have fancied him then. And that's cheating in my book."

"I didn't fancy him," Leanne protested. "I swear to God it wasn't like that. Me and you were finished way before I started liking Terry. Ask Goldie."

"Yeah, right," Zak said scornfully. "Like she's not going to back you up no matter what you say."

"Yeah, all right, she probably would," Leanne conceded. "But not about this. Come on, Zak, think about it. You know what's she's like. She knows how much trouble it's caused, so she'd tell me to admit it and get it over with once and for all, wouldn't she? Anyway, if it *was* true, she'd probably tell me to tell you just to get back at you for the way you treated me."

"I didn't treat you bad," Zak shot back. "Yeah, I made a mistake and went with someone behind your back, but I regretted it, you know I did. You just didn't want to give me a chance to put it right."

"It wasn't just that," Leanne reminded him. "You were always sniffing around other girls, even when I

340

was right there with you. But if I tried to pull you about it, you'd just laugh it off and say I was being paranoid. Or have you forgotten all that?"

"You *were* paranoid," Zak said. "And from what I hear, you haven't changed, because you're giving your new man grief about women now. Or should that be *girls*?" he corrected himself. "'Cos we all know he started *you* off young."

"You're doing it again," Leanne said, swiping at the tears as they began to fall. "Making out like it's dirty, just because you don't like it. But I was nearly seventeen when me and Terry got together."

A woman walked into the bus shelter just then. Seeing the tears on Leanne's face, she glared at Zak. Sucking his teeth, Zak took hold of Leanne's arm and marched her out.

"Pack it in," she protested as he pulled her up the road. "People are watching. Someone will call the police."

"Let them," Zak snapped. "Then maybe I'll just tell them what I know."

Yanking her arm free, Leanne stopped walking. Flinching when he turned back with an angry look on his face, she raised her chin and said, "Go on, then. If you want to give me a slap, do it. Right here in front of everyone. Then see who the police believe."

Peering into her eyes, Zak said, "I'm not going to hit you, you stupid cow."

"Yeah, well, you're going to have to if you expect to get anything out of me," Leanne hissed. "But I warn you now, I'll fight back. And when I'm done, Terry will finish you."

Sneering, because he wasn't in the slightest bit worried about her boyfriend, Zak took his mobile out of his pocket and said, "All right, I gave you a chance. Let's see what your dad's got to say about it."

Blanching, Leanne made a grab for the phone. Swinging it out of reach, Zak said, "What's up? You're not scared, are you?"

"Stop it!" Leanne pleaded. "Please, Zak, you've got it all wrong."

"Well, your dad doesn't seem to think so," Zak said, pressing down on one of the phone's buttons. "He already reckons your fella's guilty."

"All right!" Leanne blurted out. "I'll do it. Whatever you want, I'll do it. Just don't tell my dad. *Please.*"

Smiling, Zak snapped the phone shut. "You mean that?"

"Yes," she cried. "But don't expect me to ever talk to you again after this, because I hate you!"

Inhaling deeply, Zak gazed at her as she sobbed. He felt bad about doing this to her, but it was the only way to make her give him another chance. She would probably resent him for a while, but she'd realise eventually that he'd had her best interests at heart. Terry Day was wrong for her, and if this was what it took to get her to see that, then it had to be done — by whatever means necessary.

Sue's heart was lighter than it had been in a long time when Dave dropped her off back at Julie's flat. Over

342

coffee at the little café he'd taken her to — thankfully not the one she'd been in with Terry — she'd told him that she was willing to give it a go with him. And he'd been so happy that he'd turned to the three little old men who were the only other customers, and the bored-looking woman who was serving, and announced, "She said yes!" as if she'd just agreed to marry him. Which got them a free cup of tea and cream éclair each by way of congratulations.

Glad that she'd made the decision, and relieved that Dave had agreed to give her a bit of time before they told anyone, Sue was on cloud nine when she walked into the flat. But one look at Julie's face told her that the bubble was about to burst.

And boy, *did* it.

"This isn't working," Julie said, straight out, no preamble. "I've tried, but I just can't hack it. You've got to go."

"Just like that?" Sue gasped. "Even though you know we've got nowhere *to* go."

Shrugging, Julie lit a cigarette without offering her one. "Not really my problem," she said coolly. "All I know is, I've done my best to help you out, and you've just taken the piss."

"How?" Sue said. "I haven't done anything. In fact, I've been tiptoeing around you for the past week trying my best not to *breathe* too loud in case it annoyed you. So how's that taking the piss?"

Tutting, because she hadn't expected to have to justify herself, Julie said, "There's all sorts of reasons, Sue. This is *my* flat, but it feels like you and Connor have taken over since you got here. If it's not you moping about, or him stinking the place out, it's all the flaming social workers sticking their noses in where they're not wanted."

"Tell me about it," Sue retorted. "But it's not like I *want* them here, is it?"

"Maybe not, but you're the only reason they *are* here," Julie countered firmly. "And then there's the food, and the bills, 'cos you're not exactly helping out on that score, are you? It's like you expect me to keep you, and it's not on."

"I gave you money last week," Sue reminded her indignantly.

"Yeah, twenty quid," Julie snorted. "And I had to lend you some of that back for nappies. Which is another thing . . ." she went on, a hint of disgust on her face now. "He's *six*, for fuck's sake. What the hell's he still doing in nappies?"

"You know exactly why," Sue muttered, her cheeks flaming now. "So don't dare say it's my fault."

"Maybe not," Julie conceded. "But people finding out where I live is. You had no right fetching that bloke round."

"Isn't that a bit pot calling kettle?" Sue sniped, getting angry now. "Seeing as you bring every Tom, Dick and Harry you meet in the clubs back of a weekend?"

Eyes sparking furiously, Julie said, "You've got a week, then you're out."

"Wow, that long?" Sue drawled, struggling to keep the sarcasm out of her voice. "Good to know who your

344

friends are in times of crisis, eh? And it's not like none of this is *your* fault, or anything. God forbid I should remind you that it wouldn't have happened if you hadn't been so eager to shag a stranger!"

"Don't push it," Julie muttered, stubbing her cigarette out in the ashtray. "I've given you a week, and that's pretty bleedin' generous seeing as I could have just put your bags outside the door."

Pursing her lips, Sue held Julie's gaze for several moments, then turned and walked out. She felt like punching her for being such a bitch, but it wouldn't do any good. And at least she'd given them a week, so there was still a chance that the council would come through in time. Highly unlikely, but a week was still better than nothing.

Marching out of the flat now, she headed into the park and sat down on a bench near the gates. Pulling her jacket collar up around her throat, she shoved her hands into her pockets and waited for Terry to bring Connor back.

Terry was bang on time. Holding Connor's hand when he got out of the car, he carried the two bags of clothes and toys that he'd bought for him over to Sue.

Smiling tightly, she took a last drag on the cigarette she was smoking and tossed the end onto the floor. "Had a good day?"

"We've had loads of fun, haven't we, Connor?" Terry said, squeezing Connor's hand to get him to smile, because he seemed to have gone down since he'd seen his mum. And she looked troubled, too, but he sensed that whatever was going through her head, she wouldn't appreciate him asking. Handing the bags to her now, he said, "I've bought him a few things."

"You didn't have to," she said quietly.

"I wanted to," he said. "He's my boy, and we haven't had much of a chance to spend time together lately."

Taking this as a dig, Sue's lips tightened.

"I didn't mean that the way it probably sounded," Terry told her quickly. "I just meant . . . well, I haven't spent anything on the kids in a while, so I thought I'd spoil him for a change. Don't mind, do you?"

Shaking her head, Sue stood up. "No, I don't mind. And I'm sorry if I made you feel bad. I've just got a bit of a headache." Picking up the bags now, she reached for Connor's hand. "Best get you in out of the cold. Say bye to Daddy."

Bending down to kiss him, Terry felt a tug of sadness. They'd had a great time today, and even though Connor hadn't said a word Terry had really felt as if he was close at times.

"Can I give you a ring mid-week?" he asked, walking with them towards the road. "Arrange another visit?"

Nodding, Sue said, "Yeah, that would be fine. But don't just turn up, because I don't know where we'll be."

Frowning now, Terry watched as she walked Connor across the road. He hoped he hadn't offended her by buying Connor clothes. Obviously she couldn't afford to replace all the stuff they'd lost, but maybe he'd been a bit premature in jumping straight back into the provider role.

No, he told himself, climbing into his car. He wasn't going to feel guilty about that. He always *had* been the provider, and it was her who had stopped him by refusing to take the maintenance when he had offered it. She'd said that she would rather die than take anything from him, and didn't want him to think he was buying the right to see the kids. So if she felt bad about it now, tough.

Not that he was going to get into an argument about it at this early stage. But if he had the money, then he would treat the kids.

Or, rather, *kid*. Because he had no clue when he would next get to treat Nicky.

Sighing, Terry put the car into gear and went home.

He'd made two big decisions today. One: no one was ever going to stop him from seeing his son again. And two: Leanne was going to be a part of their future relationship — whether she or Sue liked it.

Leanne was curled up on the couch watching TV when he walked into the living room. Giving her a nervous smile, praying that she hadn't heard where he'd been today and who with, he said, "Hi. Have you had a good day?"

Forcing herself to smile, Leanne nodded. "Yeah, it was okay. You?"

"Fine," he said, relieved that she hadn't attacked him, because that meant that she probably hadn't found out.

"Cup of tea?" Leanne asked, getting up now and padding through to the kitchen.

"Yeah, great," Terry said, slipping his jacket off. "You been cooking? Something smells good."

"I made lasagne," she called back. "And I got you some of that garlic bread you like."

"Sounds lovely," he said, sitting down. She was acting so nice, he'd be sure that *she*'d been up to something if he didn't know better. But he presumed she was probably just feeling guilty about having spent the day with her dad. Although she needn't have worried, because he was hardly going to object — not when he knew how important it was for a child to see its father.

"Did you go to town?" Leanne asked, bringing his tea through a couple of minutes later and cuddling up next to him.

"Might have known you wouldn't forget that," Terry teased, reaching for his jacket. "Close your eyes and hold your hand out."

"What is it?" she asked, guilt momentarily forgotten in the excitement of knowing she was about to get a present.

Taking something out of his pocket, Terry placed it on her hand. Eyes still closed, Leanne's heart began to thud in her chest as she ran her fingers over the small square box.

"Open it, then," Terry said impatiently.

Opening her eyes now, Leanne's voice was tiny as she asked, "Is this what I think it is?"

"I don't know," Terry said softly. "You'll have to look at it and see."

348

Hands shaking, Leanne flipped the lid back. Gasping when she saw the ruby and diamond ring twinkling back at her, she said, "Oh my God, it's gorgeous."

"You like it?" Terry asked, taking it out of the box and reaching for her hand.

"I love it," she gasped, her eyes glistening as he slipped it onto her finger. "You know which hand that is, though, don't you?"

"I know," Terry murmured.

"But you're still married," she reminded him.

"I know that as well," he said. "But I won't be for ever. And when I'm not . . . well, I thought we might as well stop messing around and go for it. What do you think?"

Unable to look at him as the guilt settled over her again, Leanne bit her lip and gazed down at the ring.

Reaching for her when he saw the tears on her cheeks, Terry held her to him and stroked her hair. He figured she was probably overwhelmed because she hadn't expected this. But he'd surprised himself just as much as he had her, because he hadn't intended to look at rings when he'd headed into town with Connor that morning — and he certainly hadn't intended to spend that much money. But something had clicked when he'd been talking to Sue in the café, and he'd realised that he'd been holding his and Leanne's lives on hold this past year because of guilt. But if Sue could forgive him, it was time he forgave himself. And he'd already committed himself to Leanne, so this just seemed like the next logical step to take.

"I love you," Leanne murmured, her face still buried in his jumper. "You know that, don't you? No matter what happens, or what anyone says, I really do love you."

"Ditto," Terry said softly.

CHAPTER
FIFTEEN

Sue's face spoke volumes when Dave pulled up alongside her at their usual meeting place on Monday morning. Giving her a quizzical look when she'd put Connor onto the back seat and climbed in beside him, he said, "Everything okay? You haven't changed your mind again, have you?"

Shaking her head, Sue flicked a surreptitious glance in Connor's direction to let him know that she didn't want to discuss it now.

"As long as you're sure," he said uncertainly. "Because you know I'd rather you just came right out with it if you have."

"We'll talk later," she muttered, hoping he wasn't going to press her in front of Connor.

Murmuring, "Okay," Dave set off.

Dropping her outside the housing office on Alexandra Road fifteen minutes later, he offered for her to leave Connor in the car with him.

"Best not," she said, when Connor immediately began to whimper. "He's already pissed Julie off, so I don't want him winding you up as well."

Frowning when Sue pulled Connor out of the car and walked him quickly up the ramp, Dave sat back to wait for her, his mind ticking over ten to the dozen.

It had taken weeks to get her this far, and if she'd changed her mind and he had to go through the whole take-as-long-as-you-like routine again, he'd go absolutely fucking crazy. But he would do it if he had to, because he was more than halfway to achieving his goal and there was no way he was dropping the ball now.

It wasn't that he didn't like her, because he did. Well, more fancied than liked, if he was honest, because Dave had never considered it natural for blokes and birds to be mates. They had completely different interests and priorities in life, so he'd always found it best to stay the hell away from them during the day, only coming home in time for a drink and a fuck. But while Carole understood that, Sue seemed to think that he actually liked hearing her whingeing about how crap her life was. And that had started to grate on him, so she'd better be a bloody good shag by the time he got her into bed to justify all the effort he'd put into getting her this far.

But who knew . . . if she *was* good in the sack, he might just consider training her up and keeping her on as a plaything — after he'd done what he'd set out to do and destroyed Terry.

As long as she kept that weird fuck of a son of hers out of his way.

And Dave, like just about everybody else, apart from Sue, Terry, the doctors and Pauline, had no doubt that the boy was putting the silent act on as a means of getting attention. But it wasn't just this about him that irritated Dave. It was the fact that he looked so much like his father. Every time Dave laid eyes on him, it was Terry he saw looking back at him.

Still, it would be easy enough to keep the little shit in line if he had to be around. A hefty backhander with the threat of worse to come usually did the trick.

It was almost two hours before Sue came out again, and Dave could see at a glance that she'd been crying. Groaning to himself, because he was already bored off his skull from having had to sit and wait, he reminded himself why he was doing this and put a caring look on his face.

"What happened?" he asked, getting out of the car to open the back door for Connor. "What did they say?"

"That I've basically got no chance of being rehoused this side of Christmas," she told him, her voice catching as a little sob escaped. Biting her lip, she shook her head, struggling to hold the tears in. "Sorry, I've just been doing this in there, and I swore I wasn't going to do it again."

Telling her that she didn't have to worry about him, that he was here for her, Dave put his arms around her.

"Not here," she hissed, pulling back. "Connor's watching."

Backing off, Dave said, "Fine, but we need to talk, so I'm taking you somewhere where he can play while you tell me what's going on. Okay?"

It wasn't a question, it was a statement, and Sue was too weak to resist. Grateful for his strength because she could feel her life was unravelling by the second, she nodded and climbed back into the car.

Taking them to a McDonald's over in Longsight, where nobody would recognise them and disturb them, Dave sat Sue at a table in a quiet corner. Whisking Connor up into his arms then, he carried him to the counter to order himself and Sue a coffee and Connor a Happy Meal.

Watching as they went, Sue smiled sadly. She'd made the right decision. Now Connor could have two men in his life, both good, strong men who would protect him. She just prayed that Dave didn't get too attached and expect her to exclude Terry, because it wouldn't be fair.

Grinning broadly as he carried Connor, every inch the proud father, Dave felt him struggling and heard the whimpering and gave his legs a tight squeeze, hissing through his teeth, "Keep that up and you'll be sorry, you little mardy arse."

Stiffening with fear, Connor stayed stock-still in his arms as they reached the counter. Dave had really hurt him just now, pressing on the bruises that his own son had created. But if Connor had been scared of Fred, he was absolutely terrified of Dave.

Carrying him over to the indoor play area when he had collected the order, Dave plonked Connor down in the ball-pit and told him to stay there until he gave him permission to get out.

"And make like you're having fun," he snarled. 'Cos if you upset your mam, you'll have me to answer to."

Plonking the Happy Meal down on the table beside the pit then, Dave went back to Sue, still smiling, but with a light of fondness in his eyes now.

354

"Great kid, that," he said, sighing as he sat down facing her. "Wish my lads were as well behaved. But with a mother like theirs, it's no wonder they've turned out like they have. He's lucky to have a lovely woman like you as his mam."

"Thanks," Sue murmured, feeling the tears starting up again, because no matter how bad she was feeling, he always made her feel special and secure.

"Anyway," he said now, reaching for her hand across the table. "Let's have it. And no bullshit about how you're fine, because you were already upset when I picked you up this morning. So, what's going on?"

Exhaling wearily, Sue stirred her coffee slowly with her free hand. "Julie's told me to get out," she said after a moment. "When you dropped me off yesterday, she just came right out with it."

"Bitch," Dave hissed, frowning deeply. "Why?"

"You," Sue murmured. Then, correcting herself in case he thought she was blaming him, she said, "Well, not so much *you*; more *me* for bringing you up to the flat."

"I didn't even come in," Dave said indignantly. "What's her fucking problem?"

"Just the fact that I brought someone from the estate there," Sue told him, shrugging. "She's got a thing about people knowing where she lives."

She didn't bother mentioning that she'd already had a go at Julie about all the men *she* had taken back there in the year since she'd known her, because then Dave would guess that Sue had been with their mates and think she was a slag — just like everyone said.

"Told you to get your own place from the kick-off," Dave was saying now.

"I am trying," Sue reminded him quietly. "But the council reckon I'm not in urgent need because I'm staying at Julie's."

"But you told them she's kicking you out?"

"Yeah, and they said I'll need to prove it by getting a letter from her telling me to leave by a certain date."

"So get one."

"I will. But they still might not find me anywhere. They reckon I'll have to go into a hostel."

"Well, that's good, isn't it?" Dave peered into her eyes. "The way you were talking, I thought you were going to be out on the streets, or something."

"Might as well be," Sue muttered, swiping at a stray tear with the back of her hand. "Me and Terry had to live in a hostel when we first had Nicky, and it's the worst place I've ever lived in. There were mice and cockroaches running all over the beds, and you couldn't leave anything in your room without someone breaking in and nicking it."

"Yeah, but that was a long time ago," Dave said, trying to cheer her up and make her see the positive side of it. "They'll have cleaned up all that kind of shit by now."

"Will they hell," Sue said, a note of defeat in her voice. "There'll probably be rats by now. And there was a girl in the housing office just now, kicking off about them still not giving her a house even though she's been in the hostel for over a year. And she had two

356

babies, so if they've left *her* there that long, they'll probably leave me even longer."

"No, they won't," Dave said confidently. "She probably deserved to be put there. But it wasn't your fault that you lost your house, so they'll have you in and out in no time."

"They won't," Sue said flatly, the expression in her eyes hopeless. "They've told me I'm not a priority case. And because I've only got one child, I'm only entitled to a two-bed flat."

"You've got *two* kids," Dave reminded her, as if she'd forgotten.

A touch of irritation in her eyes now, Sue said, "I do *know* that, thanks. But apparently Nicky's not an issue because she's gone missing. And, according to them, it's intentional on her part, so they've got no duty towards her. And it doesn't help that she's sixteen soon."

Exhaling loudly, Dave said, "Well, you are in a bit of a pickle, aren't you?"

It was such a ridiculous phrase, and it sounded even more absurd coming out of the mouth of a big strong streetwise man like Dave Miller, that Sue couldn't help but laugh.

Looking into her eyes, Dave smiled. This was how he liked her, without all the moaning and the crying. Just laughing softly, and looking all girly and feminine.

"I've got an idea," he said, the words springing out of his mouth as soon as they entered his head.

"Oh?" Sue sounded cautiously hopeful.

"Move in with me," Dave said, shrugging as he added, "Just until you get your own place. Save you having to go into a hostel, wouldn't it?"

"No, I couldn't," Sue murmured, dipping her gaze as a blush spread across her cheeks. "Thanks for the offer, but it wouldn't be right."

"Why not?" Dave persisted, wondering why this hadn't occurred to him before now.

Reminding him that they'd only just become a couple, and that they had only kissed twice, Sue said, "I just don't think I'm ready for anything else yet."

"Behave," Dave drawled, a teasing note to his voice. "We're together now, so it's not like we won't do it at some point. But if that's what's worrying you, forget it, 'cos you can have your own room, if you want. And you can stay as long as you like. No strings."

"What about Carole?" Sue asked, surprised that she was even considering it. But while it wasn't what she would have wanted until she and Dave were sure that they were going to work out, she had to admit that it was better than the alternative.

"What about her?" Dave said, drawing his head back and frowning. "I'm not talking about *her* house, I'm talking about mine."

"I didn't know you had one," Sue said, embarrassed again, because it hadn't even occurred to her to wonder where he'd been living since he and Carole had split up.

"I haven't," Dave said, shrugging. "I moved in with me dad when I left the bitch. But he's got to be ninety if he's a day, so he won't bother you. He never even comes out of his room any more; just lies in bed getting me to fetch and carry for him."

"Oh, that's awful," Sue said sadly. "Is he ill?"

"Nah, he's just lazy," Dave chuckled. "But seriously, he won't bother you. In fact, he'll probably enjoy having a woman about the house again. Hasn't been the same since my mam died."

"What about Connor?" Sue asked, gazing across at her son. Frowning when she saw that he was exactly where Dave had left him, she tutted softly. God only knew what was wrong with him now, but he looked absolutely ridiculous sitting alone in the middle of the sea of multicoloured balls. Any normal child would have been rolling around and having fun. But not Connor. He was as stiff as a statue, his huge, dark eyes staring vacantly off into space.

"He won't disturb the old man, if that's what you're worried about," Dave said. "He's not exactly loud, is he? And, anyway, my dad's deaf as a doorknob, so it won't make any difference to him *who*'s in the house."

"I don't know," Sue said, biting her lip. "I'm really grateful for the offer, but I don't know if it's worth the hassle we'll get."

"Don't you worry about any of that," Dave said firmly. "If anyone's got a problem with it, they can come to me — if they *dare*." Pausing, he dipped his head to peer into her lowered eyes. "Come on, Sue, if we're going to give this a go, then we're going to have to come out sooner or later. And I know you wanted to wait a bit, but you're not exactly in the best position right now, are you? And no one even knows where I'm living, so you wouldn't have to worry about anyone coming round uninvited."

"Carole must have figured out that you'd have gone to your dad's after you left her," Sue said quietly. "And she must know where it is, because you were together for long enough."

"Carole's got no idea," Dave assured her. "Fact, if you asked her, she'd probably tell you that my dad was dead, 'cos that's how much she knows. My parents met her once, when we first started going out, and they hated her, so I never took her round to the house again. Anyhow, they moved out of Rusholme years back, and she doesn't know which area they went to, so it's not a problem." Shrugging now, he said, "There's nothing else I can say, except the offer's there if you want it." Squeezing her hand now, he added, "And I'd really like it if you said yes, because I really like *you*. Okay?"

"Okay," Sue murmured, gazing back at him with affection. "I'll think about it."

Winking at her, Dave said, "I've got a good feeling about this, Sue. You and me, we're going to be good together."

Sue felt the butterflies start up in her stomach, and she was surprised because that usually only happened with Terry. So maybe Dave was right . . . maybe they *were* going to be good together.

She certainly hoped so, because he was exactly the kind of man she needed in her life. Strong, protective, passionate, kind. And he genuinely cared about her kids — which was exactly what Connor needed, too.

CHAPTER
SIXTEEN

"You don't have to go," Julie said, a guilty look on her face as she followed Sue into the bedroom at the end of the week. "I was due on when I said it, and you know what a bitch I can be. I get a right temper on me about the stupidest things, but I don't mean half of what I say — you know that. Come on, mate, let's not fall out like this."

"It doesn't matter," Sue assured her, giving her a small smile of forgiveness. "Honestly, I'm not mad at you. You were right. We *were* taking over, and it wasn't fair."

"So stay, then," Julie said, her eyes glistening with tears. "Please, mate, it won't feel the same without you. You and me have been like sisters this last year, and I'm going to miss you."

Thinking that sisters didn't do to each other what Julie had done to her by not telling her the truth from the start, Sue shoved the last few of Connor's clothes into a bin bag and shook her head.

"I'll miss you, too, but it's better this way. Your flat's too small for all three of us. And the council were just going to leave us here, so you might never have got your space back."

"I don't care," Julie insisted. "I'd rather know you were safe here with me than living in some scummy hostel."

"We'll be fine," Sue lied. "I went to see it yesterday, and it's really clean. Anyway, it's only temporary until they find us somewhere permanent." Pausing now, she bit her lip before asking the favour she'd been trying to get the courage up all week to ask. "Thing is," she said. "I really don't want to get my benefits messed about again while they've only just sorted them. So do you think I could carry on getting them from here? Just until I get my own place."

"Will they let you do that if they know you're living at the hostel?" Julie asked, thinking it highly unlikely.

"I don't know," Sue admitted, not having thought it through that thoroughly. "But I can ask, can't I? And they might treat it as a special case, what with Nicky still being missing."

"Doubt it," Julie said, shrugging as she added, "But if they say yes, I don't mind. I'd still rather you just told them to forget it and stay here, though. Hostels are for losers."

Chuckling softly, Sue said, "No, they're not. They're for people like me who haven't got any choice."

"But you *have* got a choice." Julie pounced. "You can stay here."

Sighing, because she wasn't making this easy, Sue said, "You've done enough for me already, and it's time to move on." Tying a knot in the bag now, she gave Julie a hug. "Thanks for everything, you've been a good mate. And we'll still see each other, so don't worry about that. I just need to start standing on my own two feet again or I'm never going to get anywhere."

Chins wobbling as she struggled to control the tears, Julie flapped her hands in a gesture of surrender. "Okay, but you make sure you ring me as soon as you're settled. And make some friends quick so you can get a babysitter, and we'll start going out again."

Thinking that she would rather die than ever go out on the town with Julie again, Sue nodded. Picking up her bags then, she walked through to the living room and jerked her head at Connor.

Clutching at the small teddy that Tina had sent over for him a few days earlier, Connor reluctantly slid off the couch. He hadn't particularly enjoyed being here, but he'd rather stay here than go to Dave's house any day.

He'd wanted to scream when he'd heard his mum lying to Julie, telling her that they were going to a hostel. He'd wanted to run in and tell Julie where they were really going and beg her to let him stay with her instead. But the words wouldn't have come out, and he'd just have made his mum mad, because she'd already warned him not to tell anyone.

Just like she'd warned him not to be mardy in front of Dave, because then he might kick them out like Julie had.

Sniffing loudly, Julie reached down and gave Connor a big cuddle as he traipsed miserably past her.

"Bye, squirt," she whispered, the tears in her voice trickling into his ear. "And I'm sorry Auntie Julie's been a cow lately, but she never stopped loving you — you know that, don't you?"

Peering up at her, Connor tried to project his thoughts into her head through her eyes.

Please let me stay. Tell my mum you want to keep me . . . Please . . .

But it didn't work.

Ruffling his hair, Julie turned him around and gave him a little push in the direction of the door, saying, "Go on, then. Get moving before she goes without you."

Resisting with every ounce of his being, Connor twisted round and threw his arms around her fat waist.

Laughing sadly, sure that he was just letting her know that he was going to miss her, Julie prised his hands off and pushed him firmly out into the hall.

Squatting down beside him at the front door, she gave his cheek a gentle pinch, saying, "I'll see you soon, so you be a good boy for your mum." Whispering now, she added, "And tell your mum to get that man to drop you off at the end of the road. She might think he's her friend, but I don't like him, and I don't think she should be telling him where you're living. Okay?"

"Come on, Connor!" Sue called impatiently up the stairs just then. "The bags are in the car, now we're just waiting for you. And Dave's got things to do, so get a move on!"

Shoulders sagging, because there was no point trying to prolong it, Connor turned and walked down the stairs.

364

Shaking her head as she watched him go, Julie closed her front door. That poor boy didn't want to go into a hostel, but if Sue was too damn stubborn to accept an apology and do the right thing by him, there was nothing that Julie could do about it.

"All set?" Dave said when Connor was safely buckled in on the back seat.

Nodding, Sue pulled her own seat belt on and smiled. Despite her trepidation when he'd first suggested this, she was excited now. The more she'd thought about it over the past week, the more she'd realised that it was the ideal solution to her problems. Especially now that Julie had agreed to let her carry on claiming her benefits from the flat, because now she wouldn't have her money cut by declaring herself as living with a man. And therefore there would be no complications when she eventually got her own place again. She'd just change her address and make a new claim for housing benefit and council tax, and it would all be sorted.

She still had the problem of the social workers to get around. But if they kept calling round at the flat and getting no answer — and Julie would definitely ignore them — they would eventually give up and go and find some other poor family to harass.

Which just left the problem of what she was going to tell Terry.

She'd already put off the idea of him picking Connor up this Sunday by telling him the same lie that she'd told Dave last week: that the social workers were coming round for the day. But she'd agreed to meet up with him the following Sunday — back in Cheetham Hill, because she hadn't told him about moving yet. So she had just over a week to come up with a good excuse for getting out of Dave's house for the day. And then she'd have a good few hours to think about what she was going to tell Terry when he brought Connor back.

But for now, she just wanted to forget about all the lies she was having to tell and concentrate on the immediate future. So, settling back in her seat, she gazed out of the window as they drove — wandering how far his father's house was as they went right through town, past the Fitton and Grafton estates in Rusholme, and on towards Didsbury.

"Where on earth is it?" she asked when she realised that they were about to go onto the motorway.

"Wythenshawe," Dave said, giving her a side-grin. "Far enough out that no one can find me, but close enough that I can drive back any time I want. But don't worry, it's not the council-estate part. It's country."

"I didn't know there was any country in Wythenshawe," Sue murmured, feeling a little uneasy as the Manchester she knew like the back of her hand receded into the distance.

"Not *country* country," Dave laughed. "Just a bit off the beaten track, so to say."

He wasn't wrong, as Sue soon discovered.

It was a small detached farmworker's cottage, and it was barely visible from the rough lane they had to travel up to get to it, masked by a sprawling mess of overgrown trees and bushes.

"It's a wreck," Dave warned her as he turned through the gate and drove up the bumpy path. "The old man inherited it years back, and hasn't bothered doing anything to it since. But soon as he's gone, I've got big ideas for it."

Glancing up at the house as they pulled in beneath the ramshackle porch at the side, Sue felt her heart sink like a stone. It really was a wreck. And not one of the ones you saw on those auction shows on TV, which looked fantastic when they were renovated and got sold for millions, but one of the dingy old ones that nobody wanted to touch, with creepy little rooms and long narrow corridors — and probably an outside loo and no running hot water.

She wasn't far off the mark.

Stepping through into a small enclosed porch when Dave unlocked the side door, she struggled not to wrinkle her nose as the smell of mildew assaulted her. And there were other smells floating about on the air, too; rotten scents that reminded her of the bins at the back of the market, and something almost animal-like.

"I know it's a tip," Dave said, dropping his keys down onto the ledge behind the door and opening another door into the kitchen. "But I honestly think I'll make a mint off it one day."

Sue thought he was living in a dream world if he ever thought he'd make money from a dump like this, but her smile hid her absolute horror as she looked around the kitchen. The cupboards were filthy and falling apart; as was the sink, which was like a graveyard for plates and cups, all heaped together and bearing the slime and caked-on debris of whatever had been left on them when they'd been put there in the last century.

"He's a dirty old bastard," Dave said, blaming his father as if he himself had played no part in the decay. "Anyway, come and see the rest of it, then you can put your stuff away."

The rest of the house was as bad as the kitchen. Mangy old furniture nestled among a mess of newspapers, old cups and dishes, overflowing waste-paper bins, and ashtrays.

Surprisingly, Dave's own room was spotless. His bed was made, and there was a large flat-screen TV and an expensive stereo system. His clothes were all ironed and hung up, and the scent of his aftershave hung sweetly in the air, the freshness of which was due to this being the only room in the house where the window was actually open.

"The old man's not allowed in here," Dave told her when he'd unlocked the door and showed her in. "Everywhere he goes, he stinks the place up and makes a mess, so you have to keep him out if you want to keep it straight. But don't worry, I've already put a lock on your room."

Clutching at Connor's hand, Sue nodded, her heart yearning to be back in Julie's tiny, cramped flat. Or even the hostel, because either place would be better than this depressing cesspit of a house.

Hearing a shuffling sound behind her when Dave ushered her back out onto the landing, she turned her head sharply, half expecting to see a rat rummaging around in the filth. A shabby-looking old man was standing in the doorway of the room next door and as he peered at Sue, his faded eyes seemed to send out a message. Shock, fear, annoyance — she didn't know. But it certainly wasn't a welcome.

"What's up?" Dave said sharply, his chin jerking upwards as he looked at his father.

Shaking his head, Jack Miller dropped his gaze and went back into his room.

"Nutter," Dave muttered. "I told him you were coming to stay for a bit, but he must have forgotten."

"He's all right about it, isn't he?" Sue asked, acutely aware that this was the old man's house and that she shouldn't be here if he didn't want her to be. In fact, it would be a relief to use his reluctance about having her here as an excuse to get the hell out.

"Course he is," Dave assured her. "Anyway, this is your room," he said now, squeezing past her to get to the door of the last room on the landing. "It's only small, but it'll do for now." Whispering now, he added, "If you're still here when the old fucker pegs it, you can have his room, 'cos that's bigger, and Connor can keep this one."

It chilled Sue to hear him talking so glibly about his father dying, but she supposed he must have his reasons. It couldn't be easy for a man like him, who obviously liked being clean and orderly, judging by his room, to have to tolerate living with someone as dirty and lazy as his dad.

Following Dave into her room when he unlocked it now, she was glad to see that it was as tidy as Dave's, although there was far less furniture in it, and no ornaments or knick-knacks of any kind. Just a bed, a chest of drawers, a wardrobe, and a chair.

"The mattress is fairly old," Dave told her, handing her the key. "But it's clean, and I bought you some new sheets and a duvet, and that. Sorry there's no TV," he went on. "But you can come and watch mine at night when Connor's in bed. And Connor can watch the downstairs one in the day," he added, letting her know that the invitation into his room extended only to her. "Anyway," he finished, rubbing his hands together. "How about you make a coffee and get yourself used to where everything is while I get your bags out of the car?"

Standing in the kitchen a few minutes later, Sue looked around in despair. There was no way she was touching anything while it was in this state; and *no* way she was drinking out of one of these filthy cups. But she could hardly say that to Dave when he'd been kind enough to let her stay. So she rolled up her sleeves and tentatively opened the cupboard under the sink — surprised to find several bottles of cleaning fluids, a half-empty pack of sponges, and a dusty box of rubber gloves.

Guessing that they were leftovers from when Dave's mum had still been alive, Sue pinched a pair of the gloves out with her fingernails. Shaking them vigorously in case they had spiders or bugs inside the fingers, she slipped them on. Feeling better already, she removed the dishes from the sink and stacked them on the ledge. Then, dousing the sink with bleach, she set about scrubbing it.

Dave came in just then, carrying three of the bin bags, while Connor followed miserably with the last one. Grinning when he saw what Sue was doing, he said, "Now that's what we like to see, isn't it, Connor? A woman who knows her place."

Smiling and frowning at the same time as she peered round at him, Sue said, "You'd best be joking, Dave Miller!"

Winking cheekily, he said, "Course I am. I'm just glad you felt comfortable enough to get stuck in without all that usual *is it all right if I open this cupboard*, or *do you mind if I use that plate* rubbish." Then, eyes twinkling, he jerked his head at Connor, saying, "Come on, let's get this stuff up to your room while your mam gets on with her job."

Chuckling when Sue flicked the sponge at him, sending a spray of foam across the room, Dave lurched out. Glancing plaintively at Sue, Connor pleaded with his eyes for her to come with them and save him from having to be alone with Dave. But she waved her soapy hand at him, hissing, "Hurry up. Don't let him do it all himself or he'll think you're ungrateful."

Pointing to a corner of the bedroom when Connor joined him, Dave told him to put the bag he was carrying over there.

Shaking from head to toe, Connor did as he was told. Dave hadn't said anything nasty to him since that day at McDonald's last week, but he was still terrified of him.

"That's a good lad," Dave said quietly, looking down at him. "And if you just carry on doing as you're told, we'll be fine. But you're in my house now, so I don't want to hear any of that whingeing you've been doing lately. Right?"

Nodding quickly, Connor stared up at him with wide eyes.

"Good," Dave said, seeming satisfied. "Because you've been acting like too much of a baby for my liking, and it's time you started being a man. So no more whining and crying, and no more grunting at your mam, 'cos she's got enough to put up with without you upsetting her."

Nodding again, Connor waited to see if there was more. But Dave had finished with the rules. Jerking his head at Connor, he walked out of the room, saying, "Let's go see how your mam's getting on with that coffee. Then if you're good, you can stop in and watch telly while I take her to get a bit of shopping. And you can bet your life she's already making a list, 'cos that's what women do: demand, demand, demand."

Connor didn't really understand what Dave was getting at, but he sensed it wasn't good. Although Dave sounded quite nice again, like he'd used to sound before he got angry that day, so maybe he was only joking.

Following him back down the stairs, Connor peered nervously into all the dark corners they passed. He didn't want to stay here on his own, knowing that that creepy old man was in the room upstairs. But there was no way he was going to whinge to get his mum to take him along, because Dave would get mad. Anyway, if they were only going shopping, they wouldn't be gone too long. And, scary as it was, he'd rather be here than in Dave's car, because he felt sick every time his mum made him get into it, worrying that Fred would spot them and batter him for it when he eventually went back to school. And he didn't even want to think about what Fred would do if he found out that Connor was living at his dad's house.

No, not living, he corrected himself; *staying*. Because that was all they were doing, according to his mum: just staying for a little while, until the council gave them their own house. Back on the old estate, with any luck. Near his dad.

Connor couldn't wait.

"I need a mop," Sue said as soon as Dave walked into the kitchen. "And some more washing-up liquid, because this one's rubbish. Oh, and the milk's off, so I couldn't make you that coffee."

"See?" Dave smiled down at Connor. "Am I always right, or am I always right? What was I just saying about women and lists?"

"Oh, I see," Sue laughed, relieved that they seemed to be getting on so well. "Ganging up on me already, are you?"

Dave's father heard Sue's laughter floating up from below and pursed his wrinkled lips. He'd actually seen her a few times when he'd still lived in Rusholme, but he hadn't recognised her today because she'd been a teenager then, and just one of numerous girls who had occasionally walked home from school with David and his gang.

David had always preferred the company of boys, and there was a time when Jack had wondered if he was a pooftah, and all the aggressive, trouble-making behaviour was just his way of disguising it. But it wasn't. David just preferred male company — and used women for sex.

He'd met his match in that Carole one that he'd had the kids with, though, and she'd lasted a good deal longer than most of his tarts. The one time Jack and Mary had met her they'd known that she was as bad as David, so they hadn't been surprised that their sons had turned out to be loutish, ill-mannered replicas of him. But Leanne was a different kettle of fish. A beautiful, wilful child, she had been their favourite from the off — just as she was David's. And Jack still had a soft spot for her, even though he hadn't seen her in years. But he wasn't in any rush to go looking for her, because he had no doubt that she'd probably be just like her mother by now.

Hearing the front door slamming shut, Jack narrowed his eyes and listened out for David's car. Hearing the distinctive crunching sound of tyres crushing gravel a few seconds later, he exhaled wearily.

Jack's older brother Ernie had inherited this house from their dad, and when he'd died it had been passed down to Jack. And he and Mary had jumped at the chance to move into it, despite the fact that it had been almost as much of a hovel then as it was today. It was the perfect retreat for them to see out their remaining years in peace — away from David and all the trouble that seemed to linger in his wake.

David hadn't bothered them too much over the next few years, too busy with his own life to pay more than the occasional visit. And only then when he needed to tap a few quid out of his mother, if a deal had gone wrong or he'd gambled a bit too much away. But since Mary had died, Jack had scarcely laid eyes on him in years.

Then, *wham*! He leaves Carole and turns up with his bags, declaring that he might as well move in and get used to the place, seeing as how it was going to be his soon enough anyway.

It depressed Jack to know that his son was waiting so eagerly for him to die. And even more so to know that it wasn't going to happen any time soon. But what could you do when your body was determined to carry on functioning as usual? And he refused to even think about speeding the process along by artificial means — although David probably had more than enough foreign substances lying around in his room to make it very quick and painless. But Jack could never do something as sinful as that and risk losing the chance to meet up with Mary again on the other side. So he struggled on: despising his disrespectful son more with every passing day, and rarely venturing out of his room unless he thought he had the house to himself.

Like now.

Holding tightly onto the banister rail now, Jack eased himself slowly down the stairs, his bones creaking and cracking with every step. Irritated to hear the sound of the TV before he reached the bottom, he was muttering about the waste of electricity as he pushed the living room door open. Walking across to switch the TV off, he caught sight of Connor out of the corner of his eye and hesitated, his finger still hovering over the knob. If it had been one of David's boys, they would have yelled at him to leave it on — and called him a few choice names to boot, despite the fact that they were only eight and thirteen years of age. But this boy looked petrified.

"You watching this, son?" Jack asked, his croaky old voice sounding odd to his own ears, never mind the boy's, because he rarely used it these days except to mutter to himself under his breath.

Getting no reply, he left the TV on and went over to his chair.

"So, who are you, then?" he asked, taking his tobacco pouch out of his pocket and rolling himself a cigarette. "I'm David's dad, Mr Miller," he went on when Connor still didn't speak. "And I take it your mummy is David's new lady friend, is she?"

Tutting softly when he got absolutely no response, Jack squinted at Connor. Apart from the terror, there was something dark and sad in the boy's eyes, and Jack hoped it had nothing to do with David. He liked to play the big I am; the life and soul of every party; the charmer. But he was a nasty little bugger behind the façade, and he detested weakness — especially in lads. He liked them to be rough and rude, and capable of scaring the shit out of everyone — like his pair. But this little one looked like a cry-baby, and David wouldn't like that.

376

Glancing quickly around now, to make sure that David hadn't sneaked back in, Jack said, "Is there anything wrong, son? Only you don't look too happy, if you don't mind me saying. And if there's anything you want to talk about, I'm a pretty good listener."

Aware that he was staring at the man, but unable to drag his eyes away because he'd never seen anyone as old and wrinkly before, Connor didn't so much as move his head. The man sounded kind, but Connor didn't trust him. He was Dave's dad, so it might be a trick. Dave could be hiding somewhere, waiting to pounce when Connor talked, so he could prove that he'd been lying all along and get his mum to send him away.

Giving up, Jack lit his roll-up and smoked it in silence. The TV programme that had been on when he came in had finished now, and an old western starring John Wayne had started up. It was one of Jack's all-time favourites, but the boy was making him feel too uneasy to enjoy it. Sitting on the sofa as stiff as a poker, his eyes so big and dark in his pale little face, he reminded Jack of one of the children out of *Village Of The Damned*. So, finishing his cigarette, he went back upstairs to watch the film on his little black and white portable instead.

Connor gasped for breath when the man had gone. Lately, when he got scared, he'd started to make funny wheezing noises. His mum hadn't mentioned it, so she mustn't have heard him doing it yet. But when she did, she'd hate it, he was sure. Just like she hated all the

377

other noises he couldn't help making. So now, when it happened, he held his breath.

And that was why he was glad the man had gone, because he'd held it for so long this time that he'd started to feel really peculiar. His head had gone all tingly and buzzy, and everything had started to go black around the edges of his eyes.

Feeling reasonably normal again, his brow soon puckered into a frown when he felt the tell-tale signs of needing a wee. His mum had stopped putting nappies on him during the day, telling him that he was a big boy and shouldn't need them any more — and that he'd best not let Dave know that he was still wearing them at night while they were staying with him, or else.

Without the security of the nappy, Connor knew that he would have to get up and go to the toilet asap. But the bathroom was upstairs next to Dave's dad's room, and he really didn't want to go up there. There was another one that Dave had pointed out to them when they'd first arrived, but that was in a little brick shed outside, and he didn't know if he was allowed to go outside. But if he didn't he would wet himself right there on the couch, and that would be awful, because there would be no way of hiding it or cleaning it up in time.

Deciding to risk it, Connor eased the living room door open and crept back out through the kitchen and the porch. Making a dash for the shed, he pushed the door open, squealing with fear when a huge spider dropped down in front of his face. Fortunately, he'd already pulled his zip down, so when the wee immediately began to squirt out, he was able to aim it straight into the dirty toilet pan.

Pleased with himself for controlling it, he went back inside. He wished he could tell his mum when she got back, because she'd be really proud of him. But he couldn't speak, so he'd just have to content himself with knowing that he'd done it, and keep the victory to himself.

Hearing shuffling sounds on the ceiling, which told him that the old man was still upstairs, Connor wandered over to the window. Easing the dirty net back at one corner, he gazed out at the garden in astonishment. Their garden back at home had been just about big enough to swing a bat around in, but this one was vast. And there were no fences dividing it from someone else's, there were just rows of gnarly old trees, and a field of grossly overgrown grass, with a mess of brambles joining everything together like an enormous spider's web. And towards the rear, which seemed to be miles away, there was a partially visible roof of something that Connor presumed was some kind of shed or outhouse.

Jumping when he saw a movement in the bushes to the left of the window, he peered at it intently. There seemed to be something furry moving slowly in there between the roots, but he couldn't quite make out what it was.

Catching sight of a bobtail a few seconds later, he almost cried out with delight. He'd only ever seen rabbits on TV or in books before, and had never seen a real live one, and he was excited, because it was so much more exotic than a cat or a dog.

Watching it now as it snuffled through the undergrowth, Connor felt like his heart was going to burst right out of his chest when it hopped out into a clearer spot. It was so beautiful, its fur all brown and soft-looking, with little speckles of pure white every now and then.

Tapping softly on the window to get its attention, he held his breath when it stopped moving and seemed to look straight at him. Its eyes were huge and dark, just like his; and its nose was tiny and sweet and twitchy.

Wishing he could go out and touch it, just to see if it was as soft as it looked, Connor sighed when it went about its business and disappeared from view.

He looked out for a few more minutes, hoping that it would come back out. But it didn't, so he went back to the couch and tried to watch the film, which was at a loud point now; lots of cowboys and Indians chasing each other round on horses.

Yawning, he rested his head on the cushion.

"Look what Dave's got for you," Sue said, her voice chirpier than it had been for a long time as she opened the living room door a short time later. Seeing Connor lying fast asleep on the couch, she rushed in and patted the cushion beneath him. Breathing a sigh of relief when she found that it was dry, she smiled when Dave popped his head around the door.

"Flat out," she whispered.

"Must be all the excitement," he said quietly, jerking his head at her to come back out. "Leave him, he'll be all right."

"I was thinking to wake him up," Sue said, glancing back worriedly as she followed Dave into the kitchen. She didn't know how long Connor had been asleep already, and didn't want to risk leaving him too much longer because he definitely would wet himself at some point. He always did when he was sleeping.

"In a bit," Dave said, pulling her into his arms and kissing her.

"I want to show him what you got," she gasped when he finally released her. "Please, Dave. I can't wait to see his little face when he sees it. And there's plenty of time for all this later, when he's in bed."

"Go on, then," Dave relented, giving her an indulgent smile. "But don't forget what you just said, 'cos I won't."

Blushing when she felt the tingle between her legs, because it was happening every time she kissed him now, Sue grabbed his hand and pulled him back into the living room.

Kneeling down beside the couch, she gave Connor a gentle shake, saying, "Wake up, Con . . . look what Dave's bought for you."

Opening his eyes, Connor looked up groggily into hers. Then, jumping when he saw Dave standing behind her, he swallowed loudly. Had he wet himself? Was he in trouble?

"All right, little fella," Dave said, squatting down beside Sue now and taking the small box from her hand. "We thought you might need this to keep you amused while you're staying here."

Peering down at the box when Dave handed it to him, Connor's eyes widened. He couldn't believe it. He'd wanted a Nintendo DS for *ages*, but his mum hadn't been able to afford one.

"What do you say?" Sue prompted.

Gazing mutely up at Dave, Connor blinked exaggeratedly.

"Hey, did you see that?" Dave laughed. "He just said thanks with his eyes."

Thrilled that Connor was making such an effort to communicate with Dave, Sue gave him a big kiss.

Pleased with himself, because he'd just realised that his mum was desperate for him to stay on Dave's good side, which in turn meant that he would be staying on hers, Connor smiled back at her. And then he smiled at Dave — although it was harder to keep the smile in his eyes now, because there was something so scary in Dave's.

Repulsed by the sight of Terry's little mini-me gurning at him, Dave said, "Right, well, you show him how to play his game while I have a word with my dad. Then we'll give him his dinner and head off when you're ready."

Hearing this, the smile slid off Connor's face and he peered worriedly up at his mum when Dave left the room. Seeing the fear in his eyes, Sue said, "Don't worry, we're not going to be out for long. Dave's just taking me to the local for a couple of drinks to celebrate us moving in. You won't be on your own, because he's asking his dad to watch you. And you were all right with him when we went shopping, so you'll be fine. Anyway," she added, tapping the box he was still clutching, "You've got this now, so you can just stay in your room and play with it. You don't even have to see his dad if you don't want to."

Sighing resignedly, Connor gazed down at the box. He supposed he'd have to get used to her going out now that they were living with Dave, because that was what adults liked to do. And like she'd said, at least he'd have the DS to keep him occupied, so it wasn't like he was going to be bored.

Giving him one of the cuddles that felt so nice to him because they had been so few and far between lately, Sue laid her face softly on his hair, murmuring, "I know it's not perfect, sweetheart, but at least we've got a roof over our heads until we get our own house. And we will get one, I promise. But until we do, I need you to be a good boy and do as Dave says. Just one thing . . ." she went on, really whispering now, "When you see Daddy, you can't tell him where we are, or he'll get upset. And we don't want to upset him, do we? So we'll have to pretend that we're still at Julie's. Okay?"

Too warm in her arms to worry much about what she was asking of him, Connor nodded. He didn't like lying to his dad, but it wasn't really a lie if he didn't say the actual words. And, anyway, if it made his mum happy, then Dave might be nice to him, too.

Taking a bath while Sue fed Connor and got him ready for bed, Dave scowled every time his flesh touched the enamel. He hated baths and would usually go to the gym and take a shower there, because the thought of sitting in a hot soup of dead skin cells and bacteria from his arse disgusted him. And he didn't even want to think about what remnants of his *father* might be clinging to his body when he got out.

He couldn't wait to rip the bath out and shove in a high-tech walk-in shower. But he refused to spend any money on the place while his dad was still alive, because he wouldn't put it past the fucker to let him do it up and then sell it out from under his nose and piss off to some high-security retirement home where Dave wouldn't be able to get at him.

It would be simpler just to kill him, and the thought had crossed Dave's mind on more than one occasion. But he knew he'd never be able to do it. Not with his mother looking down on him. And she was, because he could feel those eyes of hers boring into him whenever he spoke harshly to the old man; hear her disapproving voice telling him to behave. And she was the one woman he'd ever obeyed in his life, so he couldn't shake off the habit of a lifetime just because she was dead.

Still, his dad couldn't last too much longer, judging by how decrepit the old fart was looking lately. And Dave could wait, because there were more important things on the agenda right now.

Like getting Sue's knickers off.

She made him laugh. He'd managed to wangle a few kisses out of her, but every time he tried to touch her she jumped, like she was a fucking virgin or something.

Like he didn't already know that she'd left the kid on his own and gone out shagging some bloke the night of the fire — *and* stayed out all weekend. And bad as Carole was, even *she* wouldn't do something like that. Which made it all the more laughable that Sue was acting so concerned about going out for a drink with him tonight and leaving the kid with his dad.

But if he had to play the game her way and act like he respected her pretend worries, then he would. Because, one way or another, those knickers were coming off tonight — and one more knife would be slicing into Terry Day's back.

And Dave was confident that it would happen, because Sue's resolve was melting faster than an ice cube in the kettle. She was already grateful to him for giving her and Connor somewhere to stay — although her face when she'd copped her first look at the place had been a picture. But she was too polite to complain, so she would do her damnedest to make the best of it in order not to offend him. And gratitude was a pretty potent tool for sanding off the last stubborn traces of resistance.

He almost felt sorry for the poor cow. Now that she'd committed herself to the idea of being his girlfriend, she really thought she'd be getting the same in return. But she was on a hiding to nothing if she thought it was ever going to develop into a love kind of thing. He would happily shag her brains out, but that was as far as it was ever going to go. Carole was the closest he'd ever come to loving any woman, and that was only because she was like a female version of him. But if *she* wasn't enough to really hook his heart, a nice girl like Sue stood no chance.

All Sue was to Dave was a means to an end: a tool of revenge to be used against her husband — soon to be ex, if Dave had anything to do with it, because he'd even go as far as marrying her, if it twisted the knife that bit more.

Whatever it took, he would make the bastard pay for putting his dirty hands on Leanne. And shacking up with her and getting her to fall out with Dave over him had just compounded the crime. And now the silly cow thought she *loved* him, which made Dave's blood boil. But he wasn't stupid enough to kill Terry over it, because there was no way he was spending the rest of his life behind bars for the cunt. He'd come pretty close a few times, though, and had only just managed to stop himself from going too far.

But beating him up hadn't been enough to get Terry to leave Leanne. And getting the lads at his works to hassle him in the hopes of making him quit his job, leaving him too skint to keep Leanne in the manner to which she'd been accustomed and send her running back to Daddy Big Bucks, hadn't worked either. So Dave had done some serious thinking, and come up with the plan to hit Terry where it really hurt — by taking *his* precious daughter, to let him know how it felt to lose someone you love with your whole heart and soul.

Unfortunately, Dave hadn't really thought through what he would do with Nicky once he'd snatched her. He'd been coked up at the time and had vaguely imagined that he would just stick her in the shed for a bit, then let her go when Terry had agreed to stay out of Leanne's life. But then it had all got a bit messy with the fire and the police getting involved, so he'd been forced to keep her. But he'd have to let her go eventually.

Either that, or kill her. And the longer this went on, the more likely it seemed that he might have to do the latter.

Dave knew that Nicky wouldn't tell anybody where she'd been or who she'd been with if he let her go, because she was absolutely terrified of him. But he couldn't risk letting the police get at her, because if they started doing tests on her there would be enough traces of Dave on her for them to nail him to the wall.

Snatching her had definitely been one of his less intelligent moves, and he wished he'd thought of getting off with Sue before he'd gone ahead and done it, because setting himself up as Daddy to Terry's kids made so much more sense from a long-term revenge point of view. But he'd done it now, so he had no choice but to see it through. And it was good that they all thought Nicky had started the fire and run away, because they'd stop looking for her before too long. So when her corpse turned up a few months down the line, a few hundred miles away from Manchester, under a chunk of concrete at the bottom of a river, there wouldn't be anything useable left on her body to link her to Dave — if they even recognised her by that time.

So, yes, everything was still working out okay. Now all he needed to do was get into Sue's knickers and cement his place in her life, then he could sit back and watch Terry implode. And he *would*, because there was no way he'd accept another man taking over his role in his kids' lives. And the more he kicked off about it, the more Leanne would get suspicious that he was actually jealous about Sue. And before too long it would all be over. Leanne would come home, and Terry would be left with nothing.

Dave couldn't wait!

Sue was just taking Connor up to bed when Dave came out of the bathroom. Blushing when she saw that he was wearing nothing but a small towel looped around his waist, she dipped her gaze, trying not to notice the broadness of his chest, or the muscular tone of his stomach. It had been a long time since she'd seen a man in such good condition, because the few she'd got anywhere near the undressing stage with over the last year had all been the weedy types she'd met at the clubs. But Dave was built like Terry, and that was what she'd always considered a *real* man should look like.

Not that she'd had too many men — despite what everyone back on the estate thought. Terry had been her first, and she'd married him — which was the ultimate in respectability in her mind. And even when he'd left her for Leanne, she hadn't gone wild as everyone had assumed. She'd just made a wild new friend. But Julie had been a big, warm, comforting presence in her life just when she'd needed it most, so she'd gone along with her lifestyle of going out every weekend and having fun, even though she hadn't actually enjoyed it all that much.

Now she desperately wanted Dave to know that she was a decent woman. And that meant keeping a tight rein on herself, even though his kisses were getting to her in a way that no other man had managed since Terry. She was his girlfriend, and it was important that he respected her, or their relationship would never be as strong as she was determined to make it.

Taking Connor into their bedroom now, she put a nappy on him and pulled his pyjama bottoms up over it. Then, tucking him into bed with his new game, she got herself ready to go out.

Kissing Connor when Dave tapped on the door a short time later, she told him to be a good boy. Then, taking a deep breath, she went out to have her first proper date with her new man.

CHAPTER
SEVENTEEN

Connor was bored. It was their second Saturday at the house, and his mum had gone out shopping with Dave again. The batteries in his DS had run out just after they had left, so he couldn't play with that. And there was nothing on TV but sport — which he hated. So he wandered over to the window and, resting his forehead against the cold glass, peered out at the jungle.

Things had changed since Dave had taken his mum out for a drink that first night. Connor didn't know what had happened, but something must have, because she'd been acting weird ever since; always blushing when Dave looked at her, and giggling when he spoke to her. And if she caught Connor watching, she'd do something odd with her eyes at Dave, and then he'd go out of the room and call for her to follow him upstairs for a "quick word" about something or other. And then Connor would hear even more giggling, and loads of banging noises, like they were bouncing on the bed, or something. And they usually fell off, by the sounds of it, because then they would start moaning like they'd hurt themselves.

It happened every day, sometimes more than once, and sometimes even at night when Connor was trying to get to sleep. He didn't see why they didn't just stop it if they always ended up getting hurt, because that was what his mum would have told *him* to do. But Dave's dad never told them off about it, so Connor presumed that they mustn't be doing anything bad.

Connor didn't actually mind being left on his own. In fact it was easier for him, because he had to be so careful not to do anything stupid when his mum and Dave were around, and he was constantly worrying about making funny noises, or needing to go to the toilet. But none of that seemed quite so urgent when he was alone.

Anyway, he couldn't look out for the rabbit when they were here. Not only because it was his secret, and he didn't want to share it, but because he had a feeling that if Dave found out that it was out there, he might never see it again — like he hardly ever saw his mum.

He'd named the rabbit Barney, and when he saw it he spoke to it in his head, trying to project the thoughts at it through the window. He'd seen it a few times now, and each time he'd felt the same thrill of excitement as the first time. Especially when Barney came up close to the edge of the brambles and looked straight at him. That made Connor feel like they were friends, which was good, seeing as he hadn't seen anybody else since he'd come to live here, apart from his mum, Dave, and old Mr Miller.

His dad had rung a few days after they had moved in, but his mum had lied and said that she couldn't let him pick Connor up that Sunday because the social workers were coming round for the day — which they *hadn't*. She'd promised to take Connor to meet him in the park outside Julie's the following Sunday, though. And that was tomorrow, so Connor was really excited about it. But he was nervous, too, because she hadn't mentioned it all week, and he was just praying that she hadn't changed her mind and cancelled it again without telling him.

He didn't believe much of what she said any more, because he knew that it could change at the drop of a hat depending on what Dave wanted. Like today, she'd promised that she wouldn't be long, but they'd already been ages. But even if they came back right this very minute, they would probably just go upstairs to play without him again.

"You got nothing to do, son?" Jack Miller asked, coming into the room just then and finding Connor slumped on the window ledge. "Every time I see you, you're in some kind of a dream world."

Turning his head slightly, Connor gazed up at him. He was no longer terrified of the old man, because he'd hardly seen him in the week they'd been here. And when he did see him, his voice was always quiet and kind. But Connor still wouldn't talk to him. They both knew that.

"I don't see why you don't just go out if you're so fascinated by it," Jack said now, going to his chair and sitting down to roll his habitual cigarette. "That's what boys did in my day — got out there in the dirt and made themselves a den."

Intrigued, Connor tilted his head.

"Oh, aye," Jack went on, aware that he'd caught his interest. "Me and my friends used to go out at sunrise, and we wouldn't come home till our mams called us in for supper. We'd be out there all day, digging trenches and fighting the Germans, or climbing trees and building hideaways. You ever had a hideaway, son?"

Connor shook his head. He'd never even heard of whatever one of them was, but it sounded good.

Sighing, Jack said, "No, I bet you haven't. That's the trouble with parents today; too quick to stick their kids in front of the computer or the telly while they get on with their own thing. Never mind letting you get some fresh air in your lungs. No bloody wonder you've all got colds and asthma." Lighting his cigarette now, he sucked on it and peered at Connor thoughtfully. "Want to go out?" he asked after a moment. Seeing the instant spark of *Can I?* in Connor's eyes, he jerked his head towards the door. "Go on, then . . . what's stopping you?"

Connor wasn't sure if he was allowed. Mr Miller was telling him to do it, but what if his mum came back and thought he'd just gone out without permission. And if Mr Miller was back upstairs by then, he wouldn't tell her any different. And Connor couldn't.

As if reading his mind, Jack said, "It's all right, son. I'll tell your mam where you are. Go on."

Walking hesitantly, Connor went to the door. Glancing back one last time, he waited until Mr Miller nodded, then dashed out.

It was icily cold outside, and the wind whipped at his face as soon as he stepped out of the back door.

Shivering, because he hadn't thought to put his coat on, he dragged the sleeves of his jumper down as far as they would go and wrapped his arms around himself.

Wandering down the side of the house, he stopped when he came to the outskirts of the jungle. It looked even wilder and higher now that he was in front of it, and he couldn't see any immediate way into it. So, walking sideways, he edged his way along the narrow track between the house and the first line of bushes, heading for the small clearing where he usually saw Barney the rabbit. Squatting down there, he peered through the tangle of roots. There was no sign of movement, but he was sure he could crawl through if he got down on his knees.

It was like a whole new world on the underside. It was still cold, but the wind wasn't reaching him, so it was nowhere near as bad. And everything sounded strangely muted, as if he were under a huge blanket. It gave him a feeling of isolation that he'd so far only experienced inside his own head, but the sensation was heightened and made more exciting by the fact that this time it was physical as well as mental. Feeling like an explorer in a lost world, far away from everyone else, he inched his way in.

Watching through the window as Connor's feet slowly disappeared from view, Jack shook his head sadly. The poor little bugger didn't have a clue how to play. And he was far too happy being by himself, which was a real sign that it happened too often.

394

Jack had picked up enough of Sue and David's conversations over the past few days to know that the boy had problems which meant he couldn't talk, but that wasn't all that was wrong with the boy, he was sure. There was some sort of deep-rooted sadness in him that went well beyond so-called shock.

But there was no point worrying too much about him, because they were only staying temporarily, from what he could gather. Although the amount of time Sue had spent in David's bedroom lately, Jack didn't think she seemed all that eager to leave just yet.

Still, he didn't mind her being here, because at least she wasn't like David's last one. And unlike David, she was respectful of the fact that this was *his* house. And she'd been keeping it nice and clean, which was a welcome change. She actually reminded him of Mary, because Mary hadn't been a big talker, either. She'd just been a nice, warm presence about the place. And Sue, with her perfume trailing in her wake and her soft voice, filled a bit of the gap that Mary had left behind in Jack's life.

Shame she couldn't break whatever spell David had woven over her and spend a bit more time with the boy. But she did love him, Jack could see that. It was just David being David; demanding all of her time and attention for himself. But he'd soon revert to his old ways, Jack was sure. All this affection he was displaying, and the talking and listening, wasn't who David really was. He was either really into this one, or he was playing some kind of game with her. And knowing David as well as he did, Jack would bet his life that it was the latter. Although with what aim in mind, he had no idea.

Connor came to a small clearing midway through the jungle. Standing up to survey his surroundings, he brushed the soil off his knees, glad that it hadn't been raining lately, because it would be so much harder to stay clean if the ground was muddy and his mum would go mad.

Turning to look back towards the house, he could just about see it through the tall grass. He couldn't see Mr Miller behind the net, but he sensed that he was there. But it wasn't a horrible sensation, like when he felt Dave's eyes on him, because this didn't feel like being spied on, it just felt like being watched over, and that was all right.

Looking in the other direction now, he realised that he could see the broken-down old shed far more clearly. It was still a fair distance away, but he could see the corrugated tin roof now, and the worn, dull metal walls. There was a small window in the side, too, with several broken panes which looked like they had been boarded over from the inside.

Wondering if this was what Mr Miller had meant by a hideaway, because it looked like the kind of place where no one would ever find you if you got inside, Connor started to push his way through the brambles that were standing between him and the building.

It took him a good fifteen minutes to get anywhere near, and it started to get really stinky before he reached it. It was a really dirty kind of smell, like a toilet that hadn't been cleaned, Connor thought. And there were other smells, like damp soil and rotting vegetables.

Somebody had been here before him, because there was a narrow path of trodden-down grass and brambles over to his right. Thinking that he would go back by that route, because it would be easier than fighting back the way he'd come, Connor went right up to the shed. The window was too high, so even if it hadn't been boarded over he wouldn't have been able to see through it. But, making his way around to the door, he found that it had a huge padlock on it, and several bolts, some way up at the top.

Going around the back, his foot slipped on loose soil and stones and he cried out as he felt himself falling. Clutching at a thick old root, he sat down with a bump. It was a steep drop, and there were more gnarly trees growing out at a horizontal angle. Through these, Connor could see the glimmer of water rushing along a narrow rocky stream. And now that he'd seen it, he realised that he could just about hear the trickling waters above the sound of the hissing wind.

And then he heard something else. A thin, pitiful crying sound.

Straining his ears, he cocked his head. It was fading in and out as the wind gusted, but it was definitely there. And it sounded like . . .

No, it couldn't be!

Clutching at the root, Connor hauled himself back up to his feet, his heart pounding painfully in his chest as his breath came in ragged bursts.

It couldn't be Nicky, because she'd run away. What would she be doing here at Dave's house?

He wanted to call out to her, to see if it really was her or if he was imagining things. But the sound wouldn't come. And anyway, he didn't dare, because someone else might hear him. And if they thought he could talk again, they'd expect him to answer all the questions they had been storing up for him.

In the distance, Connor heard the sound of a car. Knowing that it must be his mum and Dave coming back from the shops, because no one else ever drove up the lane, he lurched back to level ground and thrashed his way through to the trodden-down section. Running hell for leather back up to the house, he burst through the back door just as the car turned in through the rusty gates.

Chuckling softly when he saw the wildness of Connor's eyes as he ran back into the living room, Jack cocked his finger, beckoning the boy over to him.

"So, you'd rather they didn't know you'd been out, would you?" he said perceptively, plucking stray bits of grass and twigs out of Connor's hair and off his jumper. "Well, that's okay by me, son. It can be our little secret." Rubbing the knees of Connor's trousers roughly now, he whispered, "Slip your shoes off and stick 'em under my chair. I'll give them a going-over later."

Doing as he was told, Connor went and sat down on the couch. Seconds later, his mum popped her head around the door.

Seeing the two of them sitting in companionable silence, Sue smiled, and said, "Hi, sweetheart. I'm home." Then, to Jack, "Hello, Mr Miller. Hope he's not been any trouble?"

"None whatsoever," Jack told her, flipping a surreptitious wink at Connor. "We've just been watching the wrestling — haven't we, son?"

Smiling again when Connor quickly nodded — without looking at her, she noticed — Sue said, "Well, thanks again for watching him. I really appreciate it." Then, "Best put the shopping away. Oh, and I was going to make spaghetti bolognaise for dinner, if you'd like some?"

Telling her not to worry about him, that he'd see to himself, Jack eased himself up out of his chair. Glancing at Connor when Sue went into the kitchen, he whispered, "Did you have a good time out there?"

Connor couldn't tell him what had happened. He couldn't tell anybody, because they'd think he was stupid. But he was grateful that Mr Miller had let him go out, and that he'd covered for him just now. So, giving him a tiny smile, he nodded.

Touched, because it was the first time the child had ever smiled at him, Jack said, "Well, it looks like it's done you a world of good. So, any time you want to do it again, you just let me know and I'll make sure they don't find out. Okay?"

Nodding again, Connor watched as the old man walked slowly out. Listening as Jack climbed the stairs and went into his bedroom directly above, he sighed. Mr Miller had sounded sad just now, and that wasn't good, because Connor was starting to quite like him. He was a bit like Pauline Wilson. Old, and always asking questions, but not pushy about it, not like the other people who got annoyed when they talked to him and he didn't answer. Pauline and Mr Miller had nice eyes. At least they did when they looked at *him*, although Connor had seen Pauline look at his mum with bad eyes before they'd made friends, and he'd seen Mr Miller giving her a few funny looks as well.

But Connor still wouldn't try and talk to him — even if he had thought that his voice would work. Because, nice as Mr Miller was, he was still Dave's dad.

CHAPTER
EIGHTEEN

Nicky cried herself to sleep. She quite often did these days, because her stomach always seemed to be hurting. And her head. And her eyes.

She felt like a mole, living in a pot of foul-smelling ink, and every now and then the sun would burst through and burn holes right into her brain.

But those moments of blinding brightness were less frequent recently, because he hadn't been coming so often. In fact, there were times when he didn't come at all, but she couldn't be sure how far between they were. All she knew was that she didn't think she'd eaten in . . . well, she didn't even know how long. It could have been days, weeks, or even months.

He'd left a big bottle of Lucozade the last time he'd come, so at least she'd had that to sip at. But it wasn't going to last for too much longer, and she was having to ration herself because she had no idea when he would come again. Or even if he would. And one of these days, she was sure that he would simply forget all about her. Or just get fed up of the mess he'd created and wash his hands of her.

She didn't usually care, having almost lost the will to keep going. But she felt strange today, because she'd really thought that she had heard Connor crying out. She knew that it was probably just an aural hallucination, a memory that had flashed through with a clarity that had made it feel real, but it had stirred up all the old feelings, nonetheless, and now she was desperately longing to be back at home.

Nicky could see everything so clearly in her mind's eye; all the furniture, and the curtains, and the smoky haze that always seemed to linger above the room like a dirty net curtain. And she could smell the smoky air, and the scent of the sausages and mash that Connor had always seemed to want for his dinner. She could even smell the distinctive odour of his mattress after a thousand wettings and dryings-out. And none of it was bad; it was all just home. And she wanted to be back there so badly.

But it was never going to happen. She'd already been gone for ever, and if they hadn't come looking for her yet then they never would. Anyway, after hearing about their party, she could only assume that they had wiped her out of their memories, like people did when they lost a loved one. They're gone, so you just have to put them out of your head and get on with your own life. That was what people always said when someone died.

And she might as well be dead. She certainly felt like she was.

CHAPTER
NINETEEN

Driving into the city the next afternoon, Dave couldn't remember if he'd been down to see Nicky the day before. Or even the day before that. He was getting lax, and that wasn't good. He needed to get food to her regularly, or she was going to get ill and complicate things.

He'd more or less resigned himself to the thought of having to kill her now that it had gone too far, but he needed to be in control of the when and the how of it. It wouldn't do to have her die in the shed at the bottom of the garden. Not when there was already a bad smell down there, and the water board were slowly working their way up along the canal messing with the drainage pipes. They probably wouldn't reach the land behind the house for some months yet, but he couldn't take the chance of having a rotting corpse under their noses if they happened to come to survey the stream or something in the meantime.

So he had to keep her alive for now, and that meant feeding her. But he just hadn't had much time or opportunity to get down there, not with Sue following him around like a dog all the time.

She'd really thrown herself into the whole relationship thing, and he had to admit that he was kind of enjoying having her in his bed. Although she was surprisingly naive about sex, given her reputation, and he was actually beginning to wonder if she'd had half the men she was supposed to have had. But he was teaching her a few tricks, and she was a pretty fast learner, so it was all good. And it was great that she didn't move once she was asleep. Unlike Carole, who had kicked the shit out of him every night for years — although he suspected that half the time she hadn't even been asleep, and had just used it as an excuse to get him back for whatever he'd done to annoy her during the day.

Good old Carole. He couldn't help but miss the bitch and her vicious mouth. But there was no way he was ever going back there permanently. And, right now, he was keeping her at a firm distance, because he was on a mission and it was more important to pull it off than to keep her sweet. He would just wangle his way back into her bed when it was done. Although she might put up a fiercer fight when she realised *who* he'd been shagging behind her back this time.

But she'd find out soon enough. Everyone would. Because Dave was bored of playing Sue's *let's-just-wait-a-little-while-longer* game, and was ready to tell the lot of them and get the ball rolling. If Sue was committed, then she wouldn't give a toss who knew. And that was what Dave was planning to hit her with — as soon as he'd delivered this latest batch of powders.

Pulling up outside Frank Delaney's house now, he put the plastic bag containing the coke inside his jacket. He only delivered to his big buyers these days, the rest he passed on through his team of lads on the estate. And Frank was one of the biggest, so Dave would always deal with him personally.

Frank was taking five ounces today, and would pay in cash, which made it well worth the risk for Dave to carry it in his car. And he hadn't been stupid and gone for one of the flashy Beemers that the other dealers splashed out on when they started making serious money; he'd opted for a quality three-litre Jag instead. And the pigs never looked twice at a white man in a Jag, so he was pretty confident that he'd never get pulled for anything avoidable.

Telling Sue that he'd be back in ten minutes, and to beep the horn if there was a problem, he left her in the car and went up the path.

Waiting until he'd gone into the house, Sue slid her mobile out of her pocket and switched it on. Terry had rung earlier in the week asking when he could have Connor again, and she'd fobbed him off, telling him he'd have to wait until today. Then she'd turned her phone off in case he rang again and Dave saw his name on the screen. Checking it now, she saw several missed calls from him, and five messages — which became increasingly terse as he tried to find out what was happening regarding the visit.

There were also three missed calls from Julie, and two messages. The first asking her to ring back; the second telling her that the social services had been round for the past three days running, and had left a note through the door saying that they were becoming concerned about Connor's welfare and needed to speak to her urgently.

Switching the phone off again, Sue slipped it back into her pocket and gazed out of the window. That wasn't good. Terry would keep, but the social services wouldn't. If they were concerned, it meant that she'd been right all along, and they *had* been watching her as closely as they'd been watching Connor. And now they couldn't reach her, they would probably put him on the "at risk" register, or something. Because that's what those nosy bastards did when parents of troubled kids took back control of their lives.

Deep in thought, she didn't notice the two young boys who had just ridden around the corner on their bikes.

Spotting Dave's car, Ben Greene said, "Yo, there's your dad's motor. But who's that sitting in it? It ain't your mam, is it?"

Using the heel of his trainer as a brake, Fred screeched to a stop and peered across the road into the passenger seat of his dad's car. Scowling when he saw who it was, he turned his bike around and stood up on the pedals to give himself a good quick start.

"Wait up!" Ben called after him, struggling to get his larger bike facing the other way again.

Ignoring him, Fred raced off down the road. Jumping every kerb, and narrowly avoiding being hit by a car, he tossed the bike down on the pavement outside his house and ran inside, yelling, "Mam! *MAM!* Me dad's round at Frank Delaney's house, and he's got Sue Day in his car!"

"You what?" Carole spat, anger flaring in her eyes as she jumped up from her seat at the kitchen table. "Move!" Shoving past him, she rushed out of the house.

Hot on her heels, Fred jumped back on his bike and raced ahead to make sure that the car was still there while his mum stomped down the road, shoving her sleeves up as she went.

Sensing that it was all about to kick off, Ben Greene pedalled hard to keep up with Fred, waving for some of his friends who were just crossing the road to come and watch the fight.

"Oi!" Irene Murgatroyd yelled at him as he rode past her house where she was weeding in the garden. "Who's fighting? Better not be you lot, or I'll be straight round to see your mothers."

"It's not us, it's Fred's mam," Ben told her, too excited to be bothered to tell her to piss off, as he would have done usually.

"Who with?" she called after him as he rode on.

"Connor Day's mam," he called back.

Bustling straight round to Pauline's, Irene pounded on the door with her fist.

"There's a fight," she squawked when Pauline opened up, already bustling back up the path. "Carole and Sue are at it."

"Oh, no," Pauline groaned, an instant frown on her brow. "What on earth's the matter now?"

"No idea, but you'd best hurry or you'll miss it," Irene said, flapping her hand at her to get a move on.

Carole had just reached the car. Yanking at the passenger-door handle and finding it locked, she banged her fist on the window.

Jumping, because she'd been in a world of her own, Sue glanced up at her. Blushing guiltily when she saw her, she groaned when she saw hordes of kids and several of her old neighbours barrelling around the corner to see what was going on.

"Get the fuck out of that car!" Carole yelled at her through the window. "And don't just sit there looking at me like you're fucking stupid, 'cos I'll break the bastard glass and *drag* you out in a minute."

Sue glanced back at the house to see if Dave was coming out. But he wasn't. So, taking a deep breath, she pulled the lock up. But before she could open the door, Carole did it for her.

"You cheeky fucking slag!" she snarled, grabbing two handfuls of Sue's hair and tugging her out of her seat. "I fucking *knew* something was going on with you two, and you barefaced lied to me!"

"I didn't lie," Sue yelled back, grabbing at Carole's hands to prevent her from tearing the hair straight out of her head. "And, anyway, it's got nothing to do with you, 'cos Dave left you. And he's with me now, so get your stupid hands off me!"

"What do you mean, he's with you, you skanky bitch?" Carole screeched, holding on and pulling Sue around in a circle. "He *ain't* with you!"

Unable to free her hair, Sue kicked Carole hard in the shin. "Yes, he is," she hissed. "And he's staying with me, so get over it!"

"Stop it!" Pauline yelled, reaching them just then. "Carole, Sue . . . pack it in before someone gets hurt!"

"*Hurt?*" Carole repeated scathingly. "I'm gonna do more than fucking hurt her. I'm gonna *kill* her!"

"Oh, yeah?" Sue growled, grabbing Carole's hair now and dragging her head down. But just as she drew her knee back, intending to let Carole have it in the face, two strong arms lifted her up and plonked her down facing the opposite way.

Going for Dave now, clumps of Sue's hair trailing from her fingers, Carole whacked him across the face, screaming, "You bastard! You told me you were just giving her a lift that day, but you weren't, were you? And it *was* her in the car park at that stupid fun day, wasn't it?"

"So what if it was?" Dave said calmly, standing between the two women. "I told you it was none of your business then, and it still isn't."

"So how come you slept with *me* that night?" Carole demanded, tears in her eyes now.

Laughing nastily, Dave said, "Don't be ridiculous. As if I'd sleep with you again."

"You *liar!*" Carole gasped, unable to believe that he was fronting it out like this.

Taking Sue's arm, Pauline said, "Come back to mine, pet. You don't need to be getting involved in any of this."

"Yeah, come on." Irene joined in, giving Carole a dirty look. "Leave them to it."

Shaking them off, Sue dodged around Dave and faced Carole.

"Look, he doesn't want you, so just stop making a show of yourself and go home. And you're wrong about us, because we've only just got together, so you've got nothing to kick off about."

"Fuck off!" Carole yelled, lunging at her again.

Holding Carole back, Dave jerked his head at Sue, saying, "Go to Pauline's while I sort her out. I'll pick you up from there when I've finished here."

The kids were all laughing by now.

"Shame!" Fred gloated as Sue walked past him. "My mam battered you!"

"Yeah, just like we battered mongy Connor," Ben added gleefully.

Narrowing her eyes, Sue glared at the two boys. "That was you? I might have known it, you little bastards!"

"Oi!" Dave barked, still holding Carole back. "Just go. I'll deal with him."

Shooting one last poisonous look at the boys, Sue allowed Pauline and Irene to lead her away.

"Ridiculous," Pauline muttered, herding Sue back up the road. "Never could keep her nasty mouth shut, that one. And out on the street like that. The woman's got no pride."

Irene was more interested in getting the gossip than in slagging Carole off. Folding her arms as she walked, she peered at Sue, saying, "So, you and Dave, eh?

410

Never saw that one coming. How long's that been going on?"

"Not long," Sue muttered, keeping her head down as she felt the stares of all her old neighbours following her up the road. "Just over a week."

"And how's it going? Is he being good to you?"

"Mmm."

"Leave it, Reen," Pauline said quietly but firmly. Pushing her gate open, she waved Sue in ahead of her. Then, standing in Irene's way, letting her know that she wasn't invited, she said, "I'll just get her a cup of tea. See you later."

"Well, that's nice, I must say," Irene complained as Pauline ushered Sue into her house and closed the door. "And it was me what told her about it in the first place. I'll keep my bloody mouth shut next time."

Going into the kitchen to put the kettle on, Pauline said, "There's a comb on the shelf if you want to sort your hair out. And you'd best put a spot of cream on that scratch."

"Scratch?" Sue repeated.

"On your face," Pauline said, coming back into the doorway and tracing a finger down her own cheek to indicate where it was.

Looking in the mirror over the fire, Sue tutted when she saw the nasty red welt running from her cheekbone to her mouth. And her hair was all over the place, like she'd been rubbing balloons on it.

Taking a small tube of TCP cream out of the drawer, Pauline handed it to her. Finishing the teas then, she carried them through and sat down.

"I know it's none of my business," she said, watching as Sue put herself back to rights. "But do you really think it's a good idea getting involved with Dave? Don't get me wrong, I've got nothing against him," she added quickly. "But you know what Carole's like. She's never going to give you any peace."

"I know," Sue said quietly. "But she knows about us now, so she'll just have to get used to it." Turning from the mirror, she came and sat down. Thanking Pauline for the tea, she sipped at it. Then she said, "He's been really good to me this past few weeks, Pauline. Me *and* Connor. And I know you probably won't understand it, but I really like him."

"I'm sure you do," Pauline replied, not sure that Sue really understood what she had let herself in for. "But have you thought what this is going to mean to the kids? And then there's Terry to consider."

"It's got nothing to do with him," Sue muttered. "He's been with Leanne for a year, so he can't say anything."

"And Dave's her dad," Pauline pointed out. "So that's bound to make it even more complicated."

"Not if everyone stays out of each others' business," Sue said. "Anyway, you can't help who you fall in love with. And you can't switch it off just because someone doesn't like it."

Raising her eyebrows, Pauline said, "So, it's love then, is it?"

Inhaling deeply, Sue pursed her lips thoughtfully. She hadn't meant to say that, but now that she had, she realised that she meant it.

"Yeah, I think it is," she said. "And believe me, I didn't go into it lightly, because it was as much a shock for me to find I had feelings for him as it is for you. But he's been so good to me. And he feels the same way. So what am I supposed to do? Pass up on the chance of being with someone who really cares about me and the kids, just because Carole and Leanne have got a problem with it?"

"What about what Carole said just now?" Pauline reminded her. "About him sleeping with her the night of my fundraiser?"

Feeling a small knot of jealousy twisting in her gut, Sue tried to shrug it off. "If he did, he did. But we weren't together then, so it's not like he went behind my back or anything. Anyway, he said he didn't, and I'd believe him over *her* any day."

Sighing, Pauline said, "Well, you know your own mind, so I won't interfere. But I just hope it doesn't come crashing down on your head, because you've had a bad enough time of it lately. And so has Connor." Sipping her own tea now, she said, "How is he, by the way?"

"Fine," Sue said wearily. "Dave's been great with him, and he seems to get on well with Dave's dad as well."

"Jack?" Pauline said, genuine surprise in her voice. "I thought he was dead. I haven't seen him in years."

Cursing herself for having mentioned Dave's dad, because that could lead to Pauline asking where he was living, Sue said, "Yeah, he's okay. Anyway, thanks for the tea, but I think I should go and see what's keeping Dave."

Reminding her that he'd said he would pick her up from here, Pauline took out her cigarettes and offered her one. Taking it, Sue lit it and glanced out of the window.

"Oh, Lord, you know what I forgot," Pauline said suddenly. "I rang you a few times, but your phone was off. And that friend of yours was a bit rude when I tried to get her to pass a message along, so I didn't like to ring her again. But you're here now, so I can give it to you."

Standing up, she hurried to the sideboard and took out a tin box. Unlocking it, she took out an envelope and handed it to Sue.

"The money we raised," she said when Sue looked confused. "You never came round the morning after, and I haven't seen you since. It's not as much as I'd hoped, but it's all there. Three hundred and twenty pounds, and seventy pence."

"That's a lot," Sue murmured, blushing. "I didn't expect that much."

"Yes, well, I thought there would be more, considering how many people came," Pauline said, shrugging as she added, "But we didn't do as well on the drinks sales as we'd hoped. And between you and me, I think Irene might have been giving a lot of it away, because she was a wee bit under the influence herself by the time we started selling the alcohol. Anyway, there you go. It's all yours."

414

Sue didn't know what to do with the envelope. She didn't want to put it straight into her pocket, because that felt cheap. And she definitely wasn't going to open it and look at the money.

"Will you take some?" she asked, glancing up at Pauline. "As a thank-you."

"I most certainly will not," Pauline said adamantly. "That was raised for *you*. So you just take it and use it to buy you and Connor some new things to replace what you lost. Okay?"

Smiling at the look of indignation in Pauline's eyes, Sue nodded. "Okay. And thanks again. You've been a real friend."

"I'm glad I could help," Pauline said modestly. Then, "Did you hear anything about that appeal thing yet?"

"Not a lot," Sue told her, slipping the envelope into her pocket while Pauline put the tin box away. "The policewoman came round a couple of days later and told me that they'd had a lot of calls from people claiming they'd seen Nicky. They were going to look into them all, but she said it could take some time, because there were a lot of sightings in places like Blackpool and Scarborough. I've not heard anything since, though."

"She'll turn up," Pauline said quietly, guessing from Sue's expression that she was still desperately worried.

"I'm not so sure," Sue murmured. "And it's her birthday in a few days, and the policewoman's already warned me that they'll scale the search down, because she'll be sixteen."

Shaking her head, Pauline went back to her seat. "Beggars belief, doesn't it? You'd think they'd just go on searching until they found her, never mind scaling it down."

Shrugging resignedly, Sue said, "Apparently she'll just be a missing person once she's of age, so they've got no choice. And they haven't found a body, so they're pretty sure she's just run away."

"It's a shame, nonetheless," Pauline said, sighing softly. "And is Connor doing all right without her? I know how close they were."

"He's coping," Sue said. "Still not talking, but he's dealing with it in his own little way."

"I'd love to see him," Pauline said, smiling fondly. "Do you think you could fetch him round sometime and let me have him for a few hours? I haven't got any grandchildren, what with my Georgina preferring her career to motherhood, so I'd love the chance to spend a bit of time with him. I could take him out to the museum, or something. My John's not interested in anything that doesn't involve blood, so I've missed doing stuff like that."

Gazing at her and seeing the longing in her eyes, Sue said, "I think he'd love that. He's got a real thing about dinosaurs."

Giving her a wry smile, Pauline said, "I hope you're referring to the ones at the museum and not to me?"

"Don't be daft," Sue said, smiling herself now.

Glancing at her watch then, she bit her lip. Dave was really taking his time, and she hoped things hadn't turned too nasty with Carole. But she couldn't go back out there to find out after he'd told her to come here, so she'd just have to wait for him.

Dave had put Carole into the car and driven her off down the road to get her away from the onlookers. Parked up in Netto's car park now, he lit two cigarettes and tried to pass one to her.

"Fuck off!" she hissed, refusing to take it. "I don't want anything that's touched *your* mouth. Not now I know where it's been."

Flicking the cigarette he'd offered her out of the window, Dave said, "Please yourself." Then, peering at her, wondering how much he could afford to tell her, he said, "It's not what you think, you know."

"Yeah, *right*," Carole snorted disbelievingly. "It's *exactly* what I think. Exactly what I said when you got caught giving her a lift to the fucking hospital. *Lift*," she said again, spitting the word out. "I should have known you were lying, because you couldn't tell the truth if it was crawling around in your mouth with legs and arms!"

"Whatever," Dave murmured, wondering where she got these sayings of hers from. And what the hell they were supposed to mean.

"You're such a bastard," Carole said now, shaking her head, because she still couldn't believe that he'd just stood and denied her in front of that bitch.

"Say what you like," Dave said coolly. "But you don't know what's really going on, and you'll change your tune when you do."

"So tell me?" Carole demanded, glaring at him. "Thought not," she said after several moments of silence. "You can't tell me, because you haven't had time to think up a believable lie yet. But don't bother on my account, 'cos I don't even care any more. You've burned your bridges as far as I'm concerned, and you can just go back to your slag and leave me the hell alone."

"You don't mean that," Dave said confidently. "When you know the score, you'll have me back."

"In your fucking dreams!" Carole snorted, folding her arms, her nostrils flaring with anger. "And don't think Leanne's going to be too happy about this, 'cos she'll be fuming when she hears about it. And Terry's not going to like it, either. The shit that bitch has given that poor man this year, and now she goes and does this. And you're no better," she added. "He's done nothing to you but fall in love with your daughter. But you can't just be happy that she's got herself a lovely man, you've got to go and try and ruin his life, even though you know it'll ruin hers, an' all. Just because you're jealous that she loves him. You make me *sick*!"

Narrowing his eyes, Dave kept his mouth shut. He'd told Sue that he'd split with Carole because he'd sided with her after her fight with Leanne. But that had been nothing to do with it. It was purely down to this protectiveness that Carole was still displaying towards Terry. They'd had blazing rows about her going round to see him and Leanne, knowing full well that Leanne wasn't talking to Dave. But Carole wasn't the kind of woman you could dictate to, and it didn't matter how many times Dave told her to stay away, or how many fights they had about it, she'd blatantly carried on seeing them. So Dave had left. And now he knew that she was still on *his* side, he wasn't about to tell her what he was really up to, because she'd probably go and warn the cunt.

"Got nothing else to say?" Carole said suddenly.

Looking at her, Dave shook his head. "Nah. I think we're finished. Sorry you found out about it like this, but at least you know now, so me and Sue can get on with it in peace."

A thunderous look in her eyes, Carole said, "So, that's it? You're with Sue and fuck what I think?"

Shrugging casually, Dave said, "That's about the size of it, yeah."

"Well, what was all that shit about me not knowing what was really going on?" Carole demanded.

"Nowt," Dave said easily, taking a long pull on his cigarette and tossing it out of the window. "I just felt a bit guilty and wanted to make you feel better. But there's no point glossing over it. I'm with Sue now, and I'm staying with her."

"You are one cold piece of shit," Carole snarled, a spark of pure hatred in her eyes now. "After everything we've been through, and all the shit I've had to put up with from you over the years, you just sit there and tell me that you're with *her* now. Well, I hope you both burn in hell. And I'm going to make sure that Terry fights for custody, because she shouldn't be allowed to keep them kids. Not if she's going to have them around a dirty drug-dealing bastard like you."

His eyes flashing a clear warning now, Dave said, "You can say what you want as far as Sue and Terry and all them are concerned. But you ever grass me up for the drugs and you are one dead woman. And don't test me on this, Carole, because I fucking mean it."

He did, and Carole knew it. But she was too angry and hurt to give him the satisfaction of knowing that she would never breathe a word about his dealings. So, snorting defiantly, she said, "Don't tell me what to do, Dave Miller. Your days of trying to control me are well and truly over!" And with that, she got out of the car, slamming the door as hard as she could behind her.

Watching as she flounced away, Dave shrugged. She wouldn't dare grass him up, but she'd definitely go and tell Terry. Pity Leanne was going to fall out with him again, but he'd win her back round in time. He always did. And probably Carole, too, once she knew why he was doing this. But he could always find another tart to warm his bed if she wouldn't.

CHAPTER
TWENTY

Connor had just gone outside. Taking the easy route through the already trodden-down part, he ran down to the shed.

He'd been thinking about Nicky all night, convinced that it had been her that he'd heard yesterday. And if she was down near that shed, then she must have come looking for him.

Edging his way around the shed now, to the steep, slippery bit, he took firm hold of one of the trailing roots and pulled himself carefully around from one corner to the next, his gaze riveted on the tiny glitter of stream that he could see through the entwined branches of the trees.

It took ages, and Connor's feet slid out from beneath him several times, forcing him to cling on for dear life. Making it to the other side at last, he sat down and rubbed his sore hands on his trousers. Deflated because he hadn't seen or heard a thing, he idly reached for a fallen branch and started to whack it against one of the rocks that were scattered around. Liking the thudding sound, he did it again, and again, doing it harder and harder as the tears of frustration began to fall.

Nicky woke up with a jerk. There was a dull pounding sound coming from somewhere above and to the left of her. Was it Dave? she wondered, struggling to sit up because she felt so weak. Or had somebody come to find her at last, and was trying to break the door down?

Standing up, Nicky felt her legs shake wildly as a rush of nausea gripped her empty stomach. Swallowing it down, she tilted her head and cocked her ear up towards the roof.

And that was when she heard the sound of crying mixed in with the pounding noise.

"Connor?" she croaked, her voice barely a whisper. Coughing as soon as the word left her mouth, she doubled over and clutched at her stomach. Retching for a few seconds, she caught her breath, and straightened up. "Connor," she said again, more loudly. "CONNOOOOR!"

Feeling the blackness pressing in on her from the inside as well as the outside now, Nicky slumped down on the mattress.

Connor's head jerked up and the sob caught in his throat. He was sure he'd just heard Nicky calling his name.

Scrabbling to his feet, he gazed around, desperate to know where she was. Listening hard, he heard nothing else and wondered if he'd imagined it. But he hadn't. He *knew* he hadn't.

Opening his mouth, he tried to call back to her. But nothing came out apart from that weird wheezing sound. Taking a deep breath he tried again. And again. And again. Until suddenly it came.

"*Nicky?*"

It was only a tiny whisper that was immediately lost on the wind, but now he'd done it, he wasn't about to give up.

"*Nicky . . .*" he managed again, his voice stronger and louder. "Where are you?"

Hearing nothing after several more seconds, even though he'd held his breath and listened really hard, Connor's shoulders slumped with dejection. He *had* heard her, and she was definitely around here somewhere, he knew she was. But she wasn't down the slope by the stream — she'd sounded closer than that. But there was nowhere else to hide up here, apart from the shed. And he couldn't get in there because the door was locked.

"*Connor?*" Jack shouted just then. "You'd best come back in, son. They're on their way back."

Snapping out of his thoughts, Connor scrambled back around the side of the shed and ran down the path. He'd come back again the first chance he got. And he would keep coming until he found Nicky.

Sue was quiet as Dave pulled up beneath the parking shelter at the side of the house a few minutes later.

He'd seemed really pleased with himself when he'd come to collect her from Pauline's, and he'd been chatting all the way back, not seeming to notice that she hadn't said a word. He was just so happy that it was all out in the open, he'd said; glad that everyone knew, because now they could get on with their life together in peace, without Carole or Terry hassling them. And he wanted to take her out tonight to celebrate. Maybe back into the city, so he could show her off to his mates.

Sue was glad that he was happy, because he'd taken so long to get back to Pauline's that she'd begun to fear that he had patched things up with Carole, and that he would tell her they were getting back together. But she wasn't too happy about the way that Terry was going to find out about them.

For Connor's sake, she'd wanted to try and keep things on an even keel with Terry. But there was no chance of that now, because he'd be furious with her for letting Dave have so much access to his son when she'd denied him any. And he'd also be convinced that he'd been right when he'd accused Sue of flirting with Dave way back, and there would be nothing she could say to convince him otherwise.

But, oh, well . . . he could think and say what he liked. Dave had committed himself to her, and she had to do the same for him if they were to stand any chance of having the happy life he was so sure they would have together, even if that meant things reverting back to the acrimonious state they'd been in before she and Terry had settled their differences. And she had nothing to be guilty about, because it wasn't Sue who had cheated and torn the family apart.

Connor was on his own in the living room watching TV, and Sue could see that he'd been crying. Assuming that he was upset because she'd promised to take him to see his dad today, she sighed. She'd really meant to try and work something out, but it was hard trying to get a minute to herself since things had become so full-on with Dave. He wanted to be with her all the time, and it was difficult knowing how to say that she needed a bit of time alone without offending him. And she really didn't want to lie to him and sneak out to meet Terry behind his back, because he'd been good to her, and he didn't deserve to be lied to.

Not that it would be an issue now that they were out in the open. But Connor was the one who was really going to suffer.

Sitting down beside him now, Sue put her arm around him and gave him a cuddle, saying, "Sorry, sweetheart. I know I let you down, but we'll work something out for you to see your dad soon, I promise. It might just take a bit of time," she added quietly. "But you'll just have to bear with me. Okay?"

Confused, Connor frowned. He'd been so busy thinking about Nicky that he'd forgotten all about his dad.

"Where's Mr Miller?" Sue asked now, stroking his hair.

Connor jerked his head up towards the ceiling.

"In his room," Sue said, sighing again. "I hope you've not been disturbing him? I already feel bad that I have to keep leaving you with him, so please don't get on his nerves, will you, love?"

Sniffing softly, Connor shook his head. He didn't get on Mr Miller's nerves. Mr Miller liked him.

"Good boy," Sue said, squeezing his frail shoulders. "Anyway, let me get up so I can make you some dinner. You stay there and watch your programme."

Getting up, she went to the door. Pausing there, she glanced back at her son. He looked so sad, and she wished she didn't have to go out and leave him again. But she couldn't tell Dave that she didn't want to go out tonight. She'd just have to make an extra-special effort to spend more time with Connor from now on.

CHAPTER
TWENTY-ONE

Zak was in the bathroom when Leanne's phone rang. Jumping guiltily, she reached for it, praying that it wouldn't be Terry. It was bad enough lying to him before she left the flat about where she was going and when she got home about what she'd been doing. But to have to lie to him while she was in another man's bed was a step too far.

Relieved when she saw her mum's name on the screen, she answered it.

"Where are you?" Carole demanded. "I've been round to yours twice in the last hour."

"I'm out," Leanne told her evasively. "What do you want?"

"You're not going to believe what's just happened," Carole said.

Listening as her mum told her about her dad and Sue, Leanne's face drained of colour. "Have you told Terry?"

"Not yet," Carole said. "But I can't wait to see his face when I do. He's going to go mad."

Telling her mother that she'd meet her at the flat in ten minutes, and not to say a word to Terry if he was

427

back, Leanne switched the phone off and reached for her bra.

"Who was that?" Zak asked, coming back in from the bathroom just then with a towel looped around his waist.

"No one," Leanne said, clipping the bra shut and snatching up her jumper.

"You're not going already, are you?" he moaned, flopping down beside her and brushing her hair gently off her face.

"Don't," she snapped, jerking her head away.

"What's wrong?" He frowned. "Have I said something to upset you? You were fine a minute ago."

"Yeah, well, that was then and this is now," Leanne said tartly, pulling the jumper over her head.

"Christ, you can't half be cold when you want to be," Zak complained. "One minute you're all over me, the next you can't wait to get away from me."

"I'm never all over you," Leanne lied, pulling her knickers on.

"So what are these?" Zak demanded, pointing out the marks she'd left on his back with her nails. "Figments of my imagination?"

"So, I got a bit carried away," Leanne muttered, tugging her jeans on now. "Don't read anything into it. It's just sex — nothing more, nothing less."

"What you being like this for?" Zak asked, struggling to understand how she could go from red-hot passion to icecold indifference in the space of a few short minutes.

Shrugging, Leanne said, "I'm only doing this because you blackmailed me into it, so let's not pretend it's anything more than that."

Zak was speechless. He had really thought they were getting somewhere, and he'd certainly never forced her to have sex with him, so he was offended that she was making it sound like that. All he'd wanted was to have a bit of time alone with her, to talk about the old times, and break the ice so they could start to get to know each other again. And it had been going really well. They had shared a few spliffs, and had had a good laugh, and one thing had led to another — which she had enjoyed every bit as much as he had. So where the hell all this had come from, he didn't know.

Fully dressed now, Leanne snatched up her handbag and looked down at him. "I'm going. When do you want me to come back?"

"Just go," Zak said quietly.

Turning on her heel, Leanne marched out without another word.

Watching from his window as she came out of the front door below, Zak narrowed his eyes thoughtfully when she switched her phone back on and made a call as she walked quickly up the path. He could see that she was agitated, and wondered if the call she'd taken when he was in the bathroom had been from Terry. And, if so, whether Terry had been hassling her; trying to find out where she was and demanding that she come home. She'd certainly gone weird straight after it and, looking at her now, Zak was concerned that he might have landed her in trouble.

They hadn't talked about Terry at all since Leanne had been coming round, but Zak was still convinced that the man was wrong for her. Despite her initial reluctance to see him, she'd thawed out pretty quickly, and he'd seen glimmers of the old Leanne in her eyes when they had been having a laugh. And he'd found it odd that, after proclaiming her undying love for Terry, she'd so easily fallen back into *his* bed. And the more he thought about it, the more convinced he became that Terry had some kind of hold over her.

Wasn't that what dirty old men did when they set their sights on a young girl? Groomed them over a period of time, then entangled them in a relationship that they called love and held them fast, ostracising them from their family and friends until the poor girl believed that no one else could ever love them like he did.

But what were those kind of men capable of doing to the girls they supposedly loved if something or some*one* threatened to destroy what they had spent so long building?

Worried now about what might be facing Leanne when she got home, Zak reached for his phone. He'd promised that he wouldn't do this if she agreed to see him, but if she was in danger he wasn't going to be able to rescue her by himself.

Kelly Greene was seething as she stood in the alley at the end of Zak's road and watched Leanne walk out of his house.

She'd really thought that Zak liked her after he'd come into her house that night. They had chatted for hours, and drunk nearly a full bottle of her mum's brandy, and smoked several spliffs. They'd mostly talked about Leanne, but it hadn't overly bothered Kelly at the time because she'd have gladly talked about *anything* if it had kept Zak there longer.

She'd been wrecked by the time he'd left, so she hadn't known if anything had happened between them when she'd woken up the next morning. Disappointed when she'd checked herself to find no obvious signs, Kelly had consoled herself with the thought that, even if nothing *physical* had happened, they had still shared something special.

Sure that he would come round to see her again, she'd stayed in for the next three days, waiting for the knock on the door. But when it didn't come, she'd decided to take the bull by the horns and go round to see him. But just as she turned into his road, she'd spotted Leanne going into his house.

Wanting to know what the hell was going on, because Leanne was supposed to hate him, she'd hidden in the alley and watched the house until Leanne had come back out again — *three hours* later.

Knowing that something was definitely going on, Kelly had gone home in tears, cursing Leanne for being such a dirty, lying bitch. She already had a boyfriend, and was forever lording it up over the rest of the girls about how great he was, so why did she have to go and steal Kelly's man?

Not that Zak *was* her man, but he would have been at some point, she'd been sure about that. But Leanne had obviously heard about them getting close, and had jumped back in to stop it before it could get properly started.

Kelly had watched her going in and out of Zak's house a few times since then, but today something snapped. And as Leanne marched past, she decided it was time to put an end to it.

But she couldn't tackle Leanne by herself, so, calling round for a few of the girls from her gang at school, she led them down to the small play area outside Leanne's flat, and waited.

Terry arrived home just before Leanne.

Unable to get hold of Sue because she'd had her phone switched off all week, he'd driven over to Cheetham Hill when Leanne had gone to visit her dad that morning, determined to find out where Sue and Connor were staying so that he could confront her and get his promised day out with his son.

The girl in the café had been a great help, not only walking him down the road to show him which block Sue had been living at, but also telling him all about the man whose car she'd seen Sue and Connor getting into several times lately.

The same man who she had seen putting bin bags of clothes into the boot of the car just over a week ago, since which time she hadn't seen Sue or Connor.

Thanking her for her help, Terry hadn't even noticed her slipping her phone number into his pocket before she went back to the café. He'd been too busy worrying about the implications of the man, the car, and the bin bags.

Ringing every bell at the block until one of the tenants had finally let him in, Terry's concerns had deepened when, after pointing out the right flat, the woman had told him that she hadn't seen Sue or Connor for several days. But she had seen the social services, and they had apparently been quizzing people about Sue, trying to find out why she hadn't made herself available to them.

Getting no answer at the flat, Terry had hung around for a while, hoping that Sue's friend would come back and tell him what the hell was going on. But when she still hadn't come back after an hour, he'd given up and headed into the park across the road. And, sitting on the bench where Sue had waited for him on the day he'd taken Connor out, he'd thought everything over.

The café girl's description of the man in the car had sounded suspiciously like Dave Miller. But what would Sue be doing with Dave? She had told Terry that Dave had just given her a lift home from the hospital on the day that Connor had been discharged, and that was what Dave had also told Carole. Yet the girl had implied that they had seemed to be closer than just friends, so was it possible that they *had* been seeing each other? And, if so, how come Leanne didn't know, considering she'd been spending so much time with her dad lately? She'd been to his house three days ago, which was after Sue had supposedly gone off the scene around here.

But if Sue had moved in with him, surely she'd have seen the signs at his house?

Unless Sue hadn't moved in with him, and had only been getting a lift to somewhere else. But either way, she should have told Terry, because he had a right to know where his son was living.

The only way he would really know what was going on was if he asked Leanne to ask her dad straight out. But then he'd have to tell her how he knew, and he couldn't do that, because it would destroy Leanne to think that he'd gone behind her back like that. And he didn't want to upset her, because things had been great between them since they'd got engaged. She'd been more loving than he could have hoped in the last couple of weeks, and the sex had been amazing. Although he'd sensed that her efforts were partly due to guilt about having made friends again with her dad and spending so much time with him. But Terry really didn't mind, and wished she'd stop acting so jumpy when she got home from her visits.

He'd been sure that she would settle down eventually, and that they would find a way of keeping the two relationships separate yet equally fulfilling for her. But if Dave really was with Sue, then his and Leanne's renewed relationship would collapse, because Leanne would never forgive him for that. And Terry would be even more important to her — which would make it all the more devastating when she found out about his secret arrangement with Sue. And she would, because Dave would make sure of it — to get at Terry, and to get between them.

Making his way home when it became obvious that he wasn't going to get any answers about Sue's whereabouts from anyone down there, Terry decided that he was going to have to bite the bullet and tell Leanne before Dave did.

He just didn't know *how*.

Deep in thought as he parked up and got out of the car, he only vaguely noticed the girls who were congregated on the swings in the play area.

Looking round when one of them called his name, he squinted to see who it was. Recognising her as one of the girls Leanne had brought round to the flat on her karaoke nights, he carried on walking.

"Oi, I'm talking to you!" Kelly yelled after him, annoyed that he was trying to blank her when she was doing him a favour. "Don't you want to know what your girlfriend's been up to?"

"I'm busy," Terry called back over his shoulder, not even listening to what she was saying.

"Too busy to hear about Leanne shagging her ex behind your back?" Kelly shouted spitefully.

Still not listening, Terry opened the main door and went into the flats.

Eyes narrowing with malice when Leanne walked around the corner a couple of minutes later, Kelly shouted, "Oi, slag! Hope you're ready for a beating when you get in there, 'cos I've just told your boyfriend about you and Zak!"

"You what?" Leanne squawked, the blood draining from her face as she peered at Kelly across the car park. "You'd better be fucking joking."

Nerves failing her when Carole suddenly appeared, Kelly turned and ran, with her girls close on her heels. They might be able to take Leanne on her own, but not her and her mam together.

Grabbing Leanne when she tried to go after them, Carole said, "There's no time for messing about with your mates. We need to sort out what we're going to do about your dad."

Leanne was physically shaking now. All the way back she'd been wondering what she was going to tell Terry about where she'd been today, because he'd know that she couldn't have been with her dad once he found out about him and Sue. She'd decided to say that he hadn't turned up, and that she'd gone round to Goldie's instead. But if Kelly had told him about her and Zak, then he'd think that she'd been with him all the other times she was supposed to have been seeing her dad as well, and would want to speak to Goldie.

And Goldie wouldn't be happy about having to lie to him. Not when she found out that Leanne had been lying to *her* about Zak.

"Brazen bitch," Carole was hissing now, her own face as pale as her daughter's as she recalled the confrontation she'd had with Sue earlier. "You should have seen her, sitting in his car like she fucking owned it! But she wasn't so cocky when I dragged her out by her hair. And she's lucky your dad came out when he did, or I'd have ripped her bleedin' head off! But then he comes right out and tells me they're living together — in front of the whole *street*. So I told him to fuck right off if he thinks he's crawling back to me after this.

436

And I said he can forget about you, an' all, 'cos I know exactly how *you* feel about all this. And Terry will go mad when he hears."

"He doesn't care about her," Leanne muttered jealously.

"Maybe not, but he still deserves to know," Carole said firmly. "It's his kid, so it affects him. Anyhow, let's get inside. It's bloody freezing out here."

Leanne really didn't want to go in, but if she didn't then Terry would know that it was true and she would lose everything. She would just have to front it out and make Terry believe that Kelly was lying. And it should be easy enough, because everyone knew what a bullshitter Kelly was.

But just wait till she got her hands on the bitch!

CHAPTER
TWENTY-TWO

Dave was whistling happily as he ironed a shirt in his bedroom. Now that Carole knew about him and Sue, it wouldn't be long before Terry found out. And what better way to really stick it to him than to parade Sue around under his nose, and let it be known to the entire estate that they were a happy little family now — and that *he* had no part in it.

Pressing speakerphone when his mobile rang, so that he could talk while he carried on ironing, he frowned when he heard an unfamiliar voice.

"Hello, Mr Miller, it's Zak Carlton . . . I, er, don't know if you remember me, but I used to go out with your Leanne when we were at school."

"How the fuck did you get my number?" Dave demanded, already planning to tear a strip off whoever was handing it about willy-nilly.

"You gave it to me ages ago," Zak reminded him. "When I was still seeing your Lee and I was helping you fix that car up."

"So I did," Dave conceded. Then, "So what you ringing me for?"

"It's about Leanne," Zak said nervously. Then, "Well, more about Terry Day, really."

"Oh, yeah?" Dave said, instantly intrigued.

In his own room next door, Jack was pouring with sweat as he lay on his bed. He'd had a pain in his arm for most of the day, and his breathing had been a bit more laboured than usual. Thinking that he was probably coming down with a cold, he'd come straight back up to his room after warning the boy that his mum and David were coming up the lane. But the pain was getting worse: spreading to his chest, it was clutching at it now like a band of steel being slowly tightened.

Forcing himself off the bed, Jack staggered out onto the landing. The fear was on him now, and he could hardly breathe for panicking. Grabbing at the banister rail, he called out to Sue who he could hear moving about in the kitchen below.

Sue had just opened a tin of beans and tipped them into a pan. Putting it onto the stove, she was just lighting the gas when she heard an almighty crashing sound. Running out into the hall, she watched in horror as Jack tumbled down the stairs and landed in a heap at the bottom.

"*DAVE!*" she screamed. "DAVE, COME QUICK! YOUR DAD'S FALLEN DOWN THE STAIRS!"

Tutting, Dave told Zak that he would call him back in a minute. Clicking the phone off, irritated that he'd been disturbed when Zak was just telling him something really interesting about Terry and the fire, he wandered out onto the landing.

Sue was squatting over his father at the foot of the stairs. "Get an ambulance," she cried when she saw him. "He's knocked himself out."

Muttering, "Fucking idiot," Dave trotted down to see the damage. "How old is he, and he can't even walk down the stairs without tripping over his own feet?"

"It's serious," Sue said urgently. "He's really hurt himself. Call an ambulance," she begged again.

Tutting, Dave did as he was told and tapped the emergency number into his phone.

"Who's coming with him?" the paramedic asked, looking from Dave to Sue as his colleague wheeled Jack out on the stretcher a little while later.

"Don't look at me," Dave said gruffly. "I'm busy."

Confused by his callous attitude, and all too aware that the paramedic was disgusted, Sue said, "I'll go. *Someone* needs to be with him."

Shaking his head when she went into the living room and came back out with Connor, the paramedic said, "Sorry, but you can't bring the child. It'll be too traumatic if we have to stop en route to resuscitate."

Glancing at Dave, Sue said, "He'll have to stay with you. Either that, or you'll have to go with your dad, and *I'll* stay with Connor."

"Leave him," Dave said quickly. Catching the look of disapproval in her eyes, he added, "Sorry, but I've got a bit of a thing about hospitals since my mum died. I just can't face it."

Nodding understandingly, Sue said, "I should have thought." Then, leaning down to kiss Connor goodbye

440

as the paramedic went out to the ambulance, she said, "If it's too much for you, you can drop him round at Pauline's, if you want. She won't mind, because she was asking if she could spend some time with him when I was round there earlier."

Kissing her, Dave said, "I think I will, yeah. I've got a couple of things I need to sort out back up that end."

Feeling better now that she knew there was a reason for Dave's reluctance to go with his father, Sue said, "Okay, well, I'll ring you to let you know what's happening. But try to get over to see him if you can, because they said heart attacks at your dad's age aren't good, and you really need to be there in case . . ." Trailing off, she cast her gaze down. "Well, you know what I mean."

Telling Connor to be good now, she said, "Take a nice pair of pyjamas, and put the other stuff you need into that little zip-up bag. Okay?" Giving him a pointed look to make sure that he understood that she was talking about his nappies, she smiled when he nodded.

Closing the door when she'd gone, Dave looked at Connor. He could really do without the hassle of going round to Pauline's to drop him off, but there was no way he was stopping here and looking after him. And he wasn't going to go out and leave him and risk the little fucker setting fire to the place. So, telling the boy to go and get his things, he went up to his room to call Zak back and get the rest of the story.

CHAPTER
TWENTY-THREE

Terry hadn't said a word about Zak when Leanne and her mum had walked into the flat, and he definitely would have done if he'd known that Leanne had been sleeping with Zak. So Leanne had assumed that Kelly must have been lying to her about telling him in order to wind her up.

Relieved, she'd pushed it to the back of her mind, thinking that she would deal with Kelly later and make sure that she never did tell Terry. But right then, there were more important things to worry about. Like why Terry had become so angry when her mum had told him about Dave and Sue. Why did he care who Sue was sleeping with? Did he still want her for himself, or something?

Terry had adamantly denied that when she'd confronted him, saying that his only concern was Connor. But Leanne didn't believe him, and she'd cried, and smashed things, and accused him of all sorts. She'd even thrown his ring back at him, telling him that she'd rather die than marry him.

And the argument was still going strong now when the knock came at the front door. Ducking when she threw a shoe at him, Terry went out into the hall to answer it.

Thinking that it was probably one of the neighbours complaining about the noise, he was surprised to see Jay Osborne and a couple of PCs standing there. But when he saw the serious expression on Jay's face, his heart sank.

Unsure if *his* expression was due to dread that she'd come with bad news or to guilt because he'd realised that he'd been caught out, Jay said, "I'm going to have to ask you to come to the station to be formally interviewed about the disappearance of your daughter, Mr Day."

"*What?*" Terry gasped, peering at her incredulously. "Are you serious?"

"Deadly," the male PC told him bluntly. "So be a good lad and let's get moving, eh?"

Coming out into the hall just then, Leanne forgot all about the argument when she heard this. Rushing up to Terry, she clutched at his arm.

"I don't get this," he said, still looking at Jay. "You know I was at work when it happened. You've already talked to my boss about it."

"This isn't about the verified time," Jay informed him. "It's about the time between you arriving home from work and going to the hospital."

"I was here," Terry reminded her. "You know I was."

Leanne's heart was pounding now. She knew exactly what this was about — and exactly who was to blame. But if it was just a case of word against word, then she would swear black was blue that Kelly Greene was lying.

"We've already told you that he was here with me all night till we went to the hospital," she said now. "So why are you questioning him again?"

Glancing at her, Jay said, "Because we've just received new information to the contrary." Back to Terry now, she said, "Did you go anywhere between arriving back here and going to the hospital?"

"No," Terry said immediately. Then, remembering, he felt the blood drain from his face. "Yeah," he admitted, a helpless look in his eyes. "I went for a walk."

"Where to?" Jay asked, wishing that it wasn't true, because she genuinely liked this man and had hoped that he was completely innocent.

Running a hand through his hair, Terry said, "The late shop on Great Western Street."

"Did you come straight back?"

"No, I sat in the park for a while."

"How long for?" Jay asked. "And did anybody see you?"

"Couple of hours," Terry murmured, his heart sinking more with each incriminating word. "And, no, I don't think anyone saw me after I left the shop. It was dark, and raining, so no one was around."

Sighing regretfully, Jay nodded at the PCs.

"Terrence Phillip Day," the male officer said, taking his arm and pulling it behind his back. "I'm

444

arresting you on suspicion of the abduction and murder of Nicola Davina Day. You do not have to say anything . . ."

CHAPTER
TWENTY-FOUR

"Of course he can stay," Pauline said when Dave turned up on her doorstep with Connor and explained what had happened. "You just get yourself over to your dad. And don't worry about Connor; we're going to have a great time."

Thanking her, Dave winked at Connor and set off down the path.

Waving him off from the doorstep, Pauline smiled down at Connor. "Oh, it is lovely to see you," she said. "I was telling your mummy only today how much I've missed you, and I've got lots of ideas for things we can do. But they'll keep till tomorrow. Have you had your dinner yet?"

Connor shook his head, his eyes fixed on his garden on the other side of the low hedge. It was weeks since the fire, but the debris was still there: piles of charred wood, and glass, and bricks. And he was almost sure he could see some of his toys amongst the ruins.

Most of the top half of the house was destroyed, but the council had erected scaffolding around it as they prepared to start the rebuilding work. But even in this state, Connor would have moved back into it in a heartbeat. That was home, and it always would be.

446

Realising what he was looking at, and guessing that it was upsetting him, Pauline bustled him into her house, saying, "Come on, pet, let's get you in before you catch a cold. We'll put your things up in the spare room, then you can sit and watch telly with Uncle John while I make you something to eat." Catching sight of what John was actually watching as she said it, she quickly amended it to, "Or, better still, you can sit in the kitchen with me. I've got a couple of jigsaws you might like. Or some paper, if you want to draw?"

Nodding, Connor held her hand tightly as she took him up to the spare bedroom. He would rather be with his mum, but he was glad that he hadn't had to stay with Dave.

Sitting at the kitchen table after she'd cooked him some sausage, egg and chips, Pauline sipped at her tea and watched as Connor listlessly shoved the food around on his plate. He seemed even more troubled than the last time she'd seen him, and it broke her heart to think what must be going on inside that silent little head of his.

It must have really scared him to have seen Dave's dad fall down the stairs. Not to mention the stress he must have already been under knowing that his mummy's new boyfriend hated his daddy's guts. And then to be brought here and have to see his old house like that, a stark reminder of the awful night that had stolen his sister from him and shocked the very voice out of him.

It was all too much for a tiny child to be expected to cope with, so it was no wonder he was upset. But

Pauline would do whatever she could to make sure he had a comfortable night. And tomorrow she would take him to the museum to see the dinosaur exhibition.

Shoving her thoughts to the back of her mind when she realised that Connor was staring at her, she smiled, and said, "Everything okay, pet?"

Holding her gaze for several long moments, a thousand thoughts flitted across the dark surface of his eyes. Then, as if he'd decided something, he reached for the paper he'd been drawing on while she'd been cooking. Turning it over so that she could see the picture, he pushed it across the table towards her.

Taking her glasses out of her pocket, Pauline slipped them on, saying, "Oh, you want me to see what you've drawn. Let's have a look, then."

It was a crude drawing, typical of a six-year-old, and it took Pauline several moments to make out what the shapes represented. There was some kind of building, surrounded by what she presumed were meant to be trees. And in the centre of it there was a figure, apparently female because it had long hair. But unlike most children's drawings, the face didn't have a big smile; it had a down-turned mouth and what looked like teardrops on the cheeks.

"Is that your mummy?" Pauline asked gently.

Shaking his head, Connor carried on staring at her, his huge dark eyes desperately trying to convey the message to her.

Frowning, Pauline said, "It *is* a woman, though, isn't it?"

Connor nodded now.

It occurred to Pauline that it might be Nicky, but she hesitated about asking him in case he reacted badly to hearing the name out loud. But if that *was* who it was supposed to be, then surely he wanted her to know, or he wouldn't have shown it to her. Hoping that she was right, and that she wasn't about to upset him, she said, "Is it Nicky, pet?"

Connor nodded again.

"And is that her in your house?" Pauline probed, trying to be as gentle as she could.

A shake of the head now.

"But it is her inside someone's house?"

Another shake.

At a loss as to what to ask him next, Pauline smiled, and said, "Well, wherever she is, it's a lovely picture. You're very clever."

The hope that had flared in Connor's eyes died as suddenly as it had ignited.

Putting the picture down, Pauline said, "Shall I take that plate, because you don't look like you're enjoying it all that much? Then we can pop you in the bath and get you ready for bed, eh?"

Tears flooding his eyes, Connor got up and followed her upstairs. He didn't really know why he'd decided to show Pauline the picture, but he'd just felt like he should, because he trusted her and he'd thought that she might understand. But she'd given up trying to guess, and now he was scared that she might show it to Dave. And if Dave recognised the shed, he'd know that Connor had been out in the garden and might shout at him.

Drying him off with a big fluffy towel in the bedroom after his bath, Pauline emptied Connor's things out of the bag he'd packed. Not batting an eye when she saw the nappies, she simply put one on him, then slipped his pyjamas on him and tucked him up in the bed.

Nipping back downstairs to make him a cup of cocoa, she sat on the bed when she came back up and stroked his hair as he sipped at it. He looked so lost, the poor little thing. And she couldn't get that picture out of her head, and what he'd been trying to tell her by showing it to her.

"That picture . . ." Pauline said, making one last attempt. "Were you trying to tell me something, pet?"

Nodding slowly, Connor held his breath as he gazed back up at her. *Please let her get it right this time.*

"Do you think you know where Nicky is?" Pauline went on, her instincts bristling as she looked into those deep, dark, secret-holding eyes of his.

Connor nodded like he'd never nodded before.

"Can you tell me where?" Pauline asked.

Connor's chin began to wobble as the tears spilled over. He couldn't tell her, because he had no idea where Dave's house was. And he wouldn't have been able to even if he *had* known, because Dave would get mad at him for telling people where he lived when he'd already told Connor's mum that he didn't want anyone to know.

Sure that it was probably just wishful thinking on Connor's part, Pauline put her arms around him and rocked him gently until he'd stopped crying. Then, getting him to lie down, she pulled the quilt up around his shoulders and kissed him goodnight. Switching the light off then, leaving the door ajar so that he wouldn't be in complete darkness, she was just about to cross the landing when she thought she heard him speak.

"Was that you?" she asked, rushing back in. "Did you just say something? Can you say it again for Auntie Pauline?"

His voice barely a whisper, Connor drew on every last ounce of willpower to force the word out again.

"*Shed?*" Pauline repeated. "Is that what you said? Is that where you think Nicky is?"

Sighing with relief, Connor nodded, his sleepy eyes already beginning to roll.

"Can you talk to me some more?" Pauline urged. But the boy was too exhausted.

Rushing back downstairs, Pauline was so excited that she could barely speak herself as she told John what had just happened.

"You're imagining things," John said dismissively, bobbing his head to see the TV as she got in the way and blocked his view.

"Trust you not to be interested," Pauline snapped. "But I know what I heard. And look at this . . ." Rushing into the kitchen, she snatched up the picture and rushed back to show it to him.

"It's a kid's drawing," John grunted when she thrust it under his nose. "They all look like that."

"No, there's something about this one," Pauline insisted, waving it in front of his face. "Look at the expression on Nicky's face. And she's inside something, and he said it wasn't a house when I asked. So why would he suddenly come out and say shed if that wasn't what he meant?"

"I don't know," John grumbled. "But if you're that bothered, why don't you give that policewoman a ring? You know you've been dying for an excuse to contact her so you can quiz her about the search. And who knows, she might get a child psychologist onto it and crack the whole case."

Muttering, "Sarcastic bugger," Pauline stomped into the kitchen and lit a cigarette. Gazing at the picture again, she decided that she *would* give the policewoman a ring. She'd ignored her instincts to go and check on Connor that night, and he'd nearly died as a result. So could she really afford to ignore them now? She didn't think so.

Hands shaking, because she had no doubt that they would think she was a crazy old fool, Pauline went back into the living room to get the policewoman's number.

"What you doing?" John asked, glancing at her out of the corner of his eye.

"Never you mind," she said, hurrying back into the kitchen and closing the door. It would be hard enough making this call without him jeering at her.

Jay Osborne had had Terry put in one of the holding cells back at the station. Since he'd realised how serious this was, he'd taken her advice and opted not to be interviewed until his solicitor was present. Even though that meant being detained for the night, because the office concerned had informed them that his solicitor

452

was in London and wouldn't be back until the following afternoon.

Telling one of the PCs to make sure that somebody took Terry a cup of tea, Jay left him in the cell and headed to the canteen to get herself a coffee.

She'd really hoped that the anonymous caller who'd given them the tip-off had got it wrong, because she had genuinely thought that Terry was innocent. But now he'd admitted being awol for those couple of hours after getting home that night, added to which there had been a couple of half-hour periods when he'd still been at work during which he'd been alone, it looked like they'd have no choice but to investigate his movements.

Smiling wearily when Ann, her driver, came over just as she found herself a quiet table and sat down to drink her coffee in peace, she groaned when she heard about Pauline Wilson's call.

"Okay, well, let me just have this and we'll call in on her," she said. "And then I need to go to Cheetham Hill to let Sue Day know what's happening, because she's not answering her phone."

Livid about Terry being arrested, Leanne rooted through her pockets for the knife that Goldie had given her to protect herself with on the night of her party. Finding it, she set off for Kelly's house.

Kicking the door when she got there, she stood back and yelled, "Get yourself out here, you lying bitch!" Then she booted the door again, and didn't stop until Kelly opened it.

"What the fuck are you *doing?*" Kelly gasped, peering at the scuff marks on the door. "My mam's gonna go mad when she sees that."

"Do I look like I give a toss?" Leanne snarled.

"If this is about me telling Terry, I'm sorry," Kelly squawked, stumbling back over the doorstep as Leanne came towards her.

"It's not about that, and you know it," Leanne snarled. "It's about you grassing him up to the police!"

"I don't know what you're talking about," Kelly protested fearfully. "Honest to God, Lee, I haven't said nothing to them!"

"Your phone's ringing," Carole said, slapping Fred on the head as she walked past the couch. "And hurry up and answer it, 'cos I hate that fucking ringtone."

Jumping up, Fred ran into the kitchen to get his phone. Seeing Ben Greene's name, he grinned. "Yo, dude! Wha'ppen?"

"Your Leanne's gone off her head!" Ben squawked, sounding terrified. "She's kicking the shit out of our Kelly, accusing her of grassing up her boyfriend to the pigs. You'd best tell your mam to get round here and sort her out before my mam gets back from the pub, or there'll be murders!"

Rushing back into the living room, Fred relayed the message. Then, telling Ben that they were on their way, he followed his mum, who was already dragging her jacket on as she marched out of the door and up the path.

★   ★   ★

454

Dave was in the pub when his mobile rang. Grinning slyly when he saw Carole's name on the screen, he answered it, hoping to hear good news about Terry.

"Hope you're proud of yourself," Carole spat at him, sounding breathless as she paced down the road. "Our Leanne's been rowing with Terry all day about you and that whore, and now he's been arrested and she's kicking seven shades out of Kelly Greene over it."

"So what's it got to do with me?" Dave asked, taking a casual swig of his Scotch.

"It's your fault she's het up in the first place," Carole yelled. "So you'd best get your arse over here and sort her out before *she* gets arrested, an' all. And Maggie Greene's on her way home, so I'm going to have to deal with her. And if I do for her and get banged up, you'll have to take our Fred and Len into your little love nest, won't you? So it's your choice!"

Chuckling softly when she hung up on him, Dave finished his drink and strolled out to the car. He'd not long made that anonymous call, but if the pigs had already arrested the cunt it could only mean that they'd already suspected him of having something to do with it. And that was great, because now Terry wouldn't only have to face the fact that he'd lost his family, he'd have to accept that he'd lost Leanne as well, because they'd never survive as a couple with him behind bars. And even if Leanne was the kind of girl who would wait for him, she was more likely to go back to that lad she'd started seeing again.

Wonderful stuff!

"I'm so sorry for dragging you round here like this," Pauline apologised when Jay arrived. "I wouldn't normally have bothered you, but with everything that's already happened I thought I should let you know. And you did say you wanted people to tell you anything, no matter how small it seemed."

Assuring her that it wasn't a problem, Jay followed her through the living room and into the kitchen, leaving Ann in the car. This should only take a minute, she reckoned, so there was no point them both going in.

Handing Connor's drawing to Jay, Pauline pointed to the sad-faced figure in the centre, saying, "That's Nicky. And I thought this was supposed to be a house," she went on indicating the structure around the figure. "But Connor said no."

"He spoke to you?" Jay asked, her eyebrows rising.

"Well, not at that point," Pauline admitted. "I was asking him questions, and he was nodding or shaking his head. But when I put him to bed, I'd just come out of the room when I thought I heard him say something. So I went back in and tried to get him to say it again, and he said 'shed'."

"Shed?" Jay repeated. "Are you sure?"

"Well, almost sure," Pauline said, folding her arms now. "But it was pretty quiet, so I can't be positive."

"He didn't say anything else, then?"

"No. He just went to sleep."

Popping her head around the door just then, Ann told Jay that there was a disturbance across the estate,

456

and they were the closest unit so they would have to attend.

Asking Pauline if she could take the picture with her, Jay said, "I was about to go and see Mrs Day, as it happens, so I'll get her to take a look at it. See if she can think what it might mean."

"You know she's at the hospital, don't you?" Pauline told her, following her out.

"No, I didn't," Jay said. "Nothing serious, I hope?"

Telling her that it wasn't Sue being treated, Pauline said, "I only found out about it earlier myself, but it seems she's moved in with Dave at his dad's place, and she was there when they took Jack in, so she's gone with him while Dave dropped Connor off here." Shrugging now, sure that the policewoman was as mystified by this new turn of events as she herself was, she said, "She seems happy enough, so I'm not going to knock them. But when you see her, can you tell her that Connor's been good as gold, and to give me a ring if she wants me to keep him another night."

Telling her that she would pass the message on, Jay got back into the car where Ann was waiting for her.

"Kelly Greene's apparently being assaulted by Leanne Miller," Ann explained as they set off. "One of the neighbours called it in; reckoned they saw a knife. And the mothers are supposedly looking set to get stuck into each other, too. And in the meantime Leanne's dad's turned up."

"Funny," Jay murmured, slipping the drawing into her pocket and buckling her seat belt. "I've just been told that Mr Miller senior is in hospital, and Sue Day's with him. So what's Dave doing here?"

"Having fun watching the women scrap, knowing him," Ann muttered caustically.

Kelly had escaped by the time the police arrived. Back inside the house, she'd locked herself in the bathroom, and was crying as she surveyed the mess that Leanne had made of her face and hair in the mirror. She was going to have a huge black eye, and it would take months for the hair to grow back where Leanne had yanked a whole handful out. And Kelly didn't have a clue what she was supposed to have done.

When Leanne had started kicking the door, Kelly had been sure that she was going to have a go at her for telling Terry about her and Zak. But she'd accused her of grassing him up to the police, which hadn't made any sense, because Kelly hadn't spoken to the police. But Leanne hadn't believed her and had started threatening her with the knife. Then both of their mams had turned up and started kicking off at each other, and it had all gone mad. But when Leanne's dad had come and taken the knife off Leanne she'd gone really loco and had laid into Kelly with her fists instead. And her dad had left her to it — until one of the neighbours had shouted that they'd called the police.

Hearing the sirens as the police car turned into the road and pulled up outside, Kelly crept into her bedroom to watch what was happening through the window. There was no way she was going out there and grassing Leanne up for what she'd done, or she'd be dead next time Leanne got hold of her.

Dave had tossed the knife under someone else's hedge by the time the police car pulled up, closely followed by a vanload of uniforms. He'd have left them to it, but with some of the coke still sitting undelivered in his boot there was no way he was risking them pulling him on suspicion of trying to leave the scene of a disturbance, because then they'd have the authority to search his car.

"Right, what's going on?" Ann asked, jumping out of the car and coming straight to the point.

"Don't look at *me*," Maggie Greene said indignantly. "I've been at bingo and come home to find *her* —" she jabbed a finger in Leanne's direction "— kicking ten tons out of our Kelly."

"What have you got to say about it?" Jay asked Leanne.

"Nothing," Leanne said, shrugging nonchalantly. "She went for me, so I defended myself."

"Like fucking hell you did," Maggie squawked. "Our Ben's already told me you was trying to kick the door in. That's why Kelly come out in the first place."

Fronting it out, Leanne said, "I didn't kick any door. I was just talking to her about something, and she flipped out."

"Everything's sorted now," Dave interjected calmly, unfazed by the PCs who were standing around them in a semicircle, waiting to pounce if it kicked off again.

"Where's Kelly?" Ann wanted to know. "Let's have her out to give us *her* side before we decide if it's sorted, eh?"

Catching the dark look of warning that Dave was giving her, Maggie felt a shiver of apprehension ripple down her spine. Inhaling deeply, she said, "It's all right. There's no harm done. Just two girls having a scrap over a lad. You know how it is."

"We had a report that a knife was seen," Jay said.

"Knife?" Maggie repeated, folding her arms and looking at the Millers as if they were all on the same side now. "Don't know nothing about a knife. Do you?"

"Someone's telling porkies," Carole said, shaking her head as if she couldn't believe that people were capable of such exaggeration. "There's no knives round here. Like Maggie said," she went on, standing shoulder to shoulder with the other mother as if they were the best of mates, "this is just a silly girly thing got out of hand."

"Won't mind if we search you all, then, will you?" Ann said.

"Feel free," Dave said, holding out his arms, safe in the knowledge that he had nothing on him.

Ann patted the women down, while two of the male officers gave Dave a quick search. Finding nothing, they turned to Jay and shook their heads.

"I'd still like to see Kelly," Jay insisted.

"Sorry, love, but she's gone out," Maggie lied, praying that Kelly would have the sense to stay inside. "She said she was meeting up with some friends, so I couldn't tell you where she'd be by now."

Aware that they had closed ranks and that she was going to get nowhere, Jay sighed and said, "So I take it no one wants to press charges against anyone?"

"No," they all replied in unison.

"We'll leave you to it, then," Jay said, heading towards the car as the PCs went back to their van. Pausing there, she turned back, saying, "Sorry to hear about your father, by the way. I'm just heading over to the hospital to speak to Mrs Day if you'd like a lift."

"No, you're all right, love," Dave said, retaining the unconcerned smile, even though he could have killed her for saying that in front of his daughter, because he could already feel Leanne's furious glare burning a hole into the back of his head. Now he'd have her on his back about that as well as everything else, and he hadn't even had the chance to talk to her yet.

CHAPTER
TWENTY-FIVE

Jack had been resuscitated twice in the ambulance on the way over to the hospital and it had been touch and go for a while, the paramedics warning Sue that he might not make it. But the old man was made of sterner stuff, and he'd rallied round by the time they reached the hospital.

He was awake now, but very weak, and Sue had felt compelled to hold his hand as she sat beside his bed, even though she didn't know him all that well.

Jack was grateful for her being there, but he was also worried. Gazing at her through half-slitted eyes now, he said, "You should be with Connor, not sitting here with me."

"Connor's fine," she assured him.

"No," Jack said, shaking his head. "You shouldn't leave him with David. Please . . ."

"He's not with Dave," Sue said, a flicker of a frown on her brow. "He's staying at my friend's house for the night."

Sighing weakly, seeming relieved to hear this, Jack said, "He's a good boy, you know. But very sad."

"I know," Sue murmured guiltily. "He's been through a lot lately."

"You know he can talk, don't you?" Jack said quietly.

"No." Sue shook her head. "He's not been able to talk since the fire. The doctor's say it's psychological; after-effect of the shock."

"I've heard him," Jack insisted. "Earlier . . . calling out to someone called Nicky."

"That's his sister," Sue gasped, her eyes stinging with sudden tears as she realised that it must be true. She'd never mentioned Nicky to Jack, and Dave barely gave him the time of day, so he wouldn't have told him. So the only way he could have known was if, as he'd said, he'd heard Connor saying the name.

Licking his lips now, Jack said, "I'm tired."

"Do you want me to go and let you get some sleep?" Sue asked, sniffing back the tears.

"No, stay," he said, his fingers holding onto hers. "I meant tired of life. It's not been the same since . . ." Trailing off, he inhaled deeply and slowly.

Scared that he was taking his last breath, Sue gazed at him worriedly. "Are you all right, Mr Miller?"

"I'm still here," he said quietly. Then, "You should leave."

Sue's frown deepened. She'd just asked if he wanted her to leave and he'd said no. Now he was telling her to go. She supposed it must be the drugs confusing him, but she wished he'd make up his mind.

"David's no good," he went on, sounding sad now. "I know he's my boy, but he's trouble, and he'll hurt you. He hurts everyone who cares about him. And you do, don't you?"

"Yes," Sue admitted, feeling the need to defend Dave, because he wasn't as bad as his dad seemed to think. "I know he's not a saint," she said, "but he's been good to me and Connor, and I don't know what I'd have done without him these past few weeks. I was surprised, actually, because I've known him a long time and hadn't seen this side of him. But he's got a good heart." Smiling now, she squeezed Jack's hand. "Obviously takes after you, eh?"

There was a tap on the door just then, and Jay Osborne looked in. Feeling the heavy atmosphere in the room, she instinctively lowered her voice as she said, "Sorry for disturbing you, Mrs Day, but do you think I could have a quick word?"

Glancing up at her, her eyes filled with dread, Sue said, "It's not Connor, is it? Nothing's happened to him?"

Shaking her head, Jay said, "Connor's fine. I've just come from Mrs Wilson's and she said to tell you he's been as good as gold." Casting a quick glance at Jack now and seeing how frail he looked, she said, "Maybe we should talk outside so we don't disturb Mr Miller."

"Don't mind me," Jack said quietly, the rare hint of humour in his voice surprising Sue, because Dave had told her that his dad was a miserable old fucker — and she hadn't seen much evidence to the contrary since she'd been living with him. "I'm not going to be here too much longer, so I'm hardly going to tell anyone what you're saying, am I?"

"Don't say that," Sue murmured sadly.

"It's true," Jack said softly. "But don't worry, I won't be missed. Anyhow, come on in and say what you've got to say, love."

Jay had really wanted to discuss this with her in private, but Sue was obviously reluctant to leave the old man. And Jay couldn't blame her if he was as far gone as he seemed to think he was.

Saying, "Okay, if you're sure," Jay stepped into the room and closed the door quietly. "I'll try to keep it brief."

Pulling up a chair beside Sue now, she said, "We received an anonymous call earlier tonight, from someone who claimed to have information linking your husband to your daughter's disappearance."

"No," Sue said immediately, shaking her head. "No way. Not Terry. He loves those kids, and he would never do anything to hurt them."

Jay agreed, but she couldn't say that. Instead, she said, "We've taken Mr Day into custody, and he'll be formally interviewed as soon as his solicitor is available. But in the meantime, I need to know if there's anything you can tell me about that night which might have relevance to this new line of inquiry?"

"Like what?" Sue asked, frowning. "I've told you everything."

"Maybe you could have forgotten something," Jay said, holding Sue's gaze. "Is there a possibility that you could have seen your husband before you went out that night, for example? Or did you see his car in the vicinity when he should have been at work?"

"No, definitely not," Sue said, dipping her gaze and peering down at Jack's wrinkled hand in hers.

"Are you absolutely certain?" Jay persisted. "I know you've reported him for domestic violence in the past so, if you're worried about speaking out, please be assured that you'll have our full protection."

Blushing deeply now, ashamed to be receiving sympathy about something that had been an absolute lie, Sue muttered, "He's not like that. They were just arguments that got out of hand, and I should never have said what I said. He's a good man, and he loves his kids. He just didn't love me any more, and I lashed out. But it wasn't true."

Accepting this without question, because it was exactly what she'd suspected all along, Jay said, "I'm sure Mr Day will appreciate your honesty. But we still need to know if there's anything you've forgotten to tell us about that night. Maybe Nicky mentioned her father?"

"No." Sue shook her head. "Things had been pretty bad between me and Terry, and I banned him from seeing them."

"I understand the situation," Jay said softly. "But if you're saying that your husband is a good man who loves the children, do you think there's a possibility that Nicky might have continued to have contact with him without your knowledge?"

"No." Another shake of the head. "I'd have known if she'd been seeing him, and she definitely wasn't. Anyway, she never went out except to go to school."

"And you don't think there's even a slight chance that he might have called round to the house to see them that night; that Nicky might have alerted him that you'd gone out?"

Sue's blush was deepening. She felt terrible. If Terry had been arrested, then they must have reason to doubt his alibi. But there was no way he would have gone to the house, not after Sue had already had him arrested for trespassing. And Nicky hadn't been there when Sue had gone out — but she still couldn't admit that, not even if it led to them clearing Terry. Because then *she* would be in trouble. And it would destroy her if they took Connor away. Apart from which, Dave wouldn't want to have anything to do with her if he knew what she'd done.

Assuming that Sue's red face was the result of having had to admit that she'd lied about Terry being violent, Jay decided that there was probably nothing more that she would learn from her tonight. They would talk to her again when Terry's questioning had got under way, but they were done for now. So, thanking her and apologising again to Jack, she got up and walked to the door.

Hesitating there when she remembered Connor's picture, she took it out of her pocket, saying, "Oh, by the way, Mrs Wilson asked me to take a look at this. Apparently, Connor drew it earlier, and she was concerned about it." Handing it to Sue now, she said, "I'm not sure whether it's anything more than a display of his emotions about Nicky, but Mrs Wilson seems to think that he thinks he knows where Nicky is."

"Did he talk to her?" Sue asked, wondering if she was the only one who didn't know that Connor had started talking again. And worrying about what he might have told them already.

"Not at first," Jay said. "Apparently she just asked him questions and he nodded or shook his head. But later on, she thought she heard him say the word 'shed'." Pointing at the picture now, she repeated what Pauline had told her. "That's Nicky, and those look like trees, and we think that this must be the shed he was referring to. I just wondered if it might mean anything to you?"

Looking at the teardrops on the face in the picture, Sue felt a wave of sadness wash over her. Poor Connor. First talking to himself as if he was actually talking to Nicky. And now this. He was obviously missing her even more than anyone had realised.

"My shed," Jack murmured just then, his voice even weaker than before as he peered sideways at the picture Sue was holding. "Broken glass, horizontal trees. Boy's been going down there. Came back crying."

Jay gave Sue a questioning look. Shrugging, Sue said, "I didn't even know there *was* a shed. And I didn't know Connor had been in the garden. He was probably just wishing Nicky was there playing with him like she used to."

"David doesn't know," Jack said, clutching at Sue's hand as pain skittered across his brow. "Thinks it's his shed now," he went on after a second. "Don't tell him the boy's been down there or he'll be angry."

468

Gravely concerned as the look of pain on the old man's face intensified, Sue said, "I won't tell him if you don't want me to, Mr Miller." Glancing up at Jay now, she said, "Should we get the nurse?"

Already heading for the door, Jay said, "I'll get her. You stay here."

Calling for help, Jay stood back as a couple of nurses came into the room to minister to Jack. Mrs Wilson was convinced that there was something important about the picture, and now Mr Miller had said that Connor had been crying when he'd come back from playing down at his shed today, and Jay was beginning to think that it might be worth taking a look at it. She doubted that Nicky could really be in there, because they had searched every house and garden on the estate. But if there was even the slimmest chance that something had been overlooked she wanted to know.

Standing beside her, Sue was shaking so badly that her arm kept knocking against Jay's. Giving her a reassuring smile when the nurses settled Jack down, Jay said, "He's okay now — don't get upset."

Nodding, Sue exhaled tensely and went back to her seat.

Coming over as Sue took the old man's hand in hers again, Jay said, "I'm going to go and let you rest, Mr Miller. But I wonder if you'd mind if I go and take a look in your shed? Probably nothing there, but I'd like to see — so I can reassure Connor, if nothing else."

All too aware that he was slipping away, Jack told her to look wherever she liked. His fingers too weak to squeeze Sue's more than a whisper now, he added,

469

"Sorry, Sue, but he's got things he shouldn't have and it's time he was stopped." Pausing for breath, he swallowed loudly. "Keep Connor away from him," he murmured after a moment. "He's . . ."

"Oh, no," Sue sobbed as Jack's mouth went slack. "Please don't die, Mr Miller. Dave should be here with you, not me. Just wait till I've phoned him, *please*."

"He's gone," Jay said quietly, putting a gentle hand on Sue's shoulder. "And so's the pain. Look."

Glancing up through her tears, Sue saw that Jack's face was no longer agonised; it was relaxed and peaceful.

Swiping at the tears, she said, "I've only known him a week, so you must think I'm stupid for crying like this. But he was nice to me, and Connor seemed to like him. And I know it must have disturbed him suddenly having us move in when he'd spent so long on his own in the middle of nowhere, but he never showed it. He just left us to get on with it."

"So he didn't live on the estate?" Jay asked.

"No." Plucking a tissue out of the box on Jack's bedside table, Sue wiped her nose. "He's got a house just outside Wythenshawe. Dave moved in with him when he left Carole. Oh, God, Dave," she said now. "I'm going to have to tell him about his dad. And he was so happy earlier."

Watching thoughtfully as Sue slid her hand out of Jack's, Jay said, "Could you tell me the address, please? I'd like to nip over there before you and Dave get back, so we can take a look around without disturbing you."

Telling Jay what she needed to know, Sue thanked her for being so thoughtful. Then, walking out into the corridor with her, she went off to call Dave while Jay walked quickly back out to the car.

Jay's instincts were on fire. She hadn't wanted to say anything to Sue in case she'd got it wrong, but there was something about this whole set-up that disturbed her. She'd heard how much Dave Miller hated Terry Day for setting up home with his daughter, so could it be possible that he had had something to do with the fire as a means of revenge? Unlikely that he'd have targeted Sue's house, given that they had apparently embarked on a relationship, but there was definitely something suspicious going on. And Ann wouldn't mind trekking over there, because she'd already made it clear that she'd love nothing better than to catch Dave Miller out. And even if they found nothing but the "things" his father had said that he had but *shouldn't* have, it would be something.

"Dave?" Sue said when he answered his phone, a fresh burst of sobs catching in her throat. "You need to come to the hospital. Your d-dad . . ."

"Is he dead?" Dave asked, sounding like he didn't give a toss.

Misinterpreting the coldness as shock, Sue said, "I'm so sorry, love. But he wasn't on his own. I was holding his hand. And he'd been chatting to me and the policewoman before —"

"What policewoman?" Dave interrupted, the sound of him pulling deeply on a cigarette hissing down Sue's ear.

"The one who's been looking for Nicky," Sue told him, sniffling back her tears. "She dropped by to tell me that they've arrested Terry. And then she showed me a picture that Connor drew, and your dad reckoned it was your shed, so she's gone to take a look at it. But she said she'd be out of the way by the time we —"

"What the fuck do you mean, she's gone to look at it?" Dave cut her off, his voice furious.

"Sorry," Sue said, thinking that he was offended that they were doing this when his father had just died.

"They've got no fucking right," Dave snarled, his breath jerking now as he ran out of the pub to his car. "They need a warrant to search it."

"Your dad told her it was okay," Sue said quietly.

"Yeah, well, it's none of his business any more," Dave snapped. "He's dead, so it's mine, and it's not okay by me."

"I'm sorry," Sue said again, sure that he was just lashing out about this because of grief.

"Be at the door," Dave snarled. "I'll be there in a minute."

"Don't you think you should come and say goodbye to your dad?" Sue asked. But Dave had already disconnected the call.

CHAPTER
TWENTY-SIX

Unaware that Dave was speeding their way with a terrified Sue in the passenger seat of his car, Jay climbed out of the squad car when Ann pulled up at the front of the house. A second car turned into the driveway a few seconds later, carrying the three extra uniforms she had requested — just in case something turned up and she needed the scene to be secured for evidence.

Ann was convinced that the "things" Jack Miller had alluded to would probably turn out to be drugs, and she couldn't wait to get stuck in. But Jay just wanted to do a quick search before Sue and Dave came home, because she didn't want to cause any more distress than was absolutely necessary under the circumstances.

"Bloody hell," one of the PCs complained, walking down the side of the house and shining a powerful torch-beam on the garden. "It's going to be murder getting through this lot."

"There's a bit of a path over here," Ann said, pointing towards the trodden-down section she'd just spotted when he'd lit up that area.

Going over to it, Jay was just about to set off to look for the shed when Dave's headlights arced through the

473

darkness as he roared up the drive and screeched to a stop behind the second squad car.

Jumping out, Dave rushed towards them, yelling, "Get the fuck off my property!"

"We've had permission," Jay informed him calmly, glad that the extra PCs were male, because Dave Miller looked like he'd be difficult to contain if he exploded.

"Not from me, you haven't," Dave said sharply. "And it's my house, so unless you've got a warrant, you'd best get the fuck out!"

Running up to him, Sue clutched at his arm. He'd been too angry to speak when he'd picked her up outside the hospital, and he'd driven here like a madman. But she was sure it was just the pain of losing his father that was causing him to lash out. And guilt, for not having been there when he'd died.

"Just let them take a look," she said now. "They'll only be a minute, and then we can go inside and have a drink."

Jerking away from her, he said, "Shut the fuck up, you stupid bitch."

"Don't, Dave," she implored, still holding his arm. "I know you're upset, but there's no need to take it out on me. I love you."

"If you don't get your fucking hands off me right now," he snarled, glaring down at her. "I'll knock you out. Now fucking *move*!"

"Oi, pack it in," one of the PCs called out, walking towards them. "We know you've lost your dad, but there's no need for that kind of behaviour."

474

"Well, get the fuck out of here, and I'll be fine," Dave said through gritted teeth.

"We don't need your permission to search the property," Ann informed him, a small smirk of triumph on her face. "We've already got the permission of the owner."

"If you're referring to my dad, he's dead," Dave reminded her. "So *I'm* the owner now."

"We won't know that until we see it in writing," Ann came back at him smoothly. "Until then, we've had all the permission we need."

"I'd think about that if I was you," Dave growled. "Because I won't drop this; I'll take legal action and make you prove that my dead dad gave you that permission. And you won't be able to prove it, as you well know, so whatever you find won't be admissible as evidence. And you don't want to risk me getting away with whatever you think I've done, now, do you?"

Keeping her cool, even though she knew that he was right, Ann said, "Fine. So we'll stay right here and ring through to the station and get them to apply for an emergency warrant."

"No need," Jay said, looking Dave square in the eye. "We have cause to suspect that a child may be being held here against her will, and that gives us the authority to search without a warrant. Which is exactly what I intend to do — with or without your co-operation."

Glancing at the four uniformed coppers, Dave knew that he wouldn't be able to take them all on at once. But he couldn't just stand here and let them search the shed, because they would definitely find what they were looking for. And the chances were that the girl was dead by now, so he'd be up for murder as well as kidnapping and false imprisonment. He had to run, and run *far*. But for that he needed his passport and money, both of which were in the house.

In the box with his gun.

Knowing exactly what he had to do, Dave pulled the knife he'd retrieved from under the hedge out of his pocket and, slinging an arm around Sue's neck, pressed the tip of the blade into her throat.

"You'd all best fuck off," he barked, walking Sue backwards down the path. "And I mean it, so don't try anything funny or she'll cop for it."

Holding her hand up to stop the PCs from doing anything, Jay said, "Let her go, Mr Miller. This is just silly."

"*Silly?*" he repeated, sneering nastily as he reached the side door. "You're not at fucking boarding school now, love. This ain't *silly*, it's deadly fucking serious. You're trespassing on my land, and I'm taking a hostage to make sure you leave. Got it?"

Holding the knife flush across Sue's throat now, to make sure she didn't try and make a run for it when he took his arm off her neck, Dave took his house keys out of his pocket and unlocked the door. Dragging her inside, he shoved her through the porch and into the kitchen. Relocking the door, he slid all the bolts into place and ordered her up to the bedroom.

"What's wrong with you?" Sue gasped, stumbling on the stairs because her legs were shaking so badly. "They only want to have a quick look in the shed. They don't really think Nicky's in there. It's more for Connor's sake than theirs."

"You are one fucking stupid bitch," Dave spat, unlocking his bedroom door and pushing her inside.

"I can't believe you're being like this," she said tearfully, bouncing as she landed heavily on the bed. "You were so lovely earlier. What have I done to make you so mad?"

"You think I was lovely, do you?" Dave sneered. "Well, you're even more stupid than I thought, then, aren't you?" Never taking his eyes off her, he reached to the back of the wardrobe and pulled out a metal box. Unlocking it, he took out the gun he needed.

Sue's breath caught in her throat. "What are you going to do with that?" she gasped.

"What do you think?" Dave shot back, checking to make sure that the clip was full.

"You're not going to kill me, are you?"

"Eventually," Dave said coldly, going to the window and peering out to see what the police were doing. It was too dark to make out anything more than silhouettes, but he was pretty sure that they were all still up at this end of the garden. No doubt they'd have called for armed back-up by now, but he planned to be long gone by the time it arrived.

Taking a deep breath, Sue yelled, *"HE'S GOT A GUN!"*

"Stupid *bitch*!" Dave snarled, turning and whacking her across the face with the weapon's barrel.

Sobbing, she held a hand to her wounded cheek, feeling faint when blood oozed out from between her fingers.

"Get back downstairs," Dave ordered, pointing the gun at her head now.

Barely able to stand because her legs felt like jelly, Sue forced her body to move. Losing her footing on the last few steps, she tumbled down and landed on her knees at the bottom. Hauling her roughly up by the back of her jacket, Dave threw her into the living room.

Keeping the light off, he looked out through the nets. He couldn't see any of the police officers now, and assumed that they had all dived for cover at the mention of the gun. An Armed Response Unit would be on its way by now, and he had to get away before it arrived. But he'd left his car keys in the ignition, and he had no doubt that the pigs would have taken them by now to stop him making a quick getaway. There was plenty of woodland to hide in if he went on foot, but now that they knew he had a gun, they would follow at a distance and keep him in their sights until one of the marksmen could get a clear shot at him. So he had no option but to take them all out before the back-up arrived, and give himself a good head start.

After putting out the urgent request for armed back-up, Jay sent one of the PCs around to the front of the house to keep watch in case Dave tried to escape from that side before they arrived. Telling another to watch the side door, and the third to watch the back of the house with Ann, she picked up a large screwdriver from a heap of tools she'd noticed by the outhouse door. Putting her head down, she made her way up the path towards the shed. If Miller was desperate enough to take his own girlfriend hostage in order to stop them from seeing what was in there, then she wanted to know what it was.

Barely able to see because the moon was blanketed by a thick bank of clouds, Jay felt her way around to the door at one of the ends of the structure. Running her hands up it, she felt the padlocks and realised that she would probably need a much more specialised tool to prise them off. But it was an old shed, so the chances were that the hinges would be less secure.

Feeling her way to the other side of the door, she eased the flat end of the screwdriver between the wood and the metal and wrenched it backwards and forwards in the hopes of splintering the wood and loosening the holding screws.

Pausing after several minutes to wipe her sweaty hands on her trousers, Jay cocked her head when she caught a faint sound coming from inside the shed.

"Hello . . .?" she called, her voice a harsh whisper because she didn't want to alert Dave Miller to what she was doing. "Is somebody in there?"

Pressing her ear against the wood, she listened hard. Hearing the sound again, she was almost sure that it was a human voice, although it was so faint she could barely hear it.

"Nicky?" she said, her mouth so close to the wood that she could taste it. "Nicky, if that's you, don't worry. I'm going to have to get help, but I'll be back, so just sit tight."

Dashing back up the path now, she waved the PCs over.

Watching through the nets, Dave saw what was happening and knew that the time had come to take action.

"Looks like they've found your girl," he murmured, squatting down and resting the barrel of the gun on the ledge to get as steady an aim as he could.

"Nicky?" Sue gasped. "How — how do you know?"

"Because your nosy mate's just come back from snooping in my shed," Dave said, peering through his sights and wishing the figures would stop fading in and out of focus, because he needed to be deadly accurate if he was going to take them all out before they scattered and he could no longer locate them.

"So she *was* in there," Sue croaked. "You've had her all this time? But why? What's she ever done to you?"

"Haven't you figured it out yet, you thick bitch?" Dave snarled contemptuously. "You know what they say about an eye for an eye. Well, how about a daughter for a daughter?"

"This is about Terry?" Sue gasped. "Nicky *and* me."

"And the penny finally drops," Dave sneered. "About fucking time!"

"That's evil," Sue cried, barely able to believe what was happening. "What Terry did had nothing to do with me and Nicky."

"Maybe not Nicky, but *you* knew what was going on, and you let it happen," Dave spat back at her.

"I thought we'd sorted all that out," Sue said plaintively. "You know I had no idea. I was just as hurt as you were. *More* so, in fact."

"Bullshit!" Dave hissed. "Leanne was only *twelve* when she started babysitting for you, and she was fucking gorgeous even then, so don't try and tell me the dirty bastard wasn't already eyeing her up. And women who say they don't know what's going on under their noses are liars. You knew all right."

"I *didn't*," Sue protested, sliding her hand out and groping around for something heavy to defend herself with when he came at her, which she knew he would. "I swear on my kids' lives, I didn't."

"Like that means anything," Dave snorted. "You went out and left a six-year-old alone in the house so you could swan off for a dirty fucking weekend. And don't bother trying to lie to me about that, sweetheart. You might have fooled that lot out there, but *I* know what really happened, 'cos I already had your Nicky by then. So don't be giving me none of that *swear on my kids' lives* bullshit, 'cos you don't give a fucking toss about them."

"Yes, I do," Sue replied quietly, her fingers settling on the rim of Jack's heavy glass ashtray. "I love them."

"Shut the fuck up," Dave spat, his voice thick with contempt. "Or I'll change my mind about using you as a hostage and kill you right here and fucking now!"

Outside, Jay had just moved into the exact right position in relation to the three PCs she was talking to for Dave to take them out in quick succession.

"*JAAAY!*" Ann screamed as the first shots thundered out through the window and Jay slumped to the ground at her feet.

Instinctively shoving Ann aside, one of the male PCs grabbed Jay's arm and dragged her into the tall grass, just as a second barrage of shots flared out.

But the third burst of bullets sprayed the ceiling and walls of the living room as Sue took an almighty swing at Dave's head with the ashtray, cutting a deep gash into the flesh behind his ear and knocking him to the floor.

EPILOGUE

"Are you all right, pet?" Pauline asked, giving Sue a warm hug.

Nodding, Sue dabbed at her tears with a tissue. "It's just so sad," she murmured, gazing at the mound of earth the gravediggers had tossed over the coffin. "I keep wondering if it was us being there that stressed him out and pushed him over the edge."

"Oh, I doubt it," Pauline said softly. "I knew Jack for years before he moved, and he was a nice man. He didn't deserve a thug like Dave for a son, so if anyone caused him stress by moving in it was *him*. If anything, you and Connor probably gave Jack some comfort in his last few days. You definitely did in his last minutes, because you were there for him. And there's nothing worse when you get to mine and Jack's age than the thought of dying alone, believe me."

Thanking her, because her words had salved a little of the guilt she'd been feeling, Sue said, "He kept telling me to leave, but I didn't understand what he meant. Now I know he was trying to warn me about Dave." Pausing, she bit her lip and shook her head, murmuring, "I can't believe I left Connor with him. He could have done anything."

"Yes, well, he didn't," Pauline reminded her firmly. "He brought him to me. And that was the best place the lad could have been, because I'd have protected him with my life."

Smiling sadly, Sue reached for her hand and gave it a squeeze. "Thanks, Pauline. I'll never forget what you've done for us. And I know I don't deserve it, because I've been horrible to you at times."

"Don't you be so silly," Pauline scolded. "Anyway, never mind all that. You just concentrate on getting you and the kids sorted."

"I will," Sue murmured, blowing her nose again. "As soon as the council stops messing about and gives us the house they promised at the start of this."

Tutting, Pauline said, "They're buggers, aren't they? And I've seen three empty houses on the estate this week alone. Want me to have a go at them?" she offered then. "As chair of the association, I should think I'll hold a fair bit of clout."

"No, don't worry about it," Sue said quickly, sensing that the council might just dig their heels in even harder if they had Pauline harassing them. "The hostel's not as bad as I thought it would be. And at least the kids have got people around them all the time, so they feel safe when I'm not there."

Terry and Leanne had just arrived. Spotting them as they headed through the gate hand in hand, Pauline nudged Sue, and said, "Do you think we'd best go out the other way?"

"No." Sue shook her head. "It's not her fault, and it's time we got this sorted once and for all." Catching the look of incredulity on Pauline's face, she said, "I know they started out wrong, but they must really love each other if they're still together after everything that's happened. And they're engaged now, so even if I can't stand her I suppose I should make my peace with her if she's going to be part of the kids' lives."

"Well, you're a bigger woman than I'd be under the circumstances," Pauline said admiringly. Seeing the wheelchair being pushed through the car park just then, she said, "Oh, those policewomen are here. Will you be all right with these two on your own while I nip over and say hello?"

"I'll be fine," Sue said, stepping behind the huge angel headstone that was towering over the neighbouring grave. "But can you do me a favour, and don't tell the police I'm here? I can't face them just yet."

"Oh?" Pauline gave her a curious look.

Shaking her head, Sue cast a hooded glance in Terry and Leanne's direction, indicating that she didn't want to discuss it in front of them.

Biting her lip when Pauline bustled away, Sue prayed that she'd keep the policewomen talking for long enough for her to say what she had to say to Terry and Leanne then make a quick escape. She knew she couldn't avoid it for ever, but the last thing she wanted was to get arrested in front of them. And now that Nicky had been interviewed about what had happened that night, it was only a matter of time before they came for her and everyone found out what a terrible mother she was.

Terry was apprehensive as he and Leanne reached the graveside. They'd missed the funeral service because Leanne had wanted to visit her dad in prison that morning. Arriving here now, his heart had sunk when he'd spotted Sue. But when he'd suggested waiting until she'd gone before coming over, Leanne had insisted that she wanted to say goodbye to her grandfather. Terry just hoped she didn't kick off, because he'd had enough of all the fighting and arguing.

Sue was equally nervous, because she had no doubt that Dave would have told Leanne the truth about what had happened by now. And if *she* knew, then so did Terry. But, much as she was dreading his reaction to seeing her, she knew that she would have to take whatever he threw at her — for the kids' sakes. They would obviously have to live with him while she was in prison, and the last thing she wanted was for him to turn them against her and refuse to let her see them again. And if that meant building bridges with Leanne, then so be it.

Giving Terry a sick little smile across the grave now, she took a deep breath, and said, "Hello, Terry . . . Leanne."

"Don't talk to me," Leanne spat, glaring across at her with red-rimmed eyes — the result of seeing her dad behind bars, not the death of her grandfather. "I don't even know what you're doing here, you cheeky bitch. You're not family. You've got no right."

"I just wanted to pay my respects to your grandad," Sue said evenly, determined not to allow herself to be drawn into a catfight. "He was a nice man."

"Fuck off!" Leanne hissed. "You only knew him for a week, so don't try and make out like you were anything to him, because you weren't. Just like you're nothing to my dad."

Gritting her teeth as she realised that this was going to be even harder than she'd thought it would be, Sue said, "I know it's all been a shock, and I'm really sorry about —"

"Sorry about what?" Leanne interrupted nastily. "For getting my *fiancé* nicked just because you can't tell the fucking truth? Or for getting my dad banged up because you couldn't keep your dirty hands off him?"

"Pack it in," Terry hissed, blushing with shame when mourners from a nearby funeral began to cast disapproving looks in their direction.

Turning on him in a flash, Leanne yelled, "Don't you tell me what to do! And don't you *dare* defend this bitch after everything she's done to me, or you can forget about us — and I *mean* it!"

"I haven't done anything to you," Sue reminded her calmly. "I'm just trying to put a stop to all this arguing, that's all. If you're going to marry Terry, then the kids will be part of your life as well as his, and I've accepted that."

"Over my dead body!" Leanne squawked. "You really think I'm having those brats in my life knowing that my dad's inside because of them? You must be *mad!*"

Narrowing his eyes, Terry peered at Leanne as if seeing her for the first time. He'd been trying so hard not to blame her for any of this, and it had been difficult to keep his cool at times, especially when she talked about her dad as if he was some kind of fallen god whose only crime was to love his child too much. But there was no excusing what she was saying about *his* children now.

"You know what," he said quietly. "*I'm* the mad one, for thinking I could spend the rest of my life with you. They say the apple doesn't fall far from the tree and, Christ, have you proved that today."

"Meaning?" Leanne demanded, furious with him for arguing with her in front of Sue.

"Meaning that you're just like your dad," Terry said flatly. "*And* your mum. And to be honest, I don't know which is worse. Her, for trying to get off with me every time your back's turned. Or him, for kidnapping my daughter. Or *you*," he added coldly. "For having the bare-faced cheek to try and blame Sue and my kids for what happened."

"Oh, so it's nothing to do with *her*, then?" Leanne retorted self-righteously. "She didn't go out and leave your precious brat in the house on his own?"

"I don't know what happened," Terry replied. "And to be honest, I don't really care right now. I'm just glad they're all safe. But you don't give a toss about them. You're more concerned about the bastard who did this to them."

"Don't call my dad a bastard," Leanne warned him.

"Or what?" Terry asked, looking at her with disgust. "You'll get him to kick my head in? Sorry, love, I'm past caring. About him — *and* you."

"You'd best not be saying what I think you're saying," Leanne hissed, glaring at him with hatred.

490

"'Cos if you finish with me and go back to her after all this, I swear I'll kill you!"

"I'm not going back to her," Terry replied coolly. "But I'm not wasting any more time with you, either, because you're poisonous."

"Well, you can have *this* back, then," Leanne spat, wrenching the ring off her finger and tossing it away. "And don't think you're crawling back to me when you realise what a mistake you've made, because I'll be with Zak!"

"Good luck to him," Terry snorted. Then, watching as her eyes followed the ring's progress to where it landed in the earth covering the coffin, he said, "Oh, and in case you're thinking about sneaking back in to dig it up later, I wouldn't bother. It was only fifteen quid from the second-hand shop."

It was a lie, but it hit Leanne exactly where he had known it would, and he didn't feel any pity when she immediately burst into tears. All it had ever meant to her was another kick in Sue's teeth, and he knew that now. Although he didn't know why it had taken him so long to figure it out, considering that the first thing she'd wanted to know after he'd presented it to her was if it was more expensive than the one he'd bought for Sue.

Leanne was sobbing loudly now, her face buried in her hands. But instead of comforting her as she was expecting even after all that had been said, Terry just nodded goodbye to Sue and walked away.

Despite everything that had happened, Sue couldn't help but feel sorry for the girl. She knew the tone voice that Terry had used just now all too well, and it signalled that he had made up his mind. And he was the kind of man who never went back once he'd crossed that line. So, just as he'd said that he wouldn't be coming back to Sue, he would also never go back to Leanne now that he'd broken the relationship off. But Leanne had a long way to go before she would accept that. A long way, and a great deal of pain, when she realised what a good man she'd had and lost.

Exactly like Sue had already done.

"Don't cry, Leanne," she said now, her eyes filled with sympathy as she gazed at the sobbing girl. "You will get over him in time."

"Like *you* did?" Leanne yelled back at her spitefully, the tears stopping as abruptly as they had started. "You've been hanging around like a bad smell all year hoping to get him back, but it's never going to happen, 'cos he's *mine*!" Then, screaming, "*TERRRRY!*" she turned and ran after him.

Shaking her head as she watched, Sue's heart lurched when she spotted from the corner of her eye the policewomen heading her way. Her immediate instinct was to run, but it was too late for that. So, taking a deep breath, she turned to face them.

"She looks upset," Jay said, twisting around in the wheelchair to watch Leanne chasing after Terry as Ann bumped her across the rough grass to the graveside. "Is everything all right?"

"Not really," Sue said, glancing back at Leanne who was grabbing at Terry's arm now, only for him to shake her off determinedly.

Asking Ann if she could leave them for a minute, Jay waited until she'd gone. Then, looking up at Sue, she said, "Sorry I haven't had a chance to speak to you sooner, but I really wanted to thank you for what you did. If you hadn't stopped Dave Miller from shooting that night, we wouldn't have been able to call for help and I'd have bled to death."

A frown of confusion skittered across Sue's brow. "I'm the one who should be thanking you," she said. "If you hadn't taken Connor seriously, Nicky would have died."

"You can thank your friend Mrs Wilson for that," Jay told her, smiling conspiratorially. "She's very persuasive when she gets an idea into her head, and she was so convinced there was something to the picture that I couldn't ignore it. Anyway, the children are safe now, so it worked out well." Pausing, she gazed up at Sue thoughtfully. "But how are you?"

Blushing, because she knew that she didn't deserve anybody's concern, Sue shrugged and said, "I'm okay." Then, breathing in deeply, she said, "Look, I don't know what Nicky's told you, because she's not really talking to me at the moment. But whatever she said, it's true. This is all my fault, so if you're going to arrest me, I'm ready. Just . . . can you make sure that Terry gets the kids, please? Or Pauline, if it's too difficult for him. Only, he's splitting up with Leanne, so he might have to find somewhere to live first."

Listening to the resignation in Sue's voice, and seeing the stark sadness in her eyes, Jay decided to put her out of her misery.

"I'm not going to arrest you," she said. "I don't think it would benefit anybody — certainly not the children. Anyway, this case is purely about Nicky, and as she was kidnapped at a different location, what happened at home doesn't come into it." Pausing now, she gave Sue a long, meaningful look, before adding, "Mistakes have been made, but lessons have been learned, I'm sure."

Tears of relief and gratitude streaming from her eyes, Sue buried her face in her hands. "I'm so sorry," she sobbed. "I've never done anything like that before, and I don't know why I did it. I really thought Nicky ran past me when I was leaving, so I thought everything would be okay. But I shouldn't have left Connor, and I'll never do it again. I *swear* it."

Satisfied that Sue meant what she was saying, Jay knew that she'd made the right decision. Reaching out, she patted Sue's arm, saying, "Put it behind you and get on with looking after your family. And don't worry about Nicky. Dave Miller told her a lot of things about you that she didn't need to hear, and she'll have to work out the truth from the lies for herself. But she does love you, so she'll come round in time."

"I know," Sue murmured tearfully, making an effort to pull herself together. "And I'll just have to wait until she's ready to talk to me. But the support workers at the hostel have been great, so I'm glad she's got them to talk to in the meantime."

"She'll be fine," Jay said confidently. Then, "And how's Connor doing?"

"He's just confused," Sue told her, sighing softly. "He hasn't got a clue what's going on, but he's made up to have Nicky back. Oh, and he's nearly stopped wetting the bed."

"Well, that's good," Jay said, smiling again. "Shows he's not as stressed out as he was."

"Suppose so," Sue agreed, smiling herself now. "I'll just be glad when this is all over and we can really move on."

"Yes, well, it shouldn't be too long now," Jay said. "We haven't got a confirmed date for the trial yet, but I'll let you know as soon as we hear anything. And don't worry: Dave Miller's got *no* chance of walking away from this."

Murmuring, "I hope not," Sue wiped her nose one last time and stuffed the tissue into her pocket.

"Anyway, best get going," Jay said, glancing at her watch. "You've got my number, so feel free to call me if you need to talk."

"Thanks," Sue said quietly. Then, leaning down on impulse, she gave Jay a quick hug and walked briskly away. Casting one last glance towards the car park where Terry was still adamantly fending Leanne off, she joined Pauline at the gate.

"You didn't have to wait," she said, hoping that Pauline wouldn't start quizzing her.

But Pauline had already decided not to stick her nose in, sensing that whatever Sue and DC Osborne had been talking about it must have been personal for the uniformed one to leave them to chat in private.

So, instead, she linked her arm through Sue's, saying, "That's what friends are for. You come together, you leave together. Well, except when it's time to get on

Jack's bus," she added, jerking her head back at the graves as they set off down the road. "That's one journey we all make alone. Least, I bloody *hope* so, or my John will be hopping on board asking how he's supposed to cook his own tea."

"Won't he be more concerned about how to work the telly?" Sue asked, wondering why she'd spent so long at war with this kind, caring, dry-witted old lady.

"Oh, no, pet, he doesn't need me to show him how to work *that*," Pauline chuckled. "It's just the cooker he's got a problem with. And the hoover . . . and the kettle . . . and the washing machine . . ."